KINGDOM OF RUNES

KING MAKER

AUDREY GREY

ISBN: 978-1-7337472-8-8

This book is dedicated to the readers who hate something about themselves. I hope you know you're beautiful just the way you are.

ERIT

SOLISSIA

THE
MOTHER'S
SEA

COURT
OF
NINE

THE
GREAT
STEPPES

ASHARI

KINGDOM
OF
ICE

ISLE
OF
MIST

DRAGON-TA
STRAIT

THE FLOATING
CITY OF
TYR

MORGANI
ISLANDS

ASGARD

GULF
THRE

FEYRA'S
SPEAR

THE
DESERT OF
BALDR

B

THE
SELKIE
SEA

DROTH

REYIA

DARKLING
BAY

BAY OF
SHADOWS

SPIREFALL
CASTLE

SHADOW KINGDOM

THE
RUINLANDS

SACRED TREE
OF LIFE

FEYRA'S
TEMPLE

BLOOD BONE
MOUNTAINS

THE
WITCHWOOD

GLITTERING
SEA

KINDOM OF
VERDURE

THE BANE

DEVOURER'S
CAMP

THE SUN COURT

MANASSES

FFENDIER

DEAD MAN'S STRAIT

PERTH

FALLEN KINGDOM
OF LORWYNFELL

ASHIVIER

F THE
UEENS

MUIRWOOD
FOREST

CROMWELL

DUNE

KEN

REE

RUNE
WALL

VENASSIAN
OCEAN

KINGDOM OF
PENRYTH

VESERACK

THE MORTAL LANDS

"The stag in wood, the bear in the field, they all bow down to her. The ravens up high, the Shadowlings of nigh, they all swear oaths to her. The mortal kings, they fall, one and all, to worship at her feet. But those that don't heed the shadow of wings, the bite of fiery eyes. Her wrath will come and swallow them whole, the girl of fire and ice."

~ Translated lullaby from the apocryphal blood augur texts

ONE

The tug of dark magick woke her.

Haven Ashwood clutched her chest. Her body thrummed as if a thousand panicked moths beat against the underside of her ribs. When the brush of powdery wings became the scrape of claws, she jolted into a sitting position.

Then, like the too-long, too-sharp fingernail of something ancient, the magick tapped against her breastbone.

Tap. Tap. Tap.

Release me.

Rubbing her eyes, Haven slipped from her bed and through the silent halls of Fenwick Castle, drawn along by some invisible thread.

Moonlight seeped from the open windows. The silvery light danced across the iridescent runes that tattooed her stippled flesh, but the glow couldn't chase away the dark shadows pooling against the stone walls.

A guard leaned against the wall. His eyes were sleepy as he stared into the closest candle, watching a handful of moths drown in the wax pool.

He didn't even blink as she passed. Her magick ensured he couldn't see her. She took a strange sort of pleasure in that, even as she begged him to notice.

To stop her.

He was blind to the inky-blue veins of light spilling from her flesh. Blind to the girl with magick wandering the castle at will, covered in nothing but a muslin nightgown.

Every door that creaked open beneath her palm left her feeling a bit more lost. What was she doing awake? Her gaze shifted to the dagger inside her hand. When did that get there?

Gnarled, twisted horns of molten silver formed the hilt, the dark handle cool and terrifying inside her palm. An eye watched her between the horns, the iris bright red like embers shifting inside a glass marble. The pupil was a slash of black, and it dilated in the shadows like a real eye.

When it blinked at her, something close to terror sparked inside her heart.

A frigid breeze drifted from the closest open window as she passed two sentries near an archway of winding pillars entwined with dahlias.

Her throat clenched.

The dark magick inside the hollow of her bones stretched out in anticipation, a primordial beast awakened from its slumber.

No.

Prince Bell's room lay just beyond.

No.

Only she possessed the key to enter. She willed herself to turn around, go back to bed. To scream. To somehow alert the guards playing a game of runedice by his room. Instead she quietly unlocked the prince's door and crossed the threshold, a startling sense of panic beginning.

No.

Arched windows ran the length of the chamber, the fragile light stifled by a set of drawn velvet curtains. The prince appeared tiny curled atop his four-poster bed. Gold sheets tangled around his legs. He was still wearing the silk socks that rode up to his slim calves.

No.

A figure rose by Bell's headboard. The presence seemed formed from a tapestry of shadows, each layer smoky and nebulous and ever-changing. But behind that veil of churning darkness hid a sentience, an ancient, primordial evil that bled the air from the room and made her heart skitter sideways in her chest.

"Now," the figure ordered. His voice slithered across the silence and into her skull.

The thin wool rug was soft against Haven's feet as she obeyed, approaching the sleeping prince. The dagger was heavy in her hand. Strange runes flickered over the blade. The molten lines of red and blue disappearing as fast as they appeared.

No. No. No.

The muscles in her body fought to regain control. But the darkness was sewn into every pore, every crevice of her flesh; she was a puppet to its desires.

"What do you want?" she begged, fearing she already knew the answer.

"I want so many, many things," the darkness whispered.

Squinting, she sifted through the inky smoke, trying to discern the thing inside. For there was no doubt now—it was a monster, a creature of unimaginable horrors.

"What do you want from *me*?"

"Obedience," it purred. "Pledge your allegiance to me and I'll make you a god among gods. They will all bow down to you, a mortal queen of unimaginable power, and no one would ever dare try to enslave you again."

"Queen of what?" she hissed. "Nightmares?"

"Queen of everything."

Terror wound its way through her ribs. "I don't want to be a queen."

"No? Your thoughts betray you. You crave power over men. You want to punish them for what they've done to you. Or would you allow yourself to be chained again, Rose?"

The former nickname lodged just below her heart, a splinter worming deeper with each breath.

But this wasn't Damius, her former captor. This wasn't anything human at all. Nor was it a Noctis.

It was something else. Something powerful enough to access her memories.

"Fear doesn't work on me," she growled, glaring into the black miasma. "Whoever you are, whatever you are, I will never obey you, or anyone. I am my own master."

Laughter seeped from the black smoke, trickling along the stone walls until it pooled below her sternum. "Do you truly believe you can defy me? That you have a choice?"

"There's always a choice."

"How very naive of you. As long as the ancient magick of the Netherworld permeates your mortal blood, as long as that darkness wends through the hollows of your frail bones, you belong to me."

"Liar." But her voice was oh so soft.

"Watch and see."

Terror constricted her heart as she witnessed her hand rise above Bell's chest. The sharp edges of the double-sided blade glittered. Inside the steel she caught her reflection. Her eyes were black pits of nothing, of death.

Bell awoke with a start, his sleepy eyes widening as he took in her weapon, poised right above his heart. Despair settled in his face, and he whispered, "Don't hurt me, Haven. Please."

No, Goddess no. Not Bell.

She tried to fling the weapon from her fingers, but her body wasn't obeying. The knife shook in her hand as she struggled against the force pushing down the blade. The hard muscles of her shoulder trembled; her teeth ground with the effort until her jaw popped.

The knife's eye, the one that was the color of Netherfire, watched her. Willing her to drive its length into flesh and bone. She could feel its need for blood, for agony.

Feed me, it whispered. *Drown me in blood.*

And then something inside her snapped and the last frayed tether of control broke.

Gripping the dagger's handle, she lifted the weapon high above the prince and then plunged the wicked blade into his chest.

TWO

Screams ripped Haven from the nightmare. Her screams. Somewhere between last night and this morning, she had tumbled from her low-lying bed and was sprawled on the wooden floor of her bedchamber. A headache hammered at her skull.

Groaning, she pressed her thumbs into the tender spot just above her eyes. The pain was either from falling off the bed or, more likely, the infusion of honeymead, lilac, and clove she'd been taking to control her dark magick.

Bell had found mention of it once used by the Solis on Noctis prisoners. The foul potion was supposed to lessen her dark magick—but so far, all it seemed to do was give her migraines and leave a bitter taste in her mouth.

Someone hovered over Haven. As the sleep cleared from her vision, she made out dark button-eyes blinking down at her behind craggy cheeks and a frown. Without a word, Demelza dabbed Haven's face with a wet washcloth, tsking beneath her breath.

"The nightmares are growing stronger," her lady's maid muttered, her thick northern accent both jarring and comforting. Demelza flicked her gaze over to the open window where a cat-sized raven perched. A diamond brooch sparkled between his orange claws. "'Tis demons."

Ravius cocked his head, returning the glare. His silver eyes were way too human for Haven's liking, and they glinted with fury, leaving little doubt about Ravius's feelings on being called a demon.

Not that he needed gestures to make his thoughts clear. Something that Stolas failed to mention—one of his countless omissions—was that Ravius could talk.

At least, to Haven.

The bird squawked at Demelza, but only Haven heard his enraged voice as it rattled off in her head. *Witch, you should be flogged for your insolence.*

For the thousandth time, Haven responded inside her mind, rubbing her temples. *She's not a witch.*

Ignoring Haven, Ravius spread his wings wide and puffed out his chest, making himself as large as possible as he faced down Demelza. *I am Lochran O'Beirne. Greatest Asgardian warrior of old. How dare you challenge me, witch. Bow before me or face the consequences.*

His voice had the alluring brogue of an Asgardian and the disdainful lilt of a royal.

Stolas, if you can hear me, Haven thought. *You owe me big time.*

"Hand over that jewel you thieving Netherworld demon!" Demelza roared.

Ravius was only a raven, but Haven could have sworn a smile curved across his black beak as he bent down and snatched the brooch in his mouth. Then he proceeded to wave it back and forth.

Stolas had also failed to mention Ravius's penchant for hoarding sparkly things. She'd recently found a rather large cache of jewelry—stolen from Goddess knows how many nobles—inside a hollowed-out portion of the loveseat by the window.

Having none of it, Demelza snatched a wooden-handled broom from the corner and charged across the room toward Ravius.

An indignant squawk was all Ravius got out before he was flung out the window.

As Haven watched the angry bird disappear into the still-dark morning air, she felt some of the tension lift from the room.

"Like I said," Demelza grumbled, setting the broom back in its place and dusting off her hands. "Demons."

There was no point arguing with her maid that demons didn't lurk inside the mortal realm anymore. At least, not in the way they had been thousands of years ago, when lower demons were supposedly as plentiful as stray cats.

Now the demons were bound to the Shadeling in the darkest pits of the Netherworld. The few still here—like the djinn from Lorwynfell—were summoned before the Shadeling's imprisonment. A remnant of an era when kings had powerful enough light magick to bind demons deep below their castles to guard royal treasure.

Blowing out a breath, Haven settled her head back onto the floor. From this vantage point she could see the thick layer of dust collecting beneath the iron frame of her small bed.

"Demelza, when was the last time someone cleaned this room?"

Demelza clucked her tongue. "They refuse. Because the demons."

"For the last time, Demelza. There are no demons."

"Hmph." Demelza leaned down to wipe Haven's face again. "Says the girl sprawled on the floor like a fool."

Haven batted away the attempt before jumping to her feet. Demelza shuffled after her, thrusting the wet cloth out like a weapon, but Haven waved her off.

"It was a nightmare, Demelza. Last I checked, you can't wash those away."

"No, but you sweat when you dream." Demelza tsked as if the very idea was offensive. "And sweat not only stinks, it attracts demons."

"Goddess save me," Haven muttered as she lifted her sword hand for inspection. Even though she knew her nightmare wasn't real, her body lightened with relief as she took in the absence of a dagger—or Bell's blood.

Demelza straightened, the painful curve of her hunched shoulders smoothing out. After rifling through the tall oak wardrobe by the window, she retrieved some hideous collection of clothes they both knew Haven wouldn't wear and laid the ensemble on the rumpled bed.

"I will find you a runecatcher for your dreams," Demelza offered, "and then you must put it above your bed. Yes?"

Her words came out closer to an order than an offer.

Haven repressed the grin forming over her jaw and said, "Thank you. I'm sure it will help."

They both stared at the clothes on the bed, unwilling to admit the obvious—the runecatcher would do nothing. Haven's nightmares were beyond the reach of anything in this mortal realm.

They had been for months.

The only thing that stopped them was Stolas. Whenever her nightmares became too much, she would find herself inside his dreamscape. Her terror gone. No more horned, seeing, *talking* dagger. No more killing Bell or Archeron or Surai.

Except, the last few weeks, his dreams were closed to her, along with the small comfort they brought.

She tried not to worry over Stolas's absence as she dressed in uncomfortable silence. Demelza didn't so much as scoff when Haven overlooked the creamy gold gown and slippers for her leather pants and favorite worn boots. But she did make grumbling noises as Haven holstered small daggers at her wrists, thighs, and waist.

To appease her maid, Haven donned her newest cloak—a bright red wisp of sable—and fastened it to her tunic with a shiny gold pin shaped like a dahlia.

More daggers went into the pockets she'd sewn into the lining, and Demelza's gaze narrowed once again.

"A lady of the court should not jingle with steel," Demelza pointed out.

"Good thing I'm not a lady, then," Haven answered, brows knitted as she finished stuffing a vial of oleander poison into a hidden pocket just over her heart.

Lastly, she reached for the gilded dagger on her nightstand. As her fingers brushed the hilt, an image of the dagger from her dream flashed in her mind, and dread unfurled in her belly.

It was the same damn dagger every time. Right down to the striations etched into the huge horns and the eerie eye throbbing with magick.

The figure, on the other hand, was entirely new.

"Demelza, in the future, you will lock my door from the outside at night, and if I try to break through it, even if I seem asleep—especially if I appear asleep—I want you to take a sword and run me through. Understood?"

Any other person might have hesitated. Or at the very least feigned an unwillingness to murder so easily.

But Demelza had lost her entire village to the darkness that now rooted in Haven's soul. And even if Haven hadn't told anyone her secret—that she possessed both light and darkness, good and evil—a part of Demelza must have known anyway. Must have sensed it the same way she did her imaginary demons.

Demelza gave a grim nod and said, "Straight through the heart, m'lady. 'Tis a promise."

"And don't be sad afterward."

"No worry of that nonsense, m'lady."

"Wonderful."

Haven squared to face the dressing mirror in the corner.

For a flicker, a heartbeat, the reflection from her dream stared back. A girl wholly strange and unpredictable, ruled by a darkness she could never begin to control and a bloodlust stronger than any good that might be left inside her.

It seemed only a matter of time before that girl took over—and Haven had no idea how to stop her.

THREE

Haven reveled in the countless gasps of delight rising through Fenwick Castle, each awed murmur punctuated by laughter and enthusiastic clapping. The noble men and women packing the great hall came from the untouched kingdoms, mainly, but a few had traveled all the way from the Curse-stricken north.

The boy they came to see stood proud and tall on a dais littered with rose petals and coins. All eyes were riveted to his upturned palm.

Or, more precisely, the golden flame of magick sprouting from it.

The flame was tiny, a mere spark sizzling and spitting bright specks of light. But it promised something the kingdom of Eritreyia hadn't seen in years.

Magick.

And with it came an even more elusive thing—hope.

Grinning, the Prince of Penryth pretended to close his palm

and snuff out the spark, eliciting yells from the crowd. Hand held above his head, he bowed low and the flame grew to the size of an apple.

"Peacock," Haven muttered, although her heart swelled at the sight of him being playful and happy again for the first time since they returned.

Smiling like that, with his brocade vest and smartly tailored steel-gray leather pants—her pants, by the way, and much prettier on him—he looked every bit the dashing prince he was always meant to be.

Which explained the ring of young women thronging the dais at his feet.

The stage was new. King Horace had it built specifically for Bell to show off his magick. An octagon, each side showed off a famous scene from the mortal histories. All together it took master craftsmen from all over the mortal realm fifty-two days to shape the slab of pale quartz into the impressive monument it was now.

But their artistry and efforts were wasted. When Bell was atop the stage, he was all anyone could see. He could have been standing on a rock and they wouldn't have noticed anything different.

Golden runelight from the chandelier above—gifted a month ago from Solis traders across the Glittering Sea—flickered inside his soft, dark curls and glimmered off the three rubies adorning his new crown. The one his father now insisted he wear.

Being in front of a crowd suited him, and a pink tinge dusted the ebony skin of his high cheekbones, lifted in an almost constant smile. While performing, the sorrows of the last few months melted away.

It was just Bell, the crowd, and magick.

Haven pressed away from the wall she leaned on near the back of the crowd and caught Bell's attention. Their eyes met briefly, a silent signal passing between them as her fisted hand began to open.

Two things happened at once. Bell lunged, back perfectly straight and chest puffed out.

At the same time the magickal sphere hovering above his palm surged to the size of gourds and began spinning.

As the onlookers cried out, and Bell lifted his chin higher, mouth pinched tight with concentration, she chuckled.

One might think Bell held a sword, not magick, with that stance. A master fencer showing off his skills.

Truth was, swordsmanship had never suited Bell. But magick. Well, magick was like the piece of armor he'd been missing all these years. The crown that marked him as royalty.

Almost overnight, he'd gone from forgotten son of an aging king to a world-renowned prince adored and loved by all.

Lightcaster, they murmured. Cursebreaker. Last mortal with magick of the Goddess.

Too bad it was Haven's magick that twinkled and danced from his deft fingers, casting tiny orange flames inside his topaz-blue eyes.

But the only people in the room who knew that were Haven, Bell, and the annoyed Solis warrior staring knives at Haven in her periphery.

"Don't," Surai warned in Solissian.

Haven turned to face Surai.

She was frowning, her beautiful lavender eyes glittering with reproach. They were upturned at the corners and rimmed with long, fluttery lashes. The kind of eyes that could be infinitely kind or vexingly savage.

Right now they were the latter. And it didn't help Surai's mood that mortals kept pushing past her to get a better view of Bell.

If they knew the warrior hidden beneath the layer of silk fabric . . .

"Don't what?" Haven murmured, pretending she didn't hear the warning growl inside her friend's voice.

Surai sighed and tapped Haven in the soft part of her temple, hard. "Whatever thoughts are rattling around that rash mortal brain. Don't."

Haven glanced at Bell and then back at Surai.

The hood of her plum-colored cloak hid most of her hair, but a few sleek dark edges, shorn in grief after the death of her lover, poked out just inches above her jaw. Where the runelight hit her cheeks, runemarks shimmered, tracing beautiful iridescent glyphs and curves that spooled down her neck and into her armor-plated corset.

Haven winked. "You know better than most, there are no thoughts in my head. I'm a simple creature. Eat. Sleep. Be amazing."

Surai clicked her tongue, a divot puckering the center of her pert chin.

Nethergates. Surai only did that when she was in a mood foul enough to kill a lorrack.

"They're tired of boring displays of magick," Haven insisted, jerking her head at the crowd. "They're about to start snoring."

"Huh," Surai countered. "Who knew mortal *oohs* and *ahhs* meant boredom? You learn something new every day, I suppose."

"But look how glorious he is up there. Look at him smiling— *smiling*, Surai. When was the last time that happened?"

"Do you really want to piss off Archeron? He explicitly forbade you from performing any magick beyond flares."

"Surely he'll understand."

"Do you actually know him?" Surai scoffed.

"Well he's not here." Haven tried and failed not to sound

resentful of his absence. She didn't begrudge him leaving, but . . . she missed him. More than she thought she would.

When they returned to Penryth as Cursebreakers and heroes, Archeron refused the king's payment of gold and jewels.

All he asked for was to be given leave for the turn of three moons to hunt down Bjorn the betrayer.

He'd been gone for exactly that, which meant he would be back any day now. She was filled with both anticipation and nervousness at his return, and a part of her wondered if those months apart had changed things between them.

Not that she knew how to categorize what, exactly, that was.

"Haven," Surai said. Her voice had raised a few octaves into a pleading tone. "The mortals are children. They're impressed by anything that sparkles. Dazzle them with a few shiny tricks and be done with it."

Haven, who only took a little offense to her friend stereotyping mortals, knew her suggestion was the practical, safe option. Hadn't they done the very same thing nearly every night for weeks?

But she shook her head. "Bell deserves more than a few cheap tricks, even if they do sparkle beautifully."

"Goddess help me." Surai ran two fingers over her forehead, kneading the spot in-between her charcoal eyebrows, two perpetually arched smudges that gave her a curious look. "You haven't practiced enough. Something could go wrong."

Her friend's voice faded as another cry of excitement rose from the hall.

Haven's Netherworld magick might own her sleeping hours, but during the day, when she was awake and in control, she could make her light magick shine.

Darkness didn't define her. And this was a perfect screw-you moment to the dark magick rooted inside her.

You don't own me.

With a taunting grin, Haven drew a long, winding rune with her finger over her chest, careful that no one saw.

It was a creation rune. As she traced the lines she was supposed to think of the creature she wanted to make. It sounded simple but it was incredibly tricky, requiring concentration and focus.

When the rune was nearly finished, and the chances of messing up the creation were low, she let her attention drift to Bell.

Beneath his dark tunic, a faint throb of light pulsed. She cast a quick glance around.

Did anyone notice?

But even if someone did happen to catch the glow, they wouldn't know that Bell wore a special powerrune around his neck. One that directed her magick to him and kept up the illusion they'd been using since they returned.

Luckily, every eye save Haven's was on the sphere of fire blossoming from the prince's open palm.

The moment she finished the rune, the fire surged outward. A spinning miasma of orange and red flames that grew and grew.

Sparks became feathers. Long, proud feathers of indigo and cyan-green. The tips of its wings were peach colored, its head a distinguished royal blue.

"It's a . . . peacock," a young boy cried.

Haven's throat swelled with pride, and she ignored Surai's groan.

Last time she tried that rune her magickal peacock turned into a lumpy, half-run-over rooster that caught the drapes on fire before dissolving into the floor.

This was progress; this was wonderful.

Bell glanced at her, his face just as shocked as everyone else's.

Really? His expression seemed to be saying. *A giant peacock?*

She flicked up her eyebrows, her own message clear. *Really. A giant, glorious peacock. Just like you.*

With a sigh, Bell turned back to his fans and performed an elaborate flick of his hand. The peacock shot into the air, a plume of fiery tail-feathers trailing over the upturned cheeks of the onlookers.

A collective peal of awe erupted from the crowd as the magickal bird swooped and dove, stirring the black and gold Penrythian banners hanging from the rafters, and Haven felt her chin lift and her own chest puff out.

She shot Surai a triumphant grin. "Meet the first royal Penrythian peacock. What shall we name him?"

"Idiot," Surai muttered.

"That's a horrible name for a peacock," Haven pointed out.

Surai cut her eyes at Haven and shook her head, the sharp ends of her hair slashing at her chin—but one corner of her mouth lifted, filling Haven with hope.

It had been so long since Haven saw Surai truly smile, and she held her breath, willing the other corner of her friend's lips to finish the too-rare act.

Instead, Surai touched the offending side of her mouth, and it smoothed back out into the perpetual expression of contemplative sadness she always donned.

Haven sighed, her focus drifting through the hall.

Like always, her attention snagged on the arched windows. Ravius sat quietly on the cracked stone sill, watching the entire thing with a look of superiority. Their eyes met, and she swore the raven tilted its head to the garden far below. Taunting her with the prospect of fresh air . . .

Her pulse raced as she imagined the plush grass beneath her

bare feet, the cool breeze scented with plumeria and roses.

Despite the high ceilings and ample space, she itched to be outside. To be free. Both of the stifling crowd and the pressure from constantly hiding the truth.

Stop, she scolded herself. *Your place is here, with Bell. Wherever that may be.*

Tearing her gaze from the open windows, she focused on the runelight flickering from the sconces situated between each window until her heartbeat steadied.

Their eternal golden light—a magickal luxury the kingdom hadn't experienced since their own runelight extinguished years ago—flickered tall and regal, impervious to the wind fluttering in from the windows.

At Bell's insistence, the King had allowed the citizens of Penryth and the surrounding villages to take the runelight back to their own homes on the wicks of sallow candles.

Without the looming presence of dark magick to siphon it, the runelight would last forever.

She took in the rest of the room. Royals from all over the mortal realm flanked either side, their tables positioned so they overlooked the spectacle.

Haven recognized Lord Thendryft and his daughter, Eleeza, at the table nearest Bell's stage. Beside her, a boy no older than nine sat. By his dark skin and bubbly smile, he was Eleeza's brother.

They all wore deep burgundy, and Eleeza's sleek dark hair was pinned atop her head with a network of plum-wine ribbons that gave Haven a headache just looking at them.

Lady Thendryft's eyes were bright as she watched Bell. Her wide, beaming smile left little doubt about her thoughts on their engagement.

Well that makes exactly one of them.

At the other end of the long room, the royal family sat at the head banquet table, watching the entire spectacle. King Horace lounged in the largest chair in the middle, his cheeks ruddy from too much meat and wine.

But his eyes were still sharp as they followed his son, the same way he had since their return from the Shadow Kingdom.

An outsider might think that, after nearly losing his son to the Shade Queen, he was finally appreciating him. But Haven knew better. The king was a lot of things, but dummy wasn't one of them.

He suspected *something* wasn't right. Thank the Goddess he hadn't figured out what . . . yet.

The king's mistress, Cressida, on the other hand, couldn't take her attention off the magickal peacock.

As she followed the creature with her gaze, hardly seeming to breathe, there was a hungry look in her eyes that made Haven uneasy.

Now that magick was back in the kingdom, and it didn't belong to the Shade Queen anymore, Cressida had something else to lust after.

Her son, Renk, sat glumly beside her, his pheasant leg untouched. Frown lines etched across his high forehead, his thick brow eclipsing his beady eyes so that Haven nearly missed the bitterness glittering inside them.

Shadeling's shadow, he looked seconds away from launching over the table and strangling the bird—or Bell.

Alarm spiked her breathing as she caught the sneer twisting his face, and one hand automatically went to the new sword sticking up from the scabbard at her waist.

He didn't even bother hiding his bitterness at Bell's newfound status.

Touch him, she thought, willing her threat over the crowd and across the room, *and I'll murder you.*

Perhaps she had accidentally employed magick to bring him her message, because Renk blinked and then slid his slimy gaze to her.

A little smile twitched his greasy lips, and he picked at his teeth with a delicate bird bone, the act somehow aggressive.

What are you going to do about it? his expression taunted.

Bastard. Her fists curled at her sides as a panicky feeling frayed her senses.

In the time they'd been gone, and then the three months since they had been back, Renk had changed. Grown from a cruel, baby-faced teen to a cruel, thick-jawed man.

He's going to hurt Bell, eventually. Today, tomorrow.

Soon.

Then kill him, a far-away voice whispered before she shut it out. But her own mind was whirring with panic now, jumping from danger to danger.

It wasn't just Renk and Cressida who posed a threat. The Shade Queen was still out there, hidden somewhere dark and deep. The king proclaimed her dead, as did most of the other kingdoms, but Haven knew better.

Then there were the citizens of Penryth and beyond to consider. Bell's magick drew them in, made them crazed in a way that bothered her.

Never had Bell been more of a target . . .

A flicker of panic.

That's all it took to crack open something inside her.

She felt her insides shift, felt something poke and prod her defenses, and then a trickle of cold seeped in, settling at the base of her spine.

You can't keep me out, the darkness whispered. *I am you.*

Runes. She needed to calm down, but the idea that she could lose control set her pulse pounding in her skull, making things worse.

Now that she had powerful magick, her emotions were fragile things to be carefully dealt with—before they became weapons.

Calm down, Ashwood.

Sucking in a breath, she closed her eyes and counted runes, the way Archeron had taught her.

Illusion rune. Fire rune. Taste rune. Love rune . . .

Not helping. Her head spun; her breathing hitched; her veins tightened until they ached.

The kernel of cold twined upward, scraping over each knob of her spine, wending over her ribs and pooling beneath her sternum.

"Haven?" Surai's worried voice broke through the darkness of her eyelids, but she blocked it out as she worked to silence her mind and the fears that fed the darkness inside her.

Let me in, the voice demanded. *Or they will take everything from you.*

Three long months had passed since they saved Bell from the Shade Queen.

Three long months of healing, where she should have forgotten the feeling of panic at watching the Shade Lord take him. Should have gotten over the bubble of agony lodged below her ribcage from knowing he was being hurt, possibly tortured.

Knowing he was scared.

But now, instead of finally being safe, they had just shifted from one kingdom of monsters to a new one. Except these monsters were worse, hidden beneath masks of nobility, making it near impossible to protect him . . .

Something was wrong. She came back to the now. The room

was too quiet. That's when she realized how cold she was. The chill so deep even her marrow felt frozen.

"Haven!" Surai hissed.

Haven knew what she would see when she opened her eyes.

Still, when she finally did look, the sight sent a surge of shock straight to her core.

The peacock was gone, replaced by a sinister, shadowy form rippling across the ceiling. The oily mist slithered and clumped until a familiar shape took hold against the mosaic of stones.

Instead of beautiful feathers, long, crooked limbs sprouted from a mangled body.

As Haven and the others watched in terrified silence, wings of the deepest black spread over the room like night falling. The temperature had dropped considerably, Haven's breath spilling out in a silvery fog.

The silence became dread. Someone whispered, "gremwyr," before their voice cut off.

No one else dared say the name of the monster used by the Shade Queen, as if just saying the word would conjure it into reality.

Except it was already here, and the only person who could stop it now was Haven.

But as Haven glanced down at the bluish light seeping from her fingers and felt the thousand needles of ice prickling her fingertips, she understood she wasn't in control anymore.

Her dark magick had been set free.

FOUR

Screams erupted around Haven. The crowd surged. A few guests managed to flee, but most stood frozen in fear as they watched the magickal gremwyr scuttle across the ceiling.

Memories of Bell's runeday ceremony three months ago came roaring back. In her mind's eye, Haven saw the gremwyrs storm the temple. Saw them murder countless innocents before kidnapping Bell.

Except this time there was no weapon for her to fight back with. At least, no physical arrow or blade to pierce this creature's flesh. Because this thing, whatever it was, was a part of *her*.

Bell craned his head back and caught her attention, his bright blue eyes stretched wide with fear.

He remembered too. He was shaking. Terrified. The trauma of his capture displayed in his bared lips and shivering body.

Her throat clenched tight as she recognized the same betrayed expression from her nightmare.

Use me, the darkness whispered. *Show them how powerful you are.*

No. She shook her head as she desperately tried to rein the dark magick in.

But how? She tried calling it to her. Tried willing it back into the tiny little chunk of her soul she'd carved out to house it.

But she could feel its excitement. Feel its bloodlust as the creature stretched out its dark, monstrous body, feeding off the fear of those below.

Like a feral dog who'd been chained and starved and then finally set free, no amount of coaxing would command it to return before it sated itself.

Just like in her nightmare.

Who shall I kill? it whispered.

No one, she ordered. *I don't want you to kill anyone.*

Liar.

Someone shrieked and the gremwyr dove straight for the royal table, a streak of blue and black, talons and wings. Shadows and death.

It was headed for Renk.

Nononono

Cressida gasped and flung her arms out, knocking over a chalice of wine. With the burgundy liquid blossoming over the gold tablecloth, Renk shot to his feet. His hands lifted in a futile effort to protect his face as the great magickal beast neared.

Then the king's bastard son dropped to his knees, the scabbard of his ceremonial sword scraping the stone, and ducked under the table.

Goddess Above, this was really happening.

"Haven," Surai called, but even right next to her, she sounded distant, like she was yelling from underwater. "Haven, you need to close the door before that thing murders every mortal inside these walls."

But Haven was frozen.

For a strange moment, she could do nothing but stare at her creation, caught between the contrasting emotions of terror and awe. The gremwyr was marvelous, its great wings perfectly rendered, its face so detailed she could make out the curved fangs protruding from its lipless mouth, the malice inside the monster's reptilian eyes.

Perfect little ridges of bone spiked its hunched back.

It was darkness and hatred and fear wrapped into an illusion—it was her emotions, the ones she kept locked away, finally broken free.

The thing hovered over the table, its wing gusts blowing back the tablecloth and knocking over cups.

As if coming out of a trance, King Horace jumped to his feet. One hand on his crown, he didn't even try to feign bravery or help his family as he scrambled behind four of the royal guards.

Eleeza rushed from her table toward Cressida and Renk. A short-sword flashed in her hand as she neared—she must have hidden the weapon under her dress somewhere.

She halted a few feet from Cressida and faced the gremwyr, her face tight with terror.

Brave fool. Haven's respect for Bell's unspoken fiancée was considerably higher—but that just made her possible death harder to swallow.

Cressida, on the other hand, was a statue. The only thing moving was her marigold hair, which blew back with each wing gust of the gremwyr. Her hands splayed over the table, showing off every silver and gold bauble adorning her long fingers.

Her lips parted. Haven thought she might scream, but nothing came out. Her eyes dampened as her gaze glided over the creature, and Haven was reminded of the hungry way she looked over Archeron.

No doubt in that moment Cressida would have given Renk over to the magickal beast if it meant controlling it.

The thought fed Haven's rage.

Feeling her growing fury, the gremwyr slowly twisted its head like an owl to look back at her.

Let me kill them, it pleaded. *Just one. One would satisfy me.*

No, Haven ordered, unsure if she thought or spoke the command. *No, please*, she repeated, even as part of her wanted otherwise.

Even as she imagined Cressida's head rolling down the steps . . .

With a frustrated screech, the gremwyr flared its wings, sending the people closest to the front scurrying. But those wings were already softening, the talons along its wings ribboning into darkness.

It was changing shape again, this time into a nebulous black mist that spread through the air until the space above the table was dark as midnight. Chandeliers and rafters disappeared inside that great, billowing darkness.

Somehow that shapeless mass was more terrifying than the gremwyr or any other creature it could mimic, because she understood just how powerful the thing was inside her.

I'll never be able to control something so massive, so dark . . .

All at once the shadowy mass arrowed toward where Renk hid.

Haven gasped along with the crowd as the mist funneled underneath the tablecloth, slipping beneath the half-inch crack where the fabric met the floor. Three seconds and it disappeared from sight.

With its absence came silence. A great and terrible silence as they all watched and listened. What was it doing down there? Why was Renk so quiet?

Surai took hold of Haven's arm. "What's happening?"

"I don't know," Haven admitted. "I'm not controlling it any longer."

Surai looked at her strangely, her mouth parting as if to refute her.

A scream erupted from beneath the table and quickly died.

Haven's throat tightened.

"Help him!" the king finally ordered.

As if coming back to life, the guards surrounding the king rushed to where Renk hid. One brave soldier dropped to his knees and reached out a trembling hand to lift the bottom of the tablecloth. His head averted, probably in case Renk was shredded into pieces.

Shadeling's shadow. Please don't let that be the case.

Slowly, so damn slowly, Renk came into view, un-shredded and seemingly intact, and all Haven's blood seemed to flood back into her body.

He was okay. No blood or tattered clothing. Not a scratch that she could see.

Only Renk didn't move. Not even to breathe. He lay on his side, back to the crowd, curled into himself. Water pooled around his pants and darkened the stone.

No—not water, she realized as the soldiers grabbed his arms and hauled him up, his face drained of blood and crotch dark.

Renk had pissed himself, and Haven almost felt sorry for the king's bastard as he finally gulped down a ragged, sobbing breath.

Almost, until she remembered the time Bell's bully half-brother had murdered the pigeons Bell fed every morning out of spite. He shot them with arrows and had the cooks serve them for lunch in a pie. Or the time Renk shoved Bell down a flight of steps and said he'd tripped, breaking his arm. Bell had been too scared of his brother to tell anyone but Haven what really happened.

The list of reasons not to feel sorry for Renk was endless. And yet, as Renk ripped another lungful of air from the room, the sound strangled and painful, like he was sucking in glass, she was glad she hadn't murdered him.

Cressida ran to her son, pulling at his clothes as if somehow that would prove he was okay. Renk's eyes were unfocused and glassy, fixed on something in the distance.

Drool dripped from his bottom lip.

Other than his odd breathing, he was unnervingly quiet.

Satisfied her son was still mostly intact, Cressida whipped to face Bell—Oh, Shadeling's shadow. Bell!

Haven had almost forgot that he was the one everyone would blame, and she pushed through the crowd to him just as Cressida launched into a tirade.

"How dare you try to hurt the king's son," the king's mistress sneered. The crowd parted for her as she stormed toward his stage.

"I didn't—" Bell began, his voice paper-thin, but she interrupted him.

"Enough." She paused five feet from the prince, making sure everyone saw how she held up her hands—to ward off any more magick. "We all saw your intentions, Prince of Penryth."

"No." But his gaze collapsed under her accusatory sneer, falling to his boots. "I would never hurt Renk, no matter how horrible he is, or how much he deserves it."

"So you admit there is hatred between you?" Cressida pushed.

"That's not what I said," Bell snapped. "Stop twisting my words."

Haven was almost to the stage when Surai once again took

her arm. This time, the Solis let her ungodly strength show, and Haven flinched from the grip.

"You need to leave," Surai said. "If they find out—"

"They won't," Haven said. "And I won't abandon him to face this witch alone."

Surai's lavender eyes had darkened to the color of an overripe plum, and they slid to where her fingers bunched around Haven's arm. Silver runes flickered over Haven's flesh, bright and beautiful and forbidden.

If they weren't hidden from mortal eyes, Haven would have been executed the day she returned to Penryth.

Surai's face softened, and her grip loosened. "They will kill you, Little Mortal. And I cannot lose another."

Haven's eyes stung. Surai lost her partner, Rook, because of Haven, although Surai would never look at it that way.

Clearing the emotion from her throat, Haven brushed a hand over Surai's shoulder. "I won't leave him to pay for my mistake."

Surai grunted something in Solissian about Haven being a fool, but she released her grip on Haven's arm.

Haven turned back just in time to see Cressida say, "Or what? Will you try to kill me too, Prince?"

She needed to intervene before the crowd turned against Bell.

Loping up the steps to stand beside the prince, Haven said, "It was an accident." Her voice rang out cool and sharp, in stark contrast to her heart, which thudded against her sternum like a frightened rabbit. She let her gaze fall over the room. "Magick is temperamental. Before the Curse stole every royal child with magick, the children of the Nine Houses were trained from birth to handle it."

A murmur of consent rose from the onlookers. They adored Bell, and they *wanted* to believe her.

In a brave show of solidarity, Eleeza climbed the stage to stand beside him. She didn't say anything, but her presence was enough.

Screwing her expression into a solemn mask, Haven dragged her gaze over every face, willing them to listen. "Bell can hardly be faulted for not being taught how to lightcast. He isn't to blame."

I am, she thought bitterly. *Not him. Me.*

But admitting as much would be a death sentence for a common mortal such as herself. Only royals were allowed to lightcast. And she had done so much more than that.

If the people learned the thing that nearly killed Renk was borne of dark magick . . .

Cressida had waited for the crowd to quiet before responding. Now, she laughed even as her eyes grew cruel. "No. Whatever depravity we witnessed just now was birthed by hatred, not inexperience." With great flair, she made a point of retreating a step from Bell, as if he were something dangerous to be feared. "Did something happen to you in the cursed lands? Did the Shade Queen poison your soul, perhaps, and then send you back here as a spy?"

Haven's nostrils flared. Shadeling's witch!

Fearful whispers slithered through the hall. "He could be changed," someone said. "Who knows what happened to him over there?" another added.

A pleased smile pulled at the corners of Cressida's painted lips. So this was how Cressida would undermine Bell, now that he was in the king's favor again. Eleeza sent Haven a concerned look.

She might not be from this kingdom, but she understood the political machinations of the court enough to know Bell was in trouble.

Haven's throat tightened as Bell sent her a desperate look. "It was an . . . accident," he reiterated, but his voice was swallowed by the suspicious murmurs.

Sensing her opportunity, Cressida pivoted to face King Horace. "An accident?" Her tone was softer as she caught the king's eye. "Everyone saw the prince send that monster to kill our son. Even a king as powerful as yourself, my liege, cannot deny the truth now."

The nobles were quiet as they switched their focus to King Horace, whose face was finally regaining some of its color back.

With a flippant wave of his hand, the king dismissed his guards and strode to stand at the side of the table. His steps were confident, no trace of fear or indecision anywhere in his countenance. Now that the threat was gone, he could afford to act brave again.

He waited until he was sure he had the room's attention before speaking.

"My son, Bellamy, the crown prince of Penryth and only mortal runecaster in Eritreyia, has much to learn about magick." He cast a sharp glance over Cressida as he spoke, and his look wasn't one of appreciation. "I am sure once my Sun Lord returns to train him, his control over his powers will increase." A hush fell. "Tonight was an unfortunate accident. Thank the Goddess no one was hurt."

As Cressida understood what the king was saying—that Bell would not be punished—she went still. She knew as well as Haven that's not all he was saying. The king just publicly declared his allegiance to Bell, leaving little doubt Renk and Cressida were no longer in favor.

Cressida had played her hand—and lost.

Cressida's lower jaw trembled, and for a moment, before she contorted her face into a docile look of acceptance, something dark and ugly came over her expression.

Her focus raked over Bell. Long enough for Haven to feel the hatred simmering there. Then Cressida snapped her fingers and two guards jumped to attention, following her gestures to help Renk from the room.

Haven's hands—which at some point had balled into rocks to hide her magick—softened and stretched, allowing the blood to rush back into her fingers. She released a long sigh.

Goddess Above, she'd nearly messed everything up.

Bell's arms hung limp at his sides, his fingers clenching and unclenching as if he actually thought he was to blame. He kept shooting glances at his father, ignoring the looks from practically the entire room.

Then he muttered something that sounded like an apology and fled the stage.

FIVE

Haven tracked Bell to the stairwell close to the library. Somewhere along the way he'd discarded his cloak, and one of the guards shadowing him held it as they chased after the prince. Now that his father, King Horace, saw Bell as an asset, he had guards protecting him.

Even inside the castle.

Haven's own guards hesitated at the bottom of the stairs. She grinned over her shoulder at them, raising her eyebrows in challenge. The biggest male, a thickset soldier who might have been handsome, if not for a nose so broken it was nearly flat over his face, sneered at her in reply.

Something about the broken-nosed guard put her on edge, and she found herself keeping tabs on him whenever he was around.

Pushing thoughts of her new guard aside, she diverted her focus to Bell as she loped up to him on silent feet. She wanted to touch him, to comfort him somehow, but thought better of it last minute.

They were beyond those innocent years when they could touch without awkwardness. Spirefall had seen to that.

Instead she walked silently beside him until he stopped to acknowledge her.

"I'm not mad," he said by way of greeting, but his voice said otherwise.

"Okay, you're not mad," Haven repeated. She pretended to straighten the edge of her tunic. "But it's understandable if you are. I have no excuse. If I had stuck to the plan . . ."

"Then the citizens of Penryth would have seen yet another glittery ball, and I'd be no more special than a pyromancer." A bitter grin lifted his cheeks, and he ducked through the massive library doors and into his favorite place in the entire realm. "And it was a beautiful peacock," he added over his shoulder, "even if I take affront to the implication."

All four of their guards paused by the towering oak doors as Haven and Bell wound up the spiraling stairs to their spot near the balcony. The guards never came inside.

In their simple minds, the library was the safest place in Penryth.

If only they knew the truth. Magick was inside these books, dangerous, wondrous magick. The kind that could spark wars and fell kingdoms.

"Would you like to know its name?" Haven said at the top landing. "Surai called him Idiot, but I think that's demeaning for a bird of his stature . . ."

Her words trailed away.

Bell was leaning against the iron railing—a twisted vine of roses—his profile facing her as he studied the floor-to-ceiling rows of books. He sighed and scraped a hand through his curls before turning his attention back to her.

Even sad and angry, he was handsome. His sea-blue eyes vibrant against his umber flesh, delicate features reminding Haven of the new statues the king had acquired recently from Solissian traders.

It was an infinitely paintable face, and already she'd seen his likeness sold in the market square on miniature canvases. There were even tiny busts of the handsome, Cursebreaking prince.

Sure, they were made from cheap plaster and broke apart at the slightest touch, but Haven had three lining the window of her room.

"Bell . . ." Haven began, but her throat tightened and any apology she might have said evanesced.

He slid down the banister and sat cross-legged. "You're not going to sit?"

"Do you want me to sit?" she asked quietly.

"Of course I do," he answered, and those four words eased the panic she hadn't realized was strangling her chest.

"Fine," she murmured.

"Fine."

Flipping back her cloak, she dropped to her rear and scooted next to him.

When they were shoulder-to-shoulder, he let out a tired sigh. "I said I'm not mad, Haven, and I mean it. Unless you meant to send that . . . thing after Renk." A pause. "Did you?"

She shook her head, feeling incredibly contrite. "Renk's a complete and total droob, but I'm not that stupid. If I wanted to murder him, I wouldn't do it in public. And I certainly wouldn't let you take credit."

He dug his elbow into her ribs. "You're terrible, Haven. Renk is . . . well, he doesn't deserve that."

"Yes," she said softly. "He does. You need to be careful around him and Cressida, Bell. Especially now that you have the king's favor."

Bell stiffened, his gaze shifting to his bootlaces. "I might have his favor, but it's all a lie."

For the hundredth time that week alone, Haven bit back harsh words for the king. His sudden, newfound affection for Bell highlighted just how absent his love had been all these years.

Just like the demons the mortal kings used to keep chained below like pets, the king thought he could use Bell's powers to his advantage.

Instead of spells and chains, the king used Bell's need for a father's acceptance to control him.

"You're his son," she said, managing to keep the anger from her voice. "That should be enough."

"But it's not, we both know that." He tugged at a frayed thread along the hem of his tunic. "When we first came back, I thought I would hate him for abandoning me. But the second he threw his arms around me, the moment he declared me his son and I heard true pride in his voice, I knew that I was doomed to live the rest of my life chasing that feeling. Strange, how addicting my father's love is. Like a bittersweet drug I can't shake."

"Bell—"

"You don't understand," he added, refusing her gaze. "You can't."

He wasn't trying to be cruel, but his words stung.

"It's true," she admitted. "I don't know my parents, and I will never feel a father's love—or the lack thereof. But I know enough to recognize that you deserve better."

He swallowed, his eyes damp as they met hers. "We have to stop, Haven."

"Stop what?" she asked stupidly.

"We can't keep doing this. Pretending I have magick. Not when your dark magick is so . . . unpredictable."

The air seemed to thin. "How?"

"When I saw you perform magick in Spirefall that day, it was the most marvelous thing I'd ever witnessed." He sunk into himself, his eyes distant. "I think I knew then, deep down, that my magick was a lie. Even so. When you told me the truth, that I was magick barren, it felt like being skewered."

She rested her offending hands in her lap, studying the line of dirt beneath her fingernails. "Bell, if I could give you my magick, I would."

She had waited two weeks after they returned to tell him the whole story. The way he'd looked at her when she said his magick wasn't real . . . well, she never wanted to see that expression from him again.

"Don't you understand?" He massaged the sharp line of his jaw. "That just makes this worse. I would do anything to possess a fraction of your magick, while you don't even want it."

The words Haven wanted to say all dissipated on her tongue. She hadn't known he felt this way.

"I went along with our lie out of shame," he continued, "and because I like the way people treat me now. The way they actually look me in the eyes, like my opinion matters. Like I matter. But tonight that lie nearly got subjects of Penryth killed." He gave a scoffing laugh. "Even someone as vain and weak as me has to draw the line somewhere."

"Bell, it—I'm sorry."

"You have to leave." His voice cracked, and he cleared his throat. "I'll wait until you're far enough away to tell the king my magick has disappeared. Then, even if he suspects it was your magick, not mine, he won't be able to reach you."

Panic coiled inside her belly, growing larger with every wild beat of her heart. "No."

"If you stay here, Haven, he'll figure it out. He'll torture you until he finds your powers. He'll dig it out of you, he'll . . ."

A ragged breath whooshed from Bell's lips, and his head fell into his hands.

Haven did the same. "How can I leave when this is my home? *You're* my home, Bell. Besides the little fact that I swore an oath to protect you."

His eyes glimmered as he said, calmly, like he wasn't changing everything between them, "I could release you from your oath of protection."

His statement felt like an axe cleaving her in two. "Why? Are you mad because of Renk? I promise I'll learn to control my dark magick. I swear that will never happen again."

"You can't make that promise." His head fell back, thunking against the wrought iron banister. "You fought through horrors most can't even dream of to save me. You sacrificed everything for me. I could never be mad at you. I love you, Haven. Which is why I'm doing this."

Haven blinked as the rushing wave of panic grew louder, heavier. Never in a million years did she imagine Bell would abandon her.

"Don't you understand," he continued, his voice rattled and quick. "Something's coming. I can feel it like a . . . a shadow slowly descending. I see it in my nightmares, I see it . . . there's a crown, and these huge, black horns . . ." A frayed breath burst from his lips. "Oh, Goddess Above. I think I'm going mad."

"Bell, you're scaring me."

There was a wildness in his eyes as he met her panicked stare. "It's my turn to protect you, Haven."

Haven felt ill, her chest whirling strangely. She was suddenly all too aware of the artery throbbing at her wrist. The tightness of her lungs.

Yet the fear flooding her body couldn't hide the fact that he was right. She'd turned the problem over and over in her mind, how to keep their secret from the king.

And yet, the way he looked at them . . . the way his eyes shifted from his son to her . . .

Another outburst from her dark magick and he'd put it together. The king was a droob, but he was a clever droob.

Still, leaving wasn't an option. Bell wasn't safe. Especially now that she knew about his dreams. How long had he been having them?

"What if I find a way to . . . bind my dark magick?" she asked, carefully. As if her dark magick might hear her and take offense.

His eyes narrowed as he chewed his lip, thinking. "Can such a thing be done?"

"I don't know. I can ask Archeron when he returns."

At the mention of Archeron, Bell's lips mashed together. After Archeron left to hunt Bjorn, she'd told Bell the truth about his brother's murder at the hands of the Sun Lord.

She understood why Archeron killed Remy, Bell's older brother. Understood the atrocities that warranted such a bloody act. But Bell never would.

"I doubt a Solis such as Archeron would know much about binding dark magick," Bell said tightly.

Haven scuffed the toe of her boot against the wood floor. "I haven't been to see Nasira since she tried to kill me the last time."

The very mention of Stolas's sister and the rightful heir to the Noctis throne put Haven on edge.

"She didn't try to kill you," Bell amended, but he didn't exactly sound confident.

"What do you call sending daggers of ice to impale me then?"

"They missed."

"Only because I dove to the floor!" Haven growled, her chest tight.

If she had known the trouble that would be caused by Nasira, Haven wouldn't have made a deal with Stolas to protect her.

"What about the Shade Lord?" Bell asked, and she noticed his eyes crinkled strangely in the corners, his gaze curiously watching her response.

"What about him?" Haven snapped, instantly regretting her tone when Bell flinched.

She softened her voice. "Stolas would see me binding my dark magick as an affront. Besides, I can't control entering his dreams. We train, sometimes we talk, and then he disappears again for weeks at a time." She rolled her eyes and tried to hide her concern for the Shade Lord with a joke. "If only our deal disappeared as easily."

Her worry over Stolas was an unexpected part of their relationship. She knew either the Shade Queen or Ravenna had him imprisoned in the Netherworld and that he was being tortured.

"I don't know what changed." She picked at a ragged nail. "Why I'm entering his dreams. Maybe he calls me because he wants to check up on Nasira."

Although half the time, she entered his dreams in the midst of one of her own nightmares. Either her fear was somehow pushing her into his dreamscape, or he could sense her terror and was pulling her there.

Stolas had never discussed the specifics when they made the deal for him to enter her dreams—but she felt certain entering *his* wasn't part of the bargain.

"Then," Bell said, flicking the corner of his high collar, "it sounds like Nasira might be your only hope of controlling your dark magick."

"And if I find a way to ensure it's bound? Can I stay?"

"Yes." He sagged against the wrought iron banister. "I can't believe I even thought about sending you away. It's just . . . I panicked." Shifting, he turned to look her straight on. "But what I said is true. I'm tired of lying. We need to find a way, a plausible way, to make my father and the kingdom believe my magick has disappeared."

"And you won't miss it?" she asked. "The adoration, the applause?" She punched him softly in the arm. "The throng of screaming girls following you like cute little puppies?"

"You're the only girl who follows me around the castle, but I wouldn't use the word cute." He eyed her worn boots and scuffed pants with pointed distaste.

She chuckled. "One, that's a lie. I look amazing in these pants. Two, that might have once been true, but not now. Every girl in Penryth has fallen for the Cursebreaking prince, even Eleeza."

He pressed his knuckles into his cheeks, now bright with color. "They love an illusion, a fraud. That prince isn't me."

Before she could respond, he jumped to his feet, his back to her. "I'll see you tomorrow? I want to practice my speech for the High Council gathering in the morning."

Oh, that. Haven had mixed feelings about the new High Council, formed from the few kingdoms left standing. The fact that the mortal realm was healthy enough to even propose a rejoining of the kingdoms was a good sign. But most of the rulers would resent Bell for his powers.

If any were stupid enough to try and harm him, she and Surai were ready. But the idea made her nervous.

"I don't know how the king managed to convince the others to hold the first meeting here," Bell remarked.

They want to see the new lightcaster prince, she almost said. *They want to see how they might destroy you.*

"Anyway." He scraped his fingers through his hair and hefted the books held firmly beneath his arms up higher. "I'm off to practice and then get some sleep."

Yeah, right. If the past two months were any indication, Bell would spend most of the night bathed in runelight as he pored over the tomes held firmly beneath his arm. Then he'd show up at breakfast with dark half-moons under his eyes to rival her own.

She didn't even have to look at the titles to know what they were about. Lightcasting and the runic arts.

What he searched for inside those great leather-bound scrolls was anyone's guess. He'd been completely secretive about them, even from her. Which hurt more than she was willing to admit.

"You should try it," he added dryly.

"What? Reading?"

"Sleeping. You know, that thing where you lie back, close your eyes, and wake up *not* looking like a rumpled pile of vorgrath crap."

Stretching to her feet, she eyed the books and murmured, "You're not looking so hot yourself in that department."

"Yeah," he muttered, glancing at her over his shoulder. "Well nearly killing my half-brother was incredibly draining."

But the humor was missing from his voice.

Haven forced out a laugh. "Right. Goodnight."

She watched him go. Watched until he crossed beneath the massive chandelier and through the doors and disappeared, his guards scrambling to catch up.

Her guard, the one with the ruined nose and sneer, made a

strange face as he stared after the prince. But then he flicked his gaze to Haven, gracing her with an equally foul look.

I have to watch that one, she thought distractedly before hurrying to meet Surai for their nightly lesson.

Of course she was late, as usual.

And of course Surai would punish her for it.

SIX

The runewall buzzed with magick. Haven felt it seeping into the soles of her feet as she jogged across the top, following the line of moonstone toward the sea. Each footstep conjured a buttery gold footprint of light that receded into the stone.

She wasn't sure if she felt the energy more now because of her own magick, or if breaking the Curse had restored the power in the stones.

A shadow danced around her feet. Even though she'd grown used to the idea of being followed by an abnormally large telepathic bird, Ravius's shadow still startled her.

Why can't you sleep like normal mortals? Ravius complained grumpily inside her head.

Why can't you be silent like normal birds? she replied, ignoring the harrumph that followed.

Normal? Do I look normal to you? I am an Asgardian prince, descended from an esteemed line of warriors.

Were, Haven answered. *You were a prince. Now you're a raven. An ignominious, overly large, preening raven. One that doesn't have to follow me.*

Oh, but I do. Prince Darkshade's orders.

Haven still wasn't used to Stolas's formal term, but she wasn't sure which part was surprising. The royal title or the fittingly ominous surname.

A fox screamed somewhere nearby, and she glanced over her shoulder.

The act was more habit than anything. She'd enacted a following rune to alert her the moment someone began trailing her path. Not wanting to grow reliant on magick and lose her skills, she hardly dared use it, except for the nights like tonight.

Magick or not, she'd lost her guards the old-fashioned way. Even if they did track her, her path through the Muirwood Forest ensured her privacy.

Now that the Curse was broken, the trees were ordinary—no weeping cries or unearthly moans.

Still, people avoided the once haunted woods, including her guards. Old habits die hard.

Once she caught the gentle crash of waves against the cliffs, she dropped to the forest floor and headed toward the break in the tree line.

I wouldn't go that way if I were you, Ravius warned.

Good thing you're not me then.

Surai caught her right as she emerged from the woods.

A bright speck of gold bloomed inches from Haven's nose, blinding her.

"What the—" Before Haven could finish her sentence, she was flung onto her back, hard. The cloying cinnamon and roses taste of light magick clung to the back of her throat. Sweet and pungent, the scent burned and tingled like knocking back a thimbleful of rum.

Told you, Ravius gloated before alighting in the nearest tree to watch.

Surai grinned down at her. Her purple eyes glowed from beneath the darkness cast by her hood, bright with the promise of magick.

Even after three months, Haven still marveled at Surai's powers, now set free from the Curse's effects.

Adding insult to injury, Surai offered a hand to help Haven up. "Feeling a bit slow tonight, mortal?"

Ignoring Surai's gesture, Haven jumped to her feet and fell easily into her stance. Legs wide, arms out, palms up.

Twin pearls of light blossomed from her upturned hands. "A little warning would have been nice."

"Warnings are for good little mortals who listen to their elders." Surai winked at Haven, rubbing in her decades of age and experience.

With a wink of her own, Haven lifted her hands to her face and blew.

The buds of light fractured into a million exquisite shards. They burst toward Surai like dandelion fluff, glittering magickal weapons no bigger than a grain of sand.

Any one of which could immobilize Surai with a touch.

Last second before the magickal cloud hit Surai, she threw up a shield.

Haven's countless bits of magick bounced off the thin orange-tinged bubble and blew over the cliffs.

"Fancy," Surai muttered. "But ineffectual when you're as good at conjuring shields as I am."

"Brag much?" Haven muttered.

"When you've practiced magick for a couple centuries, you can brag too."

Haven rolled her eyes and concentrated on her right hand, constructing in her mind the sword she'd spied in the armory earlier that day. A gorgeous rapier with an emerald and ruby encrusted dragon hilt.

It was meant for Bell, a present from one of the visiting kingdoms. But just like all his weapons, he would eventually gift the beauty to her.

A giddy feeling welled in her belly as cold metal filled her outstretched hand. The invocation was perfect, right down to the ruby flames.

"Pretty," Surai said in a bored voice.

As orange fire whooshed down the length of the blade, illuminating the grass around them, Haven grinned. Veins of gold magick whirled and sparked from the inferno.

If not for the secrecy of Muirwood Forest on one side and the cliffs on the other, Haven would have never dared flaunt such powerful magick.

"Show-off," Surai murmured, her voice finally holding the appreciation Haven craved. Surai drew her own swords, twin katanas.

Flames of red magick licked the air around her weapons.

Her magick was muted and dull compared to Haven's, the well of power Surai drew upon shallower and less potent. But what the Solis girl lacked in magick she made up for in skill, thousands of years of honing her battle magick into a precise tool.

Surai lunged, and they fell into a familiar dance of thrusts and parries. Feints and jabs. Haven felt the worries from the past few weeks slip away as they practiced through the evening, mixing swordplay with Surai's helpful tips on defensive maneuvers.

Surai's talent lay in shields, and she taunted Haven with more and more elaborate types until Haven was sure her magick would run dry. When the Solis warrior grew tired of defensive maneuvers, she switched to another favorite: illusions.

Haven stared at the three enormous, shaggy brown bears approaching through the woods, their backs high enough to scrape the first level of branches, and tried to remember they weren't real.

Yet every rattle of the earth beneath her feet as one of the massive beasts took a step, every whiff of their rank carrion odor, said otherwise. Surai had filled out each beast down to the most minute detail. Golden tips softened their shaggy fur, their eyes and lips a soft black.

"Illusions are like lovers," Surai purred, appraising her masterpiece. "Once they get in your head, you're screwed."

Haven waited until the first bear was close enough to sniff her with its giant, dirt-crusted nose. Waited until its dark lips curled back, exposing spotted gums and four-inch long incisors—one chipped in half.

Then she conjured a bright orange teardrop of magick and flung it at the creatures. "Murathen!"

The ancient word meant, *be gone.*

The three bears evanesced on the breeze, sparks of their being spreading through the forest like fireflies before disappearing.

"Good," Surai said, clapping her hands. It was the first time Haven had pronounced that word correctly. "But your doubt almost cost you."

"What doubt?" Haven scoffed. "There haven't been bears in this forest for centuries."

"Then let's try with something that *does* lurk beyond the castle gates."

This time Surai constructed two magical wolves as white as the moon, with shaggy scruffs and intelligent yellow eyes. When Haven dispatched those, Surai got creative, conjuring all sorts of Shadowlings.

Dispatching Surai's illusions seemed like an easy thing. But if Haven let herself believe, even for a moment, that they were real, her magick would be useless against them.

Offensive maneuvers came next. Meaning Surai went on the attack, lobbing orb after orb of magick at Haven's head. It was Haven's job to find ways to prevent said magick from reaching her very mortal, very frail body.

The problem wasn't accessing the magick. Thanks to the tapestry of iridescent runes swirling over every inch of her flesh, she could access all the magick in the Nihl *and* the Netherworld.

She was bursting at the seams with magick.

No, the problem was not knowing *what* to do with her powers, and she flailed about, clumsily countering each new maneuver until the air simmered with the scent of burnt roses.

Surai sniffed the air and then grimaced. "Focus!"

"I am!" Haven snarled, sending a spear of red flames toward Surai's head. The Solis girl ducked and the fiery weapon exploded against a balsam tree.

As the tree groaned and toppled over in an explosion of pine needles and dust, silence fell.

Then both girls burst into laughter. Surai leapt over the fallen tree and clapped Haven on the shoulder. "Next time I go to battle against a forest, I want you by my side."

They sat on the unburnt side of the smoldering trunk, sharing a flask of moonberry tea as they worked to catch their breath. Haven was too parched to complain over the watered-down drink, diluted for Haven's mortal constitution.

The flask was hot in Haven's hand, the liquid bitter and pungent in her mouth. Ravius flew down from the trees and landed beside Surai, who took some sunflower seeds from her pocket and fed the cranky bird.

"You spoil him," Haven said, glaring at Ravius.

Ruffling his feathers, he turned from his feast to peck at Haven. *Your jealousy is unbecoming.*

Shut up, Haven responded, swatting at the oversized creature. *Or I'll put an arrow through your heart and mount you above my bed.*

You wouldn't dare, Ravius muttered, but he hopped closer to his protector.

"No," Surai countered. "I spoil you. We need to double your training, and triple the hours you spend learning the ancient language of the gods."

Haven didn't even bother groaning because Surai spoke the truth. There were three ways to channel magick. First, raw, direct channeling of magick like the orbs and flames Haven used. Second, runes. Runes were used for more complex spells. And, third, verbal magick, which had to be spoken in the ancient language.

Haven was okay at raw magick, barely passable at runic magick, and a complete failure at verbal magick.

After their breathing softened, Surai pocketed the rest of the seeds and slid her curious gaze to Haven. "Why didn't you use dark magick?"

"What?" Haven capped the flask, her throat suddenly tight. "When?"

Surai's eyebrows flicked up. "Don't play coy, mortal. Thrice I sent offensive magick near your head, and thrice you could have used dark magick to diffuse the attack. Instead you wasted energy cutting them down with your sword."

Haven unbuttoned the top two buttons of her tunic, letting

in the cool sea-infused breeze. "I'm not using dark magick anymore."

"Huh. I'm no expert in the dark arts, but I don't think it works that way."

"I'm going to ask Nasira to bind it." Haven clenched her jaw as something inside her seemed to squirm and flinch.

Surai was quiet for a spell. The soft pulse of waves lapping at the shore below the only sound.

Finally, she stood, brushing charred bits of bark from her rear.

This time Haven took her hand, letting her friend help her to her feet. A thin gold bracelet jangled on Surai's wrist, a tiny glass teardrop hanging from the chain.

Inside the teardrop glowed Rook's heart flower, a purple loosestrife.

The sacred flower was the only thing Surai kept from her dead partner. The rest of her personal effects went with Rook's body to the Morgani Queen, to be buried in the fields of Galahad in a secret location somewhere on the Morgani Islands.

"Haven," Surai began, her eyes dark with emotion. "I know it seems tempting to just erase the thing that scares you the most, but that's not the answer." Her gaze drifted to the horizon where moonlight refracted off the dark ocean beyond. "I could use magick to temper the grief constricting my heart—I've been tempted to. More than once."

"And no one would blame you," Haven said softly.

"If I lessened the pain, I would lose a part of Rook, too. Our shared memories." When Surai glanced back, barely controlled pain shimmered inside her lavender eyes. "Besides, even if I dulled the pain, it would still be there. I cannot run from it. I must face it, learn from it, master it. If I don't, that pain will master me."

Haven put a hand on her friend's shoulder, the worn leather of her vest soft beneath Haven's fingers. "Surai, your mourning is not the same as my dark magick."

"No? My grief is an unfathomable darkness that I did not ask for, but it has great power too. The power to make one cherish every second of living. Grief reminds me to hold everything and everyone I love close, because there is no promise of tomorrow."

"Does your grief make you dream of killing everyone you love, night after night?" Haven's voice came out more bitter than intended, and she immediately regretted her tone.

Surai raised her elegant eyebrows. "My nightmares only involve Rook. But I see your point. Now hear mine. Binding your magick means you are too afraid to control it. It means you are . . . scared."

The sting of Surai's words made Haven take a step back.

"It is okay to be afraid, Haven," Surai continued. "But dark magick is a part of you, and you *must* learn to control it."

"Maybe if I'd practiced the runic arts since birth like you, that would be possible. But I haven't, and now . . ." Haven held out her hands. They were empty, yet all she saw was the dagger from her dream, dark with Bell's blood. "I might be able to master the dark arts in half a decade, but by then, how many of those I love will have paid the price?"

Surai's gaze collapsed to her boots. She couldn't refute Haven's scenario was a possibility.

"I won't let that happen." Haven brushed a lock of errant hair behind her ear, more determined than ever. "Besides, I already promised the prince I would bind my dark magick."

Surai's head snapped up. Promises for the Solis were ironclad, meaning now Haven didn't have a choice in the matter.

"Well, then it's settled, I suppose." Surai blew out a resigned sigh, sending the ends of her short raven-feather hair flying from her face. "Now, where were we? Shields?"

Haven groaned. "I thought we were done for the night."

"Have you not learned anything after three months of training?"

"And have you not learned mortals need a little thing called sleep?" Haven retorted.

"Stop blabbering, lazy mortal, and show me a water shield."

Haven groaned again, but she obeyed. Pissing off Surai would only prolong their session, so Haven prepared her shield, making sure Surai heard her sighs of protest.

Goddess save her. It was going to be a long night.

SEVEN

The moon was halfway across the sky by the time Surai ended their session. Since the Solis warrior didn't need sleep, she offered to do another check of the grounds while Haven returned to the castle to rest.

Haven watched through bleary eyes as Surai transformed into her raven form, a much smaller, much less *talkative* version of Ravius. Even after three months of watching Surai transform at will, Haven was still getting used to the idea.

After Surai was a mere blip in the moonlit sky, Haven traipsed back the way she came.

The morning would come soon, along with the High Council meeting. Both events she'd rather miss, but that was impossible.

A simple energy rune would get her through the morning without sleep, but she'd grown hesitant of using magick for everyday needs. Afraid, perhaps, that once she began she couldn't stop.

Never had a mortal existence seemed so harsh until she realized all the things magick could lift from her shoulders. Sleeping. Eating. Bathing, even. All fixed by magick. If she didn't feel like walking somewhere, she could draw a speed rune that made a mile feel like ten feet. If she didn't feel like brushing her hair, a simple disentanglement rune did the trick.

Tired of people staring at her vibrant rose-gold hair? An illusion rune that changed the color to something more appropriate for the conservative citizens of Penryth.

Magick could do so many things—and yet, she was terrified of growing reliant on its benefits. On growing soft.

She traced her steps through the forest, over the wall, and across the fragrant gardens, all without any magick. Frogs croaked somewhere close by, and crickets chirped merrily.

A few revelers from the party were passed out along the benches near the second courtyard, covered in flashy capes.

They were totally unaware of the girl in their midst. Or what she could do to them . . . if she so desired.

But what she desired was sleep, and she quickened her pace toward her bed.

When the last set of gates between the gardens and the castle loomed, a strange feeling prickled the base of her spine. Despite her hurry to sleep, she paused beneath a hackberry tree and listened.

An owl hooted somewhere nearby. Otherwise, silence.

Was someone following her? Leaning down to fiddle with her bootlaces, she scanned her periphery, searching for quick movements.

Nothing.

Shaking out her shoulders, she pushed the thought away. No one was following her . . .

A shudder wracked her body. No one was *following* her.

Where were her guards?

Normally when she lost them at night, they waited for her in the gardens. Pissed and a little drunk on the flasks of plum-wine they thought she didn't know about.

Her body went cold. Something was wrong.

The image from earlier in the library began to flash behind her eyes. The way her guard looked at Bell . . .

Haven lunged toward the gate. The guard nearest the door moved to stop her. She dropped him with a fist to his stomach. The other guard went for his sword.

Haven reached for hers and pinned him with a ferocious look.

Nodding, he backed away and let her pass.

She was in a full sprint, her cloak flapping behind her. She streaked through the cobblestone courtyard and into the servant's entrance, mentally calculating the quickest route to Bell's room.

The halls were a blur of shadows and runelight. Her heartbeat slammed in her skull, mixing with the frantic tempo of her breath.

Her dagger gleamed in her hand.

Please be okay. Please be okay.

She was overreacting. *Goddess Above, let me be overreacting.*

The moment she topped the stairs to the third floor and saw Bell's open door, all her fears congealed into a lump of dread that lodged in her throat, making it nearly impossible to breathe.

Boots—someone's boots lay halfway out the door.

Were they—

Oh, thank the Goddess. Too big to be Bell's.

Relief and rage surged through her as she rushed to his room, panic constricting her vision.

As soon as she stepped over Bell's first guard, she froze. Other than a few uncovered sconces of runelight, the room was dark, the corners and background limned with shadow.

A dresser was overturned on its side. Beside it, Bell's second guard lay face down. The odd angle of his head said his neck had been broken, and a small circle of blood formed a macabre corona around the base of his skull.

Her attention snapped to the figure by Bell's headboard.

Just like in her dream.

Except the person looming over Bell wasn't Haven.

Slowly, he swiveled his head to face her. Gone was the human-like face of her guard. In its place was a demon with all black eyes and bared lips. One hand hovered above Bell, fingers curled inward like a puppet master holding strings to his creation.

She recognized the twisted blood magick Damius and the other Devourers used inside the guard's face.

Dark flickers of smoke and shadow traveled between his hand and the prince, who was awake but seemingly frozen. Bell's mouth was wrenched open in a silent scream. His hands clawed around his golden duvet.

Books littered his bed. More tomes scattered on the floor. The way they had fallen—half open, spines torn from impact—he'd been surprised while still awake.

Somehow, her guard was using dark magick. Haven felt it crawling all around the room. Heard its serpentine whispering calling to her.

For a sickening moment, she felt a tug toward the darkness the way a mother was drawn to her children.

The demon-guard snarled, the sound not even close to human, and flung a fistful of dark shadows at Haven. The oily mist broke apart into thick snakes. Runelight glittered off the black scales of the creatures as they slithered toward her, snapping the air and spitting venom.

When they neared, they raised up and spread their hoods,

casting circular shadows against the walls. But instead of striking, they paused in front of her and *bowed.*

With a wicked grin, she held out her hand, causing the demon-guard's own menacing smile to falter. When his shadows reached Haven's fingers, she let them curl around her hand like pets.

"Fool," she growled, taking a step closer. "Thinking you can use darkness against its master."

Fear—his face grew waxy with fear. His tongue darted out and wet his lips.

Another step closer.

"Who sent you?" Haven demanded.

His mouth opened as if to respond, and then his eyes bulged wide and he began to choke. Gurgling, he grasped at his throat.

Then he rasped out a laugh. "You will never figure it out, bitch."

Only a few feet separated them now.

"Tell me," she commanded.

Still holding his hand above the prince, the guard sneered at her. "Or what? I know your secret now, lightcaster. Or should I say, darkcaster? The prince is a liar and a fraud. He holds no magick . . . but you do, don't you? Wait till the kingdom hears what kind."

"Haven," Bell croaked. The hold the guard had on the prince had lessened, and Bell managed to scramble back against his headboard. He grabbed a book and held it up like a weapon.

The black snakes coiled seductively around her hand.

Use us, they begged in one voice. *We will kill him. Yes we will.*

She looked from the snakes to Bell. No dark magick. How could she forsake something if she relied on it?

Straightening her spine, she crushed the snakes' bodies between her fingers. Their rage-filled shrieks filled the air. As the dark creatures crumbled to ash, her insides writhed, and she clutched at the hollow spot just below her breastbone.

The guard grinned. "That was stupid."

Something inside his eyes, something dark and malignant, twisted her heart with dread. Still clutching her midsection, she raised her hand, palm up.

Warmth pulsed down her arm and pooled in her palm as she gathered her light magick. A wisp of flame appeared, beautiful and deadly.

In her mind she constructed a death rune.

The spark swirled and reshaped itself into a configuration of messy threads. Each thread represented a path the guard could take in life. All at once the thousands of threads began to churn, knotting in on themselves until a tiny speck of light was left, so bright it lit the entire room.

"I don't need dark magick to end you, demon. There's only one path left for you. Death."

Drawing all her energy into the flame in her hand, she lobbed the fiery weapon straight at the guard's heart.

The death rune shot straight at the guard's chest . . . and halted.

Well that can't be good.

A sinking feeling filled Haven as the death rune swerved to the left and disappeared into the runestone necklace at Bell's neck. The stone pulsed once beneath Bell's silk nightshirt.

Then the room went dark.

Shadeling's shadow.

Haven had never used a death rune before, but she was pretty sure that wasn't supposed to happen.

"The thing about a diverting stone like the one the prince wears," the guard said. "It's very easy to break the second part of the spell and trap the light magick inside the stone."

The guard's head fell back and his mouth . . . his mouth split open down to his jaw the way a snake does when swallowing prey.

A gurgling noise spilled from his throat and then slick black tentacles slipped from his too-wide mouth.

One. Two. Three . . .

Too many to count. They slapped against anything they touched, the tips tentatively touching the objects, taking them in. Their shiny bodies seemed to swell and undulate like earthworms rising from a long rain.

One of the tentacles slithered across her boot, leaving a sticky, oozing trail.

Before she could react, the tentacle lashed out, stripping her sword belt from her waist. She reached for her throwing daggers only to have those snatched as well.

"Haven," Bell whispered, dropping his book to the bed in a soft whump. "Tell me you're not doing this."

"Not me," she snarled, glancing around for a weapon.

The guard was convulsing, his chest wracked with violent tremors, as if something giant was trying to get out. More tentacles slithered from his chasm of a mouth.

So many. Where—or *what*—were they coming from?

One particularly large and slimy tentacle shot from the guard's throat and wrapped around Bell's leg.

Stupidly Haven tried to throw an orb of light magick at the slimy appendage, but the same thing happened as last time.

The weapon swerved into the runestone at Bell's chest, drawn into an inescapable prison.

Her light magick was useless.

Not relying on his companion guard, Bell had grabbed a quill pen from his desk and he was stabbing at the tentacle. "Die, you disgusting thing!"

Suddenly, warmth cut through the frigid air.

At the same time, a bright golden light lit the room, so vibrant Haven temporarily lost her vision.

Her eyes cleared in time to see a beautiful orb of magick slam into the demon. The maneuver was a simple offensive one, but the execution was flawless.

Surai!

The golden miasma of fire licked over the guard's chest, hungrily consuming the dark magick seeping from his body. As the flames hit the tentacles, they shuddered, a shriek of agony spilling from the guard's chest.

The dark creature inside the guard retracted its arms just as its host was flung backward into the wall.

The impact was so hard it cracked the stone.

The guard slid to the floor, groaned once from his now normal sized mouth, and went quiet.

"What the Netherfire?" Surai hissed, stomping into the room and zapping him with another shock of magick. His body jolted and tremored before going still. "I leave you alone for like two minutes and you're fighting blood magick demons?"

"How did you know?" Haven asked, avoiding her friend's eyes. Hadn't she just spent hours training? And yet, if not for Surai, they would have been in serious trouble.

"Ravius found me."

Haven glanced over her shoulder and discovered the bird perched on a two-foot tall marble bust of Bell. The statue was given to the prince by a tradesman.

Seeing Ravius sitting on the prince's head cut a humorous picture, and she would have smiled—if not for Ravius puffing his chest out and saying, *Thank the Shadeling I was here to save you.*

Haven barely kept from throwing a pillow at the bird's head. *I would have been just fine*, she snapped mentally.

The quill was still clutched tightly in Bell's hand, and he looked from Surai to Haven. "Can someone please tell me what happened here?"

"I'm guessing my guard was sent to steal your magick and then kill you." Haven swallowed the warm bile lapping at her throat. Taking someone's magick was hard, but not impossible.

Damius had stolen the magick from a Solis once. Not a powerful Sun Lord, like Archeron. Even a Devourer like Damius wasn't that strong. She could still hear the Solis's screams of torment as Damius ripped the magick from his chest and put it inside a jade stone.

Bell's hands shook as he set the quill onto his nightstand and then slid out of bed. His legs trembled, but he held his head high as he assessed the guard at his feet. "Why?"

Surai stepped gingerly over the thick sludge the tentacles had left over the floor and approached the unconscious guard. "He has a master, a blood mage, someone who controls him using blood magick."

"Blood mage," Haven repeated, the words sounding offensive somehow.

Damius dabbled in blood magick, but it was never his favorite. Probably because, at the time, it was assumed the old days of summoning demons with blood magick had long since passed. The door between the realm the demons hailed from had been sealed, and the demons left in their world were trapped in the pits of the Netherworld with the Shadeling, imprisoned forever.

Except, not forever, apparently.

Surai placed her foot on the back of the guard's neck. "See that there?"

Using the sharp toe of her leather boot, she tugged down his collar. A pale blue rune shone faintly in the low light. Just bright enough to make out the five coiling lines tangled together, like a nest of vipers.

In response to being exposed, the lines angrily churned and contracted, digging deeper into the guard's flesh. He let out a gargled moan.

"The blood mark," Surai hissed, yanking her boot back as if the bluish threads were *real* snakes. "Each line represents a blood slave under the blood mage's control."

"So there are more than one?" Bell muttered before releasing a long sigh.

"Blood mages keep a tight leash on their pets," Surai said. "This one must be close. Maybe even inside Fenwick. And powerful, considering the demons."

"I thought demons weren't in our realm anymore?" Haven persisted, despite the obvious evidence at her feet.

A frown twitched Surai's lips. "So did I."

"Blood slaves carrying demons?" Bell's legs seemed to give out as he half-fell half-sat on the edge of his bed.

If that were true, how could she protect Bell? The blood mage could be anyone. Anywhere. And if they were powerful enough to have five blood slaves under their command, they could disguise themselves as soldiers . . . or another guard.

That was the one thing that stuck out to her from Damius's forays into blood magick. A true blood mage could change their appearance at will, becoming anyone.

Even if she had a hundred soldiers at her command, it would be nearly impossible to keep Bell safe.

Rage propelled her toward the man on the floor.

In one motion, she plucked her sword, sticking out from beneath the nightstand where it was flung, and pressed the tip into the base of the demon-guard's skull, just above his blood mark. "So we just torture him until he gives us a name."

She could have sworn the runemark at his neck hissed.

"It's not that simple," Surai said, carefully, her tone soothing.

Haven took in the bright red beads welling around her sword tip and realized if she pressed any harder she'd kill the man.

"He'll be bound by blood magick to silence," Surai continued. "Even if he wanted to tell us, he can't."

He gurgled when he tried to respond earlier. Now it made sense why.

With a frustrated growl, Haven removed the blade from his neck and rammed it into its sheath, wishing it were his spine instead.

Think. There has to be a way.

She couldn't accept that someone with powerful blood magick had these—these *things* on a leash, ready to kill Bell. That they had infiltrated the court and could be anywhere . . . hurt anyone.

She already had Nasira to worry about . . .

Nasira. As a master of the dark runic arts, she understood blood magick.

Haven met Surai's steady gaze. "I think I might know a way to make him talk. Someone scarier than his blood master and more powerful."

Surai's eyebrows flicked up as she caught on. "No. Bad idea. Nasira is worse than a blood mage. And she loathes you."

Haven shrugged; there was no arguing that point. Apparently calling Nasira spoiled and a brat was a trigger for her, even if it was true.

"Let me handle Nasira," Bell chimed in. They both turned to him, ready to protest, but he threw his hands up. "Really. We're . . . friends. If I'm there, she won't hurt Haven."

"Friends?" Haven said. Her voice was tinny with shock. "Since when?"

It was his turn to shrug. "I go there sometimes, when I have questions about . . ." His gaze flicked to the books on the floor. "Stuff."

Haven wanted to press Bell further, but they didn't have time. Turning back to Surai, she said, "Bell will be there to act as a buffer. Besides, we'll come bearing a gift."

"The only thing that girl wants is a live human to feed off, and we . . ." Surai's gaze leapt to the guard as understanding dawned. "You can't think . . . no, Haven."

With a dark grin, Haven jerked her head toward the guard. "If we hurry, he won't even fight back. And with the demon inside him, it's really like a two-for-one deal."

"You do realize she'll probably just eat the guard and make the demon her pet, right?"

"I don't care what she does as long as we get a name."

Surai shuddered and made the sign of the Goddess—but she didn't say no.

EIGHT

Nasira stayed in an old hunting estate deep in the Muirwood. The lodge had once been used by the king's guests before the Muirwood became haunted, and was a collection of seven cabins and one larger manor. High up on a ridge and hidden by overgrown climbing ferns, the estate had long been forgotten.

Basically it was the perfect place to stash a renegade princess and heir to the Noctis throne.

"Do you notice anything strange?" Bell asked as they climbed the worn steps leading up the hill. They were steeped in darkness, the tall trees of the forest strangling any meager moonlight from above.

Haven paused. The guard was still unconscious, wrapped in one of Bell's expensive silk sheets. Surai held one end, Haven the other. She'd used a weightless rune to make his body light, but already the magick was starting to wear off, and sweat darkened both girls' temples.

Haven's arms ached as she leaned over to set the guard down.

"The woods are quiet," she said.

Surai clicked her tongue, the sound carrying through the silence. "All the forest animals refuse to come here. They are scared. They know what resides above."

Their attention drifted to the peaked roofs of the buildings above. A thin line of smoke drifted from the chimney of the main building where Nasira had carved out a nest.

Haven chuckled darkly. "My guess is she's waiting on the roofline, trying to decide if she should kill me and suffer Stolas's wrath."

Bell slid his gaze to the tree line behind them. "She prefers the tallest trees."

Betrayal tightened around Haven's heart. Not that Bell visited Nasira, but that he'd hidden it from her.

"Then what is she waiting for?" Surai asked.

"To see what we want," Haven said, sweeping a long glance over the forest before taking hold of the sheet again. "Now, c'mon. We're wasting time. Let's get this blood slave up these steps before he wakes up and starts fighting."

Before Haven could lift the guard, the sound of air rushing above caught her attention. She settled her hand on the hilt of her sword, but resisted pulling it out.

If Nasira wanted to kill them, Haven's sword would only make her laugh.

A dark shadow trailed over the skyline in wide, lazy circles. Bell was right; Nasira had been waiting in the trees flanking them. As she drew closer, her pale moon-white hair came into focus, tangled into a wild nest.

The golden gown she'd been wearing the day they met her hung in tatters, swirling around the pale flesh of her thin legs.

Whatever her and Stolas's relationship had been like, it was evident by her lack of care that he was the reason she kept herself in the manner of a queen. He was the reason she bathed. The reason she brushed her long, wavy hair.

As Haven watched Nasira land on the steps just above, a savage, predatory thing, Haven felt the sting of failing her promise to Stolas more than ever.

Haven was supposed to somehow control his little sister. To protect her and keep her safe. But here she was, wilder than any Shadowling Haven had ever encountered.

It was they who needed protection from her.

And Nasira's wings . . . Haven wasn't sure what type of upkeep wings needed, but even from here she made out the way her indigo-black feathers drooped and frayed. All manner of leaves and debris dulling their shine.

The feeling gave way to instinctual fear as Nasira's closeness registered in Haven's brain. Just like Stolas, there was something primordial and ancient about the girl that sent tendrils of fear worming around her spine.

Contrasted against Nasira's too-big eyes and pouty lips, the delicate youth and childlike innocence that clung to her, her predatory movements were all the more disconcerting.

"Goddess save us," Surai whispered—but beneath her breath. Nasira's hearing was impeccable, and she tended not to suffer insults.

Which could be anything from saying a greeting improperly to asking about her day.

Nasira slowly drew her wings in, ruffling the blue-black feathers a few times like the pigeons in the courtyard after a dip in one of the many marble birdbaths.

Then the Noctis princess extended her head, exposing her long, elegant neck, and *sniffed*.

"Why do I smell blood magick and . . . a Netherworld demon?" Nasira asked. Her Penrythian was excellent, but her words were sharpened by a faint accent. Each consonant beaten into submission.

As Haven picked out the curiosity in her voice, she relaxed a little. As long as Nasira was curious, she wasn't bored.

Bored Nasira was a nightmare.

"We've brought you a present," Haven said, even though Nasira would already know exactly what they brought her. She lifted the side of the sheet covering the guard's face. "A human and a demon. To do with what you like."

They all flinched as Nasira jumped down two steps, her wings fluttering out behind her for balance, and peered down at the guard.

A sneer hitched her lips. "I like them prettier."

Nasira flicked her feline gaze to Bell and smiled, making her preferences clear and causing Haven to put herself between the Noctis and her friend.

Bell might think the Noctis princess harmless, but he also once found a baby vorgrath in the woods and begged the King to let him nurse it back to health.

His judgment was compromised.

"It's either the blood slave," Haven snarled, "or you go back to hunting the creatures in the forest. Your choice."

Nasira frowned, and Surai responded by unbuckling the sheath straps of her katanas. A frown from Nasira could easily be followed by a volley of dark magick—as Haven had painfully discovered a few months ago.

But then Nasira shrugged and bounded up the stairs, silky tatters of her dress slithering behind her like liquid gold. "Come inside my *opulent castle*, and bring my snack."

Bell and Surai both followed without question, leaving Haven to drag the guard up the last few steps alone. The fact that she was gifting a living being to a monster didn't escape her.

But, according to the text on blood magick, blood slaves were willing participants, wholly aware of their actions. The guard inside that sheet was responsible for trying to kill Bell and steal his essence. Plus, the idiot had nearly loosed a demon on them both.

When it came to those who tried to hurt Bell, she had no forgiveness and even less remorse.

In that regard, she could be just as much a monster as Stolas's sister.

"Here's to hoping you taste better than you smell." Throwing the sheet back over the blood slave's face, Haven dragged him up the stairs and into Nasira's lair.

Haven was painfully aware that the only reason Nasira put up with Haven's orders, at least, the few times she did, was because Stolas made her promise to listen to Haven.

Still, Haven walked a fine line, never knowing when the girl would challenge her fragile authority.

It was nerve-wracking. And undoubtedly Nasira could smell Haven's discomfort as she prowled the large hall of the main lodge. The room was in disarray. Furniture thrown on its side or shredded. Pillows split down the middle in an explosion of down.

Nasira had already polished off all the casks of plum wine they'd snuck her, the empty containers—which made up half the king's summer collection of his favored drink—piled up in a corner.

That's going to be fun explaining to the king.

The skeletons of Nasira's meals, thank the Goddess all forest creatures and not human, had been cleaned and propped up in an elaborate display that hung from one of the antler chandeliers.

"And she's an artist," Haven muttered under her breath. "Who knew?"

Stolas, you owe me big time.

Nasira watched Haven from the other side of the room, where she lounged in an oversized club chair, her disheveled dress falling away mid-thigh and naked legs slung over the arm.

Her bare feet wriggled, once again giving the illusion of childlike innocence.

But the predatory way her eyes followed Haven said otherwise. Dark tentacles much like the demon's appendages from earlier prodded Haven's mind.

It took all Haven's willpower to keep Nasira from soulreading her.

"Welcome to my humble palace," Nasira called out. "Do you like it?"

Haven ignored the girl's taunt. She'd promised Stolas to keep his sister safe, not afford her the lifestyle she was accustomed.

Bell had taken up the brave job of trying to clean up the Noctis girl, and he was busy whacking at her mess of hair with a pearl-handled comb.

Nasira snarled every time he yanked too hard, but Bell shushed her and went back to brushing. After a few minutes, the comb was tangled with white hairs.

Only Bell could get away with grooming Nasira. Haven watched for a few moments longer, feeling somehow like she was invading a personal routine that had happened many times before.

How many times had Bell visited her?

Clearing her throat, Haven picked up a bleached rib bone from one of the only intact side tables and examined it. "I see you're keeping well fed?"

Nasira tsked, her lower lip dropping into a pout. "None of the animals will come near this area of the forest anymore. The boundaries you set need to be expanded."

Maybe that's because you're a monster. Haven chucked the bone to the floor with a loud *clang.* "Out of the question."

Expanding Nasira's hunting range meant an increased risk to the citizens of Penryth.

The boundary consisted of fifty square miles of woodland, all the way to the sea. Only she and Nasira could see the runes carved into the trees that made up Nasira's prison. Haven wasn't foolish enough to think the runes were too powerful for Nasira to overcome, if she really desired breaking them.

She'd chosen to obey the perimeter—for now.

But how long could she go without hunting?

"What about the provisions we send?" Haven reminded her, drawing near and flopping into a chair facing Nasira. A fire smoldered in a giant gaping fireplace a few feet away, the smell of smoke and ash heavy to the point of coughing.

Above, the head of a huge elk stared down at them with glassy eyes.

Nasira hissed. "Gruel and long dead meat that stinks of decay? Stolas never deigned to treat me so poorly. Did he not tell you what I eat?"

Stolas hadn't told her a great many things when it came to his sister.

Haven shared an impatient look with Surai. They could deal with these problems another day. In a few hours, the sun would rise and she would be in a roomful of the kingdom's most powerful mortal rulers, any one of which could be a blood mage in disguise.

"Nasira, I'm giving you what you want: a live human to feast on. He has powerful magick and there's a demon inside him. It's a win-win."

Nasira examined her fingernails, which were more like talons than mortal nails. "And what do you *win*?"

The long sigh Haven released sent wisps of her rose-gold hair away from her face. Nasira might only look like a barely pubescent mortal girl, but she was already centuries old.

There was no outmaneuvering her, or sweet talking her, so Haven simply said, "I need to know who his master is."

"Why?"

"You mean, other than the fact that there's a blood mage running loose in Penryth?"

Nasira raised an ashy-blonde eyebrow.

"Because he tried to kill Bell," Haven admitted, "and there are four more blood slaves just like that one ready to finish the job." Saying it aloud made it all the more real, and Haven felt the pulse at her wrist jump.

Nasira was still slouched in the chair, looking for all the world like she didn't care, but her toes stopped their wiggling, and her nostrils flared.

Tugging her legs down, she curled them beneath her bottom and shook her head. "Blood magick is . . . unpredictable. Even power as magnificent as mine can't break the spell that prevents the slave from saying his master's name. There must be something else you want?"

Haven loosed a nervous breath. There was, actually, something else she wanted from Nasira, but saying it aloud felt so . . . permanent. "Can you bind my dark magick?"

Nasira frowned. "Bind it? Whatever for?"

Haven glanced at Surai and then back at the Noctis princess.

"Personal reasons."

"Does Stolas know?"

Haven didn't respond, but her face gave her away.

Nasira laughed, a wicked sound, and then clapped her hands together. "He'll be furious. For that reason alone, I'll do it."

Relief poured through Haven, but that emotion immediately gave way to something rawer. A strange, heavy feeling she couldn't shake.

Bell had finished with Nasira's hair, which now fell over her shoulder in a luminous river of ivory, and had begun working on her wings. Apparently, there was a smaller soft-bristled brush for wings, and Bell meticulously ran the instrument over each feather until they shone.

Nasira's eyes narrowed to slits as she leaned back, practically purring.

"So, that's it?" Haven asked, relieved that it was so easy. "So, do we do it now or . . .?"

Nasira rolled her eyes. "By the Shadeling's horns. You truly know nothing. Of course we can't bind your dark magick now. I need time to prepare. There are herbs to collect, poisons to procure. Come back tomorrow night. Normally the preparation would take longer but . . . since I have nothing else to do . . ."

Nasira's lips bared, making her thoughts on that subject—and who was to blame—clear.

Done with grooming Nasira, Bell rested the little brush on a side table and turned to face Nasira. "You won't hurt her, will you?"

Nasira's eyes twinkled. "Of course I'll hurt her. Binding her dark magick will feel like dying, as it should. She's imprisoning the most powerful force in the realm, something most mortals and Solis would kill for. That's not something that happens without pain."

Bell sighed. "Yes, but will she be alive at the end?"

"She might circle the fringes of the Netherworld, but she won't die." Nasira gave a flippant wave of her hand, as if all of the details of Haven living or dying were unimportant. "You have my word."

Bell whirled to face Haven, his mouth twisted with worry. "Haven, I don't like this. Please, don't bind your dark magick just for me. We can find another way."

Haven shook her head, wishing she could explain why she had to do it. Wishing she could show him the unrelenting nightmares that plagued her nearly every night. And then there was Archeron. Right before he left to hunt Bjorn, they'd spent a night together—or tried to, at least. Mid-kiss, Archeron had recoiled, her dark magick so strong he'd sensed it. Afterward, he'd promised her that, as horrible as her dark magick was, he could look past it.

But that was months ago, and now her shadowy powers were stronger.

Haven knew, deep down, that Archeron could never truly accept that part of her. And she didn't blame him.

"I have to, Bell. It's for the best."

Surai had been quiet during the entire exchange, but now she advanced on Nasira with an intensity that had Haven ready to retrieve her sword.

"Forgive me, Princess, but the word of a Noctis means very little to me." The look Surai gave Nasira reminded Haven that, while Surai might be working through her grief, she still wouldn't mind murdering a few thousand Noctis to ease her pain. "If Haven doesn't make it back from your cabin tomorrow, I will remove your wings, slit your pretty little throat, and then hang your head above the fireplace like the creature you are."

Nasira clapped her hands together. "Oh, wouldn't that be lovely? A much-improved vision compared to that ugly thing"—she nodded her head to the elk head staring dumbly down at them—"don't you think?"

Nasira's voice shivered with delight, not a shred of fear or anger to be found.

She truly thought the idea was . . . *funny.*

Haven shuddered. Nasira was so powerful that a threat from an established warrior such as Surai was nothing more than a joke to the princess.

Stolas might have kept his monstrous sister in check, but how in the Netherworld were *they* expected to rein her in? A mortal new to magick, a barren human prince, and one cranky Solis soldier with barely a fraction of Nasira's powers?

If Archeron were here, he might tilt the balance of power in their direction. But the minute he stepped foot on Penrythian lands, he would be enthralled to the king.

She had to find a way on her own to deal with Nasira.

Surai turned on her heels and stalked away, making Nasira's grin stretch even wider. But one corner of her lips twitched, just enough to send dread coiling in Haven's gut.

The procedure for binding her magick was more dangerous than Nasira let on. Was that Nasira's intention? Let Haven die?

With Haven dead, the boundaries she set for Nasira would be useless, and Stolas couldn't be mad at Nasira for breaking them. He couldn't even be mad at Nasira for letting Haven do something so dangerous—it was her choice, after all.

Nasira would be free to roam as she pleased. Murder as she pleased. And the only thing lately she seemed to desire more than human flesh was the freedom to procure said human flesh. To hunt with abandon and slay without restraint.

The weight of this new thought pressed down on Haven, reminding her how very tired she was.

She rubbed her temples. *Goddess Above, you're going to pay for this, Stolas.*

As if Nasira felt Haven's newfound reservations, the dark princess glanced her way. A yellow ring similar to Stolas's rimmed her now silver eyes, making her seem more beastly than ever.

"Come tomorrow eve after the moon crests the highest ridge." Something dangerously close to excitement flickered across her adolescent face. "I'll be ready."

To kill me? Haven wanted to ask. Instead, she nodded, clenching her hands into fists as steely resolve took over.

One way or another, Haven's dark magick would be snuffed out. Either with her successfully binding it—or with her death.

NINE

Fatigue gnawed behind Haven's eyes, her movements slow and heavy. As they neared Bell's chamber, she held up a hand and approached alone. Just in case.

The door creaked open, startling three maids who were just finishing scrubbing his floor.

If they had any qualms about what they must have found— demon slime and blood—they hid their unease behind stoic faces. She shooed them out, all too aware of the way their eyes lingered on her. The way they created a wide space between Haven and themselves as they lugged their soapy buckets dark with blood.

They were scared of her. Or perhaps they assumed she was responsible for the mess they'd found.

If only they knew what you really are, a voice whispered. *They'd be terrified.*

Bell slunk inside and surveyed his room as if the demon was still inside his chamber. Sagging against the frame of his massive cherry wardrobe, he assessed himself in the mirror.

"Shadeling's horn, I look hideous," he lamented, running fingers through the soft black curls adorning his head. Their eyes met in the mirror. "So do you, by the way."

She chuckled, circling the bed. As she did, her gaze snagged on the massive books piled on top of Bell's nightstand, where the maids must have put them. She ran a finger over one, titled *The Lineage of Lightcasters*. "Is this what Nasira is helping you with? Lineages?"

Bell followed her gaze in the mirror, and a wrinkle formed between his thick eyebrows. "She does have a lot of time on her hands."

Even though she knew it wasn't meant as a barb, Haven bristled. "Would you have us let her loose on Penrythians?"

"No." Bell rubbed the back of his neck. "Look, forget it, okay? You know how I am with research. I have her compiling a few things for me, histories and such, since my duties don't allow time for such things."

"Okay." Haven forced a smile. There was more he wasn't telling her, but now wasn't the time to pry, as much as she wanted to. "I'm going to freshen up. Meet you at the High Council?"

A grin transformed his tired face. "Absolutely. But first, do you still have those beautiful red leather pants with the gold embroidery I had made for you? The ones you haven't worn a single time?"

"They're still hanging in my closet, flashy and garish as the day they were made. Why? Want to borrow them?"

Bell's face was bright as he said, "You know I look better in them than you do."

Bell's wardrobe was monitored by the king, who ensured the clothiers only offered him conservative options. Which meant

Bell raided her closet whenever possible.

"I'm not sure the High Council can handle you in those," she muttered.

Bell laughed, a flash of the happy prince she remembered before he was taken by a monstrous queen. "Guess we're about to find out."

As she slipped out the door and headed to bed, she could almost believe the dark storm clouds over her friend were finally starting to lift.

TEN

Haven knew she was dreaming, although she couldn't remember what had come before. She also knew what she would find in this dream.

Or, rather, *whom*.

"Stolas?" she whispered, wending around the same bent trees she passed every time she was called inside the Shade Lord's dreams. The other side of the trees revealed a crystalline cove, half-moon shaped, carved at the base of a forest-lined mountain.

Stunning black grains of sand shimmered at her bare feet, bright as black diamonds, as she padded over the dark shores and into the lake. Ripples surged outward, making the silvery moon reflected inside the water's surface dance.

The dark water was cool against her calves, but not unpleasant. The surface stirred with Goddess knows what, but Haven knew the creatures below wouldn't hurt her.

Not while their master protected her.

This was Shadoria. A place of shadows and mist and dark, wondrous magick. Of obsidian mountains that reached for the strange green skies and dense, haunted forests.

This was where Stolas grew up, where his family had ruled for millennia. Right up until they lost the war and the Sun Sovereign gave the island to the mortal realm. When the Shade Queen escaped from the Netherworld through the rift, the Sun Sovereign destroyed Shadoria with magick rather than let it fall into the Noctis's hands again.

This was a memory of the land before it was ruined, a pocket preserved by Stolas's mind.

As the island centered in the middle of the lake came into view, Haven quickened her pace. Fireflies swarmed above the sandy protrusion of land like sparks from a fire, rising from the tall blue-green grasses and into the starry sky.

Just like all the other creatures, they were attracted to Stolas and his dark, endless magick.

Haven waded until she reached the island in the middle of the lake. This small tuft of land, crowned with a tiny castle of onyx and strewn with children's toys, was a remnant of Stolas's childhood.

It was also where Haven found the Shade Lord each time.

A pang of dread unfurled inside her belly as she rounded the corner of the miniature castle and saw him. The many ravens perched around him took to the night in a violent whoosh. One brushed her cheek with its wing.

She forced down the cry that gathered in her throat and walked calmly toward the broken prince, wiping any pity she might have felt from her expression.

"Oh, you've come. Again," Stolas said dryly. "How wonderful."

He lay on his side in a patch of tall marsh grass. Her heart clenched as she saw the way his body was twisted, his usually pristine clothes marred with dirt and darkened with old blood. The ceremonial armor he'd been wearing at Spirefall was pitted and bent, the once lustrous metal dulled with grime.

Something was very wrong if Stolas allowed himself to appear so unkempt. She'd once joked with him that he must have an army of tailors and personal servants to keep him looking sharp—to which he'd told her he employed no less than five trapped souls in the Netherworld for his wardrobe alone.

Schooling the alarm from her face, she flopped onto the grass beside him. "Not sure why you always act put out when I come here. You're the one who calls me."

"I'm fairly certain that's . . . not true." His voice shook, and he tried to hide the way his breathing hitched.

He was in severe pain.

But pointing that out—or trying to soothe him somehow— would only make him snap at her and then disappear. She knew from experience.

Usually when she appeared in his dreams, it was after one of her nightmares. But occasionally, she arrived to find him badly wounded. His magick drained so completely that her gaze never left his chest, thinking each breath would be his last.

But, no. Whoever tortured him was not that merciful. They refused to let him die. Torturing and maiming him over and over until he finally faded off into . . . this place.

The only remaining pocket of the world that he could hide from the agony.

"Here to read me more of your books?" he asked, but beneath his annoyance she caught a hint of hope.

"If you'd like."

"What I'd like is a scalding-hot bath, maybe a nice aged red wine, some lovely music. Think you can manage that?"

"No, but I can tend to your wounds."

"I'm not in the mood." There was a finality to his voice that scared her.

"Well, I don't care if you're in the mood or not. If you're going to keep dragging me into your dreams then I'm going to take care of you."

His eyes fluttered shut, ashen eyelashes brushing the sharp curve of his cheeks. She took that as defeat.

Haven's throat ached as she scooted closer to Stolas. His silver-white hair had grown several inches longer than normal, reaching past his chin, the wavy locks tangled with sweat and blood. His full lips were pale and cracked. His clothes torn.

Reaching out, she carefully ran two fingers along his temple. The moment her fingertips connected with his cold skin, he growled low and deep, but she fought yanking her hand away.

Instead, she carefully began stroking his hair, brushing the tangles from it. Her hands shied away from his horns. Not because she was afraid of the thickset curved things—their ends were blunted and surface smooth—but because touching them seemed intimate somehow.

"What are you doing?" His voice was like two boulders colliding, the warning inside clear.

"Everyone deserves to feel cared for," she answered. "Even you."

She should have been scared by his primal tone. The way his growls became more guttural. But staring down at him, wounded and near helpless, face mired in agony, all she could think about was how this was her years ago. A terrified little girl with no hope, no escape from her misery.

If someone then had shown just a tiny scrap of love for her . . .

if they had cleaned her wounds and spoken kindly to her . . .

"Stop," Stolas ordered.

"What?"

"Grinning like you're my savior. Running your filthy fingers through my hair while I'm too weak to stop you does not make you a saint."

"No, but killing Morgryth would."

He stiffened, a muscle in his jaw trembling. "I would take care not to speak of such things."

"She's alive, isn't she? Where is she keeping you? The Netherworld?"

His nostrils flared. "You know I do not have the answers you seek, yet you keep asking anyway."

They'd gone over this a million times. Whoever held him kept him imprisoned in darkness. Ravenna was most likely complicit, but beyond her, he didn't know.

Whoever held him, they had the powerful Shade Lord under near-total control.

Lifting onto her knees, she took the wet hem of her tunic and began wiping at the flakes of dried blood crusting his neck. His cheek. Thanks to his powers, his wounds had already healed. When she dragged the bunched fabric over the razor edge of his jawbone, her stomach lurched at how very thin he'd gotten.

Each brush of the cotton fabric over his body elicited low snarls that made her hands shake. But his eyes slid shut.

It was the same every time. He showed up bloody and broken on the island his father had made for him, shattered near the breaking point.

Sometimes he made scathing remarks. Sometimes he managed a joke. Usually he simply glared at her with annoyance. But always—always it felt like a forbidden dance. Trying to keep him calm in his most vulnerable state and not get eviscerated in the process.

When she was done cleaning the blood from his upper body, she moved to access his back.

The layers of shadow swirling behind him should have warned her off. As soon as she neared where his wings should be, a roar split the air.

She was flung back, hard. The force was so strong it snapped her head and stripped her breath away.

She landed on her butt with an *oof.*

His eyes were wide open. And red—bright, feral red. His voice was inhuman as he snarled, "Enough." The jagged edge of his tone smoothed out as he added, "Please."

She held up her hands. "I won't touch you anymore, unless you want me to. Would you like me to read now?"

"Like is the wrong word."

She rolled her eyes. Hurt or not, there was only so much of his moodiness she could stomach. "Yes or no?"

He nodded. A ragged sigh fled his lips as his head fell back to rest on its grassy cushion. That small bit of magick when he pushed her away must have exhausted him. One of the fireflies landed on the tip of his horn, its belly glowing brightly.

Haven approached carefully, her heart skittering in her chest. She tried not to stare at the inky cloud hovering just behind him. Tried not to think about what lay beyond that sinister veil.

What it was hiding.

She couldn't imagine Stolas without his wings. From the little she understood about the Noctis, their wings were their most prized possession.

Please, Goddess, let them still be there.

Settling close to the injured Shade Lord, she made sure not to touch him this time, even by accident. Stolas had always been savage when wounded, but this was by far the worst she'd ever seen him.

Drawing her hands up, she imagined the latest book she and Bell had read together, some boring history of the Nine Houses. The tome appeared in a cloud of dust. As soon as she began reciting the words from the first chapter, she heard Stolas scoff.

"Not this droll thing again," he muttered, managing a scathing tone even near death.

Haven rolled her eyes. "I can only conjure books I've read recently, and Bell's on a mortal houses kick. I can make up a story, if you'd like?"

"Shadeling below, please don't. I've been tortured enough already."

She chuckled and began reading again. Boring stuff. Replete with the most excruciating details of every mortal lord, right down to what they had for breakfast.

After a time, Stolas's breathing slowed and the sharp planes of his face softened.

"No more," he finally said, but his voice was, if not content, then no longer pained. "Tell me about your life in Penryth. Have you and that preening Sun Lord declared your undying love for one another yet?"

"Oh, shut up." She nearly smacked him with the heavy book before catching herself. "I cannot wait for you to fall in love so I can tease you mercilessly."

After a few heartbeats of silence, she glanced down to see him staring at her with a strange, almost sad expression.

"What?" she asked.

"Do you really not know that my story is over?"

Her throat clenched, the emotion giving way to anger. "Don't talk like that. Like you've already given up. You—"

"Stop," he ordered. "My life ended the moment Morgryth killed my parents and I was consigned to the Netherworld, forced to be its lord. I became a monster that day. Why do you continue to deny what I am?"

"That isn't your fault."

"Do you really think that's true? That I didn't enjoy tormenting the souls under my reign? That I didn't take pleasure in the creative ways to hurt them? I will never experience love the way you do . . . because I will never deserve it."

Staring at this creature, this beast of horns and pain and shadow, Haven saw something different than what he imagined. A boy caught between darkness and light, dreams and nightmares, cruelty and redemption.

"You were once a prince," she said softly. "If you are ever freed from those bonds you can go back to that life, can you not?"

Something crossed over his face. A darkness so encompassing, so hopeless that she wished she'd never mentioned love.

"No, Beastie. That prince no longer exists. If I were let loose upon your world I would burn it to ashes without a single sliver of remorse."

"Then why? If you're beyond redemption, if you're the monster you claim, why am I here now?"

"Because my story may be over, but Nasira's has just begun."

She set the book down in the grass where it instantly disappeared. "I'll never give up on helping you, Stolas."

"Odin's teeth, you're an incessant creature." He groaned softly. "Keep my sister safe and out of trouble. That's how you help me." His eyes had returned to their faded silver color, ringed in gold, and they fixated on her. "Tell me. How is she?"

"Wonderful as always," Haven muttered. "A total delight. She's only tried to murder me once, which I assume is her showing restraint."

He laughed, the sound devolving into another groan. "She's the direct descendant of a Noctis Empress, heir to the dark throne. Did you think she would be docile like that Sun Lord you keep on a leash?"

"No, but you could have warned me about her thirst for blood and murder."

"I thought common sense would prevail."

"Oh? What about Ravius and his inability to shut up? That would have been helpful to know up front."

His eyes brightened to amber, the color Haven was learning meant Stolas was happy—as much as someone like him could be. "Ah, my old friend. How does he fare in Penryth?"

"Well he hasn't been made into a pie . . . yet." Spreading her legs out in the grass, she released a long breath. "How in the Netherworld did you two become friends, exactly?"

"Living, he was Lochran O'Beirne, an Asgardian warrior with royal blood and a talent for bloodshed renowned across Solissia. His most famous trick was using tracking ravens to find his enemies."

"So, you made him a raven in the afterlife."

Stolas's lips pulled into a grin, but it didn't reach his eyes. "I had just been made Lord of the Netherworld, and my rage coupled with my boredom made my methods of torture particularly creative. For Lochran, I turned him into a raven and let his previous victims hunt him. It was rather clever, if I do say so myself."

"When did that change?"

"I was young and lonely. And he wasn't terrified of me the way others were." He managed a half-shrug, then glanced at the ridge of mountains behind them. Pale light settled over the jagged peaks. The moment the sun broke they would both awaken in the real world from sleep. "That is a long story, and I'm afraid we're running out of time."

The heavy despair in his voice chased away the levity of the past few minutes. Something about it made her say, "I'll see you again, won't I?"

Clenching his jaw, he propped his body on his elbow. The pain from that small act was etched into his face, but he refused to lie back on his side.

"Only the Shadeling knows how you've been able to enter this protected fold of my dreams. At first, I found it an inconvenience. You appearing with the stink of your nightmares still clinging to your body, your fear perfuming everything. But then . . ." A ragged breath escaped his lips. "If I'm being quite honest, you are the sole reason I have lasted this long."

Haven swallowed, an invisible fist pressed into her diaphragm. "What are you saying, Stolas?"

"I'm saying thank you, Beastie. Thank you and goodbye. The time has come to end our little . . . whatever this is."

"No." Her voice sounded so very small; the tug of fear that she might never see him again startling.

"You don't have a choice in the matter, I'm afraid." The resignation in his voice terrified her. She should have been overjoyed at not coming here anymore, but all she could think was how alone he would be. Hurt and alone and suffering, just like she'd been in those Devourer tents.

"Why?"

"Because this . . . this happiness I feel here, with you—it is a light that draws things out of the shadows. Vile, evil things I feel just outside my cell."

"Stolas, you're scaring me."

"I sense a wave of despair coming, Beastie, a dark ocean of terror that will swallow everything you hold dear. The most I can do is hope it does not find you or Nasira."

Before Haven could respond, the sun breached the mountains, sending golden rays spearing across the lake. As the light brushed her flesh, she began to disappear.

"Wait, please. Don't do this, Stolas."

"I'm afraid it's already done."

Stolas fell back onto the grass, his energy spent. Diaphanous rays poured over his ruined body, even more shattered than she'd realized. Bruises mottled his arms and chest, cuts and welts mapping his body.

And his wings—his poor, beautiful, perfect wings. They'd been stripped of feathers completely. What remained was a shredded, bloody, broken mess of bones.

Her stomach clenched at the horrific sight.

"If you see me again, here or somewhere else, do not trust me. Do you understand?"

Before Haven could respond, she awoke to the sun spilling through her window, Stolas's words etched into her mind.

ELEVEN

The High Council was set up on the wisteria-laden terraces outside, overlooking the tiered gardens. Now that the Curse was broken, the seasons had returned with a vengeance, and spring was in full bloom. Below the marble railing pulsed a vibrant world that set Haven's heart on fire.

The scent of it all made her a bit woozy—or perhaps that was not sleeping more than four hours a night for the last three months.

Rubbing the back of her neck, she settled against the far end of the terrace, leaned against a pillar, crossed her arms, and watched.

Ten royal guards were posted along the wall. At her insistence, there were ten more in plainclothes, masquerading as nobles. Surai stood eagle-eyed on the other end of the patio, near a tinkling fountain. And the shadow of Ravius swept over the long banquet table brimming with sweet wine, cured meats, and dried fruits as he patrolled the grounds for anything amiss.

None of it felt like enough. Not with four more blood slaves and a blood mage on the loose.

When the High Council members began trickling through the double arched doors wreathed with roses, Haven stiffened. Most of the members were men, rulers of their kingdom with royal lineages as long as their elaborate capes that trailed around their ankles.

A few had allowed their wives to attend, but of course they stood demurely behind their husbands. Not allowed to sit, nor speak, apparently.

Lord Thendryft was the exception. Once led to his high-backed seat near the far side of the table, he demanded another chair be brought out for his daughter, Eleeza.

Haven bit her lip to keep from smiling as the servants nervously fluttered around in search of a suitable chair. When one scurried back over with a footstool, Eleeza lifted one curved eyebrow and he scampered off to find something more suitable.

She deserves a throne, Haven decided, before realizing that Eleeza was in line to someday have the biggest mortal throne of all. The throne of Penryth, as queen to Bell.

As if conjured from her thoughts, two trumpeters appeared to announce the royal family. Haven's fingers flexed around the hilt of her sword as she watched Cressida enter the terrace first, escorted by Renk.

Cressida wore a creamy gown of mulberry silk with an empire waist bordered with pearls, her hair plaited above her head. Renk wore a military uniform dripping with medals—despite having never fought in a true war.

As they were escorted to their seats near the head of the table, Renk slid a glance at Bell's empty place next to King Horace's seat. Something dark and twisted flickered just beneath his dead eyes, and Haven had to bite her cheek to keep from lunging at him and ramming a blade through his black heart.

The darkness inside her jumped at the idea, and she steadied her mind with deep breaths.

Not today, evil.

She regained control just as Bell ducked beneath the wreathed entryway. True to his word, he looked marvelous. A crown of silver rose from his dark curls. Two ruby encrusted dahlia cloak pins fastened an airy white cape of silk to his shoulders, and a matching belt sparkled from his startlingly red leather pants.

A high collar fringed with gold finished the look.

The high lords all rose at once. Haven tensed. Watching for any hint of magick. A too-quick movement. The brief flash of steel.

Instead, the entire table burst into applause as murmurs of "Cursebreaker," rippled through the air.

A frown tugged King Horace's face as he entered two steps behind Bell, the king's confusion over the early applause evident. Obviously, he wasn't prepared for Bell stealing the praise he thought rightfully belonged to him.

Two servants pulled out the chair for the king. The second he sat, Cressida was in his ear, whispering.

Only the Goddess knew the words that spilled from her red lips like a slow and steady trickle of poison, but Haven could guess.

Look how he steals the adoration that rightfully belongs to you. Look how they love him instead of you. Look how he plans to usurp you one day.

Let me kill the bitch, a quiet voice whispered, but Haven steeled the prison inside her where the darkness lived and focused on scanning the others.

If her dark magick escaped again in such a public manner, Bell would have no choice but to send her away for good.

After a few minutes, the table quieted and the king spoke. A long droning speech about Bell breaking the Curse. His strength in the face of evil. His unflappable bravery.

Of course, he didn't mention Haven or the other Solis. As soon as they'd arrived back in Penryth after breaking the Curse, the king had begun his campaign to downplay everyone's part but Bell's.

Haven didn't mind—although the luxurious gowns and baubles the king sent her as a reward were still in her closet, untouched.

With the grandstanding over, the real discussions began. Matters of the realm that hadn't been dealt with in decades like trade agreements and treaties were broached. After a full two hours of this, the king broke the discussion with sweet meats and candied nuts.

This was followed by a mind-numbing discussion on borders, and another painful hour commenced of lords squabbling like children while agreeing on almost nothing. The Penrythian sun grew angrier by the hour. A lavender swath of velvet was drawn above the table for shade, to little effect.

Haven cringed, willing Bell to interject his views into the mix. Oh, he tried a few times, but the table had descended into a shouting match, with a lord from Dune accusing one of his neighbors of crossing Dune's borders for trade without proper tithes.

If only they would all shut up . . .

A smile tugged her lips. Yes, if only.

Pretending to clasp her hands, Haven drew a silence rune over her palm. The moment her finger finished the two overlapping circles, a curtain of quiet fell.

A few of the nobles clawed at their throats, mouths still open as they continued shouting, like that would make a difference.

Bell threw a knowing glance her way.

Go, she mouthed.

Bell straightened the crown atop his head as he stood. Surprise registered in the king's eyes, which soon narrowed into annoyance at the interruption.

"As the crown prince of Penryth," Bell began, "I have something to say."

The steadiness in his voice eased some of the tightness in Haven's shoulders.

Cressida sneered at the prince. Beside her, Renk's fat lips gaped open and closed like a fish as he tried to say something undoubtedly foul.

Watching his father's mistress and half-brother squirm, a corner of Bell's lips twitched up. "As you know, I was taken by the Shade Queen. As I was flown over the many kingdoms outside our walls, I witnessed firsthand the destruction and pain the Curse wrought. In light of such atrocities, I have a few proposals."

Right at that moment, Haven felt the spell lift, allowing Renk to spit out, "Who are you to propose—"

The king held up a hand, silencing Renk as easily as if he possessed his own sort of magick. "Quiet, boy. I will hear what he says."

Bell seemed to grow two inches with pride at that, and he nodded before continuing. "First, I would like for all the kingdoms to waive their annual tithes for five years, to allow the farmers and villagers to renew their trades and fields. Many lost sons and daughters, and they need time to rebuild."

A murmur stirred the lords, but Bell persisted.

"Second. Many of the citizens across Eritreyia are starving. For much of the land outside our walls, it will take years for the soil to heal enough to grow anything. In the interim, I propose taking ten percent of the grain from the royal storage and handing it to the citizens north of the runewall."

Pride welled inside Haven as she watched Bell speak. Although they had discussed ways to rebuild not just Penryth, but the mortal realm, Bell never informed her of his propositions.

"Third. Now that the Curse is broken and the Shade Queen has fled, the creatures that once took refuge in the Shadow Kingdom have once again broached our borders."

"It's true," a ruler from Veserack added. "We've caught five pixies in the traps outside our walls alone. They raid our food stores, cause all sorts of mischief, and are hard as roaches to kill."

"Shadowlings are one thing," Bell said. "But creatures of light like the pixies and the selkies once lived among us."

The ruler from Veserack cut a sharp look at Bell. "What are you suggesting? That we invite them into our kingdoms? What's next? Should they receive invitations to our balls? Sup with us at our tables? Perhaps a seat at the High Council?" His gaze slid over Eleeza. "Goddess knows almost anyone can earn a chair these days."

"No, Lord Montclaire. I propose we give them land from each of our territories, sovereign land where they can rule beside us as allies of the mortal kingdoms, sworn to arms if war comes back to our shores."

Haven found herself holding her breath, the promise she made to the pixie, Mossbark, fresh in her mind.

"Allies?" Renk sneered. He tilted his drink back and took a noisy swig of wine. "Allies against what, exactly? Didn't you tell us a quaint little story where you vanquished the Shade Queen? You said her forces have been thrown back in the Netherworld where they belong, and that you saw the Shade Queen fall."

Murmurs of ascent filled the table.

"I think we're all a bit confused," Renk continued. "Did you break the Curse and defeat the dark queen or not?"

Bell shook his head. "I never saw her die."

"Right." Renk's fat lips curved into a smirk. "So when you want to become a hero you spin one tale. Now that you want us to do what you say, you spin another. Which is it, Bell?"

"I told you." Bell glared at Renk. "She just . . . disappeared."

"So you cannot be sure she survived?" Lord Thendryft asked, not unkindly. "Surely if she were still alive she would have retaliated by now?"

"No." Bell tugged at his collar. He was growing flustered, the horrors from that day slowly creeping in. "No, she had these . . . these cages."

"Right," Renk said. "The humans you said you saw in Spirefall. The ones she was building an army with? Where is that army, Prince? Or was that a hallucination, perhaps? Something she instilled inside you to create fear and panic among us, even after her death."

"No." Bell tipped his chalice up to his lips, only to discover it empty. He set it back on the table, loudly, and motioned a waiter for more water.

"Are you her creature," Renk persisted, "even in her death?"

"No." Bell's hands clenched the edge of the table, his desperate gaze going to the waiter with the pitcher of water.

"Do you want us to live under her shadow forever? Is that it?"

"No!" Haven flinched as Bell backhanded his empty cup, sending it tumbling over the table and clanking across the stone terrace. "Stop twisting my words, Renk! Don't you understand? She's coming for us and if we can't stop squabbling over borders and taxes, we'll never stand a chance."

Silence. Not the kind created by magick, but the kind garnered from pity and embarrassment. They thought he was insane, that he'd lost his grip on reality. She could tell by their too-big smiles, the way none met his eyes.

And she couldn't even blame them. His eyes were wild, his breathing sharp. His crown sat askew on his head.

For anyone who'd never been to Spirefall, who'd never witnessed the depravities and evil firsthand, it was hard to understand such raw fear.

Defeated, Bell sunk back into his chair, shoulders slumped.

Oh, Bell. Habit had her peeling from the column she rested against to aid him—

Yes, rush to his defense. That won't look bad for him at all.

Growling, she fell back against the marble in defeat and watched, helpless, as Renk sneered in triumph at his half-brother.

Goddess Above, how she wanted to boil the bastard alive.

But, of course, that would be even worse. So she gritted her teeth and did nothing. The terrace was painfully quiet. One of the servants retrieved Bell's chalice from the ground and brought it to him.

Even after another servant filled the glass with water, Bell simply stared in the distance.

Just when she thought the silence would stretch out forever, the doors to the terrace slammed open and a manservant rushed over to the king. Sweat dampened his temples, his chest heaving as he labored to breathe.

"Take a breath, man," the king ordered.

Ignoring his king, the manservant bowed low. "Apologies for the interruption . . . my liege. But there are riders approaching."

"Riders?" King Horace fixed the servant with a cold stare. "You interrupt our council to inform me riders travel our road? Unless the four horsemen of Odin are approaching, you will not interrupt our council again."

"Yes, my apologies." Somehow the manservant scraped lower

than he already was, until Haven thought he might actually kiss the king's embossed leather boots. "Not the four horsemen, my liege, but an entourage of . . . Solis."

"Solis?" the king demanded, a strange mixture of hope and doubt softening his voice. His sharp gaze went to the city gate, far below and just barely visible from the table. "Here, in Penryth?"

The manservant lifted his head just high enough to give a quick nod. "There's more. At least two Sun Lords ride with them, and one carries the Sun Sovereign of Effendier's banner."

Haven's heart lurched, and she knew—she just knew that one of those Sun Lords was Archeron.

TWELVE

Over a decade—that's how long it had been since the Effendier Sun Sovereign had graced the mortal lands with her banner. The prospect of an entourage of Solis led by two Sun Lords was enough to make even the stodgiest of the nobles on the terrace flush with excitement.

Haven was leaned over the marble railing, her hands fisted around the thick, knotty vines of wisteria looping around the banister. Her lungs felt paper-thin, her pulse thready along her wrists. She couldn't decide where to focus—on the apex of the kings' road where they would surely pass, or the gate.

Someone cried out and the entourage came into view. Suddenly Haven found it impossible to look, and she whirled around, forcing herself away from the balcony.

She crossed the floor, posted up behind Bell, and waited. And waited. After a while the crowd moved back to the table. The king, ever one to play it cool, stayed seated. But his eyes kept flicking to the entryway, and he nervously finished off his wine.

Haven took a steadying breath, pushing her excitement over Archeron's return aside. She needed to focus on this new development, turn it over in her mind.

If the Sun Sovereign of Effendier had banner men in Penryth, that could only mean one thing: she wanted to forge new alliances with the mortals. But why now?

Before she could ponder reasons, the royal trumpeters hurried over to the doors. One nearly dropped his trumpet. The doors parted. Both trumpeters stopped mid-blow as they beheld the Solis passing beside them.

The first Solis to enter was undoubtedly a Sun Lord, his resemblance to Archeron so striking that Haven nearly thought it was him. But then her gaze slid hungrily over his face, the refined jaw not quite as blunt as Archeron's. The high, delicate cheekbones, pale blue eyes, and long, thin nose. Gold cuffs engraved with flowers adorned his ears, and the runemarks over his tawny skin were thinner and more elegant than Archeron's.

Disappointment rocked her, and she released a frustrated breath, focusing back on the Sun Lord.

Well over six-foot tall, he wore the purple and gold colors of Effendier. Golden hair a shade lighter than Archeron's honey-wheat fell around his wide shoulders. The blond tips brushed the collar of his crystalline breastplate, which was undoubtedly created from azerite and made Cressida's expensive collection seem like trinkets.

Only the best for the Sun Sovereign's court.

He assessed the table and its occupants with lazy sweeps of his bored gaze. His lips curled with amusement, as if he found the crowd of mortals staring open-mouthed at him humorous.

Haven had looked the same way at two roaches fighting over a crumb on a table once—before crushing them both with her boot.

Someone stepped behind the Sun Lord and Haven felt her breath catch.

Archeron. His sun-bronzed face bore the effects of long days riding in the elements, and there was something around his eyes, a tightness perhaps, that she didn't remember before. Unlike the other Sun Lord, Archeron sported a simple leather vest, scuffed and marred. His pants were worn, faded from the sun and frayed from weeks of nonstop travel.

A scruffy gold beard ran the length of his jaw.

His gaze scoured the room with a quiet desperation before falling on her. For the briefest of seconds, it was only Haven and Archeron.

The terrace faded away. The people, the food, the hot sun. All of it simply gone.

She smiled, a single breath fleeing her lips. Rare vulnerability flushed her cheeks as he stripped her bare with his hungry gaze. She'd almost forgotten the surge of excitement his presence elicited. The way it warmed beneath her skin and made breathing twice as hard.

Goddess Above, why was she so hot? Sweat slid down her shoulder blades.

She could swear that his nostrils flared as he took in the scent.

The hardness around his eyes softened. He started to smile . . .

"Archeron," the king called, shattering the spell between them. "Come to your master."

Rage flashed inside Archeron's emerald green eyes as the king snapped his fingers, calling Archeron to him like a cur.

Bastard. If she could have murdered the king at that moment and gotten away with it, she would have.

When Archeron hesitated, the ring on the king's finger pulsed red. At the same moment, a pained shudder rippled across Archeron's face. He seemed to be trying to resist the command.

But how could he? A sliver of his soul was entombed in that ring and resisting its command was impossible.

Don't struggle, she silently pleaded as bile lapped the back of her throat.

Perhaps after three months away, he'd forgotten how strong the king's power over him was. Or perhaps after experiencing freedom again, he couldn't bear to put back on the yoke of his enslavement.

Not without a fight.

No one dared move as they watched to see if Archeron could refuse. A muscle flexed in his jaw, his entire body shaking with the effort. Sweat beaded along his brow, now grooved in agony.

With a loud groan, he dropped to his knees. Pain etched into every line of his face. The veins in his neck corded.

Still he resisted.

On the other side of the balcony Haven caught sight of Surai, a hand to her mouth.

All at once, Archeron's body began to contort. His back arched, his chest flaring and head snapping back. His eyes—Goddess Above, his eyes were rolled back in his head.

"Enough," Haven whispered.

Her words were meant for the king, but they found their home in Archeron. A breath gurgled from his throat and then he gave in, his rebellious spirit fading with every step toward the mortal king.

Each foot closer seemed to rub away some of his luster, revealing the raw shame beneath.

Haven flinched, jerking her head to avert her eyes. As her gaze skittered over the others, she found Surai looking as disturbed as Haven.

As far as Haven knew, Surai had never seen Archeron bent to the king's will. Not like this. Now a thousand emotions seemed to flash across Surai's face: horror, grief, and fury contorted her expression until Haven worried her friend would murder the king herself.

Haven understood all too well the feeling. Witnessing Archeron's will be overridden by magick felt *wrong*. Deep down in her soul. And she couldn't help but remember she was the reason Archeron was still bound to the king. Still a puppet to his cruel whims.

The other Sun Lord watched Archeron join the king's side with emotionless eyes. Behind him, four more Solis gathered. Two males and two females. They threw curious glances over the mortal food and clothing, and Haven couldn't help but feel lacking, somehow.

All of this—all of their mortal opulence and finery, the luxuries Cressida and the king took great pains to procure and treasured as signs of their greatness, felt like vapid baubles beneath the condescending stares of the Solis.

"Please," the king said, sprawling back into his high-backed chair and sweeping a hand over the table. "Take some food and refreshment after such a long journey."

"That is not necessary." The Sun Lord performed a curt bow for the king, the perpetual upturn of his lips making the refusal seem very much like an insult. "Our visit here will be brief, I imagine."

For some reason his gaze slid to Bell. Situated behind the prince, Haven bristled, ready to run the Sun Lord through if he so much as moved in the prince's direction.

While the king still reclined lazily in his chair, one pinky circling the rim of his goblet, his eyes danced with excitement. "Indeed. So, tell me, Sun Lord. *Why* are you here?"

"I am here on behalf of the Sun Sovereign of Effendier," the Sun Lord replied cryptically.

The king's thin lips pressed together, the skin at the corners puckering. He understood what Haven did, trade talks would take days—if not weeks.

This was something else entirely.

Again the Sun Lord let his attention drift to Bell, and a heavy feeling settled in her belly. She tried to meet Archeron's eye, but he stared straight ahead.

The Sun Lord stretched his long neck, rubbing at some invisible cramp. "You are the fifth mortal kingdom we've visited since entering your realm, but I have to say, out of all the possible mortal candidates"—he flashed a saccharine grin at Bell—"You are the one I've been most excited to meet, Cursebreaker. I hear your magick is . . . extraordinary. It must have been to defeat Morgryth."

The artery just below her jaw jumped. "Candidate?" Haven blurted, alarmed. "Candidate for *what*?"

The Sun Lord kept his intense gaze on Bell as he said, "Who is chirping in my ear?"

Finally, from her periphery Haven saw Archeron turn to her. Even without looking she felt his warning expression.

Too bad. The smirking Sun Lord and his cryptic smugness had already worn out its welcome.

"Who might *you* be?" she snarled, lifting her eyebrows. She barely made out Archeron's face twist in horror at her lack of manners, but she was beyond caring. "Or do you go by 'Sun Sovereign's Emissary'?"

He cut his eyes at the king. "I was told you kept your females in this realm as docile as you've made my poor cousin, here."

Renk chuckled. "That's not a female."

The Sun Lord turned his head to appraise Renk. When the Sun

Lord finished his assessment, his pale blue eyes were icy. "Oh, but she'd make quick work of you, wouldn't she, boy?"

Renk looked first to the king then his mother, but not even Cressida was brave enough to contradict the Sun Lord's words.

The whisper of a smile lifted Bell's lips, and the Sun Lord noticed, his own soft lips responding with—if not a true smile— an upward twitch.

Then he cast his sharp gaze on Haven. "I am called Xandrian Lightstead. At the Sun Sovereign's behest, I have traveled your realm, visiting each of the Nine Houses for mortal candidates to enter the Praetori Fiernum, the Gathering of Fire tournament, as has been their long-standing right."

Spider legs of dread prickled the base of her skull. The Praetori Fiernum? Had she read about that somewhere?

"How many other candidates from the Nine have you procured?" Bell asked softly.

"Exactly none," Xandrian answered. "And I've been to all but here and House Volantis. It seems Morgryth was successful in purging the mortal houses of lightcasting blood. Of course, every single mortal lord claims their ilk has magick, especially once they learn the prize for winning the trials, but the results have been . . . disappointing, to say the least."

"Prize?" Renewed interest sharpened the king's face. "Refresh our memories on what that is. It has been ages, after all, since a tournament of this nature was held."

"Yes, did I not mention that part yet? Silly me." A sly grin brightened Xandrian's face, and in that moment, he looked so much like Archeron. A younger, more conniving, less broken Archeron, before his enslavement to the king siphoned some of that spirit. "The Gathering of Fire trials have been held every half millennium for as far back as our history serves. Candidates from all of Solissia and the mortal realms used to gather to vie for their right as reigning lightcaster and leader of the Nine."

The king inhaled sharply; Cressida's eyes glittered with greed. Even Renk seemed impressed, his mouth hanging open limply.

"But the court of Nine was destroyed," Cressida hissed. "What trick is this?"

"No trick." Xandrian examined his fingernails. "As far as Morgryth knew, the lands of Shadoria where the court of Nine used to reside were destroyed. Only it wasn't. When the Shade Queen and her Noctis army broke free from the Netherworld years past, the Sun Sovereign had it shrouded in magick. Not destroyed, merely hidden."

A hushed murmur went over the table.

"There's a catch, though, isn't there?" Haven asked quietly. "For those who enter this tournament?"

Another grin, only this time the smile didn't reach his pale blue eyes. "There's always a catch with the runic arts. For the chance to compete, not only must you possess magick, but you must impress me with it—something not easily done even by the most skilled Solis lightcasters."

"Explain what that means in its entirety, cousin," Archeron added, and the solemn tone of his voice had Haven clenching the back of Bell's chair.

"Glad to clarify, cousin," Xandrian said with another clever smile. "The moment you perform your magick for me, Prince, you are bestowing rights to that magick on the Sun Sovereign. If chosen, you cannot change your mind. You must enter the trials. Win and all the glory of Solissia will be heaped upon your shoulders; lose, and—if you survive—you belong to the Sun Sovereign, a vassal to Effendier, to live out your remaining life serving us."

A hush fell over the table.

"And if the prince fails to impress you?" Archeron demanded.

"Fail," Xandrian continued, his gaze never leaving Bell, "and not only will you be denied entry into the trials, but your access to the Nihl will be severed. Permanently."

"He'll be . . . stripped of his magick?" Haven clarified. Her heart hammered so loudly in her skull she barely heard her own voice.

"Wholly and completely," Xandrian replied.

The table erupted in shouts. The king ran his thumb and pointer finger down his jaw, contemplating the situation.

Renk grinned, obviously thinking this to his advantage.

If Bell had any magick, that might be true . . .

If he had any magick.

Haven and Bell came to the conclusion at the same time, and they shared a long look. Bell didn't have magick, but he needed a plausible story as to why suddenly his magick was gone. That would free them both from this farce.

Underperform and Bell's magick would be stripped. *Wholly and completely.* No one would be suspicious because the entire kingdom would have an excuse. And Xandrian would have no idea that when he closed the door to the Nihl inside Bell, he was closing the door on a magick-barren mortal.

This chance offered a way out for both Haven and Bell. Still. Something didn't feel right. It was too easy.

She flicked another glance at Bell, unable to force the hesitation from her mind. But before she could convey her feelings, Bell stood, a nervous smile lifting his cheeks. His knuckles whitened as he clenched the side of the table. "I, Prince Bellamy Boteler of Penryth, accept your terms."

Archeron's head whipped around to glare at the prince. "Prince Bell, I do not think you understand—"

"Sorry, cousin," Xandrian said with a grin that settled deep into Haven's gut. "The deal has been struck. Now, Prince of Penryth, ready to impress me?"

THIRTEEN

The display of magick was moved to the gardens below, on a long stretch of lawn near the fountains. Weeping willows and hedgerows hemmed the crowd in a loose circle surrounding Bell and Xandrian. The entourage of Solis reclined against two of the largest trees, watching behind bored eyes and feline smiles.

A few female courtiers stopped in front of the Solis, pretending to fix a stocking or remove a twig from the ridiculous satin slippers they wore. But the Solis didn't even bother hiding the disdainful curl of their lips as they regarded the many layers of clothing plastered over the women. Their painted-on faces and coiffed, impossibly tall hair.

In comparison, the female Solis were dressed for comfort. Delicate gold-armored breastplates. Long wisps of gauzy silver and gold fabric. Large swaths of exposed skin, bronzed by a land renowned for its sun and ridged with lean muscle.

They ignored the wanton stares of the noble men of Penryth,

who had probably never seen so much bare flesh in their miserable lives.

All carried only one weapon.

Their magick was weapon enough.

Attendants quickly lugged ornate chairs across the lawn for the king and Cressida. Only after both had been helped into their seats—an act requiring only two servants apiece to hold up each one's cape so they didn't sit on them—could the demonstration begin.

Haven edged as close to Bell as possible. Sweat dampened her temples and pasted her tunic to the small of her back. The scent of honeysuckle and loamy soil made her dizzy.

She shouldn't have been nervous; how hard would it be to underperform magick?

Even so, her hands shook as she wiped them on her pants, leaving dark streaks of sweat. Everything was happening so quickly. Too quickly to think it all through.

At least Bell seemed confident. His white cape spread out on the grass behind him, his shoulders back and head held high. With a broad grin, he swept out an arm, whatever joke he made muffled by her pounding heart.

The throng of nobles and Solis heard it, though, and a collective chuckle filled the air.

Even Xandrian, who stood ten feet away looking every bit a god, cracked a smile. But it didn't reach his icy eyes.

"I see that you know how to make the crowd laugh," Xandrian said, rubbing the pad of his thumb over the sharp edge of his jaw. "But it's not them you need to regale, prince. It's me."

"Right." Bell cleared his throat and twisted his hand palm up. Then he screwed his face into a tight mask of concentration.

Haven had plenty of time to decide which runespell she would cast on the way across the gardens. It had to be something boring and generic, the kind of magick anyone with a powerful enough runestone could employ.

Ready to be underwhelmed, Sun Lord?

Something flickered just above Bell's palm. A fiery butterfly. It was kid's magick, the kind that once thrived even among the most magick-barren. Meant to make children laugh and babies smile.

But Xandrian wasn't a child. And he certainly wasn't smiling as the delicate golden butterfly spread its wings and began fluttering toward him.

The crowd was still as the magickal creation neared the Sun Lord. No one breathed a word as the butterfly fluttered teasingly around his brow before landing on his long, straight nose.

And no one saw Haven direct it there with her eyes, either.

A furrow wrinkled the king's forehead, his hands flexing over the edge of his chair arms.

Standing to his right, Archeron stared at her, his expression livid. The intensity of his anger seemed a bit much . . .

Then again, she seemed to have a way of annoying the Sun Lord beyond reason.

"Bravo," Renk cheered, stepping into the circle. "You have given us a . . . butterfly. How manly of you."

A few laughs trickled from the nobles. But mostly, they were quiet, as confused as the king must have been on the lackluster choice.

Xandrian hardly dared move as he pulled something the size of an apple from his pocket. The multi-faced device was shaped like a heptagon and made of azerite. Clear gems sparkled from its surface, one for each side.

He spoke a word she couldn't hear and the device snapped open. Using his other hand, he carefully plucked the butterfly off his nose, trapped it inside his palm, and transferred the creature into the device.

A trill of alarm·surged through her. Trying not to move too fast, she quickly drew an undo rune on her palm to destroy the magickal insect—but it was already lost to her. She felt the tether between their magick snap, an icy wall closing off any further access to her creation.

Xandrian watched Bell with unblinking eyes as the device in his hand began to light up. Each stone flashed as they glowed one by one until a constellation of lights flickered over his breastplate.

Tearing his gaze from the prince, Xandrian looked down at the golden cage, every single stone alight, and blinked.

An emotion as close to surprise as she imagined he could feel flickered across his face. He tilted the device in disbelief, examining every glowing stone as their light danced across his face.

Then he pocketed the cage and slowly looked back up to meet Bell's wide-eyed gaze. "Congratulations, Prince Boteler of Penryth." Xandrian's voice was soft, unsteady, as if even he couldn't believe what he was saying. "You and your magick now belong to the Sun Sovereign."

A cheer went up from the group. Haven fought to clear the panicky darkness circling her vision as she struggled for breath. When Haven and Bell locked eyes, the confusion on his face matched her own. The crowd surged to congratulate Bell.

Before she could react, the Solis circled to flank the prince. As they began prodding him across the lawn, he angled his head back to catch her eye once more.

I'll fix this, she mouthed.

But the declaration felt hollow. A lie of the worst kind. Even muddled by shock, she understood Bell was now as bound to the Sun Sovereign of Effendier as surely as Archeron was bound to Bell's father.

FOURTEEN

After the magickal demonstration, things moved rapidly. Bell was taken to pack his things while the royal family did the same. They were going with him, of course. All the way to Effendier.

To participate in magickal trials. Without magick.

You really screwed this one up, Ashwood.

Haven had to rescue him somehow. Help him escape the Solis and then flee.

She tried to get near the prince, but the king had soldiers to keep curious eyes back. That now included her, for reasons she didn't understand.

The soldier barring Bell's door glanced down at her hand, positioned on the hilt of her dagger. Fear flashed across his eyes, but he didn't budge.

"I'm sorry," he said. "I have my orders."

"Whose orders?" she demanded, squaring her shoulders. "The

king's?"

He shook his head but refused to give her details. Even at the threat of steel. Whoever had given the order, he was more terrified of them than her.

She wasn't about to give up, though. Going against all sense of dignity, she yelled Bell's name until she thought her voice would shred. When that didn't work, she shoved past the poor guard and began pounding on the door.

That's exactly where Archeron and Surai found her, hammering away at the heavy wood and contemplating how much trouble she'd be in if she battered the prince's door down.

Surai, it seemed, wasn't barred from seeing the prince. A fact that irked Haven immensely.

After promising Haven she would find out what was going on, Surai slipped past the guard, winking as she did. The moment Surai closed the door behind her, Archeron stalked toward Haven.

"You," he growled, crooking his finger at her like a weapon. "Come with me."

The guard lobbed a you're-in-trouble grin at her. Snarling, she followed Archeron to a quiet corridor.

"They won't let me see the prince," she hissed as soon as they were alone.

He raised an eyebrow. "I'm well aware."

"And what was that earlier?" she continued. "I did the easiest magick spell there is, a child's trick. How in the realm did that win him over?"

He pinned her with a glare that could fell giants. "He wasn't judging Bell on his performance. He was testing his powers, sampling the purity of it. But you would have known that if you'd taken two seconds to ask me."

"Oh . . . runes." Her head fell back. She should have expected that. "The box."

"Yes, the box—or what we like to call *ignis arca*, a fire taster in the mortal tongue. I tried to warn the prince," he added, his voice softening. "I would have told you on the way to the gardens, but the king . . ."

A pang of guilt hit her as the shame in his voice became clear.

"Wouldn't allow you to leave his side," she finished for him.

His nostrils flared as he nodded. "Three months away was just long enough to remind me of the exquisite joy freedom brings. Now, being enthralled to him feels like a living death."

"I'm sorry," she whispered, the anger coiled inside her body relaxing as she remembered what this must be like for him.

"It's not your fault."

"Sure about that?" She couldn't help but remember how he entered the Cursed lands to break his enslavement to the king and then ended up using that one opportunity to save her life instead.

"Stop. You are not to blame."

Thinking about the Curse brought her attention to Bjorn. "Did you find him?"

He knew who she meant, and a shadow darkened his face. "No. The betrayer must be in hiding." He shook his head, as if dislodging Bjorn from his mind, and held out his arms. "Now, I have waited a painfully long time to see you, Little Mortal. Come here."

A command. One that she happily obeyed. Shivering, she closed the distance between them until his warmth engulfed her. He slid an arm around her waist and pressed her into him.

Months on the road had left him smelling of leather and salt, and she found herself dragging in deep lungfuls of his scent like a fool.

He chuckled. "Are you . . . sniffing me?"

"Just making sure you don't smell as foul as you look."

He slipped a wide hand beneath her tunic. She shivered as he trailed the calloused pads of his palm over her waist and around to the small of her back.

A gasp slipped from her lips, and he laughed again, the sound like a drug. "Liar," he whispered, running his nose along her neck. "I look amazing and I smell divine."

She nipped his shoulder. "Peacock."

He growled, trapping her against the wall as his tongue entered her mouth. Her lips parted in welcome. Her body pressed into his, hungry for the feel of him. There was nothing gentle about his kiss, but she matched his ferocity, exploring his mouth with newfound courage.

For months she had dreamt of doing this. Touching him. Feeling his body against her. Consuming him in every way possible.

Now she lost herself to the sensation. Her troubles slipping away as easily as dirt in a hot, soapy bath. His wide, capable hands slid down to cup her bottom. At the same time, his mouth moved on from her lips to her neck, exposing the flesh just below his sharp jaw.

Runes shimmered down the side of that bronzed skin, silvery swirls that seemed to move as she watched. Dancing for her. Only her.

When his lips left her neck and returned to her mouth, he had hardly begun to kiss her before he stiffened.

His lips went hard and pulled away.

He angled his body to force space between them.

Something inside her stirred. Her dark magick slithering and uncurling, rejecting his light magick's closeness.

Had he felt it?

A glance up at his face and she knew he had. He tried to hide it with a smile, but there, deep inside his emerald eyes—revulsion.

"You felt it again?" she asked, shame surging through her. She felt dirty, gross. Like the blackness seething inside her body was smeared across her face for all to see.

"Yes." He raked his fingers through his unkempt hair and tugged at the ends. "Your dark magick must be growing stronger."

With a frustrated sigh, she pulled away, flattening against the wall. Archeron let out a breath to match her own.

Then he flicked a glance over her face, recognized her embarrassment, and said, "I can handle a little bit of dark magick."

"What about a year from now? We have no idea what my powers will be like then."

"We'll find a way to stop it. Whatever it takes."

That reminded her of her deal with Nasira, and she flicked up her eyebrows as she glanced up at him. "What if I could bind my darkness somehow?"

He was quiet for a breath, but he couldn't mask the hope that flicked over his face. "Is such a thing possible?"

"Maybe."

"If that's true, and you could somehow snuff out that side of your magick, that would make things between us . . . easier."

A tug jerked her core. A tiny part of her had hoped he'd say it didn't matter. But of course it mattered. She harbored something depraved, something bloodthirsty and horrible.

Who wouldn't want that removed?

"How do you manage then with Avaline? She's part Noctis, which means she has dark magick, right?"

He rubbed the back of his neck. "No. She's still a mortal descended from one of the Nine Houses, and her magick originates from the Nihl."

Another pang of disappointment hit her, but she hid the emotion, focusing on the obvious next question. "Did you tell her?"

"Who? Avaline?" A little smile played across his lips. "Yes."

"And?"

His hunt for Bjorn had taken him straight through his betrothed's kingdom, and he'd promised to inform her of Haven.

"And," Archeron began, slowly, teasingly, "I found her in bed with two lovers when I arrived, so I think she was amenable to the idea."

"She said that? With words?"

"She said that. With *words*."

That should have eased the tension in her chest, but if anything, talking about Avaline only made things worse.

How would she ever get used to the idea of another woman?

If she didn't already owe Archeron so much, if he hadn't given up everything to resurrect her . . .

She blinked. *No. That wasn't why she stayed with him at all.* Archeron was good and kind, *and* beautiful, there was no denying that.

He gave up everything for her. She could sacrifice her pride for him.

She toyed with the button of her tunic. "Good, because if she isn't okay with it—"

"What?" Archeron growled, suddenly pinning his arms on either side of her head. "You would give me up?"

Haven was completely serious as she said, "You know I would."

It was his turn to blink, his golden brows gathering. "Well, then I suppose it's a good thing we Solis don't see our partners as property like you mortals, to be given away and taken back at our whim."

"You're engaged, Archeron."

"Yes, but I'm also immortal. We've both agreed that we are not yet ready to wed for at least five hundred more years . . ."

Five hundred more years. He spoke of half a millennium as if it were a few months. She would be dead by then, her body broken down to dust, any memory of her long forgotten.

Sometimes she forgot how different she and Archeron really were. Sometimes she wondered if being together was right.

He gave up everything for you.

Haven ducked beneath his arms. She didn't care what Archeron said, she'd never get used to the Solis's liberal views on marriage and monogamy.

"I think," she said, flipping around to face him, "that we should focus on the problem at hand. Bell."

"Agreed," he grumbled.

"I think the king has banned me from seeing Bell."

"It was Cressida, actually," Archeron amended, his playfulness evaporating. "I overheard her ordering Bell's guards to keep you away. But it's worse than that." He paused, watching her closely. "She wants to prevent you from joining Bell in Effendier. She's already petitioned the king to keep you here—and he's agreed."

Her mouth filled with invisible sand. "Why?"

"Because Bell is weaker without you, and she's hoping for him to fail. If he does, he remains part of my mother's court indefinitely."

"Giving Renk the opportunity to take his place in this court."

"Precisely."

"But why would the king agree to that?"

"Because, Little Mortal, the king thinks now that his son has magick, he doesn't need your protection anymore. He wants the world's eyes on the Cursebreaking prince of Penryth and not you."

"Runes." She released an angry breath. "I should have expected this."

Archeron picked at a piece of dust on his vest. "We can pass off my magick for now as Bell's, but that will only go so far. Once they enter the trials, my magick will be useless. They have wards in place to prevent the audience from interfering."

"Can you petition your cousin to have him disqualified?" she said, desperation making her words come out jumbled and quick. "Perhaps even . . . your mother?"

"No. He's locked in by a covenant of magick. Only my mother can release him now, but it's more likely the sun would plunge into the Glittering Sea than her find such grace. She has no love for the king of Penryth, and possessing his son will give her immense pleasure."

Haven gouged her knuckles into her temples and sighed. "I've totally screwed him this time, haven't I?"

"Yes," Archeron agreed, not affording her an ounce of pity. "You have. But give me time to figure out a plan."

"Us," she corrected. "I'll be there too. It might take a few days to find passage—"

"No," he snarled, closing the little bit of distance between them. "What do you think will happen the moment my cousin figures out Bell's secret? Think, Haven." He tapped the corner of her temple, making her flinch. "He'll realize whose power he sampled, and he will not hesitate to execute you, as is the law."

"I won't let that happen."

"No? How, exactly?" He shoved a hand through his hair. "This proves why you should not enter the Solis Court. You have no idea how it works there, the level of scheming, the ancient magick. There are hundreds of powerful Sun Lords and Queens all vying to impress my mother. Lightcasters who have spent centuries perfecting the runic arts. Someone like you would only make things worse."

"Someone like . . . like me?" She could hardly talk through her anger. "What exactly does that mean?"

"You know what it means. The dark magick inside you . . . never mind." He frowned. It looked like he wanted to say more, but then he waved his hand and turned to leave. "I have to go."

"You're just going to leave?" she asked. Her head was spinning, her heart lurching erratically in her chest.

His back was turned, shoulders stiff. "I don't have a *choice*."

Oh—*oh*. The king was calling him.

She watched him slip down the hallway and disappear, wishing she knew the words to call after him. He would be departing soon, perhaps now, and she didn't want their last few words together to have been in anger.

She kicked the wall, wincing as hard stone connected with her big toe. All these months, all the imaginary conversations and scenarios she'd planned for when they finally met up again—and they ended up fighting.

Bravo, Ashwood. Way to make your reunion truly spectacular.

The idea that perhaps Archeron was right—she would only make things worse in Effendier, gnawed at her. She'd already messed so many things up. The incident with her dark magick escaping. Her nightmares. Now this.

She was a royal screw up with nobody to blame but herself.

Still. She knew deep down that if she let Bell sail off to Effendier alone, she would never see her best friend again.

FIFTEEN

Haven perched above the main gates to the castle, hunched down along a curved section of sun-faded stone beside a marble lion wreathed in wilted black dahlias, and watched the royal entourage pass below. They moved slowly through the iron gates, a trickle of horses and bright velvet riding into the dusk-painted canvas of muted golds and pinks.

Silence permeated the group. Broken only by the soft clop of the horses' hooves and the swish of their tails against the flies.

Ravius sat heavy and dour on her shoulder, a manifestation of her foul mood.

What a boring display, he remarked inside her head. *I've seen funeral processions with more liveliness.*

Ignoring the pesky bird, she scoured the long line of horses and nobles for Bell's chestnut stallion, or the prince's new snow-white cape he would certainly be wearing. But a crowd of well-wishers hemmed in the road, and when she saw him—sitting proud atop his horse and squinting against the fading sun—he quickly disappeared beneath the gates before she could so much as call his name.

Only Haven recognized the hard curve of his smile as fear. Only she spotted his hands bunched in his lap, whites of his knuckles bright as he clutched the reins.

He was terrified.

News had already spread of the prince's invitation to the tournament. Apparently it was considered a great honor to be chosen.

Given that she wasn't allowed to see the prince, she'd spent the last few hours before they left poring over the texts for mention of the Praetori Fiernum trials. Only a measly chapter in a Solis History book mentioned the secretive trials, and it was vague, at best.

But she'd learned a few important things already.

One. Mortals rarely made the cut. For a mortal from one of the Nine Houses, being invited was a huge honor, as the trials were held once every century.

Two. The trials were brutal. While the details surrounding the trials were shrouded in mystery, there were two accounts of contestants dying most horrifically.

Three. Only once had a mortal won the trials and the chance to preside over the House of Nine. Bartholemy of House Courtenay. He ruled for seventy-two years and seven days as King of the Nine Houses.

Four. The average number of contestants seemed to be around fifty, and the average number of finalists who walked out alive at the end was closer to fifteen.

Basically, when she inadvertently made Bell a contestant, she'd consigned him to death.

She waited under the fading sun until the last of the court rode past, but Archeron wasn't among them.

Her heart ached at the thought of not seeing him one last time, especially when she'd just been reminded how wonderful it was with him around. Arrogant and annoying as he sometimes was.

Ravius fluttered off as she hopped down from the gate, defeated. She was just about to cross the cobblestone path when a rider thundered toward her, a cape of purple whipping in the air behind him.

She recognized the pale gray Alpacian mare with the azerite horns immediately, and she lunged into a sprint to meet the rider, practically leaping into his arms.

Archeron pulled her into his lap. "Couldn't leave without saying goodbye," he murmured into her ear.

"You need to protect him," she said, taking his square chin between her fingers until his warm green eyes couldn't look away. "There are forces out to take his magick and his life. A blood mage—"

"I know." His voice was gentle. "Surai told me everything. I'll take care of him, Haven. I swear on my life I'll do everything in my power to keep him safe."

She nodded, chest tight. "Will you stop at Skyfall Island? Xandrian mentioned that was the last House of the Nine."

"No. Now that he has Bell, there's no need. My mother only specified one mortal for the trials."

Has Bell. Has *him, for rune's sakes.* Like a possession one might acquire, a nice new hat or a shiny new pair of boots.

Haven swallowed. He'd be in Effendier sooner than she imagined. "Tell him to be strong?"

"Of course."

"And . . . that apology extends to you as well." She brushed her lips over his. At some point since they last spoke, he'd found time for a bath and a shave, and his face was smooth against hers. "I don't want to fight."

He chuckled. "That wasn't a fight, Haven. Look, I'll be back soon and we can figure this out. But, for now, just stay put."

"I can't do that, Archeron. You know that."

His eyes narrowed to green slits, and he grasped her jaw between his fingers, forcing her to look at him. "Goddess help me, Haven, if I see you in Effendier . . ."

A warning hung at the end of his sentence.

"I mean it," he added softly. "If for no one else then do this for me. If I lost you . . ." A snarl ripped from his chest. "You are the only thing now keeping the darkness at bay. Do you understand?"

She wanted to argue but his anguished tone suppressed the words in her throat.

"You might be able to fare against the Sun Lords and Queens at court," he continued. "You may well manage to hide your magick for a time. But I know my mother. She will see through your illusions to the abominable magick beneath, and she will destroy you for it."

Abominable magick.

The word stuck in her gut, and she shook her head. "But if you knew me, you'd understand I can't do that. Bell is my family. I went into Spirefall and broke the Curse for him. Do you really think I won't come to his aid now?"

His nostrils flared. He seemed to think of a million responses before settling on these words: "If you come to Effendier, you won't only lose me, Haven, you will die. And this time there won't be a wish to save you."

Archeron's mare stomped anxiously, pulling at the bit and swinging her head side-to-side. Like his horse, Archeron was growing antsy to leave. His gaze skipped to the horizon, now a thin band of orange, where the others made a delicate, curving line.

As much as she wanted to assure him she would stay, she couldn't. Not without lying.

She slid from the saddle. The moment her boots slapped the uneven cobblestones, a feeling of being adrift hit. The emotion lingered as she watched him spur his horse into a gallop.

And it remained long after he'd disappeared into the delicate shroud of darkness creeping over the land.

Ravius descended from the treetops and landed hard on her shoulder. He pecked at her ear a few times and then settled down low.

He's a pretty thing, Ravius teased. *If bulging muscles and pillowy lips are your fancy. Not as regal nor as clever as my master, Prince Darkshade—*

"One more word," she growled, "and I'll make you into a pie."

He squawked with displeasure, but there was no snappy retort. A wise choice, considering her mood.

Nearly everyone she cared about was gone, and she couldn't protect them from her mistake. Archeron was risking his neck just knowing about Bell's deception, much less helping him continue deceiving the Sun Court. And given he was already ostracized from his homeland, what would happen if they caught him?

How much farther could he fall before he broke completely?

And Bell. He was about to be thrown into a battle he wasn't ready for, in a land brimming with the most powerful magick in the realm.

If they didn't discover his fraud on the way over, and he somehow survived the political machinations of the Sun Court, he didn't stand a chance in the Netherworld of making it out of the trials alive.

Not without someone inside the trials feeding him magick—and it was more likely Nasira would become a saint than a contestant would share their magick with the prince.

Night completed its descent, bringing a chill to the air and a strange sense of a world changed. Drawing the lightweight cape around her shoulders, Haven went to switch clothes and find Surai.

As she slipped in and out of the shadows, a plan began to form from her conversation with Archeron earlier. A wonderful, dangerous plan.

There are wards in place that prevent magick from the crowd outside the trials . . .

But he'd said nothing about a contestant *inside* the trials.

Now she just needed a way to enter the tournament as a contestant. As she heaved herself up the wide marble steps leading to the palace, each leg seemingly filled with sand, a headache began to form behind her eyes.

The pain blurred her vision, and she almost didn't notice Surai leaned against the frame of the gilded doors until she was on top of her. Without a word of greeting, Haven explained the plan.

When she was finished, Surai released a long, grievous sigh. "We will die. All of us. You know that, right?"

"Not if everything goes according to plan," Haven insisted.

"But everything won't go according to plan. It never does." Surai tugged at the ends of her dark hair. "You don't know the Sun Sovereign. She's every bit as ruthless as the Shade Queen."

"I'm not afraid of her."

"You should be." Surai paused, worrying Rook's heart flower at her wrist. "Haven, you are the only person I have left other than Archeron, and I will follow you to the ends of the realm. But I have to ask. Have you not done enough for this mortal prince?"

Haven glanced at the sky, remembering that same view ten

years ago, only then she was terrified and lost. "If not for Prince Bell, I would be a slave or worse. But he didn't just buy my freedom; he clothed me, he fed me, he insisted I was educated and protected. When I awoke screaming from my nightmares, he told me I was safe. That I would always be safe. When his father tried to send me away, more than once, he refused to eat until I was brought back. The only reason I am alive—the *only* reason—is because of his kindness."

"He is a moral and good prince," Surai admitted. "A rarity for mortals."

Haven's throat ached with emotion. She'd never thanked him for saving her, not properly. Now it was all she wanted. "If it was Rook, or even me, what would you do?"

Surai didn't even hesitate as she said, "I'd follow you both to the ends of the realm."

"Then it's settled. We're going to help the prince . . . and maybe, if we're lucky, when all of this is over he'll be a king."

A frown tugged on Surai's lips, but she nodded. "You're a good person too, Haven Ashwood." Haven went stiff as Surai wrapped her in a hug. "A little naive, but that's because you are a baby in terms of years lived. Now, let's just pray to the Goddess that goodness doesn't get us all killed."

SIXTEEN

Surai went to prepare for travel, and Haven wearily made her way to her chamber. Demelza was waiting for Haven, slumped in a hideous green brocade chair mending a pair of Haven's pants. Her halo of curls stuck out at all angles.

The moment Demelza took in Haven's tense expression, her forehead grooved and she began muttering about a bath.

"No bath," Haven groaned, flopping onto her hard mattress. "Don't have the time. But some fresh clothes would be wonderful."

A sigh of longing tinkled from her throat as she imagined her porcelain tub brimming with water, lavender and verbena scented steam wafting from the bubbly surface. After going weeks without a proper bath in the Cursed lands, she now found herself taking a minimum of two baths a day.

That was all about to change. Haven threw a tired gaze at her pants. Why hadn't she discovered a magickal rune for taking off clothes? Surely one existed. And if it didn't, that was a travesty.

While she wriggled out of her sweaty clothes, Demelza rummaged around her wardrobe until she found an outfit she deemed worthy.

When Haven was fully dressed, she fell back onto the bed and closed her eyes. Her world spun with all the things that needed to happen—but she was suddenly so tired.

This not sleeping thing was catching up to her.

"You have a problem, yes?" Demelza said, her astuteness not the least bit surprising.

"Yes. Problems, plural." Haven cracked her neck. "There's something I have to do to save the prince. But doing it will hurt the *other* person I love—and probably end in my death, at least, according to him."

"And what happens if you do not do this thing?"

Haven's jaw clenched, and she let out another breath. "Then the prince will become enslaved to a faraway queen—if he doesn't die—and I live forever knowing he did so partially for my mistake."

Demelza let out a slew of words in her native tongue that Haven guessed to mean you're screwed.

"Exactly," Haven added.

Demelza's skirt swished softly over the floor around the bed as she paced. "Then you must do this thing, even if it kills you."

"I know. I just wish I could make *him* understand." An image of Archeron's stubborn face came to mind.

Demelza snorted. "Men are pliable as clay . . . given the right *touch.*"

Haven nearly choked on air. "Not this man."

"All men." Demelza's voice held an amused lilt that made her sound younger, freer. "Even preening Sun Lords." *How did she know about Archeron?* "But you need not worry about that yet. You must eat and rest and then do this thing."

Haven's eyelids fluttered open to the feeling of someone lightly tugging her hair. Haven froze as she watched Demelza—an upside-down version—brushing Goddess knows what from the tangled curtain she once called hair.

"If you refuse to keep your hair neat," Demelza chided, "then you should at least keep it braided."

"It was braided this morning."

"You do it wrong." Demelza yanked on a knotted strand, causing Haven to yelp. "Let me fix your hair and it won't come undone for a year."

"If I have any left after you're finished."

Demelza only yanked harder.

This is what it's like to have a mother. The thought was as fleeting as it was bittersweet. Her mother was gone, probably dead. Trying to substitute her with the first mortal woman who showed Haven kindness was foolish and cruel.

And calling Demelza's attack a kindness was a stretch . . .

"You are hungry, yes?" Demelza waggled her eyebrows. "I will send for some food."

Massaging the tender spot just above her eyes, Haven sat up. "Just some fruit, and maybe some of those pastries I like. And can you pack me a light bag. I'll need . . . travel clothes. A few gowns." She cringed at the last request. "One or two of my jewels—you may have to search the cushions."

Demelza lifted a sharp eyebrow. "Travel? In this state?"

"It can't be helped, Demelza."

"The thing you must do?"

Haven nodded.

"Then I will go with you." Demelza planted her hands on her

wide hips.

Surprise made Haven's tongue forget how to work, and she cleared her throat before managing, "No, Demelza, it's not necessary."

"There are demons involved, yes?"

"A few, but—"

"I go."

"No, Demelza. Your job doesn't require you to take such risks. Not for me, not for anyone."

Demelza launched into a long string of curses in her mother tongue, followed by, "Understand? I go."

Haven didn't understand, but she had never seen Demelza so adamant about anything, and she quickly decided against fighting her. "It will be dangerous."

"I am not scared," her lady's maid snapped, slapping a hand over her chest to show how brave she was.

"That's not—never mind. If you insist on going, I can't stop you." Haven stretched to her feet, her body complaining with every move. It was time to meet Nasira. "Come along. You can see firsthand the dangers I speak of."

Hopefully Nasira could scare Demelza into some sense.

Surai met them in the courtyard. She glanced at Demelza, shifted her gaze to Haven, and then just shook her head. Without a word, they made the trek to the hunting lodge.

Normally Surai and Haven climbed the runewall and traveled through the Muirwood before backtracking around the western side of the palace. But Demelza couldn't climb the two-story high wall, so they took a more direct approach.

Demelza followed quietly behind Surai, keeping pace with the girls. Her spry steps surprised Haven, but then again, she must have walked up and down the stairwells of Fenwick fifty times a day, at least.

The canopy of branches and tangled vines above strangled the moonlight, swathing them in darkness. At one point Surai threw up an illumination orb to light their way, the golden light casting a strange pallor over the forest.

If Demelza was surprised by the sudden display of magick, she didn't show it.

When they began to climb the ridge leading up to the hunting cabin, Demelza's lips thinned.

"There are demons here," Demelza whispered, surprising exactly no one.

"Worse," muttered Surai.

Haven thought Demelza might have a heart attack when Nasira appeared looking every bit a demon. From the primordial yellow glow of her eyes to the dark wisps of magick dancing around her.

The spread of her midnight wings seemed to swallow the stars as she swirled in tight circles above them, her childish laughter echoing off the rocks. Her long ivory hair swirled around her head like a crown of snakes.

Before Haven could blink, Nasira speared toward Demelza.

The impact of the small girl slamming to the rocky path seemed to rattle the entire mountain. The gust of her wings sent Demelza's springy curls flaring back and her threadbare brown cloak whipping out behind her. Sand and tiny rocks sprayed their faces and made Haven blink.

To Demelza's credit, she didn't so much as flinch.

Nasira cocked her head sideways at Demelza. "If this is my meal, I'm disappointed. She smells like shoe polish and old leather."

"Who are you to speak of stench?" Demelza demanded, lifting a fleshy chin. "When you reek of sulfur and decay and twisted magick?"

"Enough." Haven slipped between the two, ready to access the dagger hidden inside her sleeve if Nasira misbehaved. "Nasira, there's been a change of plans. I haven't found another blood slave for you. The prince was taken—"

"Taken?" Nasira interrupted, a sly smile revealing sharp teeth. "Does taken mean willingly volunteered in your language?"

"You were there?" Panic lanced her side as she imagined Nasira around all those innocent mortals.

"Of course. I smelled the cloying magick of the Sun Lords from miles away." She grinned brightly. "And, technically, the boundaries don't apply to soulwalking."

"Did any of them see you?" Surai demanded.

Nasira let out a scoffing laugh. "I am the heir to the Noctis throne. I know how to soulwalk without being noticed, Solis."

Demelza's leather-brown eyes widened at Nasira's exclamation. *Finally, something that rattles the hardened woman.*

Ignoring her, Haven said, "I'm going to Effendier to help Bell. First, I need you to do what you promised, Nasira."

Nasira's dark eyebrows met. "You can't be serious. Do you know what giving up your dark magick means? You're ordinary, with the same magick as any Sun Lord. Ordinary *and* unskilled. How could you want that?"

Tightness clenched Haven's chest as indecision crept through her. To survive Effendier and win Bell's place in the tournament, she would need every bit of magick she possessed. Her twin magick—light and dark—made up for her lack of experience.

Without it, she was much weaker.

The dagger from her dream flashed in her mind. The twisted blade, jagged edge wet with blood. The crooked horns and red eye pulsing in time with her heart.

Archeron's voice clanged inside her skull. *Abominable magick.*

She flinched as she glanced down at her hand, expecting to see the weapon there now. Expecting the cold metal against her flesh—and the rage and bloodlust that came with it.

Her body went ice-cold.

As long as she possessed dark magick, Archeron would never truly trust her. And she didn't blame him. If she didn't restrain it somehow, there was a chance that evil power would break down her will. It could turn her into an instrument of terror; it could hurt people she loved.

That could never happen.

"I've never been more sure of something in my life. Bind it, rip it out, erase it completely. Whatever it takes to kill the darkness inside me."

"I can't kill it, but I can restrict the doorway to access your dark magick. *Only* . . ." Nasira dragged the word out for emphasis, "if you let me come with you." Haven opened her mouth to protest but Nasira cut her off. "The deal was I get all the blood slaves. Since that won't happen if I stay here, I'm going to Effendier."

"Not a chance in the Netherworld," Haven snapped.

"I'll be good; you won't even notice I'm there. Please, I want to help." With a menacing frown, Nasira crossed her arms over her chest. "Prince Bellamy is my . . . friend."

Nasira spoke of friendship as if she were talking about a stray dog that wouldn't leave her alone.

Surai scoffed. "Your friend? I don't think you know what that word means, Noctis."

Nasira's wings flared as she cut her eyes at Surai. The Noctis bared her teeth at the Solis. "If I wasn't being good right now, I would make you pay for saying that lie."

Surai touched the spot between her eyebrows and then flicked her fingers at Nasira—basically the middle finger in Solissian. "You could *try*. And that's exactly why we're not taking you along. How long until you decide being good is boring? Or that Sun Lords have magick you want to sample? I will not expose Effendier to your depravity."

Nasira's hands balled into rocks at her side. "As if you could help Haven. I've seen mortals with more magick."

"My powers might be dull," Surai hissed, "but they helped me slaughter hundreds of your kind, all of them just as arrogant and stupid as you."

"Enough," Haven ordered, exhaling loudly. "You're both formidable . . . which is why I need both of you." Surai's mouth fell open as she pivoted to face Haven. "As much as I hate the idea, with my dark magick gone, we may need Nasira's . . . gifts."

A dark cloud passed over Surai's face; Nasira clapped her hands together with delight. Demelza, for her part, was sliding her ever-widening gaze from girl to girl, looking for all the realm like she might pass out and tumble down the mountain.

"I'm going to go pack!" Nasira called, as if this were all just some magickal adventure she was going on with friends. "Follow me and we'll bind your magick. We must hurry before the moon begins to ebb."

As Haven trudged up the steep path, Surai glaring fiery pits into her back, Ravius landed on Haven's shoulder. *I have a joke for you,* he began in that thick brogue. *A mortal girl, an Ashari scout, the heir to the Noctis throne, and a clever raven walk into a tavern.*

Haven rolled her eyes, not in the mood for the bird's dark humor. *You forgot Demelza.*

I didn't forget her; she annoys me so I left her out.

Whatever. Haven jerked her shoulder, trying and failing to dislodge the feathery nuisance. *And the punchline?*

He hopped from claw to claw before hunkering down low. *Oh, it's hilarious: they all die.*

I think we have different ideas about what's funny, she snarled.

Ducking beneath the low doorway into the lodge Nasira called home, Haven vowed not to let that happen.

She'd escaped hell and somehow managed to carve out a tiny piece of happiness with her friends, and she wasn't about to let one mistake ruin everything.

SEVENTEEN

Archeron's hand was hot and steady on Bell's back, but the kind gesture did nothing to stop Bell's lunch from ramming up his throat and into the Glittering Sea. Bell bristled under the weight of the touch.

Any other time he would have protested being consoled by the very same hand that sent his brother to an early death, but currently he was too weak to bother.

Bell had never vomited so much in his entire life. The first day at sea he'd hidden in his cabin attached to a bucket. When his unwanted offerings filled the rough wooden pails to the brim, Archeron dutifully carried the bucket above and dumped its putrid contents overboard.

On the second day Bell decided it was less effort to lose the bucket and heave the pitiful contents of his stomach directly into the frothy, impossibly blue sea below.

Which meant he practically lived on deck.

Being above seemed to help. He'd grown used to the overpowering sea air—a wet, briny assault on his senses—much preferred to the stench below decks. He'd learned to enjoy the way the merciless sun braised his cheeks and darkened his skin. The way the stars at night lit up the entire sky.

After the horrors of Spirefall and that unending grayness, the constant light was a balm for his soul.

But it wasn't helping now.

Archeron removed his hand and frowned. "I've never seen anyone purge themselves as much as you, Prince."

His words felt like a declaration: Prince Bellamy Boteler can't even sail without proving himself unworthy.

Wrapping one arm around his belly, Bell jaunted toward the hull. His fingers just barely curled over the salt-crusted wooden side before he was dredging up the biscuits and figs he'd picked at for lunch.

Three times, four . . . finally he stopped counting. After each episode, he watched his vomit splatter the sea below. But staring at the moving water made him dizzy. And being dizzy made him throw up.

Thank the Goddess everyone else was below deck, and the retinue of ships carrying the royal court were too far away to witness his humiliation. Public puking was high on his list of things to avoid.

"Can you scrounge up more of that bitter tea?" Bell groaned. The potent moonberry tea the Solis drank took the edge off his nausea.

Hesitation deepened the worry line that made a V between Archeron's thick eyebrows. "I shouldn't leave you alone . . ."

"If the blood slaves were going to attack, they would have by now. Unless they're trying a new method—murder by puking."

Bell groaned as the ship listed sideways and his stomach clenched tight. "I'm . . . starting to wonder."

Archeron didn't even crack a smile.

"Plus, I have this." Bell lifted his arm, flashing the bracelet with mortal runes engraved into the leather. "If anything truly threatens me, and it possesses magick, I can protect myself."

The night of his attack by the blood slave, he hadn't been wearing the bracelet. That had been a mistake. His powerrune, the one Haven gave him for his runeday—and the one that condemned him to Spirefall—hid safely between the sewn leather.

To anyone but him, the piece looked like the common runebands soldiers wore for luck.

After a lengthy pause, Archeron finally decided Bell would be safe for a few minutes alone and left. Bell was glad for the break from Archeron's presence—and not just because he despised him.

Much easier to wallow in misery and self-pity when no one was around.

When Bell had first learned of Archeron's involvement in his brother's death, it had come as a huge shock. After all, Archeron had given up everything to save Haven. How could he be both a murderer and savior?

But he'd simply come to the conclusion that the Solis were capable of affection for their human counterparts—when it suited them.

Still, despite Bell's obvious discomfort in Archeron's presence, the Sun Lord shadowed Bell's every move. He did manage not to interact with Bell unless it was absolutely necessary.

They formed an odd pair, but Bell filled the awkward moments trying to mend the huge gaps in his Effendier history.

How long had the sovereign ruled? How many heirs did she have? Who was their biggest ally?

The Sun Lord had answered Bell's constant string of questions with rare patience. But when those questions moved to the subject of the tournament, Archeron had grown tight-lipped.

"Let's hope you never make it to the tournament," he'd replied, suddenly curt.

Yep, I'm going to die.

If only he'd had a chance to talk to Haven. Right after Xandrian had announced Bell's acceptance into the tournament, he'd been swept away by soldiers and ordered to pack.

When Haven hadn't shown up later, he had assumed she was busy packing too.

It was only after the ship set sail and he went in search of his friend that he realized she'd been banned from traveling with him—for reasons he still didn't understand.

Other than Archeron, Bell rarely saw the Solis. The ship had been divided into halves: one side mortal, one side Solis. And the two halves had done a wonderful job of pretending the other didn't exist.

Now all Bell's time was spent trying to keep busy so he didn't think about the trials—or just how screwed he was. Grilling Archeron. Reading through the books he managed to pack. Avoiding Cressida and Renk.

And emptying his stomach into the ocean.

An ocean that any other time he would have marveled at. At night, their ship carved a luminescent trail that lit up the waters. During daylight the water seemed to shine from within, a vibrant impossible blue.

Then there was the lingering scent of orchid and citrus, buried beneath the usual marine smell.

The exotic perfume stuck to his hair and clothes and, when he picked it out over the stench of vomit, left him with an odd serenity.

He chanced a look at the waves, mesmerized by the rainbow shimmer that emanated just below the surface of a ten foot swell before another bout of nausea hit.

The muscles of his abdomen trembled as he rested his cheek against the plank. *How very princely of you, Bellamy.*

"Wow, Barfamy, I never realized just how fitting that name is for you."

Squinting against the harsh sun, Bell pivoted to face the male voice. As soon as he made out Renk, adrenaline flooded his body. "Wow, Renk. You'd think after all these years you could come up with something more creative."

Renk's upper lip curled into a hateful sneer. The unrelenting sun had painted his normally pale skin an angry red, his eyes glassy and slightly unfocused. Even from here Bell could smell the stink of ale on his breath.

Since the horrible incident with Haven's magick, his half-brother had been different.

And not in a good way.

"You know," Renk said, his face going strangely slack, "I haven't forgotten what you did to me. How you humiliated me in front of everyone."

There was a veiled warning in his words that made Bell's whole body go tight with alarm. They were on the deck of a ship. Alone. No witnesses.

The only thing to stop Renk from shoving Bell over the side was a moral code—something Renk simply did not have.

Renk began to walk toward Bell. Each step stretched his gash of a smile.

He was mere feet away when a sultry chuckle to the left made Renk halt. Bell already knew who it was before he turned to face the laughter, and an odd mixture of dread and relief flooded him.

The Sun Lord—more like Sun God—was propped against a mast, his long body leaned back to catch the sun. A creamy-white tunic brought out his tawny skin, and the silver-blond hair at his temples had been woven into thick braids.

His eyes were ice-blue slits as they appraised Renk. Then he flicked two fingers toward the hatch leading below deck. "Leave. Now."

Bell fought back a smile as Renk scurried across the deck.

When his attention returned to the Sun Lord he was met with the same callous expression reserved for his half-brother. Bell had never seen anyone so beautiful—or so cold.

A tingle formed at the base of Bell's skull and then the Sun Lord's lips sliced into a cruel smile.

"I'll never understand how your kind survive," Xandrian began. "A little ocean and you're brought to your knees. A little bloodshed and you betray your allies. A little Curse and you hide behind a wall and wait to die."

Cold, beautiful, and an asshole. Just my luck. "Not all of us hid behind the runewall."

"Being taken against your will does not count, Cursebreaker." Xandrian flicked imaginary dirt off the front of his shirt. "I find it curious that four Solis broke the Curse yet you and your father will have the realm believe it was all your doing. Mortals are so predictable in their lies."

"You keep saying you," Bell replied, "but not all mortals are the same."

"Aren't they? All I see are a rude, cowardly, bland people who are as empty as your stomach on the inside." Xandrian's focus drifted to the collar of Bell's shirt.

Ducking his chin, Bell followed Xandrian's stare to the dark, semi-circular stain marring the top of his tunic. Wonderful. This was his last clean traveling top, or had been, and there were still five days of sailing left.

"I have a shirt you could borrow," Xandrian offered. "I might be escorting you to a certain death, but only a true sadist would make you wear that filthy thing."

Any other time, Xandrian's dark declaration would have bothered Bell. But something about vomiting one's guts up made it hard to care about much else. Even impending death.

Bell tugged at his collar. "Thanks for the vote of confidence."

All at once, Xandrian left the mast and drifted toward Bell, moving in that strange, fluid way Archeron did. But whereas Archeron was a panther, all brute strength and grace, Xandrian was light, nimble. A leaf blowing on the breeze.

When he got to the side of the ship, Xandrian's gaze gravitated to the sea. Something flashed inside his eyes. Not happiness. More like longing.

In profile, his jawline cut a sharp edge, the perfect straightness of his long nose apparent. Golden ribbons snaked through his braids, their color matching the amber flower cuffs ridging his ears. And two tiny diamond runestones flickered from his right earlobe.

Bell could have sworn the waters calmed under Xandrian's steady attention, as if he willed the choppy azure waters into a slick pane of glass.

Perhaps he did.

"You know," Xandrian said as he looked out into the horizon. "One siren rules over all sea creatures. This watery queen is as gorgeous as she is bloodthirsty, and she demands a sacrifice from every traveler. So before each sailing we slice the pad of our thumb and drip our lifeblood into the waves on shore."

"I don't believe in such things," Bell said carefully. He didn't want to mock Xandrian's culture, but he also didn't want to come off as some naive mortal who fell for every story.

"I know her and she would take great offense to that."

"A real siren queen?" Bell tugged at his curls which had grown riotous under the constant watery spray. "Forgive me if that's hard to imagine."

"You're about to enter Effendier, the land of sun and magick and creatures well beyond your *imagination*, so you had better start believing, Prince." His gaze flicked over his ruined shirt once more. "Neptannia takes her offering one way or another. Better a nicked thumb than a ruined shirt."

Bell groaned as his belly flip-flopped, sending acrid bile surging up his throat. Embarrassed, he just managed to clamp his jaw and keep it down as Xandrian watched behind those guarded eyes.

Shadeling's horn, if he sailed again in a hundred years it would be too soon.

One of the Solis emerged from below deck and called Xandrian over. The Sun Lord had only traveled a few steps when he paused, head turned in profile.

"Why did you choose a butterfly?" Xandrian asked softly, his voice troubled as if he'd been pondering the question for a while. "Your magick is perhaps the purest I've ever sampled, which in and of itself is remarkable. You could have done anything . . . yet you performed an unimpressive child's trick. Why?"

Bell's throat tightened. "Perhaps . . . perhaps deep down I was afraid."

Close to the truth.

"Hm." A divot carved between Xandrian's pale eyebrows, the only wrinkle on his otherwise flawless skin. "Did you know, Prince Bellamy, that if you took your eighteen years of life and multiplied them by fifty, you would still not have lived as long as

I have." He turned his head so that his face was fully hidden, his expression a mystery. "Remember that next time you lie to me."

Bell's heartbeat crashed against his skull as he watched Xandrian plunge below deck.

He knows he knows he knows—

No, how could he? *Calm down and think this through.*

Xandrian guessed something was off but he hadn't discovered exactly what—yet. All Bell had to do was play it cool and pretend his magick was his own until they figured out a plan. They had five days onboard plus seven days in Effendier before the tournament started.

Surely that was enough time to come up with a solution.

Another shudder wracked Bell's gut and he doubled over, dry heaving. The violence of it jerked tears to his eyes.

For a moment, he thought he caught a flicker of coral and teal beneath the waves, the flash of sunlight off a golden crown.

For a delusional second, the tinkling of laughter mixed with the crashing of waves.

Then Archeron returned with the tea, the dark purple contents steaming from a brass tumbler. Bell forced the stuff down his throat. Wiping his sleeve across his mouth, he stumbled down the ladder to his chamber below, Archeron in tow.

Waiting on his cramped bed was an immaculate shirt the off-white color of the seashells that lined the rocky Penrythian shores. The moment Bell's fingers brushed the neat collar, a swarm of golden butterflies rose from the gauzy fabric. Thousands and thousands of them. An endless stream of gossamer-winged beauties that filled the room until a sea of wings batted at Bell and Archeron.

"Blasted creatures!" Archeron growled, swatting at the creatures before jerking a hand at the door. The door flung open, and the magickal insects drained from the room in a loud whoosh.

When only a few remained, Archeron let his head drop back, muttering, "Xandrian."

Bell leaned against the wall, a butterfly settling on his shoulder. "Why would your cousin play such a trick?"

"Because he has taken an interest in you, Prince." Archeron glanced at the open door and then flicked his fingers again, sending the heavy wooden thing slamming shut. "And in my experience that is never a positive thing."

Bell was about to speak when a small butterfly landed on top of Archeron's head. Maybe it was the contrast of Archeron's strength with the creature's frailty, but Bell found his lips stretched in a grin.

Archeron's frown made Bell's smile grow.

Only much later did Bell realize that, for the first time since he set foot on this blasted ship, he was smiling.

EIGHTEEN

One second fiery claws of pain were ripping through Haven's body.

The next, the agony was gone and she was in Stolas's world, that dreamscape of Shadoria she had assumed was a figment of his mind.

Now, though—now that she knew Shadoria hadn't been destroyed after all, she wondered if this place he brought her to was also real somehow.

Did Stolas know Shadoria still existed? If so, what would he do to reclaim it?

The lake water seeped through her pants and chilled her legs; gooseflesh ridged her bare arms. She watched ripples distort the face of the moon in the water. Something meaty and slick brushed her thigh, and she quickened her pace to the island.

Only the small protrusion of land was different than before. The grass was withered, the toy castle in disrepair, the wood rotting and glass windows shattered. The stench of decay rose from the brambles that had grown over the soil.

A breath leaked from her throat, the misty cloud illuminating what she should have already felt—the air was freezing.

Her heart spiked in her veins. Something was wrong.

"Stolas?" she whispered, fear tickling her neck. "If you're playing a trick on me, I will carve out your kneecaps and use them for bowls."

Silence. Where were the ravens? The fireflies?

If you see me again, here or otherwise, do not trust me.

The thought hit at the same time she picked up a gravelly sound, almost like a . . . growl.

Do not trust me.

The snarling rumble grew, filling the air and lifting the hairs on her arms. Louder and louder until she felt the primordial noise in the hollow of her bones.

A warning. *Run.*

She tried to move, but her legs were stuck. Literally. The thing in the water, the creature she'd never worried about before, now had its slimy tentacles manacled around her legs.

It was holding her there for him.

Him.

Her hands scrambled at her waist, and a growl of her own spiked the night as she found her waistband empty of blades.

What kind of dream didn't have weapons? Balling her hands into fists, she struck the arms of whatever Shadowling held her. At the same time, she tried to kick her way free.

Impossible. Her punches didn't even make the thing flinch.

A snarl burst from the brambles. She closed her eyes, expecting Stolas to appear any moment. She refused to see him this way.

But then the growling stopped. A word whispered over the

water, something in an ancient language she didn't know, and the creature released her legs.

"Wait, Stola—"

Then she was lying on her side on Nasira's couch with Surai hovering over her. The overwhelming metallic tang of blood filled her nostrils. Fire seared her back where Nasira's talons had cut.

Memory of where Haven had been right before her nightmare floated to the surface. Her dark magick . . . Nasira . . . the pain.

"Thank the Goddess, you're alive," Surai exclaimed, taking Haven's hand.

Nasira bounced on her toes beside the two girls. She'd changed into a pink chiffon gown with embroidered bell sleeves and a low-cut neckline. Two kinds of strappy leather heels hung from her fingers. "See, she's alive." She flashed Surai an impatient, told-you-so grin before returning her gaze to Haven. "She was like seconds away from cutting my throat. Now, onto the important details. Which shoes go better with this outfit?"

Haven stumbled from the couch. The pain brought her to her knees. "Is it done?"

"What?" Nasira cocked her head. "Oh, yes. Your dark magick is now bound. Congratulations. You're now half as strong as you used to be. Now." She waggled the heels in front of Haven's pain-blurred vision. "Ivory or beige?"

Haven just managed to meet Surai's enraged stare before she collapsed.

NINETEEN

Haven twisted in her saddle, trying to find a comfortable position. The gauze pressing down the length of her spine helped protect her wounds. Still, just the brush of her shirt against her rent flesh sent fire coursing through her body.

Seven runes were carved into the flesh of her back. Compliments of Nasira's talons. Haven had managed to hold steady, burying the pain, until Nasira engraved the seventh rune into the tender flesh at the base of Haven's spine.

The agony from that one swept Haven into unconsciousness and straight to Stolas. When she awoke, the ritual was done, she was still alive, and the door to the center of the Netherworld was sealed tight.

No more dark magick.

Was that why Stolas had been so different? He was either supremely angry over her decision to bind her dark magick, or he didn't recognize her without it.

Assuming that was Stolas in her nightmare and not someone else. But, no. He insisted his dreamscape was impenetrable by anyone but her.

The third option was less ideal. Whoever had him had finally broken him to their will.

He had warned her . . .

Shaking her head, she pushed Lady Pearl into a trot despite the lancing pain the action caused.

Moving was agony. Breathing was excruciating. The sweat that rivered down her shoulder blades and soaked through the bandages and into her fresh wounds was continuous torture.

It wasn't just the pain that bothered her though. She felt the absence of her shadowy powers as acutely as she felt the deep, furrowed wounds in her flesh.

Surai drew up beside Haven on Aramaya, her dead lover's horse. Ravius was nestled behind her on the saddle, resting in her shade after gobbling an entire purse of safflower seeds, the spoiled beast.

"Stop looking so sorry for yourself," Surai chided.

Haven let out a groan. "Surai, your heart is a black pit that rivals the Netherworld."

"You chose to bind your magick. Now you must endure the consequences." Surai slid her gaze to Haven's back, where a few dots of blood stained her tunic. The skin around her lips softened. "I can make a salve from the yucca plant. It grows along the cliffs—"

"No," Haven interrupted. "Thank you, but I can't afford anything that helps my skin heal."

When Nasira drew the runes into Haven's skin, she failed to mention she would have to have the symbols redrawn every night. The problem was Haven's light magick. The moment her skin was damaged, her magick worked to mend the cuts.

Every night since, Surai had been forced to trace the ancient symbols with her sharpest blade, reopening the scars.

But even with the added pain, Haven was more determined than ever to keep her dark magick bound. Especially since binding the wicked side of her magick had also stopped her nightmares—not counting the strange incident with Stolas. No more horrible dreams involving the horned dagger. No more blood staining her hands.

No more murdering her friends.

There were also no more shared dreams with Stolas, and his absence weighed heavy on her mind. She replayed his warning in her head. Turning it over and over trying to see it better.

He said there was a wave of despair coming. A dark shadow that would swallow them all.

Worst of all was his declaration that she couldn't trust him— and her suspicion that he was right.

The worries eddied around her skull until she forced any thoughts of the Shade Lord away. There were more pressing matters to deal with. Like finding the elusive Skyfall Island and then convincing them to go along with her plan.

Since Bell's abrupt departure, she'd had days to scheme on how to save him. Convincing Surai had taken some doing, but in the end, even the cautious Solis warrior had admitted approaching the House Volantis was their only option.

Haven took a long gulp from her waterskin, replaced it in her satchel, and then tucked the brim of her floppy hat lower to block the sun's harsh light. She'd grown used to flaunting her hair at court, but she still wore her beloved hat for occasions when the sun seemed particularly angry—like now.

A wonderful briny breeze wafted through the canyon walls. The sea was near.

Tall sandstone cliffs of pale yellow rose on either side, forcing Aramaya and Lady Pearl close together. Lady Pearl flicked her gray tipped ears at Aramaya. Then she canted her head sideways, her pink nostrils flaring as she sniffed her friend.

They'd only been on the road for two days but already the two horses were thick as thieves. They'd gotten into the supplies while everyone slept the previous night. After nibbling the bags of dried beans and sugar, they consumed half the oats and all the moonberry tea leaves.

Apparently something inside the berry was like a drug for the horses. They found the mares in the morning passed out with swollen bellies, their muzzles stained purple and pupils blown.

Valuable hours passed before the horses were able to stand.

Not a great start to the trip.

Up ahead, Demelza sat hunched on Surai's horse. It had taken the poor woman a full day to get used to the height of the Alpacian horse, but she still clenched the reins tightly, her eyes trained on anything but the ground.

It didn't help that Nasira liked to dive close to the horses just to watch the scared beasts whinny and buck. So far, Nasira had proved less than helpful, and Haven was glad the girl spent most of her time soaring above.

"The Untamed Depths," Demelza muttered, using the name Northerners preferred for the Glittering Sea, the body of water that separated the mortal lands from Effendier. Relief was evident in her voice as she performed the sign of the Goddess. "Thank the Goddess no harm befell us on our journey here."

If Demelza thought the journey to the shoreline was hard, how would she survive Effendier?

Haven urged Lady Pearl forward. The moment she cleared the cliffs and the long stretch of azure shorelines filled her vision, the pain in her back eased away.

Haven had been to the rocky shores and gray waters that flanked Penryth to the south and east many times. But this sparkling jewel of water, framed on three sides by gray-black cliffs, was something else entirely.

The water was an impossible blue, the kind that didn't look real.

"Beautiful, isn't it?" Surai asked, her lips quirked proudly. "The Glittering Sea is one of the marvels of our realm. I still cannot believe you have never seen it."

"It's . . ." Haven didn't have the words. They drew closer to the sparkling waters, Haven shielding her eyes from the bright flares of light that flickered off the waves and pulsed from deep within.

When they were close enough that the frothy waves lapped at Lady Pearl's hooves, Haven paused to glare up at the sky.

"Where is it?" Haven asked.

A furrow settled over Surai's forehead as she smoothed out a folded map of the mortal houses, squinting at the hastily scribbled sketches.

"Based on the moon cycle and this old map, the floating Island of Volantis should be . . . here." Uncertainty clipped Surai's voice. Legend suggested that Skyfall Island, gifted to the House Volantis by Freya herself, moved with the lunar cycle.

Just then, a small shadow glided over the sugar-white sands toward them. Haven flinched as Ravius rammed into her shoulder, the impact igniting the scabs at her back.

"Welcome back," Haven muttered. "Although I was rather hoping you'd fallen into the sea."

Hopping from foot to foot, Ravius pecked at her ear. *I suppose that means you don't want to know where Skyfall Island is?*

Haven turned her head to stare at the giant bird. "Of course we want to know," she said aloud. "Why do you think we traveled all this way?"

Perhaps you should open your eyes then.

"They are open."

Yes? But do they see?

Haven shut her eyes, rubbing the spot just above her left eyebrow, and opened them again. She focused on the horizon, letting her attention drift as she forced her eyelids open against the bright glare of the sun. Surai did the same.

There. A shimmer in the clouds. A shifting of the sky.

Haven blinked and a soaring slab of rock appeared over the ocean. Set nearly a mile offshore and floating on its blunted tip, the mountainous obstruction reached so high into the air that it speared the clouds. Crystalline water poured down its sides, haloing the floating island in rainbows.

"Can you see that?" Surai asked, her voice wavering. Demelza was staring at the floating island as well with a stern expression.

"Yep," Haven replied. "But how will we get there?"

Ravius shot from her shoulder toward the shore. As he did, something began to materialize on the beach. A small sailboat. It appeared ancient. The sea spray had stripped all the paint from the wood, and amber sea lichen clung to the warped surface. A ragged sail, bleached bone white, fluttered lazily from its mast.

With a loud squawk, Ravius landed on the top of the mast, ruffled his feathers, and gave Haven a pointed look.

Surai cast a suspicious glance over the boat. "Should we follow Ravius or . . .?"

"Only if we want to die," Demelza grumbled, making the sign of the Goddess.

Nasira dropped to the beach, her wings sending the horses skittering back. "Speak for yourselves. I'm looking forward to meeting the villagers of the island."

Surai glared at Nasira. "Tell me she's not coming."

Haven pinched the bridge of her nose. "Nasira will fly above the island and only attack if I signal her, right, Nasira?"

"Right," Nasira said, flashing her teeth in a grin. "Wait for the signal. You can count on me."

Haven sighed. She hated leading her friends into the unknown, and there wasn't a place any more unknown than Skyfall Island. The inhabitants hadn't been heard from since the Curse began.

Even before that, the people that lived above the clouds were isolationists who only came down for trade and the occasional war. Rumor had it the sky people possessed wings and dragons. Rumor also had it they were suspicious of strangers.

If Haven had learned anything in her short life, it was that the unknown very frequently was worse than imagined. Spirefall had seen to that lesson.

Once they boarded the sailboat, she could be leading her friends straight to their deaths.

But she needed to make a bargain with the sky people. More accurately, she needed to make a deal with one of their royal daughters.

It was the only way she could see to help Bell.

TWENTY

The moment Haven and the others were inside the boat, a strong wind filled the ragged ivory sails, making soft fluttering noises as the hull dislodged from the white sand. They glided silently across the still waters.

Haven released a breath, her eyes never leaving the floating mass of rock growing closer with each blink.

When they neared the rock, the boat slowed until it came to a full stop. Mist and clouds clung to the top of the stone, hiding what awaited them above and providing reprieve from the merciless sun. Water cascaded down the black granite and sprinkled in the still blue ocean.

"Sweet Goddess Above," Demelza muttered, wiping at the sweat darkening her sandy curls.

"Sure we have to do this?" Surai grumbled, letting her scowling gaze travel the floating island face to where it disappeared. "I read about these mortals once. Apparently there isn't much food to be had on their island so they send their dragons to hunt for them. Want to know what their favorite meal is?"

Haven shrugged, trying to hide her unease. "Chicken?"

"Other mortals. Which means I'm safe but you two . . ." Surai made a cutting gesture across her throat.

Demelza hmphed at this.

Haven cracked her neck and glared at the veiled world above. "I'm sure they're perfectly friendly and well fed."

They all flinched as a thick rope slid noisily down the rock face and plopped into the water. Another followed. Then two more. Ripples surged across the still azure water.

Without a word, Haven slipped the ropes through the metal loops fastened to the boat's side and tied them using sailor's knots.

Surai glanced over Haven's handiwork and flicked up her eyebrows. "Impressive."

Haven grinned. "I'm not just a pretty face, you know."

When the ropes gave their first tug, jerking the boat into the air, Haven's stomach flip-flopped, and she lunged for the mast. Surai's mouth grew taut, and a hand fluttered over her olive-skinned throat.

Demelza, for her part, held firm. Maybe bringing the woman with them wasn't such a bad thing, after all. Besides all her incessant mothering—she'd insisted Haven eat the elk jerky and pull from her flask every few hours.

Haven focused on anything but the ever-receding sea below. The algae-pocked face of the rock, smoothed from years of waterfalls cresting its side. The mountains in the distance. She didn't truly feel the terror of their predicament until the clouds enveloped their boat, submerging them in a white world so thick, she couldn't make out Surai a few feet in front of her.

Something cut through the curling mist. A flash of black

feathers; a high-pitched laugh.

Nasira.

For the first time since her arrival, the Noctis girl's presence didn't irritate Haven. Quite the opposite. The Skyfall people might have dragons, but she had a Noctis Queen.

A sudden screech pierced the thinning air. Then, like emerging from a lake of white, the clouds and mist fell away. They were near the top of the land mass, and she could make out windows carved into the rock face. They passed one close enough to peer inside; faces around a small wooden table stared wide-eyed at them as they passed. The yeasty tang of fresh-baked bread drifted from the small kitchen.

More faces peeked from the rooms inside the rock. Children. Adults. The elderly. All had sun-bronzed skin, bright turquoise eyes the color of the ocean, and varying shades of red hair.

The boat stopped ten feet from the top of the rock. A crumbling set of narrow stairs with rusted handrails led the rest of the way. Haven went first, running her fingers over the dragons carved into the granite, their serpentine bodies worn smooth.

Once Haven ascended the last step, she helped Demelza up, then Surai, before turning her attention on the land. Her head swam; her lungs ached. The air up here was different, thin and watery.

"I don't like it here," Surai growled.

Demelza tsked. "We agree on one thing at least, Solis warrior."

Haven surveyed the landscape—but thanks to the wall of dense mangrove rimming the perimeter of the cliffs, there wasn't much to see.

She flicked her gaze to the cloudy sky, searching for any sign of Nasira, and when she lowered her attention back to the mangroves, it was already too late.

Over ten warriors surrounded them. Heavyset, with sunbaked skin and dark hair, they looked nothing like the fair, red-haired House of Volantis she'd read about. Alarm trilled through her as she continued examining the soldiers. Their helmets were crafted from skulls—dragon skulls, by the looks of them—and they wielded arrows and spears. Probably poisoned.

By the way they were grinning, definitely poisoned.

The largest male, a thickset imposing man clad head-to-toe in red armor, jerked his head toward a gap in the foliage. "Come."

TWENTY-ONE

B ell had always assumed the Penrythian sun was hot, but the heat from Effendier beat down like an angry god, the fiery disc they called a sun a violent shade of reddish-orange raging in a cloudless azure sky. He'd long traded his beautiful silk tunics for a vanilla linen undershirt, but his sweat still pasted the airy fabric to his back and chest.

At least his sea sickness had finally abated. It was just like him to find his sea legs right as they were disembarking—or, more likely, he was too enamored with the mythical city rising from the sea to feel his nausea.

Wiping at his brow, he propped his elbows on the side of the hull and glanced at Solethenia, the capital city of Effendier and home to the infamous Sun Court. Their fleet of ships had entered the canal that wound through Solethenia at dawn. Mortals and Solissians alike filled the decks, all vying for a view of the famed city.

Even the king had come above deck to view Solethenia. He

stood to Bell's right. Never had Bell seen King Horace look awed into silence, but there he was, completely still, lips pressed closed and eyes glimmering. A collective hush had fallen over the deck as their armada glided through the foreign architecture, the only sound the soft fluttering of sails and the gentle lapping of water against the ship's hull.

Bell cast his gaze over the city. *I could never tire of this view. Never.*

Marble buildings made from stone whiter than clouds and flecked in gold engraved against the skyline, spires and towers rising nearly to the clouds. Arched bridges and a network of smaller waterways veined the city, the vibrant blue contrasted sharply against the ivory buildings. Sunlight glinted off copper domes, and tongues of amber and red runeflame danced from countless lanterns.

The city was huge, a hundred times larger than Penryth. Bright purple and gold fabrics fluttered from open air windows, and vines of every color draped from the gilded roofs and plaster balconies. Flowers were everywhere. Running rampant over the city, perfuming its briny air, settling in every crack, every free space of land.

For a breath, Bell shivered, remembering Renault's secret garden. The few happy memories he had of his captivity coming to the surface.

"You okay, Prince?" Eleeza asked. She stood with her father to Bell's left, seemingly unaffected by the city's immense, overwhelming feat of architecture and beauty.

"Yes, I—" Bell shifted his gaze to his father, back to Eleeza. "I think the pollen here affects my allergies."

The pollen affects my allergies? Bell cringed at his words.

Eleeza stared in amusement at Bell before settling that

impertinent look on the city. "I think I'm going to like this city."

Bell would have agreed, if not for the other thing. The tournament. He curled his fingers over the dark wood banister, a tendril of anxiety worming through his gut. He didn't trust Archeron to save him from this mess.

The Sun Lord had murdered his brother, and it didn't take a genius to see how much Archeron despised Bell's father. Whatever had happened between Haven and Archeron on the journey to Spirefall, whatever solace they found in each other, this world would tear it apart.

And when that tether between them broke, there would be nothing stopping Archeron from revealing Haven and Bell's lie.

Bell startled as a hand brushed the small of his back. He knew before he turned who he would see—Xandrian. The beautiful Sun Lord's face was unreadable as he nodded to the dock up ahead where a crowd gathered. White seagulls flocked around their feet and swarmed the air above them.

Standing at the front were Solissian soldiers called the Gold Shadows. He'd read about them. They were more assassin than soldier, working for the good of Solissia behind the scenes.

Why were they here? "What, do they think I'll turn and run?"

Xandrian chuckled, but the sound was dark and humorless. "I don't know, Prince. Will you?"

Bell let his gaze slide over the Gold Shadows. Even from here, Bell could see they weren't smiling.

The king broke from his trance and released a breath. "Look at them, boy. They've all come to see the might of Penryth."

"Correction," Xandrian drawled. "They've all come to see your son, the Cursebreaking mortal prince."

Bell stiffened as he awaited his father's displeasure at being outshined.

Instead, a pleased smile crinkled the king's eyes, his face pink with sun and misplaced pride. "See. Already your esteem has reached the insufferably proud Sun Sovereign. Go, change into something more appropriate to your station." The king snapped his fingers, summoning Archeron behind him. "Find me my embroidered cloak—the green one, not the red. And my matching coat. Make it quick."

Archeron's jaw clenched so hard it could slice wood, but he obeyed.

Bell went to follow the Sun Lord below deck. A few days ago, Xandrian had a servant clean Bell's shirts with a magick spell; even the Solis servants had more magick than him.

"I'll go with you," Eleeza offered cheerfully. "I'm good at picking out attire."

"So am I," Bell responded, trying not to sound as cross as he felt.

By the hurt flashing inside her eyes, he failed. "I know the Solissian customs," she insisted, jutting out her chin. "Colors signify certain things to them. Let me help."

From the corner of his eye, Bell caught Xandrian watching the awkward exchange with a bemused expression. Bell's jaw tightened. "You may find this hard to believe, but I am quite capable of dressing myself."

"I didn't mean—" Her nostrils flared, but she pivoted to face the growing crowd swarming the docks. "You know what? You're right. Forgive me."

Before disappearing below deck, Bell caught Xandrian's stare. The expression in his face had transformed from amusement to something darker. A cautious frown that confirmed for Bell that his father was wrong; the Sun Sovereign's guards weren't here to celebrate the prince. They were gathered to take his measure.

He could don the most luxurious outfit in the realm and it

wouldn't matter.

Bell flexed his magickless hands by his sides, knowing just what they would find. A barren lightcaster, hated by his father's mistress and half-brother, reviled by his father, and so disrespected that even his intended thought he couldn't dress himself.

TWENTY-TWO

The moment Bell stepped off the gangplank to the dock, he knew he'd made the wrong choice in clothes. The ebony silk tunic soaked up the sun's anger and purged it into his body. But it was more than just the sun that told him his choice was wrong—it was the way the Solis crowd stared at him. The amusement crinkling the corners of their exotic, jewel-colored eyes.

Especially the Gold Shadows.

Bell shadowed Xandrian as he led the procession of the court up a pale stone staircase carved into the wall that separated the canal from the city.

Tilting his head, Xandrian swept his eyes over Bell's outfit. "Did no one tell you what black signifies here?"

Bell let out a pent-up breath and snuck a glance back at Eleeza—who was grinning smugly.

"Someone tried, but I was too stubborn to listen. Do I even want to know?"

Xandrian's lips tilted upward. "In the Sun Court, the colors we adorn ourselves in reflect our magick. Wearing black means you are barren, Prince. Not a drop of magick inside those hollow mortal bones."

Bell swallowed down a groan as they swept past the crowd and into the streets. When they crested the final stair and the full spread of Solethenia came into view, including the castle, a wave of wonder crashed over him, eclipsing his embarrassment.

Sunlight flickered over the moonstone city, catching in its sprawling buildings and canals and lighting the gilt domed roofs like bonfires. Hundreds of temples rose to the sky, the most famous cathedral rivaling the palace in size and beauty. Between the ivory structures, the vibrant hue of green gardens and parks and ponds flickered.

But it was the famous Sun Court palace that drew his eye. Set in the middle of the city, it rose higher than the mountains in the distance. Bridges and walkways spiraled and wound through the city, all leading to the giant structure.

"Is that . . ." Bell breathed as his eyes made out the gray branches reaching out from the palace like snakes.

"The Donatus Atrea," Xandrian finished, "or as you mortals call, the Tree of Life."

The Tree of Life. The castle had been built around the tree, with many of its branches and part of its trunk incorporated into the moonstone. But even a building of that size couldn't cover it.

While some of its trunk and limbs were hidden in the castle, the rest meandered through the city, entangled so deeply in Solethenia's meshwork of bridges and buildings that Bell lost track of it. The tree's massive limbs twined around bridges and across waterfalls; they stretched across rooftops, circled statues, and sprouted through windows of cathedrals.

"I thought the Donatus Atrea stood separate?" Bell asked, remembering the canvases in Penryth depicting a lone tree.

"At one time, it did. But the Donatus Atrea has a will and a mind of its own." Xandrian flashed a lazy smile. "Luckily, its magick reshapes our walls and city around it. Otherwise, I cannot imagine my aunt's annoyance at having to pay the masons guild to rebuild again and again."

At the mention of Xandrian's aunt, the Sun Sovereign, a dark shadow fell over Bell, despite the sun's glare.

Haven didn't say much about her time searching for Bell, but she was very explicit when it came to Archeron's mother. The sovereign was every bit the monster the Shade Queen was and deserved to die a slow, miserable, fiery death.

Haven's words.

Bell grinned. Thank the Goddess Haven wasn't here. He could only imagine the fireworks that would fly if those two met. Haven would end up on the executioner's block in a day.

They ascended a courtyard overlooking a vast network of waterfalls that fell away into the heart of the city. Pavilions had been erected overlooking shiny gold cushions and marble tables laden with strange fruit cut into stars and sprinkled with white orchids. Wisteria as big as his head and other flowers Bell couldn't name twined around the white marble banisters.

In the middle of the courtyard ran a rectangular pond filled with the largest, most colorful koi he'd ever seen.

And all around the courtyard milled people; exotic, beautiful Solissians from all five continents. The sound of their contrasting accents rattled the air, an explosion of strange dialects and voices that stirred his curiosity.

As soon as Bell entered the crowd, the voices stopped.

Uncomfortable silence descended as the crowd looked from

Xandrian to Bell, who now very much felt wilted with sweat and fear.

"Ah," came a strong female voice. "The final contestant from the mortal realm."

A woman emerged from the bodies, the onlookers parting in her path. Behind her trailed seven Sun Queens, each one regal in their own right. They had hair of the purest gold, skin tawny and darkened by the sun, and long, lean bodies chiseled with muscle. Gauzy purple and gold fabric draped their bodies, baring their lithe waists and thick, supple thighs.

The Sun Sovereign's daughters. Their skills as warriors were renowned, as was their beauty.

But compared to the Sun Sovereign they shadowed, they were plain.

Bell shifted his gaze to the sovereign, air hissing through his teeth. Like the others, she was long limbed and imposing, but everything about her seemed to shimmer and draw the eye. Her gown, a metallic gold silk that split to her navel and up her thighs, made the others' attire appear common. Golden armor adorned her waist, accentuating strong hips, and a heavy azerite and gold necklace that could ransom a king draped down her long neck.

"Beautiful, is she not?" Xandrian whispered in Bell's ear, but there was something unsaid in his words.

Bell looked closer. For, although she should be described as beautiful, his mind rebelled at the word.

"She is . . ."

Disappointment flickered over Xandrian's face. "Ah, so you do not see through it. A pity."

"See what?"

"Her enchantment spell, of course. Do you truly think she looks like *that*?" Humor laced his voice, humor and resentment.

"I assumed your magick would easily break through her enchantment. Here . . . allow me."

Xandrian twisted his hand in the air. A rune appeared, stringy and glowing, like threads of fire. The rune evanesced, but the spell remained.

This time, when he saw the Sun Sovereign, her true form came through. Surprisingly, she wasn't ugly like he'd expected from someone using a beauty glamour. But she wasn't beautiful either.

She was somewhere in the middle, her features too strong to truly be considered graceful, her nose too prominent and forehead too high.

Before Bell could ask why she would worry over beauty when she could have any man, the Sun Sovereign was upon them.

Xandrian dipped in a bow.

Bell followed, along with the entire Penrythian court.

The Sun Sovereign laughed, and Bell could have sworn the sound stirred the wisteria plumes and hundreds of small cherry trees strewn across the courtyard.

"So this is the Cursebreaker," the sovereign said. Her eyes bore into him, and he could have sworn she was searching for his power. "They say your magick is wondrous. That it felled my enemy, Morgryth, and sent her crawling into a hole to die." Her true eyes were a pale, almost faded green, like dried out moss blanched in the sun, and they slid to Xandrian. "You tested his magick. Tell me, Nephew. How did you find it?"

Xandrian unfolded from his bow and straightened his spine. Bell noticed how Xandrian looked just past the Sun Sovereign, avoiding staring directly into her eyes, as he said, "It was lackluster, my Sovereign. Just like most things, the mortals embellished his prowess and skill. It will be enough to enter the contest, but nothing that would bring our court honor."

Bell tried to swallow but his throat was too dry and he nearly choked. Why was Xandrian lying?

"How unfortunate," the sovereign said. "Still, our court will find a use for him one way or another. Whatever magick trickles through your veins, Prince, it now belongs to the Sun Court."

Bell fought the smile that flickered behind his lips. She could have all his magick. Every last drop of that nothingness that haunted him.

The sovereign tilted her head, and something flickered behind her eyes as she stared at someone behind Bell. Her mouth ticked up cruelly, her eyes going hard. Wrinkles spiderwebbed from the corners of her eyes like cracks in porcelain.

Archeron stepped forward and stretched into a languid bow. Xandrian's gesture had been smooth, practiced, but Archeron's . . . his was different. Almost a mockery of Xandrian's.

Oh, he bowed low. So low the scabbard of his sword dragged across the white tiles. And his head dipped in supplication so that his honey-gold hair, worn loose about his shoulders, swept to cover most of his face.

But his eyes were anything but submissive as they lifted to the sovereign.

A tremor rippled beneath her glamour, hidden from most of the court. The humid air crackled with morbid curiosity. Everyone had to know Archeron's story, and they waited to see how his mother would welcome him.

Without a trace of affection, the sovereign raked her gaze over her son. Then she slid her eyes to the king. "King Horace, I see my son still attends you. I imagine, after all this time, that he is quite good at answering your beck and call."

"Oh, yes," Bell's father agreed, scratching at his neck. He'd worn a heavy coat weighed down with embroidery and jewels, and his sweat-damp skin was flushed pink. "He is most useful."

"And I imagine you were the one to send Archeron to help break the Curse?" she persisted.

"Indeed. I orchestrated everything. Why, I even sent my son's personal guard to help."

"Oh," she purred, somehow speaking without moving a single part of her body besides her lips. "How generous of you."

Bell fought a cringe as his father prattled on, oblivious to the sarcasm.

Through it all, Archeron didn't move. His face a statue of disinterest. Other than the slight tic of his temple, he was impervious to the entire ordeal. Probably from years of practice at her side.

No wonder he left her court years ago. Bell had only been here ten minutes and he already felt diminished somehow.

Even so, Bell had to look away. He had no love for Archeron, but whatever game the sovereign was playing, it was cruel. And his father was the only one who was clueless. Even Cressida realized they were being belittled, her garish red lips thin and brittle as she tried to hold back her anger.

Perhaps realizing his father to daft to react, the sovereign released a bored sigh and turned to the crowd. "Eat, drink, enjoy the festivities. Tonight we meet all the contestants and they may regale me with their talents. To the winner goes one wish to help them through the tournament. But those who fail to impress me will lose their spot before the contest even begins."

Did her gaze shift to Bell when she said that? By the way Archeron met Bell's stare, two deep lines etched between his lowered eyebrows, she most definitely did.

A sick feeling pooled in his belly, and he pressed a fist just below his sternum, the sweat leaching through his shirt into his hand. If he was worried about how he was going to survive tonight, how would he ever make it through the tournament?

TWENTY-THREE

Haven shifted on her toes as she scanned the group of Skyfall villagers surrounding them. Unlike the warriors, who were fitted with scaled armor, most of the people wore cotton and leather, similar to what the commoners wore in Penryth.

The landscape, too, was not what Haven was expecting. Normal looking trees, rocks, and brush one could expect from any mortal kingdom.

Perhaps the stories she'd been told about the island had given her the false pretense of something exotic, something beyond her realm of imagination, and she couldn't help but feel disappointed.

Which, considering the spears and blow darts the natives closing in held, that was the wrong emotion. Fear was probably more apt—or at least caution.

Two women with fiery red hair plaited around thin, decorative bones rushed from the circle, waving their spears at the strangers.

"What are they saying?" Surai hissed.

Haven glanced at her friend, resisting the urge to unsheathe her sword. "How would I know?"

"You're mortal," Surai insisted, as if this somehow meant Haven could speak every mortal language in the realm.

"They wish us prosperity," Demelza said. "Wait, no. They wish us death. Sorry, it has been years since I heard this foul language."

Haven almost expected Ravius to say some smart remark on her shoulder before remembering they'd left Ravius on the boat. At his insistence. He, too, had heard the rumors about the Skyfall people's legendary appetite for anything that breathed.

With a sigh, Haven stepped forward, hands held high. The gesture sent the crowd surging back.

"Why are they so skittish?" Surai demanded, her voice threaded with unease.

"I don't know, but it can't be us. As far as they know, we're women, weak and powerless."

Surai chuckled. "I'll show them weak."

Haven held in her own chuckle as she faced the crowd. "I would like to speak with your king," she called out, trying to make her voice strong but unthreatening. When nothing happened, she beckoned Demelza to translate.

Before Demelza could come up with the right words, a mountain-sized man stepped from a nearby tent. His long, dark red hair was adorned with jewelry carved from bones, and it fell well past his shoulders. Deep-set dark eyes glittered behind a sun-weathered face. He was mid-fifties, at least.

On his arm was a girl around Haven's age. Her beauty contrasted against the man's rough exterior. Haven bristled as she spied the delicate chain that wrapped down her neck to the man's shoulder. It jingled with every step she took.

Grinding her jaw to hide her distaste, Haven focused back on the large man. This was the ruler she needed to speak with.

Unsure of their customs, Haven fell into a bow. "I come from Penryth," she began, "under orders of Prince Bellamy Boteler."

When Haven stood, the burly man's distrustful expression hadn't changed. But interest flickered inside the girl's fern-green eyes. Interest and what looked like hope.

Standing on her tiptoes, the girl whispered in the man's ear. Frowning, he barked something at her in his guttural language, and the girl cast her eyes on the ground. But not before Haven caught the disgust and loathing in her face.

"Come," the man said in broken Solissian. "We will talk in tent."

If Haven didn't possess magick, she might have balked at the idea. Even with Haven's swordsmanship and Surai's skill, once they were confined in such close quarters, it wouldn't take much to overwhelm them.

But Haven did have magick, and it surged at the thought of being useful as she followed the man in charge through the maze of tents. Haven's magick was a last resort. Using it meant risking word of her blasphemous skills leaking out.

But Skyfall was an insulated island, and she would take that chance if it meant saving their lives—and wiping the smirk from the cruel man swaggering in front of them.

He led them to a towering tent set in the middle of camp. Smaller tents littered the ground around it. The tang of wet dog and burning meat filled her nose and made her uneasy. A cloying, sickly-sweet incense clung to the air inside, the intensity of the scent nauseating.

"For the dragons," Demelza whispered before coughing. "The Skyfall traders who visited my city reeked of it. They use it to keep the dragons calm."

Dragons. The word sent her heart into a tailspin, and she

scoured the room, sifting through the layers of smoke, until she found it.

The creature was tiny, no bigger than a large cat. His coloring was similar to fire, hues of orange and yellow and crimson blending together in a stunning mixture. His eyes were slitted, a pink tongue hanging limp from a parted mouth. A long chain similar to the girl's shackles bound the creature's ankle.

The girl swept a stealthy glance over the dragon, and pain shuddered behind her tight expression. She watched the obviously drugged creature for a moment longer before sliding her gaze back to her captor.

The man fell back onto a large terra-cotta cushion, the movement jerking the girl down to his side. He spread his massive legs wide, rested his hands on his knees, and stared up at them. "Sit. We talk, yes?"

Cursing, Demelza settled her tired frame on a cushion opposite the man. Surai just glared at the man before posting up against a tent pole, her eyes full of violent intent as she observed him.

Under the watchful eye of several rough looking warriors who had joined them, Haven chose the most comfortable cushion, dragged it close to the man, and then sat on the edge to face him.

"I come with a proposal for the House of Volantis," Haven began. Her eyes stayed on the man, but she watched her periphery. Searching out the shadows for quick flashes of movement. Anything that required her to retrieve the long blade that waited just inside her sleeve.

The man's eyes narrowed, and then he spread his arms wide. "I am Kranth, ruler of this island."

Haven bit her lip to hide her frown. "But you are not from House Volantis?"

The girl, Haven noticed, sat a little straighter.

"House Volantis is . . ." Kranth shrugged his big shoulders, the scaled armor he wore squeaking, and slid an amused glance at his warriors. "How you say, fallen? No more? Obliterated?"

Runes. Frustration tightened the muscles in Haven's shoulders, but she forced herself to sit tall. "That's a pity. I was prepared to make a bargain with a daughter of the House of Volantis."

Kranth laughed, but his eyes remained hard. "And who are you to make bargains?" He made a dramatic show of looking over Demelza and then Surai. "I see two frightened girls and an old, ugly woman."

Demelza let loose a string of curses.

Haven smiled. "Do I look frightened, Kranth of the House of nothing?"

He rested one of his big elbows on his knee and propped his stubbled, square jaw on his palm. Then he stared at Haven, letting the full force of his cruelty show in his dark eyes. "Not yet, but women too stupid to know when they are in danger. That's why I took the eldest daughter of House Volantis for myself, then threw her siblings and parents off the cliffs." He tapped his temple. "Stupid."

"But you're not?" Haven asked. "Stupid, I mean."

"Doesn't matter. I am powerful, and I have soldiers, many, many soldiers."

Haven's skin crawled, her fingers curling into her palms. "Even with soldiers, that seems like a mighty feat for a man such as yourself. Taking out an entire House of the Nine."

He grinned. "Not so hard when their magick dried up and their dragons grew tiny. Then they just like us."

A sharp spike of fury surged up Haven's middle. The thought of a man such as this, a cruel, ignorant thug, destroying thousands of years of culture and lineage just because he could made her want to rip out his intestines while he was still alive.

Oblivious to the threat right in front of him, the idiot continued, describing in horrifying detail what he did to the royal Volantis family.

The girl's face was rigid but composed as she listened to Kranth describe her family's overthrow and murder. There was strength there, Haven decided. She would help them if she could.

The girl's gaze slid to Haven's, then flicked to the two lamps near the dragon. Dark purplish smoke spilled from the golden lamps' mouths.

Understanding dawned, and Haven caught Surai's eye. A jerk of Haven's head, and Surai understood too.

Without magick, Kranth had to restrain the dragon with the incense. But if the creature were awakened . . .

As Surai drew near the lamps, Haven turned to the girl. "What is your name?"

The girl blinked as if she hadn't been asked such a thing in a while. "Renfyre of House Volantis"—her head lifted high—"last of my line. My friends call me Ren."

"Friends?" Kranth released a slew of guttural reprimands in his language, the violent clash of consonants ripping through the air. Once more, Ren ducked her head low, but her eyes held fire. Fire and vengeance.

"Ren," Haven said, ignoring Kranth. "I've come to make you an offer. I need to . . . impersonate you to enter a contest of magick."

The stool Kranth lounged on scooted back as he stood; a curved blade glittered in his hand. His warriors had slipped closer behind Haven. She could feel them drawing near, undoubtedly with blades of their own thirsty for her blood.

Anger turned Kranth's voice gravelly as he said, "What could you offer the last heir of Volantis for such a trick, girl?"

Haven's eyes never left Ren's as she answered, "Freedom."

As understanding dawned, Kranth's eyes widened. At the same time, Haven felt a soft whisper of breeze as the closest warrior swung his blade at her back.

TWENTY-FOUR

Without turning, without breaking eye contact with Ren, Haven froze the guards in place.

Kranth was too busy staring at his immobile guards to notice Surai snuff out the first lamp, then the second. And he hardly spared her a glance as she lifted one of the door flaps at the back of the tent to release the haze of smoke.

His focus was riveted to Haven. "Witch," he growled. But all he got was a step in Haven's direction before Ren leapt to her feet. Grabbing the chain that linked them, she wrapped it around Kranth's neck and jerked back, the iron biting deep into his flesh.

Surprise wrenched his mouth wide. Glittery anger sparked inside his dark eyes. He lifted his knife to hack at Ren, but Haven flicked it from his fingers using magick. She could have broken his neck with a snap of her fingers, could have killed him in a thousand ways, and she would have enjoyed it.

But it needed to be Ren who finished him, and Haven wouldn't steal that vengeance from her.

Kranth stumbled forward. His fingers clawed at his throat, raking so hard he drew blood, but Ren was strong, despite all he had done to her.

Or maybe because of it.

Behind Haven, the guards stirred. Her immobilizing spell was wearing off. Before Haven could produce another spell, something stirred the air. Haven looked up in time to see a flash of red.

The dragon didn't make a sound as he attacked. His shiny black claws sunk deep into the first warrior's collarbone, establishing a firm hold before he attacked the guard's face. A gust of wind burst across the tent as the dragon flared its wings, hiding much of the carnage. But the gut-churning sounds of bone crunching and flesh rending left little doubt what was happening.

A brief surge of unease slid through Haven as she realized the dragon was attacking the face because it knew the warrior's armor would make anywhere else impenetrable.

Which meant the dragon was highly intelligent.

A strangled sound drew Haven's attention back to the second warrior. He watched his compatriot with slack horror, his paralyzed face at odds with the terror brimming his eyes. He managed to move his arm, to get the serrated dagger he held up . . . but it was no use.

The dragon moved on to him, killing him in seconds.

It was quick, efficient, and utterly unnerving.

Haven wrenched her gaze away from the bloodbath and back to Kranth. He was still conscious, still fighting, but his eyes were glazing, his hands slackening. The purple shadow of death stained his bloated face.

A few more seconds and he slumped over, his big body draped

sideways over the cushions.

Ren smiled, but there was a sadness in her eyes as she said, "Thank you."

Haven's focus went to the dark veins snaking down Ren's neck. They were coming from beneath the chain.

"No!" Haven lunged for Ren—

Ren collapsed, gasping for air. Her dragon tried to fly to her but he came to the end of his chain, his wings flapping wildly as he struggled against his binds, screeching in obvious distress.

Haven rushed to Ren. Her hand was cold, the life fading from her eyes.

"The chain must have linked her life to his," Surai hissed, coming up behind them.

Demelza began to pray in her northern tongue.

"I'm sorry," Haven whispered, shocked to find the edges of her eyes wet. She'd barely known the girl, but something about the fierceness in her eyes reminded Haven of herself.

Ren was clawing at her wrist. Something glittered in her shaking hand. An iron bracelet with an emerald pendant made to look like a dragon's eye.

"For the tournament," Ren breathed. "I always wanted to have . . . magick. Now I do."

Haven's throat ached as she took the jewel, easily worth a fortune.

A snap sounded as the chain broke off from a stake in the ground. The dragon darted to Ren's shoulder, the fierceness from moments ago fading away as he nudged her head, whining low.

Ren turned her head to stare at her dragon, tears streaming down the corners of her green eyes. "You're free, now. Free."

A few seconds later, her eyes glazed over and the last daughter of House Volantis died.

Haven blinked down at the poor girl, freed at last. "Why would she kill him knowing the consequences?"

With a snort of contempt, Demelza stalked over to Kranth and spit on his body. "Because she would rather be free, even if it meant death, than live a moment longer chained."

Haven was surprised by Demelza's outburst. She was also surprised to find her cheeks slick with tears. Clearing her throat, Haven focused on the next step. She could impersonate Ren in the tournament and no one would know the difference. Skyfall Island was cut off from the rest of the world, even more so now.

But everyone knew the royals of House Volantis had dragons.

"We need to grab the dragon and leave," Surai said, her focus drifting to the front of the tent, where any minute a guard could enter and discover Kranth dead.

Haven shook her head. "We set him free, like she wanted."

"But they will expect a royal from House Volantis to have a dra—"

"No." Haven's voice was final. "He goes free, and then I tell the truth. There are no more dragons on Skyfall Island." Ren's bracelet tinkled as Haven slipped it over her wrist. "Besides, I have this. Only a royal daughter of House Volantis would possess it."

Surai didn't argue. The dragon was still on Ren's shoulder, his agitation growing stronger by the second. Haven performed a quick fire spell that melted away his chains. As soon as the shackle around his ankle was gone, he shook his leg, testing the new weightlessness.

Then his clever eyes fell on her and he took to the air, disappearing out the back exit.

"We should do the same," Demelza urged.

As they fled the rear of the tent, Surai glanced at the sky. "As much as I hate to say this, we need Nasira to distract the guards while we escape."

Haven sighed. She had hoped not to use Nasira. But the sociopathic Noctis had her uses, and this was one of them.

Lifting her hand in the air, Haven gave the signal that let Nasira off her leash. In response, a dark shadow speared across the grounds, flickering between tents like some corporeal Netherworld demon.

"We have our own dragon," Haven muttered.

Demelza made the sign of the Goddess, while Surai whispered what had to be a prayer. But Haven looked straight ahead. The warriors that had taken over the island and killed Ren's family deserved everything that was coming to them.

The screams that followed were worse than anything that had transpired in the tent, and for a breath, the unwanted ache of pity crept in. But all it took was remembering Ren, the bruises mottling her flesh, the wasted muscles of her arms and legs from being bound for Goddess knows how long, and the brittle emotion faded.

After a while, the terrified cries grew fainter and fainter until there was nothing but silence.

Silence—and the occasional tang of coppery blood carried along the breeze.

TWENTY-FIVE

Haven couldn't help but wonder if she'd made a mistake letting the dragon free. Impersonating Ren to enter the tournament seemed easy enough. How hard would it be to pretend to be someone else? Surai promised she could teach Haven the proper spells to hide her identity from anyone from the mortal realm who might recognize Haven.

She'd toyed with hiding her identity from Archeron as well— runes, he was going to be absolutely pissed—but in the end, she needed his help.

It wasn't any of those things that gave her pause. No, it was something else entirely. The House of Volantis was known for three things: Fire magick, dragon shifting, and their dragon familiars.

Haven had the fire magick thing down, and her inability to shift into a dragon could be explained by the Curse; everyone would expect her to have lost some powers. But it was the bonded dragon that threw everything into jeopardy.

Haven let her head fall back, her eyes taking in the stars to calm herself. The horses were tired, and their progress was slow. She could feel Bell in trouble, feel it in her bones, yet an entire sea lay between them.

"The portal should be close," Demelza said, sensing Haven's frustration. "If what your Solis friend says is true."

Surai, who was riding silently beside them staring straight ahead, narrowed her eyes but didn't respond.

Questioning Surai's honesty probably wasn't the fastest way to become friends, but Demelza mistrusted anyone not mortal.

"Surai is the most honest person I know," Haven assured Demelza, spurring Lady Pearl into a trot. Lady Pearl whinnied, stamping at the sandy earth beneath the tall grass. Haven flexed her fingers over the reins and pushed on, the nerves tangled inside her belly tightening with each step. "The question is, will we have enough magick to use it?"

According to Surai, the portal hidden inside the cave on the northernmost tip of Dune had been there since the dawn of time. Once, she claimed, the people of Skyfall Island possessed enough magick to use it to cross the Glittering Sea to trade with the Sun Court—when they didn't choose to fly there instead.

Fly. Haven still couldn't get over the idea of mortals shifting into dragons. From what she'd read, they didn't always transform into their full form, choosing sometimes just to sprout wings.

Wings, for rune's sake.

But Haven didn't require anything as miraculous as the ability to fly. She simply needed to save one unlucky prince from a mess of her own making.

If Bell thought the outside of the city was overwhelming, being inside the Sun Palace was like falling into a frozen lake of luxury—the beauty, the opulence and wealth ripping the air from his lungs and making him feel close to drowning.

"Here is the Great Hall of Emissaries, where dignitaries from all over the realm are entertained," the Solis male leading them said. A short, soft man with slim arms, a shaved head, and an effeminate face, Bell guessed he was an indentured slave from one of the islands that made up Freya's spear.

Rumor had it they castrated the slaves, making the men soft and diminutive.

Bell's father, who had already changed into a deep jade green ensemble with puffed sleeves that made him look ridiculous, paused to take in the high, arched ceilings. Like many of the other rooms they'd already toured, murals decorated all the available wall space not taken by art.

Half-clothed Solis and Noctis, engaged in all manner of life, from sparring to making love, sprawled over the plaster and stared at them inside ornate golden frames.

Renk pointed at an image of two Solis men locked in an embrace and snickered. "Who knew the Solis were so perverted?"

"You know," Bell remarked. "Not everyone shares your warped views, Renk."

Renk slid his oily gaze to Bell, a cunning smile on his lips. "You fit right in here, Bellamy. Maybe there's a painting of you somewhere here. Who knows what deviant vices you picked up in Spirefall."

Gritting his teeth, Bell turned his attention back to the tour. He wasn't going to let Renk ruin this experience.

They trailed into another room, this one with high, open doorways leading into a courtyard, one of seemingly thousands with balconies that overlooked the city. Bell's head spun as the sun hit his face. He felt adrift inside the labyrinth of interconnecting rooms, eddying like a leaf caught in a whirlpool.

How in the Netherworld would he find his way back to his apartment, much less make it to the banquet tonight on time?

When they first arrived, the same guide had taken Bell to his rooms. Because he was a contestant, he stayed in separate quarters from the rest of the Penrythian court. His housing was a three-story building set in one of the many courtyards, near the edge of the drop. From his window, he could look down into the waterfalls that fell hundreds of feet below.

"Well how do I look?" a lilting voice asked.

Bell snapped from his reverie and focused on two soft chestnut brown eyes and a full, teasing mouth. Eleeza. Her thick hair was wrangled into a tight braid that fell down her back, and she'd changed into a sunset-red ensemble. The fabric was gauzy and light, and just like the Sun Queens from earlier, it flowed around her hips and breasts, leaving little to the imagination. Contrasted against her dark skin, the color was striking.

Bell cleared his throat. "You look like . . . them. I mean, not the same, mortals can't really look like they do . . ."

His words trailed away as he took in the sullen downturn of her lips. "I made it. It took me hours and had me seriously wishing I'd paid more attention during my sewing courses." Her eyes brightened. "Do you . . . like it?"

Bell flicked up his eyebrows. "Sure."

Again, the fleeting look of something—disappointment?—flickered across her face. "I'd seen illustrations from years ago how they dressed, so I ripped the fabric from my petticoats and sewed like mad on the ship." A small hand fluttered to her waist, the only indication she wasn't quite as comfortable in the revealing outfit as she let on. "I thought your brother's eyes were going to tumble from their sockets when I walked out here."

Bell chuckled. "Good ol' Renk. Subtlety eludes him."

Eliza smiled. "I have a feeling a lot of things elude him."

Just then, a group of Sun Lords strolled into the courtyard. One Sun Lord was the center of attention, regaling the others with a story, his movements graceful and proud. The others seemed to hang on his every word, laughing and gesturing in a bid for his attention.

As if he could feel Bell's stare, the Sun Lord halted mid-sentence and met Bell's eyes. Xandrian went still, and Bell's heart was in his throat as he waited for a reaction. A cruel smile. A look of disdain.

Instead, for a fraction of a second, something sparked inside the Sun Lord's sky-blue eyes, and his lips slid into a rare smile. A *real* smile. As if, taken by surprise, he didn't have time to conjure his usual smarmy response.

Xandrian's grin faltered, slowly breaking down into a blank mask, before he gave the faintest of nods and turned back to his admirers.

The action was so small that it could have been all in Bell's head.

Still, his chest swelled as if a rush of air filled him, and he turned away before Xandrian could catch Bell's own lips curling upward.

When he looked back to where Eleeza had been, she was gone. And then their guide began ushering them from the courtyard to another opulent part of the palace before he could try to find her.

As Bell's boots clicked loudly on the marble tiles, and they plunged deeper into the palace, his heart ticked strangely in his chest. Somewhere in a nearby room, an ancient clock chimed, the ringing sound echoing through the open chambers and

reminding Bell that in a few hours, his magick would be tested—
and he hadn't seen Archeron since they arrived.

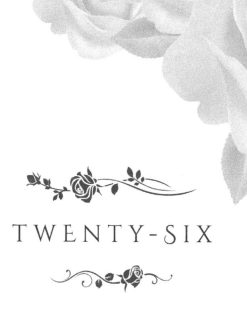

TWENTY-SIX

Archeron had thought he was ready for the Sun Court. That all the years away, and his accomplishments since then, would salve the deep, unending agony that came from his banishment. Yet the moment he picked up the scent of Effendier's shores, the perfume of orchids and brine and ancient magick, something inside him had broken open.

A scab he thought long healed.

He appraised himself inside the oblong wall mirror, his eyes settling first over his tall, supple boots, decorated in emeralds, then the long jade tunic, split open to reveal his tanned arms and chest. A golden brooch shaped into the crest of the Sun Court—a sun with flowering vines for rays—rested in the hollow below his sternum, holding the flimsy fabric together.

Xandrian had the clothes sent over, either from pity or, more likely, a sense of pride. Even a banished son of the sovereign must look the part.

But seeing himself how he used to look when he was a courtier was akin to seeing a ghost, and Archeron felt the stirrings of an emotion he'd managed to stave off all his years in the mortal kingdom: shame.

It clung to him as he stalked the halls of the palace, a stench he felt sure wafted off him in waves. Everyone could smell it, see it. The son his mother never wanted, the boy his sisters tormented and tortured, now a slave.

The thought infuriated him. All he had given to his mother, all the battles he'd waged for Effendier, all the victories in her name, all the times he loved her when she deserved hatred . . .

She deserves everything that comes to her.

He startled at the thought, no . . . the *voice* inside his head. The same soft male voice that had been invading his dreams at night. It started as whispering inside his ear as he lay down, caught in the slippery web between awake and asleep, the words so faint they could have been the rushing call of the sea outside his window.

But now—now it was no longer faint. Now he could no longer blame the voice on the sea.

I should never have come back here.

Jamming a thumb into his temple, he stalked through the humid chambers of a bath house, ignoring the Sun Queens basking at the edge of the pool with their easy smiles and beckoning eyes.

Enslaved or not, he was still a son of the sovereign. He could have any woman he wanted. Once he would have taken foolish pride in that fact.

Not now.

He wanted no part of his mother's court, including the courtesans, every one of which would report back to her.

He'd nearly forgotten how stifling the Sun Court was. The constant feeling of being observed; the sovereign's spies watching everything. Taking note. Looking for ways to spin it.

The uppermost courtyard was busy. Foreigners from all over the realm clumped on lounge chairs and divans, seeking shade beneath the silk pavilions. Another pool shaped like a panther brimmed with courtiers he didn't recognize.

His boots hardly made a sound as he stalked across mosaic tiles, over a wooden bridge, and into his favorite part of the entire castle.

The atrium was like an entirely separate world. Set slightly apart from the palace and suspended off the balcony, it drank in full sun from sunrise to sunset. The heat was balmy, the air laden with moisture, and the floor was glass, meaning all one had to do was look down and their guts twisted into a knot—but he found comfort in the sensation.

Better to feel the terror of knowing you were one glass pane away from death than to feel unwanted and unloved.

Memories of coming here as a child to escape his sisters came to mind. Like most of the palace, they couldn't handle the sensation of walking over air.

His sisters despised him, perhaps because he was illegitimate, although many of them were as well. More likely because they sensed his mother's deep hatred for him and what he represented.

The Sun Sovereign went through husbands like an addict goes through moonberry tea. Every union strategically devised to ensure her offspring manifested the greatest powers. The legitimate girls she kept, honing their skills until they were lethal. The most skilled lightcasters she kept as her private entourage; the less fortunate Sun Queens she married off to her allies.

But the males of her line died before they ever took a breath of Effendier air. If the rumors were true, a powerful seer once told his mother a son would be the cause of her death. In response, she used more seers to divine her offspring's gender before birth. All the males in her line were aborted.

Only, sometimes the seers were wrong. Sometimes, mistakes were made.

Mistakes like him.

The few other males who slipped through, if they weren't outright killed, eventually disappeared from court. Usually, their magick was easy to forget, meaning *they* were easy to forget.

Not him. Even from an early age, his magick had been remarkable. Before his mother had realized just how powerful he was, he displayed his skills in court. Once it was known, she couldn't just hide him away like the others.

Instead she allowed him to stay at court and tortured him mercilessly for it.

"I thought I might find you here," a female voice called. He recognized the sound of Avaline's voice immediately.

"Avaline." He bowed his head toward the Queen of Lorwynfell and his betrothed, drinking in her features. Most of the courtiers startled at her sleek black hair and pearlescent skin, the glorious wings that jutted unapologetically from her back. They were smaller than the average female Noctis's wings but no less commanding.

It didn't help that she insisted on wearing all black leathers knowing what that color meant in this court, or that it made her impossible to blend in.

But Avaline wasn't one to shy away from her lineage or who she was.

Grinning, she plucked the half-opened bud of a plumeria from a nearby tree and nestled the fragrant flower into one of the sapphire pins in her hair. "I can still remember the first time we made love here. It was right over there, beneath the canopy of climbing roses."

"Yes, I remember. The thorns left scratches in my ass so deep I thought it would scar." He flicked his gaze to the flower in her black hair. "You know, my mother would decree your hand be taken off for stealing that bud."

The blooms inside were used by her mages and alchemists to make poisons and various weapons. Most were forbidden to grow outside the palace. Each one could fetch the same price as a sturdy, sea-faring ship.

Avaline twirled the flower in her hair and then, with a wicked grin, plucked another. "Well, then. Now she will have to take off both my hands, so at least I will have matching stumps."

Archeron laughed, and any awkwardness he feared from their last encounter, or the years leading up to it, faded. "Somehow, even without hands, I still think you'd find a way to best any Solis in a fight."

"You know it." The flower inside her Heart Oath amulet pulsed, the sacred crimson flower nearly glowing. Her eyes shifted to his heart flower hanging from his neck. If she noticed the wilted ends of the cerulean petals, she didn't give any indication. "Goddess Above, I've missed you, Halfbane."

He pulled her into a fierce hug, savoring the feel of muscles and flesh beneath his arms. "I think I liked you better when you were a skeleton."

She drew just far enough away to punch him in the shoulder. "And I liked you better before you went and fell in love with a mortal."

Archeron rubbed his lower lip. For some reason, thinking of Haven in this place felt wrong. Thank the Goddess she was safe in Penryth, although only the Shadeling knew what mischief she was causing.

"Jealous? That's unlike you. Growing sentimental, are you?"

"I'm curious," she amended. "What sort of woman could capture you wholly when the Archeron I remember could blow through the entire stable of a brothel in a week's time."

Archeron snorted. "As I recall, that was *once* after our victory in Bremire, and you helped me. Besides, the last time I saw you, you were covered in the bare flesh of two Asgardian males."

She arched a wicked eyebrow. "Three. One was sleeping in the other room. Apparently I tired him out. Actually, they all fell asleep after you left. I was this close to fetching you back." Her voice turned soft, wistful. "It would have been like old times, Halfbane."

The nickname conjured memories of a different life when his worries were limited to surviving the next battle, running out of drink, and finding a nice warm bed—and body—for the night. Sometimes Avaline joined him. Sometimes she had her own company to entertain.

It was how their relationship worked, and why he had never minded the idea of being bonded to her in marriage. Neither of them loved each other, not in that way, at least. But there was love there, of a sort. The love of a comrade in arms, a fellow soldier who had saved his life as many times as he'd saved hers.

He respected her and she respected him, and mutual respect went a long way when it came to being with someone for thousands of years.

Avaline ran a hand up his arm, trailing a long finger over his shoulder. Her dark wings fluttered at the contact. He admired the feathers, not actually black but the deep gray color of the clay from the Ashari steppes. That color and size, along with her missing horns, were the only thing that distinguished her as a halfling, part Noctis part mortal.

"You could always keep up with my appetites, remember?" she asked, trailing her finger beneath the edge of his jaw. "Actually, I'm starting to think you are the only Solis male worth anything these days."

A smile stretched his face, but it felt hollow. Gently he guided her hand away. "I'm banished from my own court, reviled by my mother, and enslaved to a mortal king. If I'm your baseline on desirable males then you should probably reach higher."

She laughed, a tight, bitter thing. He caught the way her jaw tightened, the anger in her dark eyes. "You are more powerful and more deserving of the throne than any of the Sun Queens in this court. I'll never forgive your mother for what she's done to you, or your sisters."

A familiar tug pulled at his core.

The throne.

Once upon a time, when he was young, stupid, and ambitious, it was all he wanted. To one day succeed his mother and rule Effendier the way it should be ruled. To guide his homeland beyond his mother's greedy vision into an empire that the other Solis nations would happily serve—not because they were afraid, but because they believed in the same things.

Even when he roamed the realm as a soldier, fighting the Noctis, the option was there. Tangible and so real he could feel the throne beneath him. Feel the greatness for Effendier at the tips of his fingers.

It didn't matter that he was illegitimate, or younger than most of his siblings. The heir to the Sun Court wasn't judged by birth order, but by magickal ability.

But then everything changed. The war happened, and then Remurian died, and he was cursed to serve the mortal king. Any rights he had to the throne shattered that day.

Now the idea of ever being Sun Sovereign was an impossibility he wouldn't dare hope for. Just thinking about it opened an ache inside him so deep he felt as if he were dying.

"There are seven Sun Queens waiting to claw the throne from my mother's fingers," he said, managing to keep his voice steady, "and I am enslaved to King Boteler. Deserving or not, I will never sit upon it, Avaline."

Avaline nodded as if she understood, but her eyes shone with disappointment. "Oh, you have changed, Halfbane. Your cowardice is unbecoming."

The teasing cruelty in her tone made his jaw clench. Sometimes he forgot how vicious she could be. It used to take a lot to bring out that side of her, but now . . . now she seemed poised to explode at every turn.

With a tired sigh, he dragged three fingers over his chin; he'd shaved as soon as he arrived to better blend in with the shaved Solis and the skin was startlingly smooth. "Why are you here?"

She stripped the flowers from her hair, dropped them to the paving stones below, and ground them beneath her boot. "Oh, didn't anyone mention it? I've entered the tournament."

"Why?"

"Do you know what I could do for my kingdom if I won and became Queen of the Nine? What I could do for you?"

Archeron blinked. The old Avaline would have died before she took on such a thing. But so much had changed since then, and they were both very different people.

"Why so surprised, Halfbane? Or do you think I can rebuild my kingdom with the help of the mortals around me?" Anger flashed inside her eyes. "I was denied a seat on the High Council, did you know that? They despise me for my heritage. Every plea, every bargain I try to make turns to ash. They will give me nothing so I will take it any way I can."

"I wasn't aware," Archeron said, feeling helpless. He was in the king's meetings, he attended every banquet and every hunting party, yet he was powerless to sway the king in any way.

"Of course you weren't. You're a puppet, a slave without an ounce of power. You may be okay with that, but I will fight any way I can to right that injustice and restore us to our rightful places in the realm."

A headache was forming, muffled whispers slithering inside his mind. "Enough, Avaline."

"Why so worried? Afraid I'll show up your mortal king's pretty little son?"

"Prince Bell is not like the others."

A cunning grin found her face. "No? His family murdered my brother, your friend. The Halfbane I remember would have rejoiced in the humiliation of his killer's son." Pivoting on her heels, she strode down the path, the soft black cape she wore trailing at her heels. As she ducked under the spindly branches of a moonberry tree, she called out, "Don't let this girl make you soft, Halfbane. You know what your mother does with soft males."

He would have followed after her. Would have made her talk to him until her anger wore off and they parted allies once more. But before he could so much as take a step, a sharp tug jerked inside his heart, his spine stiffening as a gnawing pain began to eat through his insides.

The king was calling him. If he fought the command, the agony would intensify until he was doubled over. Only someone who'd had a piece of their soul trapped in one of those rings could understand the terrible, unrelenting pain of such devious magick.

His heart startled into a gallop as a thousand invisible needles jammed into the hollow of his bones and threaded through his gut. Stabbing, stabbing . . .

He fell to his knees. A single groan leaked from his mouth and then the pain ripped the air from his chest. Darkness slipped in and out of his vision; sweat soaked his feverish skin. It felt as if his soul was being jerked from his body, peeling away from his insides the way a hunter peeled off a rabbit's skin.

Only one way to make the torment end.

Struggling to his feet, he stopped fighting and obeyed. Each step closer to the king, each second nearer to giving his body over to the man he despised most in this world, filled Archeron with loathing. A vile hatred so monstrous he was afraid what would happen if he ever let it out.

As he rounded the hibiscus plants, their cloying smell clinging to his throat, a flash of movement caught his eye. Instinctively, his hand went to the dagger at his waist. He flicked a cautious gaze toward the cluster of palm trees near the corner.

There. He stiffened as he took in the Noctis male: huge leathery wings spread wide behind the figure, casting shadows over his face. But Archeron recognized the monster from Spirefall, the high-ranking soldier under Morgryth.

The Noctis flashed a strange grin at Archeron before slowly fading out of existence. Archeron barely had time to double-check that the Noctis was truly gone before he was pulled along the king's string, dragged from the atrium and into the bright courtyard.

He scoured the courtyard for the intruder as he walked, hiding the deep unease that had settled between his shoulder blades.

One question turned over in his mind. Why would a Noctis underling for the Shade Queen be in Effendier?

TWENTY-SEVEN

Bell had grown up hating banquets and parties. They were stodgy, formal affairs where everyone sat in a dim room and congratulated themselves on being rich, privileged droobs. They all pretended to listen as the king regaled them with hunting stories, and then feigned not to notice Renk drunkenly groping their daughters before passing out in a pool of his own vomit.

But the parties at the Sun Court were different. This—whatever you could call what was happening around Bell—was a celebration of life.

They were outside on the largest courtyard balcony Bell had visited thus far, a large stretch of grassy park with gorgeous cherry trees, wild roses, and tangles of wisteria clumped everywhere imaginable.

From here, the collection of waterfalls that drained into the middle of the city were visible, the water spray painting rainbows across the sky. Tables had been set up in the middle of the courtyard, and half-clothed Solis men and women strolled around them.

No, strolled was the wrong word. They frolicked and chased one another like deer playing, the sight so bizarre that Renk, who was placed across from Bell at the royal table, had yet to close his mouth.

There was no formal dance floor. Instead, groups of musicians were scattered in different corners, Solis swaying to the haunting tune of lutes and lyras and the occasional fiddle. The sound of laughter, rushing water, and the instruments converged to create an enchanting effect that made Bell feel both sleepy and alive.

"Runes, how do they live in this infernal heat?" the king asked, waving a paper fan painted with blush-pink orchids. Stubbornly, he refused to wear the light, breathable linen clothes offered to all the Sun Court guests, and he looked miserable beneath a heavy, embroidered coat.

Cressida raised her eyebrows at the entire scene. Of particular interest to her was the giant pool shaped like a sun in the center of the balcony. The bottom was some type of clear material that displayed the city far below.

Runelight flickered from the crystalline surface, the pool emptying into rivers made to look like rays. The rays streamed outward through the courtyard, winding round and round in dizzy spirals. One such little river streamed by their table, and two Solis males drifted by, completely naked.

Something about Cressida's hungry gaze as she watched them pass, the way she didn't even bother to hide her lust, made Bell feel sick. His father was too preoccupied with his fan and the heat to notice. Or perhaps it was the dark purple moonberry liquor Cressida kept pushing toward him that dulled his senses.

And Archeron . . . the Sun Lord looked ready to bolt. A bitter smile did nothing to veil his discomfort, the muscles of his neck and jaw so tight they would soon start spasming. The king ordered him seated next to Bell, in case he needed help with his raw magick.

If only his father knew the truth. When dusk fell—which was any minute now—the contestants would all perform magick to entertain the sovereign. But Bell's magick would come from Archeron, conveniently funneled through his necklace.

Because of the crowd, there was no way to practice beforehand. Bell had absolutely no idea what to expect. He kept hoping Archeron would give him a signal, or acknowledge Bell at all, really. But he just kept staring ahead with that blank face and those distant eyes.

Eleeza was seated across the table from Bell with her father. She'd spent the last half hour ignoring Bell and picking at the tray of exotic fruits on the table, but when she noticed him watching a troupe of Ashari warriors performing a dance with katanas, her pout transformed into a grin.

"They say the Ashari royals are given tiny katanas at birth," Eleeza said. "Each year, a new katana is given, and they practice keeping the weapons with them everywhere. When they turn eighteen, they're gifted the twin katanas they'll spend their life with. If they lose one, it's considered a horrible dishonor, and the only way to get that honor back is to kill oneself."

"How stupid," Renk commented, stabbing a dark plum with his knife. "It's just a sword."

Eleeza shared an annoyed look with Bell before countering, "The blades of these swords are said to hold the courage and wisdom of their ancestors before them. Losing even one is a tragedy for the entire line."

Bell wondered briefly if Haven's friend, Surai, had such

weapons. At the thought, he found himself grinning. "Where did you learn that?"

She lifted her chin, her beaded red and black earrings swaying around her neck. "You're not the only one who likes to read, Prince."

"Shadeling's shadow," Renk groaned. "You two are perfect for each other. Too bad, Lady Eleeza, that you don't have the right parts. Isn't that right, Barfamy?"

Heat sizzled over Bell's face as Renk dropped his hand into his lap. The table covered the act, but it was obvious he was grabbing his crotch.

The crude gesture made Bell's jaw grind until his teeth felt close to snapping; a tide of fury rushed over him, an all-consuming hatred that made him glad he didn't have magick.

If he did, in this moment, he would surely find a way to murder his half-brother. Or, at least, make the offending appendage fall off.

To Eleeza's credit, she didn't blush or avert her eyes. On the contrary. She pinned Renk with a superior stare, somehow using just her haughty expression to highlight Renk's stupidity.

Renk frowned, jerked his hand away, and then found a spot opposite Eleeza to observe.

Maybe one didn't need magick after all when it came to felling droobs like Renk.

Just then, a horn sounded, and one of the Sun Sovereign's daughters leaned over the railing from the mezzanine above. "My mother welcomes the courts from each great nation under her divine rule. Tonight is your chance to show the entire realm your greatness."

Bell swallowed, a hollow ache rising in his throat. Never had his barren veins felt emptier than now. Never had his lack of magick been on such display. His nervous gaze flickered over the upper balconies of the mezzanine where the Sun Sovereign and her inner court dined, but from this angle, he couldn't see much.

Goddess Above, he prayed, tilting his face to stare at the heavens. *Please don't let me fail.*

A tangerine and pink haze smeared the sky as the sun melted into the sea, lighting a thousand sparks across the glassy surface. Poets had long written about the Effendier sunsets, and any other time, the stunning image would have calmed his nerves.

But nothing, not even the most stunning sunset he'd ever seen, could tamp down his feeling of impending doom. Especially as the other Solis contestants stood from their tables and began walking toward the open area directly beneath the mezzanine.

Perspiration slicked his armpits and hands. He suddenly wished he'd asked Archeron about the Solis sense of smell, because surely they could pick up the fear rolling off him in waves.

The musicians went silent as the contestants strode across the lawn, the air suddenly somber. Every Solissian nation was represented. The group of Ashari tributes went first, their gorgeous kimonos flowing around them like liquid silk as they marched in front of the mezzanine. There were at least twenty of them.

Bell watched, trying his best not to show his awe at each show of magick. A lithe, smiling-faced girl with purple eyes drew all plums from the tables into the air above the mezzanine. When the last dark fruit joined the rest, the air erupted in flutters as the plums became pale gray doves.

Most of the doves alighted in the many cherry trees, but a few landed on the marble railing of the mezzanine, their coos filling the quiet.

The sovereign didn't appear, and a frown darkened the girl's face before she moved off the grassy stage.

More amazing tricks. Goblets turned into long-tailed red lizards that darted beneath tables. Smoke from nearby torches intertwined to become a full-sized man who leapt onto the mezzanine before dissipating on the salty sea breeze. The spears of the nearby Gold Shadows became serpents inside their hands.

Still, the Sun Sovereign did not appear.

The line in front of Bell was growing smaller. Releasing a tight breath, he eyed the stage. His fate rested twenty feet ahead. He tried to keep his eyes from wandering to Archeron, sure that someone would see the truth of his magick if he kept looking at the Sun Lord. But Archeron hardly seemed to notice the contest at all. He had his favorite dagger, the one he constantly picked his teeth with, and was stabbing the blade between his fingers. Faster and faster.

A few times, the blade went awry and nicked his flesh, Bell was sure of it. Because the Sun Lord's flesh was hewn stronger than a mortal's, a regular blade wouldn't split the skin—but it would still hurt.

Yet the Sun Lord didn't seem to notice. Didn't even flinch.

Shadeling's horn, I'm screwed.

If only Haven were here. She was the only person in his life who never let him down. And he'd resented her for it. Guilt bubbled up inside his chest as he recalled how poorly he'd treated her recently.

How could he end up hurting the one person he loved the most?

Only a few contestants stood before him now. A Morgani warrioress with a black band striping her eyes; an Asgardian woman with a shaved head, light golden armor, and a short leather skirt; and a male from Ranth Island, one of the smaller islands of Freya's Spear. Several gold piercings flashed from his nose, ears, and bottom lip.

A hand rested on Bell's shoulder, and he slowly turned, assuming it was Archeron finally come alive. Instead, he was met with blue eyes the color of the sea below and an amused smile.

"Word of advice, Prince Bellamy," Xandrian said. He tugged the high collar of his robin's egg-blue tunic; the piece was split down the middle and held together by a belt embroidered with turquoise and white orchids. "Try very hard not to underwhelm my aunt. She's not particularly fond of mortals, nor butterflies, for that matter, and she's in one of her mercurial tempers."

"I have a feeling she's always in one of those," Bell remarked before remembering who he was speaking with.

Another amused grin. "It's like you know her." Reaching out, Xandrian straightened Bell's shirt. "Then you will also know she doesn't appreciate having her magickal prowess eclipsed either."

"Meaning?"

"Meaning impress her, lightcaster. But don't overdo it."

"Thanks, because that's not confusing at all. Don't underwhelm her, don't overdo it. One might think you're trying to unnerve me into failing."

Xandrian laughed, and Bell couldn't help but notice how his stomach fluttered at the throaty chuckle. "Now why would I do that when I find you so entertaining?"

Bell watched Xandrian stroll away to join the pack of friends from earlier. A few of the men whispered in his ear before appraising Bell.

Never had Bell felt so small, so trivial. A plaything for gods to be passed around and toyed with.

It took everything Bell had not to sneak a glance at Archeron. His heart throbbed in his chest, each shuddering beat so forceful he nearly gasped.

Could one die of panic?

He was about to find out. Only one contestant remained, and the sovereign had yet to even appear over the balcony. The Morgani warrioress conjured a griffin of magick, the beast flying low as it dove toward the woman. Last second before its dark claws sank into her, she felled it with an arrow.

And then the Morgani contestant was walking from the grassy stage and Bell was alone. His palms dripping with sweat, his face on fire as adrenaline swept over his skin. Darkness had fallen seemingly all at once, the sickle-shaped moon and fat stars above casting the courtyard in a delicate silver haze.

Bell could hardly feel his legs as he stepped forward. His hands felt so completely hollow, his lack of magick a shadowy darkness he was sure everyone could see.

Don't look back at Archeron. Don't look back at Archeron. Don't—

Nerves got the better of Bell, and he tilted his head to the right, just enough to glimpse the Sun Lord's face.

Only . . . Archeron was standing up. His normally handsome face twisted into a grimace, eyes dark with rage and something else—pain.

Their eyes met briefly, a flash of panic surging between them. Where was he going?

And then Cressida snapped her fingers. "The king ordered you to fetch me more wine, Sun Lord."

For a few more agonizing seconds, Archeron fought the order, his eyes riveted to Bell. Then the Sun Lord groaned, a shudder wracking his body, and set off toward the serving tables in the distance.

Bell could have sworn Cressida's lips puckered cruelly as she rested her defiant gaze on him.

He didn't have time to turn over what her actions meant, if she knew his secret or just had horrible timing. Nor did he have time to think up an excuse, something to say to give him time for Archeron to return.

Fear had set in. A dark, spiraling terror. The reality of what was about to happen overwhelmed his mind, his senses, his everything, until one thought reverberated through his skull: *The entire realm is about to discover I'm a fraud without a single drop of magick to my name.*

The sovereign was about to be underwhelmed indeed.

TWENTY-EIGHT

Xandrian watched the mortal prince behind lidded eyes, arms folded across his chest. There was something off in the prince's demeanor, hints of panic bubbling beneath the surface. Bell's fingers clawed at the end of his outstretched arm, and his other hand kept reaching for his hair, as if to tug at the black, unruly curls askew on his head, while his gaze kept skipping to the libations table.

Strange, that one. Like most mortals, he wore his emotions like armor, not even bothering to hide his weaknesses. In the Sun Court, emotions were weapons and displaying them was tantamount to giving them away.

Xandrian took in each flare of Bell's nostrils, each time his eyes lingered on something, each shuddering breath.

Something was wrong.

It was a shame the signet ring the prince wore on his wrist also prevented Xandrian from soulreading his thoughts.

Or perhaps not. He relished the puzzle, the challenge of peeling back the prince's layers to discover what hid beneath. Because if Xandrian was sure of anything, it was that the prince harbored a great secret.

The prince took a step back. His fingers curled in on themselves. Where was the divine magick Xandrian had sampled, the one that had been the first sign there was something remarkable about the prince?

Murmurs stirred the air. The mortal king shifted in his high-backed wooden chair; it was the first time since he'd arrived that his mouth wasn't molded in a proud grin. How Prince Bellamy had come from such a worthless slug of a man was a mystery.

Xandrian switched his attention back to the prince, but something had changed in him. His shoulders were squared, his arm had steadied. He stared silently at the flame of orange magick writhing inside his palm, a hint of surprise in his parted mouth.

Xandrian grinned as he awaited whatever performance the prince was about to deliver.

It had been too long since he had something so interesting to entertain him.

Bell knew at once the girl was Haven even before the runespell hiding her identity fell away. He would recognize that swagger anywhere.

She and Surai stood at the edge of the crowd near a rowdy group of Asgardians. Both women wore cowled cloaks that stood out from the rest of the crowd.

Beneath Haven's red cloak glittered a sleek gold breastplate of scaled armor. Before the spell fell away, her hair was a dark, unremarkable brown, pulled back into a braid. Her features, too, were plain; round face, muddy brown eyes; an ill-defined nose and thin lips.

What was she playing at?

He felt the magick inside his palm before he saw it. The sliver of flame danced almost happily, and he wondered how something so small could bring about such relief.

She beamed at him, not even a smidge of guilt for having defied the Sun Lord's orders and come here. And then he knew what would happen next.

No, Haven. Don't show off. Stick to your silly peacocks.

But her grin warned the opposite; she was about to overdo it.

Runes. As soon as he felt the surge of heat inside his flesh, he flicked the flame toward the courtyard, hoping somehow to minimize the magick. It streaked through the air, dove over a servant's head, and sank into the azure waters of the pool with a loud sizzle.

Had something gone wrong?

Time stretched out, punctuated by the loud, erratic beats of his heart. Someone laughed. Bell bit his lip to keep from looking again at Haven, afraid Xandrian would notice. The Sun Lord hadn't stopped watching Bell since they arrived.

Wonderful. I've managed to create a flame that drowned itself. Bravo.

That wasn't exactly what he meant when he wished Haven wouldn't overdo it.

The laughter became murmurs. Bell followed the stares to the middle of the pool where the water rippled. A few drops lifted into the air. A few more. He found himself holding his breath.

The ripples became a wave, small at first. Then bigger and bigger until it shot into the sky . . .

Bell could hardly look at the shimmering miasma of crystal blue as it writhed and danced above the crowd.

All the water from the pools had been drained, but Haven hadn't stopped there. No, cups were emptied. Fountains drained. Even the koi ponds had been utilized, although Haven had been kind enough to take the fish with them, so that hundreds of bright orange, red, and yellow fish swam inside the water.

Someone gasped and Bell turned to see the spray from the collection of waterfalls coalescing.

Bell tried to look calm instead of surprised, but it was hard to hide his shock at the amount of water in the air. Especially as it began to split off and shape itself. Molding and forming into . . . people.

Arms and legs came first. Then faces and intricate details, right down to the buttons on their clothing and their eyelashes.

The water figures held weapons—spears and swords and longbows.

Just as Bell spotted the wings on some of them, the water soldiers began to face off. It was a . . . battle. And not just any skirmish, Bell realized, but the famous battle of Tyr atop the floating Asgardian city.

Every creature he could think of was present: Inside the Noctis ranks were Shadowlings and all manner of Netherworld demons, while the Solis side brimmed with animal shifters, dragons, griffins, and other light world creatures like the pixies and selkies.

Silence pervaded the entire courtyard as everyone craned their necks to watch the bloody match between the Solis and Noctis armies. Sun Queens and Shade Queens fought to the death; legions of gremwyrs streaked the air beside wyverns and dragons; Sun Lords tilted their heads to the sky and blew into massive, spiraling magickal horns.

Sneaking a glance at Xandrian, Bell barely had time to catch the near-imperceptible downturn of the Sun Lord's lips before two figures broke off from the melee.

In the tale, the battle lasted a year and a day. It finally ended when Freya's favorite daughter, the Sun Queen Siffia, fought and killed the Noctis General, Renbane. The stories claimed that during the fight, Renbane was overwhelmed with Siffia's beauty.

That he fell to one knee and pledged his love—right before Siffia cut off his head.

And that's exactly what happened. Haven poised the entire scene right above the mezzanine, forcing the Sun Sovereign to watch. Bell noticed a few of the sovereign's Sun Queens rush to the balcony, ready to defend the sovereign in case this was a trick.

But they stood down on some unknown signal.

And Bell, along with the entire crowd, watched, transfixed, as Siffia lifted her infamous sword, Lightsinger, and parted the Shade Lord's head from his body.

The moment the blade cleaved through the watery neck of the Shade Lord, the figures above burst into a fine mist. The droplets of water swirled through the air as they returned from whence they came; the fish once more swam happily in their pond.

The silence that followed was maddening.

Bell ran a hand through his curls, wild from the humidity, and shifted on his feet. Minutes seemed to pass as he waited for the Gold Shadows to wave him off the lawn toward the other contestants.

Instead, a sound above drew his focus to the balcony where he met eyes with the Sun Sovereign. Her hair was pulled back and woven into her crown, a lovely, delicate piece of spun glass with pearls and sapphires made to look like orchids. A purple slip of gossamer draped over her body, held together by pearl-inlaid pins.

A jolt of adrenaline shot through Bell. He was fairly sure he would never get over how unnerving she was. The ancient, almost bored look in her expression only a god should possess.

As if she'd seen and experienced too much.

"Congratulations, Prince," she said, her cold expression not matching the playful lilt in her voice. "You may ask for anything from me to help you win this tournament—within reason, of course. Come, join me for a drink."

Bell somehow managed to nod, keeping his face neutral, as his thoughts spun wildly. To the left, the Gold Shadows were already taking away contestants who failed this first test.

Contestants with *real* magick.

Bell watched it all in stunned silence, never feeling more like a fraud than now. When the Gold Shadows came for him and began escorting him toward a set of sweeping marble stairs that led up to the mezzanine—and the sovereign—he caught Xandrian's stare, shuddering at the look there.

Disappointment. Supreme, utter disappointment.

As if he had failed some stupid test.

TWENTY-NINE

Haven slipped through the Solis crowd with ease. In Penryth, going unnoticed was a much harder endeavor. She was a girl soldier with rose-gold hair who preferred knives to jewelry. But here, where females were many times more lethal than the males and at least thirty different languages, customs, and attire was on display, she could blend in.

She hardly even needed the cloak she wore, but she hadn't been sure the veiling runespell that hid her face would work. Not until she passed by Archeron near the refreshment area a few minutes earlier. She had nearly grinned when she took in his handsome face, but she caught herself just in time.

He'd given her a once over and then looked *away*. Not a hint of recognition in his eyes.

That was when she became sure of the spell.

That was also when she felt confident her decision to follow Bell here was right.

Archeron had obviously been forced away by the king right at the time Bell needed the Sun Lord most. If she hadn't been here . . .

Running a hand through a few loose strands of hair, she darted through the remaining crowd separating her from Bell. The wounds running down her spine had started to scab, and the movement broke them open.

She winced, but the pain faded as she caught sight of Bell. He stood on the third stair, three Gold Shadows leading the way to the sovereign.

Slipping behind him, she whispered in his ear, "Ask the sovereign for Renfyre Volantis to enter the contest."

When he tilted his head to face her, his face hardly seemed surprised. So he must have seen through her illusion.

Surai said the runespell protected her identity from anyone who would harm her with the knowledge. She could only assume Archeron would have seen through the glamour if he'd looked longer.

"Are you okay?" he demanded, pausing mid-stride. "You look like you're hurt."

She realized her mouth was tight, shoulders bunched to combat another wave of tenderness from her back. "I'm fine. Just do what I ask."

"Why?" The Gold Shadows were still ascending the stairs, but any moment they would turn and notice the prince had halted—and that she was talking to him.

"Because doing so will benefit you greatly," she whispered, turning sideways as if to go back down. Already she could feel eyes on her. A Sun Queen standing between two males, her gaze sliding to Haven. An Ashari male watching her beneath the brim of his hat.

Archeron once said his mother had a thousand spies in her own court. A thousand spies who looked for anything that would reap favor from the sovereign.

Afraid one of the spies was listening to her conversation, she had to be incredibly careful with every word she spoke.

Before she could read his reaction, a tall Gold Shadow turned and grabbed Bell by the shoulder. A wave of protectiveness overwhelmed Haven, and she grit her teeth, drowning the urge to sever the soldier's offending arm from its socket.

Oblivious to the threat a few feet away, the Gold Shadow jerked his head to the mezzanine. "Get up there, mortal Prince. She won't bite."

The other Gold Shadow, a female with pale hair braided to her waist, grinned. "Unless you want her to. She likes pretty things such as yourself, although I very much doubt you could handle her, boy."

Boy? The Gold Shadows lack of respect irked Haven, especially since it meant she and Bell would have to work that much harder to gain their admiration. Bell had a long way to go to earn his place as a King of the Nine.

"And what do you want?" the Gold Shadow demanded, sliding her battle-hardened gaze to Haven. The girl didn't even bother hiding the way her hand went for the hilt of her sword. "Be gone, mortal."

Haven forced her face to slacken and her eyes to go flat as she retreated down the stairs, even as her fingers itched to take that sword from the girl and lodge the blade in her throat. Sighing, Haven worked the anger from her body as she made her way through the courtyard.

Surai waited near a fountain carved to look like a selkie wrapped around a man, dragging him below the sea to munch on.

Goddess Above, Haven hated selkies.

Surai startled at Haven's approach. "Did you tell him?"

Ever since they'd gone through Demaria's portal—named after the mortal lightcaster who founded it—Surai had been jumpy. Haven wondered if her nerves stemmed from anxiety over Haven's disguise, or knowing she would run into Rook's estranged mother and court.

"He knows what to ask for." Now sure of her disguise, Haven tugged her hood back, sighing as the sea breeze cooled the sticky sweat along her neck and hairline. To anyone watching, her hair was a ruddy, unremarkable brown, her features forgettable. There was nothing that bored the Solis more than plainness.

"Are you sure?"

"I couldn't outright ask him, for obvious reasons." Stupid, freakish Solis hearing. "But he figured out my intent."

"Let's hope for all our sakes, or our trip here has been for naught." Surai plucked a flute of fizzy pink liquid from a servant's tray, ignoring the disdainful sneer from the servant, who was used to serving Solis royals and highborns, not Ashari scouts. "Nethergates, I thought that trick you did was going to backfire. What made you decide to do the battle of Tyr?"

Haven shrugged. "Archeron once said the battle was depicted in his mother's private sitting room. You wouldn't put something you'll see every night on a wall unless you like it, right?"

Cracking her neck, Haven settled on the edge of the fountain's lip to wait for Bell. Surai lifted another fizzy drink from a passing tray and sagged next to her. Both girls were worried. Demelza had taken Ravius and left to find accommodations in the city, while Nasira flew to a collection of caves far away from the city.

Just thinking about Stolas's sister gave Haven a headache, and she rubbed her temples. Bringing Nasira here was stupid. She was a Noctis, and a royal one at that.

Demelza had given Nasira her worn brown cloak to cover the girl's wings, and they'd runemarked her horns to disappear from sight. But it wasn't enough. If anyone became suspicious . . .

She dipped her hand in the cool water, remembering the way it shimmered in the air. How alive it had all looked. All those years listening to Bell recount the most famous battles from the Shadow War had paid off.

"We almost didn't make it," Haven murmured as a gold and black fish nibbled her fingers. "A few minutes later and Bell would have lost his place in the tournament and become the sovereign's property."

"Archeron wouldn't have left Bell without a good reason," Surai said.

"I know. I saw him near the wine tents." Haven frowned. "He didn't even recognize me."

Archeron should have seen through her runespell. Then again, perhaps the spell was protecting her identity from Archeron since her magick sensed he would murder her for coming here.

As if conjured by her thoughts, Surai tugged Haven's arm and gestured toward the balcony, where a furious Archeron was looking left to right. She almost didn't recognize him at first. His Sun Court attire—vibrant green silks draped over his torso and airy linen pants—so different from his Penrythian leather pants and tunic.

At seeing him, a timid smile found her lips. But then his furious gaze snagged on her and he barreled toward them, arms clenched over his chest.

Goddess Above, he was pissed.

Smile fading, she leapt to her feet just as he arrived. Pissed was an understatement. He appeared seconds away from murdering her with his bare hands. A sheen of rage glossed his eyes, the vein in his temple throbbed, and his lips were bared revealing blindingly white teeth.

Haven's hand was wet as it wrapped around the dagger at her waist, a string of defensive excuses ready on her tongue.

Surai started to jump to Haven's defense, but Haven waved her away.

"You idiot," he hissed. His chest jerked angrily with each breath, a spray of red blotching his neck. "Tell me I'm mistaken and it's not you. Tell me you didn't directly defy my orders."

Orders? She bristled at his tone, his aggressive posturing. Her fingers tightening over her dagger hilt of their own volition. He would never hurt her—she knew that—but her instincts took over.

"How did you guess?" Surai asked softly, the caution in her voice startling. She was trying to distract some of his ire—trying and failing. He didn't so much as glance at Surai, his gaze burning into Haven.

Then, with a dark grin, he leaned down and sniffed her. Sniffed her, for rune's sake.

"Do you think I don't know your smell by now, Haven?" His voice had gone unnaturally soft, quiet. "That I don't know the way your body moves, the way you tilt your head or bite your bottom lip right before you laugh?"

Haven released a steadying breath, her fingers uncurling from her blade. This was just Archeron, not a monster. She could talk to him. "What would you have me do, Archeron? If I hadn't been here . . ."

She stopped before she all out accused him of failing Bell, but she didn't need to. She could see the frustration and guilt in his eyes. The pain. In fact, the more she studied his face, the more alarmed she grew at the dark shadows pooled beneath his eyes, the distant expression, the way his gaze never settled on hers.

His pupils were large and unfocused as he stared behind her at something. "I only care about you, Little Mortal. *You*. Not him."

"He's my brother," she reminded him, willing the Sun Lord to look at her. Willing him to understand why she had to come.

"And he's the son of my enemy," he growled.

She stared open-mouthed at him, sure she'd misheard him. He had promised to protect Bell. An oath to her. That meant something.

Yet she knew the story . . . how Bell's father had killed Archeron's brother-in-arms. She just assumed he would put aside his hatred of the king for *her*. That whatever they had was strong enough to shatter the deep-seated prejudices against the king.

How naive of her. How very, very silly.

She pressed the heels of her palms to her eyes. Her feelings for Archeron dulled her judgment. Of course Archeron would have trouble protecting the son of the man who murdered his best friend. The man who cruelly enslaved him, made him do trivial, demeaning tasks just to shame him.

"Look, I didn't mean—" He slammed a hand through his hair, tugging the ends. Someone had strung jade runebeads into his honey-gold locks and they clicked softly beneath his fingers. "I vowed to do what I can for the prince, and I will."

"No, I shouldn't have asked you to take on my responsibility," she said, more confident than ever she made the right decision coming to Effendier. "I'm partly to blame for Bell's mistake, and now I'm here to fix it."

Archeron suddenly went very still, his head canted to the side. "What is different about you?"

"I did it," Haven said softly. "I bound the other half of my magick—the half you hated."

Archeron nodded. "Good."

Surai was looking from Archeron to her.

If Haven had imagined Archeron's ire would soften, she realized now how mistaken she was. His enmity had simply transformed into a bitter finality. There would be no more yelling, but that didn't mean she was forgiven for coming here after he expressly forbade it.

"I need you to listen, Archeron," she said, forcing the words out. "I'm only going to say this once, and then I'm done apologizing. Do you understand?"

His eyes narrowed, and she forced the rest out before she lost her nerve. "I'm sorry. I'm sorry that my being here hurts you. I'm sorry that you have to worry about me now. But if I have to choose between my oath to Bell and our relationship—I choose him every time."

"Of course you do." A dark smile tightened his lips. "And I have an apology for you. I'm sorry I didn't shackle you in the dungeons before I left."

Haven's throat ached as she watched him glide through the other Solis, quickly blending in with the crowd.

"That went well," Surai remarked dryly.

Haven threw a wistful stare at where he disappeared, a part of her hoping he would reappear and apologize—a real apology this time.

But, no. Perhaps this was probably better. Or at least simpler. Sever their relationship early before it complicated things. He would forgive her eventually, and they could resume their friendship.

Hopefully. If he didn't . . . she needed his alliance to make this all work.

Groaning, she gouged her knuckles into her temples, her thoughts whirling with everything that had to fall into place to

Welcome to Evermore Academy where the magic is dark, the immortals are beautiful, and being human SUCKS.

After spending my entire life avoiding the creatures that murdered my parents, one stupid mistake binds me to them for four years.

My penance? Become a human shadow at the infamous Evermore Academy, finishing school for the Seelie and Unseelie Fae courts.

All I want is to keep a low profile, but day one, I make an enemy of the most powerful Fae in the academy.

The Winter Prince is arrogant, cruel, and apparently also my Fae keeper. Meaning I'm in for months of torture.

But it only gets worse. Something dark and terrible looms over the academy. Humans are dying, ancient vendettas are resurfacing, and the courts are more bloodthirsty than ever.

What can one mortal girl do in a world full of gorgeous monsters?

Fight back with everything I have—and try not to fall in love in the process.

CPSIA information can be obtained
at www.ICGtesting.com
Printed in the USA
LVHW101738090622
720900LV00016B/478/J

keep Bell alive.

Gain access to the tournament. Shield her identity, find a way to use magick in the tournament, and lose at the very end.

Which meant she would belong to the Sun Sovereign.

Surai must have been having the very same thoughts because she pressed a cool hand on Haven's shoulder. "Last chance. We can leave this place with its court of vipers and spies. Your prince—"

Surai's words fell away as they both jerked their attention to Bell striding across the lawn. Haven's heart fell; he was frowning.

Haven rushed to him, trying and failing to look calm. "What did she say?"

She felt her world crumble as he shook his head, but his words were the opposite of what she expected. "*Renfyre* of House Volantis, you are now a contestant in the Gathering of Flames tournament."

THIRTY

Haven would meet the Sun Sovereign that evening with the rest of the contestants. There was some sort of swearing in ceremony, a promise bound in magick, but she didn't have all the details.

"Too bad Archeron is still pissed," she muttered, kicking her boots onto the low wooden table. A metal plate rested on her stomach, hardly any trace of the five biscuits and two blood sausages she devoured left except for a few crumbs. Ravius was busy collecting the morsels he could find littering her pants. "He could tell me what to expect tonight."

"One," Surai remarked. "Expect Archeron to be furious for weeks . . . if you're lucky. He may never forgive you. Two, no one knows what to expect with the sovereign. She changes up the tournament every century. You might be going to a banquet or the first trial. And three, get those filthy boots off our breakfast table."

"It's not like the table can get any dirtier," Haven remarked, eyeing a suspicious maroon stain marring the varnished wood.

Demelza looked up from the rock-hard biscuit she'd been staring down all morning. "Thank the Goddess, someone has manners here."

Frowning, Haven slid her heavy boots off the table. Her favorite leather pants clung to her long legs, and although it was early morning, sticky sweat already settled behind her knees and thighs.

They were taking breakfast at the Runefire Inn, the only place Demelza found last night that could take them. The island was full for the tournament, the taverns and inns brimming with foreigners all here to support their nation.

A representative of the sovereign had somehow tracked Haven down early this morning to give her a letter. The beautifully inscribed note requested her presence with the others in the evening, and promised her lodging in the mortal contestant housing.

That was the one major benefit of being a contestant; she got to stay in the same place as Bell. As a royal, or someone masquerading as one, no one blinked an eye when she insisted her assistants come with her.

Surai took a careful sip of her tea. Nose crinkled, she made a face, spit the mouthful of tea into the metal tumbler, and sighed. "This tea tastes like a Lorrack's breath. And I think I just spotted a crawler on that wall, right by the suspicious looking yellow stain."

Crawlers were similar to the roaches in Penryth, only three times as big. The only thing more jarring than crawlers were the cat-sized lime green lizards that infested the city. Haven had discovered one on the edge of her bed this morning and nearly screamed like a boy.

"You try finding a place with vacancy," Demelza snapped, her grumpy gaze shifting to Ravius. "Or that takes filthy, thieving birds."

The poor woman was hunched over a stool where she'd been complaining about the hard beds ruining her back since they awoke.

Haven stretched, pain shooting down her spine. Surai cut open the runemarks imprisoning her dark magick once again last night, and the wounds hurt worse than before. But she would take any amount of pain to ensure her friends were safe.

With breakfast done, they all stood and stretched. Everyone had a busy day ahead. Demelza was supposed to go shopping for Nasira. Once Demelza collected the long list of items Nasira swore she needed—silk sheets, a handheld mirror, gowns, a bottle of perfume that could only be found in Solethenia—Demelza would take them to the spoiled girl. She was stashed on the western coast, far away from the city and its inhabitants.

Haven could only imagine her annoyance at having to devour rodents and small livestock, but it was better than children.

Surai was off to scour the massive public library near the center of town looking for runespells Haven could use in the tournament, as well as any histories on the trials.

Haven, for her part, was anxious to explore the city. And not just for the things she needed—a runespell tablet, runeink, new clothes, a pain salve for her wounds, and more gauze—but because she was in Solethenia, the famed jewel of Effendier and most beautiful city in the realm.

She wanted to soak it all in. Wanted to know that places like this existed. Places where the Curse had never tainted the air and drained the magick.

Perhaps in a city like Solethenia, the heavy shadow of Spirefall and Morgryth might finally be lifted.

Just before Haven slipped out the door, Surai took her arm. "Be careful. The sovereign has eyes everywhere."

Haven glanced back at her friend. She thought about telling her she'd already spotted at least three spies—one near the bar, one at the table next to them, and one by the kitchen door.

Instead, she winked. "Always."

Haven joined Demelza on the way out, laughing under her breath as the woman peered at Nasira's two-page list.

Just as expected, two of the spies followed them, staying far enough back that Demelza didn't notice.

Haven waited until they crossed an arched bridgeway, the railing entwined with white jasmine and pink wisteria, and then paused while Demelza and Surai walked ahead. Biting her lip, she dipped her fingers into the mud and drew a runespell into the marble foundation.

A soft rushing noise from the azure water below was the indication her spell was working. Ravius startled from her shoulder as the sluggish water suddenly surged to swallow the bridge, his wings flapping loudly as he alighted on a nearby weeping willow.

A grin stretched her face. Being able to use her magick in public was like wearing a corset for years and then removing it.

She could finally breathe.

It was *exhilarating*.

The two spies following her halted, their expressions dark. They glanced her way, but she pretended to be as confused as they were by the sudden flood.

A prickling sensation sizzled at the base of her skull; they were trying to soulread her.

The prickling became sharp, insistent stabs attacking her temples, behind her eyes, the back of her skull. Gritting her teeth, she rebuked the attempt, surprised by how easy it was.

After working with Stolas, other people's magick felt dull and weak in comparison.

Speaking of . . . wasn't there a word he taught her to use when someone tried to soulread her?

She waited until she felt one of the spies stroke her mind, his attempt softer, as if he could sneak inside.

"Foetor," she whispered.

The spy closest to the bridge suddenly doubled over, his mouth wrenched open as he dry heaved.

Haven grinned as she caught up to the others. A neat party trick, but it did the job.

The sun had barely risen, but the city was alive. The cry of seagulls mixed with the blare of ships' horns and the occasional clattering of carriages.

Across the canal, the palace rose like a quartz mountain into the sky. The main city was inlaid into a hill, Freya's temple crowning the ridge. Gilt domes and ivory buildings were woven together to create an impossibly beautiful tapestry.

This side of the canal, the city flattened out in a ring. Shops lined the narrow streets, quaint stone buildings squashed together, heat already shimmering the air over their colorful copper roofs.

Once the balmy morning air warmed her blood, the half-risen sun burning like fire through the cityscape, Haven split off from Demelza and Surai and entered a busy side street. Her boots were soft against the slick cobblestone surface. A petite woman with a ruddy face was sweeping the sidewalk in front of a tea shop. Haven talked her into opening early and sampled a spicy hibiscus tea paired with honey balls, a famous Solethenian pastry.

She bribed Ravius with half of the delicacy to deliver a message to Bell, a folded-up note scribbled with a promise to be there tonight.

Afterward, Haven spent the entire day perusing this side of the city. She sampled exotic cuisine—raw fish wrapped in seaweed and black rice—from the Ashari district, found a pair of leather boots dyed emerald she knew Bell would adore, had her fortune read by a seer who was obviously a fake—he predicted she would be happily married with children soon—and spent way too much money on three runetablets.

Apparently they were all the rage in Solethenia.

Haven lugged everything up a massive hill and across a wide bridge toward the center of town. The air cooled as the sun dipped below cliffside apartments in the distance. Had she really been here all day?

She paused near the top of the hill by a fountain to readjust the bags on her arm. The sculpture in the center of the water was of a young woman held in the arms of a Noctis male. Unlike the hundreds of statues around the city, these were unkempt. Lichens and age darkened the statues, the marble chipped and worn, especially around the detailing of the feathers on the outspread wings.

Feathers. Which meant this couldn't be Odin, Freya's lover turned enemy. Odin's wings were leathery and bat-like, all claws and bone.

She read the inscription on the gold plaque: *Freya in the arms of Varyssian.*

Varyssian? The name stirred a memory inside Haven. But before she could examine the thought, a Solissian male stormed by and cursed at the statue.

That's when Haven noticed a man watching her. He wore dull brown monk's robes, his face plain but not bad to look upon.

He stood in the archway of the building beyond. It wasn't a temple, exactly—not with its sagging thatched roof and crumbling clay walls. But she felt a pull toward the place anyway.

The man smiled, the wrinkles around his eyes deepening.

Something about the kindness in the smile, the way his eyes shone with genuine love, made Haven uneasy.

The man was a stranger, a spy for the sovereign, for all she knew.

Shifting the canvas satchel across her shoulder, she pressed on toward the palace. She'd let the enthralling city muddy her sense of time, and now she wouldn't be able to go back to the Runefire Inn and change.

Darkness fell all at once, just as she entered a long bridge. So long, in fact, the end was hardly visible. Unlike the ornate marble ones, this bridge was made of glass, giving an unobstructed view of the waterfalls on all three sides. The raging waters fed into a chasm hundreds of feet below.

The roar swallowed all other sound and made her feel wrapped in a cocoon of rushing air.

"Perfect place for a glass bridge," she muttered, forcing her feet forward as a fine mist cooled her cheeks. A bubble of nausea lodged beneath her sternum as she neared the center of the structure, and she fixated on the first sprinkling of stars above rather than look down.

Haven had never feared bridges or heights, but after falling into the rift crossing into the Shadowlands, she couldn't cross a long bridge without her mouth going sand-dry.

She really needed to learn a flying spell.

Quickening her pace, she found herself almost jogging. The bridge was empty, the palace ahead a glowing beacon driving her forward. Copper lanterns brimming with runelight threw golden discs in her path.

She was halfway across the bridge when she saw the figure. A dark cloak veiled their tall form, hiding anything distinguishable.

She whirled on her heels to go back, but another figure waited for her there as well. Just like the first, he was clad in dark fabric that moved sluggishly in the wind.

This was a coordinated attack. She would have to face one of them—and she would do it happily.

Her sword sung from its sheath, moonlight trickling down its double-edged blade. She debated retrieving the second sword at her back, but, no, magick would be more effective here. Something—the change in the air, the way the hairs ridged on her arms—told her the two beings possessed strong powers.

That's okay, so did she.

The orb of magick inside her palm lit the bluish-gray night sky, the heat from the flame cutting through the cool air.

Judging she was closest to the assailant straight ahead, she faced the figure, heart racing as she prepared to charge. Already, she had a volley of offensive runespells ready to release.

Working with Surai was finally paying off.

Only the dark figure wasn't attacking. He was bent in the path, scribbling something along the sides of the bridge, the pathway—

No! She whirled around to discover the same for the other assailant. Eerie blue filaments of magick swirled and danced, growing bigger. The whisper of chanting stirred the air.

A shadow of foreboding came over her, and her breath caught as she broke into a sprint—but it was too late.

A horrendous crack rent the night, and then the bridge began to split down the middle.

THIRTY-ONE

Bell tried not to stare at the huge clock on the other side of the room. Tried to ignore the ticking that seemed to worm inside his bones. The crystal piece was shaped like the sun and seemed to run on magick alone. Any other time he would have marveled at the invention, but now . . .

Haven was late. Incredibly, undeniably late.

And, while Haven did have her own sense of time, when it was something this important, she would be here.

"Something bothering you, brother?" Renk asked, not even bothering to hide the glee in his voice.

"Only the sight of your flat, smashed-in face," Bell replied, surprised by how calm he sounded.

"You know, I cannot wait for this entire unholy court to witness you fail. Then the realm will know what the Penrythians do—you're a pathetic, useless coward who can't even control his magick."

Bell forced himself not to react, and soon, his half-brother turned his attention to the goblet brimming with fermented moon-thistle, the creamy drink served in the afternoons.

Glancing down at his lap, Bell uncurled his fist until the note inside was visible, delivered to his window at dawn by Ravius. It was wrinkled, smeared by sweat, but Haven's near-unintelligible handwriting was visible.

I'll be at the palace by dusk.

Swallowing hard, he crumpled the paper in his damp palm and pocketed it. The sun set three hours ago.

Something was wrong.

Bell blinked, wishing there was a way to dim the impossibly bright lights flooding the cavernous ballroom. The pulsing magick emanated from countless drooping flowers, similar to the clustered wisteria bud, that hung from the thick branches veining through the room. The cloying, sticky-sweet scent drowned the air and made his head spin.

The tree of life. He'd seen its heavy branches snaking through the palace, some wider than he was tall, its delicate gray bark peeling away to crimson skin. They wound through the castle in seemingly random patterns, dropping from the ceiling, wrapping around pillars. In some places they made the swollen branches part of the furniture, piling cushions and blankets along the thick branches to make seating.

Still, he had yet to get used to the idea of a magickal, sentient tree.

The contestants and their courts were gathered inside a cavernous ballroom, each with their own tables and sitting area, and the jarring sound of foreign dialects made it hard to hear the person across the table. Banners hung over the sections, announcing the nations.

Above Bell's table hung the Penrythian banner, three dahlias over a curved sword, the black flag blowing in the breeze coming from the nearest balcony. His father and Cressida sat beneath the silky banner, two mortal royal guards on either side of them, their pages ready for instruction.

Behind them, Archeron leaned against the quartz wall, arms tangled over his chest.

Other than the bitter tilt of his lips, there was no emotion in his handsome face.

Bell's gaze snagged on the near-empty table at the back. Unlike the long marble table beneath his elbows, this one was made of an ashy wood, and was considerably smaller. It was an afterthought, brought in for House Volantis.

Bell still couldn't believe the sovereign had granted his request. Although part of him suspected she agreed out of curiosity more than anything.

A contestant requesting for another mortal house to join the contest was odd, and technically meant more competition for Bell.

The sovereign would want to puzzle out why.

Bell shivered, remembering how she watched him quietly for thirty wild beats of his mortal heart. Erratic, desperate shudders she surely heard. And when she finally approved, a slow, almost animalistic tick of her head, he rushed from her presence, gulping air and clutching his chest.

Xandrian had brushed Bell's arm on the way out. Bell could still hear the words as if the Sun Lord were whispering them into his ear all over again.

Whatever dangerous game you're playing, it's not going to end well for you.

Bell refocused on the now and realized his fingers were clenched around the jeweled goblet in front of him, his shaking hand sloshing the fermented moon-thistle onto the table.

He once again looked to the House Volantis table. The quiet Solis warrior friend of Haven's, Surai, met his eyes. Worry welled inside her lavender eyes, her focus sliding to the double arched doors across the room.

Goddess save them all.

Bell had gotten used to the assaulting din of languages, metal clinking, and laughter, so when all of that abruptly died, he felt his heart tumble strangely inside his chest. When he looked up and realized that all eyes were on him, including the sovereign's, a dull sense of panic hit. Beside her stood the royal cupbearer, Lysander, a Sun Lord and the sovereign's favorite, if court gossip was to be believed.

"Prince Bellamy of House Boteler, twenty-first of your name, please come to the front," Lysander called out, before sitting on a purple and gold brocade cushion at the Sun Sovereign's feet.

She lounged on a gold throne that gave the illusion of flames, atop a dais of glass surrounded by water filled with all manner of fish and aqueous plants.

He'd heard a few courtiers whispering earlier that the water was spelled to make anyone who touched the water fall in love with the sovereign. Lanterns shaped like lotus flowers swirled in the running water, their soft light illuminating the shiny flesh of the male concubines lounged around her.

Unlike Lysander, who was more or less covered in a white tunic and long flowing pants, they wore strips of sheer fabric around their waist, showing off lithe torsos and ropy, muscular thighs.

They also wore thick golden collars around their necks.

"Go, boy," his father barked. "What are you waiting for?"

Renk sneered at him, whispering beneath his breath, "When

you're enslaved in her service, do you think she'll make a special collar just for you?"

Bell found the courage to stand. To push himself down the aisle, passing tables of Ashari and Asgardians, the formidable Morgani with their tall, handsome queen, the savage tribes of Freya's Spear, each with their own customs and language.

When he neared the marble steps of the dais, a Gold Shadow broke off from a pillar and hissed, "Naeli."

Kneel. He didn't need to understand Solissian to know the word.

But he wasn't fast enough, apparently, because the female slammed her hand into the back of his neck, digging her fingertips into the tender points at the base of his skull until he dropped to his knees.

He bowed his head, trying to slow the frantic hammering of his heart. The ragged pull of his breathing.

The sovereign unfolded from her fiery throne. Moving as one, her concubines slid waist-deep into the water. Four of them helped the sovereign across, and two more held up the seafoam blue gossamer of her skirt.

Through his dark curtain of lashes, Bell watched them deposit her on the other side of the river, mesmerized by her glamour, her godlike presence, despite his fear.

"You asked for a wish, Prince," the sovereign said, straightening the azerite crown over her gilded hair. "A strange request to add another House of Nine to the Praetori Fiernum. I would have been fair to deny you. Mortals are not beloved here, not after the last war." She threw a pointed glance at his father before continuing. "But, I, in my benevolence, granted this for you, son of my once enemy. Is this not true?"

Bell wasn't sure if he was allowed to look at her when he spoke or stare at the ground.

He chose the second, safer option. "Yes, my sovereign. Your generosity is not forgotten."

"No, no, beautiful mortal boy. Call me Lilith. We are friends here, are we not? For why else would you travel all this way, pledging yourself to my service, if we cannot trust one another?"

His throat was closing up. "Yes, my sovereign. We are friends, and allies, and my kingdom is grateful for the invitation to the Gathering of Flames."

"Ah, but I do wonder. You see, my only condition for such an odd request was for this new contestant to appear tonight with the others. And yet, I look around and I do not see her. Does Renfyre from House Volantis think she is above the other Solis nations?" When he failed to answer, she snapped her cold gaze to where Surai sat. "Perhaps I should call forth Renfyre's court, small and unimpressive as it is, to answer for her rudeness?"

Bell shut his eyes and exhaled. This was bad. He had absolutely no idea how to respond. Sorry was a fool's response. Making excuses would only make him look weak and bumbling. He could say nothing . . . sometimes nothing was better than something.

Whatever he said, it wouldn't be enough.

THIRTY-TWO

Haven screamed as glass shards embedded deep into her flesh. There was nowhere to run, nothing to grab onto, no way out of this mess. She tried to think, to conjure a preservation spell or perhaps an undoing rune.

But her mind went blank, adrenaline chasing her thoughts into circles. She simply hadn't had enough time to work those advanced runespells.

More glass showered her face and hair as the top of the structure disintegrated. Another groan as the bridge shuddered, sending her careening. She was on her knees. Her fingers bloody from the glass. Glass everywhere.

Then the ground simply gave way, and she was falling. Her stomach tightened, another scream lodged in her throat. It felt surreal, falling. Like moving in slow motion.

The roar of the falls enveloped her. Her hand curled around a thick splinter of glass she must have grabbed when searching for a handhold. Dragging the shrapnel over her forearm, she hastily drew what she thought was a rune for flying.

Nothing happened.

The water rose to meet her. A churning din of angry waves swirling in a whirlpool that would surely drown her. If the fall didn't kill her.

Moments before she hit, she felt something encircle her waist. Her body jerked at the sudden stop in motion, knocking the air from her lungs. On instinct, she struggled against the hard steel cage she felt wrapped around her. At least, until she spotted the midnight black feathers in her periphery and felt the prickle of dark magick at her back.

"Hello, Beastie," Stolas whispered in that insouciant voice. But it couldn't be Stolas. None of it made any sense.

"Stolas?" she said, sagging against his chest.

They were rising from the watery abyss at a rapid pace, the wind from his wings buffeting her hair around her face. The fine spray from the waterfalls cooled her cheeks.

After the shock of the attack, and then the terrifying adrenaline rush from falling, she was sure she was dreaming. Hallucinating. Already dead. There was no way Stolas was here, in the Sun Court, his enemy's stronghold. He wouldn't be that stupid.

A low growl rumbled her back. "Stupid? I could say the same to you. What mortal troubles have brought you all the way across the Glittering Sea to Archeron's homeland?"

"You soulread me?" she hissed.

A dark chuckle. "You're practically throwing your thoughts at me."

"I thought I was about to *die*."

"Who said you're not?" His arms tightened around her waist.

"You wouldn't dare kill me," she replied, hoping it was true.

"Otherwise you'd be stuck with me in the Netherworld for an eternity."

"Perhaps I only want to drain your essence until you're hovering between the two realms."

A sliver of fear chilled her blood. Especially after their last encounter.

If you see me again, do not trust me.

Slowly, she slid the two daggers at her waistband into each sleeve of her tunic, ready at a moment's notice to wield them—if necessary. Yes, she had grown to trust Stolas, but he was still a self-admitted monster, and she'd always known the time might come that he could turn on her, their fragile bond evaporating into dust.

The palace was just above, the moonlight reflecting off the quartz stone and making it seem to glow from within. Vining flowers clung to the walls and hung from the many balconies.

She gasped as he suddenly banked right toward the largest waterfall. They shot through the dark curtain of water, the shock of cold punching the air from her lungs.

Darkness. She drew an illumination rune into her palm, and two orbs of golden light blinked into existence. They grew until they were the size of melons, bobbing in the air as they trailed Haven. The cavern was huge, the light from the orbs lost in the infinite darkness.

"Where are we?" she asked.

"Just one of the many subterranean tunnels beneath the city," Stolas replied, his breath tickling her ear. "The previous Sun Sovereign, King Aramos, had them built as escape routes for the city during attacks."

He dropped them onto a ledge large enough for at least twenty people. As soon as her feet touched the ground, she pulled away from the Shade Lord's grip and whirled to face him. The closest orb threw harsh shadows over his sharp features.

Still . . . something inside her leapt at the familiarity in his face. His ever-changing eyes, which were at this moment a deep, violent shade of yellow.

"You're safe," she breathed, forgetting she was supposed to be afraid of him. Her heart swelled with happiness. He was healthy, no more pain. And his wings . . .

Without thinking, she reached out to touch them. Her fingers got inches from running over their sable softness before he snapped his beautiful wings closed.

"What's the matter, Stolas?" she demanded. "How did you escape?"

"I didn't, I'm afraid."

In the span of time it took her to blink, she had her daggers in her hands. But it didn't matter. He was too powerful. She watched the daggers slip from her grip and then . . .

THIRTY-THREE

A sudden hush made Bell open his eyes. And then a familiar, haughty voice echoed through the hall.

"If anyone should be punished for my tardiness, surely it's me."

Bell turned in time to see Haven striding through the tables toward them. She was limping, a slight change in her walk only he would notice, and there was a tightness in her face he didn't like.

Or maybe that was because her glamoured mask had yet to totally fall away, and he was unused to seeing the plain features and lank brown hair that made her forgettable.

He checked her over for anything alarming. Her hair and clothes were . . . wet. And the golden doublet she wore was torn at the arm and flecked with blood, as was her face and chest. The small amount of bleeding hinted at superficial wounds.

By the time she was within touching distance, her true face broke through. The transformation from unremarkable features and dull hair to the riot of wild, rose-gold locks was startling, and

Bell fought reacting somehow.

Could others see it?

A quick glance back at his father, Cressida, and Renk eased his worry. They stared at Haven with slightly curious expressions; if they saw her through her spell, surely their reactions would be different.

Haven sank into a low bow, thinking of what she could say to appease the sovereign. The truth would be helpful, and the evidence of the bridge's destruction would surely back up her story, but she hesitated to mention the attack . . . because she couldn't remember what happened *after* the bridge fell.

She had absolutely no idea how she survived. Or what she did for the three hours that had passed since night fell.

In truth, she should be dead. A fact that irked her to no avail. All that training and one single bridge was all it took to almost kill her.

Almost.

Runes, she hated bridges.

Her clothes were damp, meaning at some point she'd gotten wet. But if she'd fallen in the water, the impact alone would have broken every bone in her body. Had someone saved her? If so, what did she do for all that time? And why would they wipe her memory afterward?

Haven swallowed. If she denied the incident, she could fall right into the sovereign's trap. The sovereign could have orchestrated the entire thing or her spies might have witnessed what actually happened.

Lying about it was out of the question.

A memory danced below the surface of her consciousness, just beyond her reach.

"Well?" the sovereign said, her syrupy-sweet voice barbed. "Why have you made us all wait for your arrival? Is your magick so special that you do not have to follow the same rules of this tournament that the others do?"

Haven straightened to a stand. Looking at the woman who enslaved her son to a corrupt king, it was hard to hide her disgust, but somehow she managed to make her face appear meek. Her posture submissive.

Lowering her gaze, she said, "I was attacked on the way here crossing the glass bridge."

"Attacked? By whom?"

"I don't know," she answered honestly. "They used dark magick to destroy the bridge, and then I . . . fell into the water."

She arched an eyebrow. "Pray tell, how did you survive?"

"I performed a preservation spell," she lied, hoping the sovereign's spies hadn't witnessed the event. She was thankful for her ability to ward off soulreading as the sovereign mentally probed her mind.

Light magick caressed her defenses, soft, intimate strokes that hinted at unchecked power.

"And how did you not drown?"

One side of Haven's mouth tilted up. "I'm a good swimmer."

Scattered laughter filled the silence. But it quickly died when the sovereign didn't join in. "And you have no idea who might have done this, Renfyre of House Volantis?"

Haven squirmed under the false name, sure the sovereign knew it was wrong somehow. How to answer?

There was something, but she wasn't sure if it had anything to do with the attack. In fact, this entire incident had left her reeling with uncertainty, a feeling she despised.

Slipping her hand into her pants pocket, which was still extremely damp, she closed her fingers around a glossy black feather. Even limp and wet, she'd recognized the quill by the sheer size.

This was no raven's feather.

Jerking her hand out, she shook her head. "No. Other than Prince Bellamy, whom I only recognize through the tale of the Curse, and those from my court, I don't know a single soul here, or why anyone would want to harm me."

"A curious thing, that. Why did the mortal prince request your presence?"

As planned, she said, "I heard he'd been chosen and I sent a messenger to his entourage with the request."

"And why is winning this magickal contest important to you?" she mused, her eyes hardening.

Haven made sure the giant dragon's eye emerald was on display at her wrist as she said, "My people are oppressed by another tribe. My family is dead—"

"And your dragons?"

Haven fought the urge to look away from the sovereign's intense stare. She released a long breath. "Our dragons are gone. So you see, winning is the only way to save my House."

A half-truth.

The sovereign seemed to contemplate that for a few breaths. Her gaze flitted to the bracelet at Haven's wrist, held there.

Haven waited, heart in her throat.

Once she was formally announced as a contestant, Bell would be that much safer. She chanced a glance at him, their eyes meeting briefly.

But when she returned her attention to the sovereign, her hopes shattered. The Sun Court ruler wore a malignant grin that could terrify the Shadeling as she said, flippantly, "No, I do not think I will give you that chance now, mortal girl. Go home."

Rage surged inside Haven, and she had to quickly tamp it down. But not before the sovereign saw it and smiled.

Smiled, for Nihl's sake. She was enjoying this.

A thousand responses hovered on Haven's tongue. Each one would probably get her executed. But before she could say or do anything rash, a horn cut through the night. Followed by a second and then a third.

Gold Shadows spilled from the dark corners of the room, the blades from their weapons gleaming beneath the lights. The Solissian word *Noctari* rang through the room like a curse.

Noctis.

On instinct, Haven put herself between Bell and the balcony where soft thuds echoed off the stone.

Runelight lamps were scattered throughout the courtyard outside. One by one, the magickal light snuffed out.

Shadows writhed and grew. As she made out the first winged form engraved against the deep blue canvas of stars, her thoughts went to the feather in her pocket. But these wings were sharp, angular, sporting horns and talons meant for gashing open flesh.

These were the skeletal, leathery wings of her nightmares.

Twin blades whirled in her hands. Without caring who saw, she lit the double-edged steel with light magick. Around her, the courts all did the same, displaying their vast array of magick and weapons. Surai rushed through the crowd to stand next to Haven, her katanas glowing faintly.

Haven threw a shield over them, and Surai reinforced it with her own.

Bell held his heavy ceremonial sword out at an awkward angle.

He glanced at her with worried eyes. "Are you okay?"

"Yes," she assured him. "I'll explain later."

Bell flicked a wide-eyed gaze toward the balcony. "Are those . . .?"

"Party crashers," Surai mumbled, scowling at the approaching Noctis. The skin around her eyes tightened as her gaze fell upon a gremwyr scuttling along the arched ceiling. Her body went still, her entire focus on the creature as she removed a throwing dagger from her boot and aimed it at the monster's head.

The shadow of Rook's death was written all over Surai's face.

An inky mass funneled into the room from every open window and door, converging in the rafters above. Ravens.

Their cries drowned out the sound of chaos below.

A figure approached, sending the crowd surging away from the largest balcony. One figure became two.

Wings silhouetted both.

Bell suddenly went very still, his only movement the sword shaking in his hands. The tiny tremors flickered shards of light over his anguished face.

His throat convulsed as if he were choking. "How did—how did she find me?"

Haven nearly asked who before she made out the pale, bloodless skin and membranous wings tipped with talons. The thick tangle of waist-length hair so black it seemed to swallow the light.

Ravenna Malythean.

The Shade Queen's daughter wore a gruesome crown of bleached bones, blood-red rubies splattering the delicate piece. Dark armor the metallic hue of scarab beetles clung to her body, somehow managing to look foreboding and beautiful. A cloak of the deepest tar-black pooled behind her like spilled ink. The fabric seemed to move, and Haven shuddered as she made out the writhing mass of scorpions, beetles, and spiders.

An onyx runestone necklace glittered at Ravenna's throat, threads of bluish-black magick curling around the jewel.

And then Haven glanced at Ravenna's companion and the air sucked from her chest.

Beside her, looking more fitting of a crown than anyone else in the room, was the Lord of the Netherworld, Stolas Darkshade.

THIRTY-FOUR

Haven felt frozen, as if the world around her had turned to ice. Or perhaps it was the shock of seeing Stolas, healthy and alive, his gorgeous wings restored to their stunning glory; even the Gold Shadows hesitated in the presence of the infamous Lord of the Netherworld.

Or maybe it was his otherworldly beauty. The jagged onyx of his crown contrasted sharply against his wavy, moon-white hair, neatly trimmed at the sides, the top left long enough to sweep over his forehead. Once again, he wore the ostentatious regalia from Bell's runeday, his oil black armor shining beneath the runelight.

The feathered cloak he so despised, the one made from the wings of his mother, draped proudly from his wide shoulders.

On one of those shoulders perched Ravius, the traitor.

Haven released a sharp breath, and Stolas's dark gaze whipped to her. There was nothing in his stare that spoke of their friendship, their shared past. Only a feral savagery that pitted her gut.

He looked away like she was nothing.

He doesn't recognize me.

Which meant the identity spell was working—and that he was a danger to her.

As he swept into the room, the runeflowers dripping from the tree of life began to wilt and blacken, curling in on themselves. The Solis crowd surged away from the dark couple.

Opposing magick swelled to fill the room as everyone readied themselves for the oncoming battle.

"Regretting making that bargain with him, yet?" Archeron asked, coming up beside her.

He had yet to retrieve his sword, and the magick that danced inside his palm was barely a spark. King Horace must have ordered him to protect Bell, but Archeron wasn't about to rush doing so.

"What is he doing here?" she said, more to herself than Archeron. "He was . . ."

Broken, near death, she almost finished before thinking better of it.

If Archeron was pissed now, she'd hate to see him when he discovered she still shared dreams with the Shade Lord.

As far as Archeron knew, those had ceased when the Curse was broken.

Archeron's jaw hardened, and he slowly slid his longsword from its sheath, his gaze never leaving the Shade Lord. "Causing mischief and chaos. It's his specialty, believe me." He cut his eyes at her. "Didn't you know? Or did you assume when you made a deal with the Lord of the Netherworld that he was tame?"

Gritting her teeth, she forced her attention back to the Noctis. The crowd had surged against the far wall. Gold Shadows flanked the sovereign, who had conjured an iron shield engraved with shields and a giant sword.

She was smiling as she approached Ravenna and Stolas.

Haven drew closer, hoping her disguise held against someone as powerful as Ravenna. Behind Ravenna and Stolas, the Noctis court gathered. Wings of leather and quill fluttered and flared as the Noctis prepared for a fight.

Haven had never seen the enslaved Seraphian race, and she studied them for differences from their Golemite brethren.

Their armor was similar, a light black metal carved into skulls and grimacing, monstrous faces, but the bit of flesh she could see was streaked in faint, bluish-white runes that glowed. Occasionally, their eyes would pulse with the same luminescent magick.

The ghoulish procession halted. A few Noctis sporting exquisite custom armor joined Ravenna and Stolas. Haven recognized Magewick, the horrible Shade Lord from Spirefall.

He was huge, larger than she recalled, all muscle and wings. He wore his ebony hair slicked back, showing off his widow's peak. With his high cheekbones and eerie blue eyes, he might have been handsome—if not for his cadaverous flesh and membranous wings, the leathery skin so thin she could make out the black veins beneath.

She clenched her sword pommel, starbursts of white capping her knuckles.

If this ended in a battle, that ugly, winged bastard was the first to die, followed by Ravenna.

Head held high, the sovereign strode to meet the Noctis. In a gesture surely meant to show she was unafraid, she left her soldiers behind, meeting Stolas and Ravenna alone. Light radiated from her silhouette, seeping into the air around her.

When the sovereign was within striking distance from Ravenna and Stolas, Ravenna must have felt the light magick because she bared her teeth and retreated a step.

Stolas smiled, a lazy, irreverent thing. "Lilith, you are looking resplendent, as always."

He fell into a sweeping bow, the act showing off the silver caps adorning the tips of his horns. Threads of blue magick radiated from the strange jewelry.

The sovereign swept her eyes over Ravenna, who refused to bow, before meeting Stolas's bored gaze. "And you haven't changed much since last we met. I am a bit disappointed that the rumors aren't true—Ravenna doesn't keep you on a diamond-studded leash."

Haven watched Stolas for any sign of anger, but his face held its perfectly sublime expression. "I am well trained."

Fresh anger coursed through Haven as she remembered him bloody and half-dead, curled in the grass like a child, his wings stripped of their beautiful feathers, his hollow bones snapped.

I'm well trained.

Had Ravenna finally broken him?

The thought cut deep. She couldn't imagine the pain and suffering it would take to make the Shade Lord Ravenna's creature, especially considering what Morgryth had done to his family.

The sovereign tilted back her head, showing off her delicate neck as she laughed at Stolas's joke. But the action was forced, stilted, and when she stopped, her eyes were cold. "Your newfound subservience aside, I'm afraid your presence here has violated the terms of our truce. No Noctis may enter Solissian controlled territories, no shadowling or demon may cross into our borders. And yet, here you are with all your ilk. Is it a war you want, Demon Lord?"

At the dark title, a tremor rippled over Stolas's jaw, just enough that Haven noticed.

"War?" Stolas arched an elegant ash-white eyebrow, and Haven recalled trying to draw them once. "As fun as that might be, I've come here for an entirely different reason."

The sovereign laughed, all poise and calm as she swept her arm over the banquet tables laden with fruit and wine. But the Gold Shadows didn't relax. If anything, their grips on their weapons tightened, and they edged closer, faces stoic.

"I admit, the spice cakes are very good. Might that be the reason, *Noctari*? If so, please, you are welcome to enjoy the spoils of our land."

"Enough," Ravenna said. "We haven't come here to taste your disgusting food. We've come to claim my husband's rightful place in the Gathering of Flames."

Husband. Just the thought of Stolas forced into marriage with Ravenna right after his parents were murdered—it was enough to make Haven daydream about taking the daughter of the Shade Queen apart piece by piece.

A hush fell over the room; even the ravens seemed to stop their squawking. Haven's mind whirred as she tried to piece together what was happening. Why Stolas would want to enter a tournament that . . . *Oh.*

The winner ruled over the Court of Nine in Shadoria. *Shadoria.* His stolen homeland. The one he had assumed until recently was destroyed.

Haven's heart was racing as she strained to see over the crowd. The sovereign looked less than amused as she fixed her dead gaze on Stolas. "I am afraid the selections have already been made. Pity, but maybe next century?"

Stolas smoothed two fingers down the sharp edge of his jaw. "The Mother's Law states you must have one participant from each recognized kingdom in the realm. Last I checked, you did not have someone from the Darkshade line. Unless I'm mistaken?"

His voice was a low purr, equal parts warning and charm. He was daring her to challenge him.

"But you are—"

"Last surviving heir to the Darkshade line and prince of the Seraphians?" Stolas finished, every word dripping with smugness.

"I was going to say Lord of the Netherworld," the sovereign barked, her unhappiness at being interrupted clear.

"I am many things, Sun Sovereign. One might call me multi-faceted."

Haven held her breath as she struggled to determine which way the argument would go. It was clear by the army of Noctis inside the palace, as well as those darkening the sky, that if the Sun Sovereign dismissed his claim, there would be a great battle here followed by all-out war.

But if she allowed him to enter the contest . . .

Bell couldn't win. Not against him. Because *she* couldn't win against the mentor who'd taught her everything, not to mention the Lord of the Netherworld.

The corners of the sovereign's eyes tightened, reminding Haven the way a cornered Lorrack might look. "And where is the Shade Queen?"

"Dead," Ravenna answered, not even bothering to look sad. "Killed by the Curse."

"Liar."

Haven whipped around to see Bell approaching Ravenna, his sword held out and ready. His eyes were glossy, wild.

"Liar," he repeated softly. Never had Haven seen him so determined before. So filled with rage. "Liar."

Ravenna's lips were stained black, and they twisted into a

smile. "Hello, boy. You smell as sweet as I remember, like roses and death."

If Haven ran to stop Bell, she risked outing her identity. She glared at Archeron, who should have been reining the prince in—not standing in the distance watching Bell lose control. Surai, too, was submerged too deep in her hatred and grief to act.

Despite the risk, Haven was about to step in when Xandrian slid behind the prince. Gently, Xandrian pressed Bell's sword down until it hung limply at Bell's side. Haven couldn't see what he whispered into Bell's ear, but whatever the Sun Lord said, it woke Bell from his trance.

The moment Bell sheathed his blade, the air seemed to deflate from his body. He retreated back to Surai and Haven's protective shield.

Once again, a thick, suffocating silence draped the room. Right before the sovereign gave her answer, she caught Haven's eye. Let her stare linger.

That couldn't be good.

Then the sovereign turned to Stolas and said, "Stolas Darkshade, son of Empress Darkshade, surviving heir to the lost Seraphian throne, you are now entered into the Praetori Fiernum. But remember, if you lose, you belong to me for a mortal lifetime."

Stolas's blithe grin made it seem he'd never doubted her answer. "As much fun as that would undoubtedly be, Sovereign, I don't expect to lose."

Haven shuddered at the hungry look the sovereign gave Stolas. She could only imagine what the sovereign would do with Stolas if he were under her service.

But Haven's revulsion quickly turned to anxiety. With her out and Stolas in, Bell was more screwed than ever.

Someone called Renfyre's name, and it took Haven a breath to remember she was pretending to be Ren . . . and that she should probably answer.

Haven looked up in time to see the sovereign striding toward her, parting the crowd like a serpent in a den of mice. Her seafoam blue skirt swept behind her, exposing a long stretch of bare leg up to her hip; glorious silver runemarks shimmered down the length of tawny flesh.

"My sovereign," Haven breathed, ducking into a hasty bow. A part of her wanted to stay bowed forever. There was a cunning look in the sovereign's eyes that made Haven uneasy.

"Renfyre of House Volantis, welcome to the tournament."

Haven nearly flinched as the sovereign conjured a buttery yellow coreopsis, the hardy flower of Volantis, and pinned it to the damp breast of her tunic. She forced a stilted smile. The sudden change of heart should have made Haven happy, but she understood there would be a price attached.

One that undoubtedly had to do with the Shade Lord, and one she most assuredly couldn't pay.

THIRTY-FIVE

Haven was tired of bowing. It wasn't the act itself that bothered her so much as the momentary vulnerability that came with it—with her head lowered and eyes on the ground, anyone could strike.

"Enough of that," the sovereign said, waving her hand in the air. "I didn't bring you up here to watch you grovel."

Haven rose to her full height, tucking her hair behind her ear. If she'd had time she would have braided the stiff mess, wild from her ordeal earlier, but the sovereign requested her presence before she could so much as change clothes.

Or find Archeron and give him an earful, which is what she had been on the way to do before Lysander intercepted her.

The royal cupbearer shadowed the sovereign, anticipating her every move. He brought her a cream white velvet cloak when the night air brought a chill; he pulled out her chair, provided cushions for her feet, and even fixed an emerald-encrusted barrette in her hair when it fell slightly out of place.

"Then why did you bring me here?" Haven asked. *Here* was in the rooftop gardens just outside the sovereign's personal chambers. Plumeria and night-blooming jasmine perfumed the air, and songbirds called to one another. It was a world away from the city below, a chaotic mess of soaring cathedrals, arching bridges, and labyrinthine streets.

Amidst the shadows cast by the towering architecture, runelights winked like stars, the overly-large moon skipping spools of silver over the rivers veining the city. Somehow Solethenia was even more magickal at night.

The sovereign beckoned Haven to a cobalt tufted stool. Haven settled on the edge, ready to bolt, if necessary. She'd already marked possible exits at the stairs, a balcony thirty feet below to her left, and a domed glass skylight fifty yards away, on the other side of a meandering pool.

Leaning forward slightly, the sovereign steepled her hands. Cool air blew strands of the sovereign's blonde hair back, making her look practically . . . mortal. Not some flawless, ancient being who controlled the largest empire in the world.

Then again, Haven had been surprised by how *almost* normal the sovereign appeared in the first place. Most Solis were stunning compared to mortals, the same way cut and polished gemstones claimed little resemblance to their raw, uncut versions.

But the sovereign, while maintaining the Solis muscular, tall form, had a mortal's diminished beauty. As if a shadow of imperfection veiled her face.

"Your magick has already broken through my beauty glamour, I see," the sovereign remarked.

Haven blinked, unsure how to answer without offending her.

"I had nine sisters, and every one rivalled Freya in looks and ethereal charm. All of us were raised to catch the eye of the Sun Sovereign, King Haverus III, but I . . . well my father hid me in the back. I was plain, you see, and not very charming, not very nice to look at compared to my sisters."

"So you created a beauty spell to win him over?" Haven asked, trying to recall the little she knew about the Sun Sovereign's husband.

"No," the sovereign said, running a finger over her thinning lips. "While my sisters were relying on their appearance, I honed my cunning. While they learned to accentuate their slim waists and darken their cheeks with magickal spells, I learned things. Precious things. Who hated the sovereign, who wished him harm, who his enemies were."

"And then you presented him with that information?" Haven asked.

The sovereign grinned, a distant look in her eyes. "No, fool, I presented him with his enemies' heads."

Haven flicked up her eyebrows, begrudgingly impressed. "So why go to the trouble to look beautiful now?"

"Because everything is a weapon, Renfyre. Especially beauty. If used correctly, it's the most powerful weapon a female has."

Haven nearly reached up and touched her cheeks before remembering her own glamour. Sweat grooved the lines in her palms. Surai had said the longer she used the identity spell, the weaker it grew. But Haven was hoping that meant she had weeks, not hours, before it started to fade.

"Do you know how many Praetori Fiernum tournaments there have been?" the sovereign asked. She had leaned back in the divan, one arm rested on the gilded back. Her azerite jewelry glittered between her breasts. "Seventy-seven, counting this one. They began with our great and true Goddess, Freya, and, once she ascended to the Nihl, continued in her honor."

265

The sovereign lifted a glass of moonberry liquor to her lips, and Haven did the same, if only to wet her dry mouth. She was relieved as a watered-down version washed over her tongue.

She needed all her senses.

"It is true that the Seraphians have always been invited to the tournament, and once, perhaps, they could have been trusted with that responsibility. But, now . . . well now the Seraphian race is no more."

"But what about Stol—the dark prince?" Haven probed.

An amused smile tugged at Lysander's lips where he stood behind the divan, but the sovereign's eyes darkened at the mention of Stolas.

"I met him once, Stolas Darkshade, when his mother visited our court," the sovereign said. "We were allies once against Morgryth, for all the good it did her. Do you know what I remember? A vain, self-righteous boy who skipped meetings to read poetry, requested the finest of everything, and tormented our Gold Shadows with his dark, devious magick. Still, he might have shown promise, more so than his savage sister . . . but then, well, you surely know the rest."

The sovereign tilted her head and gazed into the night sky, and Haven wondered how deeply she had cared for Stolas's mother.

"That beautiful, arrogant prince died the day his mother did." The sovereign lifted her glass and finished off her moonberry drink. Then she blotted her lips on a napkin. "Do you understand what I'm saying, Renfyre?"

Unfortunately, Haven thought she did, but she needed the sovereign to say it.

"If Stolas Darkshade wins this tournament," the sovereign continued, "the balance of power will be overturned. The mortal realm will be controlled by Ravenna's puppet, the Lord of the

Netherworld. War will be inevitable, your realm's destruction assured."

"What are you asking?"

"I'm asking you to kill the Lord of the Netherworld. That, my dear mortal child, is the price of your entrance into the tournament." She flicked her long fingers toward Haven, muttering strange words under her breath, and a shock of magick scuttled down Haven's spine. "There. I've added an oath of silence spell. Break it, tell anyone about my order, and all the bones in your body will turn into glass that shatters at the lightest of touches."

"If I say no?" Haven asked, hiding every bit of panic she felt.

The sovereign's nostrils flared, the only indication of her surprise. "Refuse my offer, and I send you away from my court . . . but not before wiping your memory of this incident and binding your magick forever."

The world around Haven seemed to spin, a slow shift of the sky, as if it were separating from their world. Peeling away. The breath felt strange in her chest, almost heavy, the blood in her veins sluggish and hot.

There was no turning back from this.

Strangely, her pulse seemed to slow, a calm descending, as if she'd always known deep down her relationship with the Shade Lord had to end.

With all her heart, she ached to refuse the order. To lash out at the sovereign for even suggesting such a thing. In truth, she wanted to plunge a dagger into the sovereign's throat.

Even without Haven's dark magick, she might be able to kill the sovereign with the element of surprise. Lysander didn't pose much of a threat. Her concubines even less.

But it was that rashness that had gotten Bell into this mess in the first place. Biting her cheek, she focused on the pain until the rage ebbed.

Perhaps she could talk the sovereign out of this crazy idea.

But what could she say? *Stolas is my friend? I trust him? He's harmless?*

Besides, none of those things were true now. Maybe they had never been true.

She dragged a hand through her hair, fingers catching in the tangles, ripping out strands. She hardly felt the pain.

There were so many questions she wanted to ask Stolas. If only she could talk to him. And something tugged at her, a memory she couldn't quite grasp. Then there were his own words warning her *not* to trust him.

And, finally, there was the fact that Bell's life hung in the balance. The only way to save him was to enter the tournament.

And yet . . .

"What if I fail?"

The sovereign frowned. "That would be a pity, Renfyre. I suppose I would have to find a way to punish you. Or perhaps that prince who requested your place in the tournament, the one you pretend not to care about."

Haven loosed a breath. *Touch him and die*, she wanted to snarl. Instead, a steely resolve came over her, and she lifted her eyes to meet the sovereign's. "I'll do it."

"Good girl," the sovereign murmured. Her gaze immediately wandered to the pool where her concubines waited, and she waved Haven away without even looking at her.

As Haven crossed the tiled pathway toward the marble stairs, she glanced over her shoulder. The sovereign was already at the pool's curved edge. She'd slipped off her diaphanous dress, and only her azerite jewelry and crown were left. Starlight danced off them like silver sparks.

After that, Haven looked away.

THIRTY-SIX

Haven sat half in half out of the window ledge of her room, her boots propped on the frame. Her apartment was bigger than her room in Penryth. There was a bedroom, a sitting area with golden stools for seating, and a bathroom.

And the view wasn't bad either. Far below her unfurled the student's quarter, Montisol. A collection of colorful pink and green restaurants and bars surrounded the copper roofed university, the amber building nearly as big as Fenwick Castle.

Student apartments rose behind the university, the sandstone structures set along a sluggish, winding river.

Archeron once mentioned Alexandrian University as a place she might attend. She watched the students crisscross the campus, marveling at how different their lives were from hers.

Right about now, a simple, uncomplicated life sounded grand. She thunked her head against the hard plaster and closed her eyes, but when she did, images of the bridge breaking apart flashed behind her eyelids. The sound of the horrible crack as the glass shattered rang through her skull. Her insides hollowed out as she remembered falling. That strange and terrifying rush of plummeting toward a certain death.

And then . . . nothing.

Nothing.

After discussing the incident, she and Surai both agreed that the attack was probably orchestrated by the same person who was after Bell. The dark magick ruled out the Solis, and her assailants didn't have wings, which ruled out the Noctis.

"They could have hidden their wings beneath their cloaks," she muttered to herself. But why do that if she would be dead anyway?

She pulled out the feather from earlier. The shaft was bent from being inside her pocket all night, the soft filaments dulled.

"How do you fit in?" she asked the thing, twirling the hand-length quill between her fingers.

Everything seemed connected somehow to Stolas.

Stolas. Her mentor. Her . . . friend.

The moment she left the sovereign, Haven had wracked her brain for ways around the order. Kill the Lord of the Netherworld.

That in and of itself was an impossible notion—but murdering her friend seemed even more far-fetched.

And, yet, how many times had he tried to warn her what he was?

If you see me again, here or somewhere else, do not trust me.

Haven glared at the feather in her hand. Warm magick pulsed against her palm as she lit the dark quill on fire. Opening her fingers, she watched the wind take the burning plume, watched as it spiraled into obscurity.

The smell of yeasty bread and burnt coffee dragged her out of her dark thoughts. Demelza set the rolls and gilded mug onto the nearest side table. "Stop playing with fire and eat."

Haven wasn't sure which one was more dangerous; playing with fire or trying Demelza's rank-smelling coffee, but all she said was, "Thank you, but . . . I'm not hungry."

The thought of food repulsed Haven. She'd spent the last hour in the window, letting the breeze roll over her, trying not to think about what she had to do. About Stolas and the bridge and the contest and how, somehow, she'd managed to make her and Bell's situation *worse*.

I'm like a curse.

Demelza made a sour face. "Stop feeling sorry for yourself and drink. Do you know how hard it was to find Penrythian coffee in this unholy place?"

If Haven didn't consume *something*, Demelza's mothering would become unbearable. Haven accepted the coffee. The heat from the porcelain mug felt wonderful against her fingertips, but when she put the steaming liquid to her lips . . .

Haven spit the stuff back out. "What's in here? Horse piss?"

Demelza squared her shoulders. "Special northern remedy for exhaustion. Drink. It will fortify you for the coming trials." When Haven hesitated, she said, "*Drink.* Now."

Gagging, Haven forced the bitter stuff down.

The door creaked open and Surai appeared. "I can't find the prince. The maid said he hasn't been in his room since this morning."

Setting aside her foul drink, Haven slid from the window and fastened her cloak to her tunic. There was only one place Bell would be at this time of night. "I know where he is."

Surai crossed to the door. "I'll go with you."

"Surai, you really don't have to," Haven said, sliding on her weapons' belt and buckling it. "I think I'm safe in the palace, at least."

Surai scoffed. "If you believe that, you're a bigger fool than I thought. At this point we have to assume you and Bell aren't safe anywhere."

Haven groaned. A part of her wished Surai didn't know about the bridge attack. Now she would insist on accompanying Haven everywhere when it was Bell who needed protection.

"Fine. Just don't complain when you're stuck in a library in the middle of the night, bored to tears."

Surai arched an eyebrow. "The library?"

"Yes. I'd bet my favorite boots he's there."

"Well it's a good thing I just happen to know where the palace library is located."

"Wherever that boy is, hurry back," Demelza urged, hanging a bubbling cauldron of foul-smelling liquid over the fire. "You need a bath and then sleep."

Surai grinned at Haven, speaking Solissian as she quipped, "Princepella, does she tuck you in and read you bedtime stories too?"

Princepella was *princess* in the common mortal tongue.

Haven made a crude gesture as she brushed past Surai into the hallway.

Bell took a careful sip of the steaming drink the library worker just brought him. He was pretty sure it was a form of coffee—but nuttier and bolder than the coffee in Penryth, less sweet, with a strange floral aroma he was starting to enjoy.

Only in the Sun Court did they serve free beverages while you read. He turned the page of the slim hard-backed book splayed on the table; seven more spread in front of him. Empty cups and runelight votives filled what little space was left on the table.

The faint glow of runes pulsed from the spines of each book. Bell knew at least one of them was a translation rune that allowed him to read Solissian.

After months of speaking with Surai, he was fluent enough to get by, but reading the language was something else entirely. The other runes, he assumed, were protection spells.

These books were priceless, after all. And it seemed no coincidence the limbs of the Tree of Life crisscrossed the library like arms holding a child. Protecting it. He'd noticed the tree seemed to favor certain areas of the palace and city, like the cathedrals, museums, and parks.

Stools scraped across the tile floor as a table of patrons left. The balcony was almost empty. On the other side of the floor-to-ceiling glass window, the crowd from earlier had left, only a few souls left wandering the library.

He pressed the pads of his thumbs into his eyelids. How long had he been here? Hours and hours. It had to be late, but the Solis rarely slept, meaning they stayed up well past midnight. And that energy was infectious.

Only, if even the Solis were leaving now, it had to be really late . . .

The night had cooled to a pleasant temperature, the canvas of stars above providing enough light to read by. The library was set into a mountain behind the palace, the only way to reach it by a long, slender bridge. After what happened to Haven, Bell hadn't relished the idea of crossing it.

But books were worth a little risk, and he needed their calming effect tonight. Craved it. Haven would laugh at what she called his addiction, but books soothed his soul in a way people never could. And not just because he could lose himself between their pages—no, it was so much more than that.

Inside stories was the promise of truth . . . and hope.

Bell was about to close his book and reach for another when he felt the heaviness of someone's gaze.

That someone slid onto the stool to the right. Xandrian picked up Bell's current read and examined it. *Indigenous Plants of Effendier and Their Uses.*

"This looks . . . titillating," Xandrian drawled. "I assumed you would be searching for details on the past trials like all the rest of the contestants here."

Bell glanced over the few remaining patrons once more. Now that Xandrian mentioned it, Bell recognized a few as fellow rivals. The Ashari contenders sat at a table near the iron railing. And a table full of Asgardians were just behind him.

"Perhaps I'm confident enough in my magick that I don't need more information," Bell said, trying to project the confidence he spoke of. Though he wasn't sure why he cared what Xandrian thought.

"So you're reading about the native plant species for entertainment or . . ." His icy blue eyes lit up. "Wait. You aren't planning to poison the other entrants, are you?"

"Would that make me more interesting?"

A dark chuckle. "Infinitely."

Bell suppressed a grin. To anyone on the outside, his choice of reading had to look odd. But the extract from the night rose thorn Renault gifted him was running low, and he needed more now that the Noctis were here.

"I promise to only poison the ones with wings," Bell answered smugly.

He could still hear Ravenna's screech of pain after his dagger—coated with the thorn paste Renault made him—slid over her arm. A mere nick, yet it had nearly incapacitated her.

He was done researching ways to access the Nihl. As much as it killed him to admit, he was barren. It was time he accepted that and found other ways to fight against the Shade Queen's forces.

He might not have magick, but he had something that might aid in the fight against the Noctis.

He was tired of making Haven bear the load of his helplessness. Tired of not being able to help her. Just the memory of her going missing yesterday, the queasy panic that had overtaken him . . .

He was done not fighting back.

Xandrian didn't even bother hiding his amusement as he shuffled around the other books to read their titles. "Let's see what other interests you have, Prince." When he got to *Runespells for Enhancing Elixirs*, he paused, the amusement draining from his face. "Who unlocked this book for you?"

Bell tugged on a wild strand of hair, the curls beyond combing. "No one."

Xandrian's strange blue eyes narrowed. "It contains magick forbidden to mortals. You would have needed a key to unlock it."

"I didn't know . . ." The book had been wrapped in an iron jacket, and that jacket *had* been locked, but the lock opened easily enough—not that he would tell Xandrian any of that.

Bell squirmed beneath the Sun Lord's shrewd gaze. "Don't you have friends to be gallivanting with or something?"

"Gallivanting?" One of his neat blond eyebrows flicked up.

"I just mean, I always see you in a pack." *A pack of adoring males who hang on your every word like you're a god,* he didn't say.

Xandrian ran a thumb over his lips as he glanced at the stars. "You are not the only one who finds solace in this place."

The words hit too close to home. "I'm not—I'm just researching."

A smile played across Xandrian's lips. He loosened the ties of his high collar and leaned back. "I saw how the Shade Queen's daughter affected you earlier. I suppose *she* is the Shade Queen now, if we are to believe the dark witch Morgryth is actually dead." His gaze dug into Bell, searching for what, Bell hadn't a clue. "There's no shame in finding this place peaceful, Prince. I think it's the most beautiful spot in all of Effendier."

Bell had no words as Xandrian slid from his stool. Runelight danced inside the faint outline of his runemarks, the silvery light from the stars darkening his golden skin to pewter. His long pale hair was the color of spider-silk, and it fell over his shoulder as he glanced back at Bell.

"Tomorrow the training begins at dawn. My aunt assigned the greatest lightcaster in court to be your mentor, but he's a notorious hardass. Might want to rest."

Bell watched him go, wondering who Lilith appointed as his mentor. Whoever they were, they'd undoubtedly be her spy.

THIRTY-SEVEN

Haven stood with Surai on the other side of the glass windows watching Bell and Xandrian from the library. Bell's shoulders were tight, his hands gesturing when he spoke—a sign he was agitated or nervous or both.

But he was also smiling rather a lot.

"What could they be talking about?" Haven wondered aloud.

Surai released a low growl. "Nothing good considering it's Xandrian."

Haven raised an eyebrow. "What aren't you telling me about Archeron's cousin?"

"Do you remember the fountain we passed in front of the library?"

Haven nodded. The statue inside the deep pool was a beautiful woman riding a serpentine sea monster, surrounded by selkies, sirens, and other bloodthirsty sea creatures.

"That was Neptannia, youngest and prettiest sister of the

sovereign. Neptannia's particular magick was controlling water and all its inhabitants. It was a rare, highly sought after power, as you can imagine."

"He who controls the sea controls the world," Haven said, still watching Bell.

"Yes. And her sister, Lilith, didn't like that. By then, she was a major contender for the hand of the Sun Sovereign, King Aramos. But Neptannia was beautiful beyond even Solis standards, and it was said she had the skill of a siren to woo any male. Lilith had already secretly killed off her other sisters in various, unprovable schemes, so Neptannia had a curse drawn that whomever spilled her blood would lose their magick."

"That must have pissed Lilith off," Haven mused, remembering how bitter the sovereign had seemed when talking about her gorgeous sisters. Although she conveniently left out the part about murdering them.

"Yes, and when the then sovereign had this library built for Neptannia, Lilith realized she had lost. He loved Neptannia. On the verge of losing everything—the kingdom, the king, everything she had worked for—Lilith came up with a clever plan. She couldn't kill her sister without forfeiting her magick to the curse, but she could make her disappear. You see, Neptannia loved Lilith, despite her cunning ways, and when Lilith invited her younger sister to the cliffs of Sandrian to amend their relationship, Neptannia went."

Haven shuddered imagining Archeron growing up with a mother like Lilith in a court such as this.

"As a sign of her devotion and willingness to foster peace, Lilith gave her sister a necklace, a lovely abalone shell engraved with sacred runes. But the necklace was cursed, and the moment Neptannia placed the chain around her neck and the dark runestone touched her breast, she was thrust into the sea. Forever condemned to the waters as a siren."

"And Xandrian?" Haven asked. "How does he fit into the story?"

Surai's eyes darkened. "Lilith spread rumors that Neptannia fled with a lover. The then sovereign, Aramos, was heartbroken. In his grief, he married Lilith. And then, one day, the sea parted and Neptannia delivered Xandrian to Effendier's shores."

"The sovereign's son?" Haven gasped.

"Lilith hadn't known her sister was pregnant with King Aramos's child, but once Aramos saw the baby and had his runemarks checked for lineage, Lilith couldn't deny Xandrian was his. Solis children bear specific runemarks unique only to their parents."

Haven stared at Xandrian across the balcony. He was perched on his stool, lithe body erect and rigid, jaw tight. Unlike Archeron who always appeared relaxed, almost bored, Xandrian looked ready at any moment to fend off some attack.

Now Haven understood why. Growing up in this Goddess-forsaken court, under the rule of an aunt who betrayed his mother, must have been psychologically draining. "He should hate Lilith."

"He should, but she's kept him close over the years. Molded him as her own. Turned him against his own mother. Now, he's the sovereign's most trusted advisor and spy."

Haven drummed her fingertips silently along the glass, her gaze shifting to Bell. She felt worlds away from her friend, and it wasn't just the thin pane separating them. In truth, it started the day he was taken by the Shade Queen.

Or, perhaps, before. She couldn't tell anymore. Couldn't remember a time when things weren't strained between them.

Bell smiled again—beamed, really—and made some quip that sent the corners of Xandrian's lips curling upward.

"Should I interrupt or . . .?" Haven asked, glancing at her friend.

Surai shook her head. "No. Let him be. We see he's safe, now we should return home."

"Safe? You just said Xandrian is dangerous."

"Some dangers the prince must navigate for himself. Yes?" When Surai saw Haven's expression, she squeezed her arm. "You'll see. He may not hold a sword well, and Goddess knows in a fight with anyone other than a child, he would die horribly, but he's had plenty of time dealing with snakes in his own court to learn how to navigate characters like Xandrian."

True. Cressida and Renk had accosted Bell nearly every day of his young life. Haven remembered when she had accidentally broken Cressida's hand mirror. She and Bell were playing knights and monsters in the king's chamber when Haven's elbow knocked the beautiful azerite mirror to the stone floor. Cressida heard the shattered glass from her bathroom and came running.

Without hesitation, Bell took the blame, knowing Cressida would have him secretly whipped. Bell never told his father about the punishments because that would just make them worse.

It was only now, looking back, that Haven realized just how much Bell protected her from Cressida and Renk and their endless tormenting.

Drawing away from the glass, Haven released a long sigh. "You're probably right."

"I am always right. Now, back to your apartment where Demelza can draw you a milk bath strewn with rose petals and then tuck you in, *Princepella*."

Haven punched Surai's shoulder, drawing a strange look from

a Solis reading on a nearby couch. "Careful or I'll tell her you *like* her coffee."

As they exited the library, Haven flicked a glance at Bell.

Please, Freya, she prayed, *keep him safe.*

THIRTY-EIGHT

Haven awoke in a panic. She was crouched on the floor beside her bed sobbing. Crying so hard her chest ached and she couldn't breathe. Her eyelids were puffy, cheeks slick, and sweat pasted her hair in strips across her forehead.

What had she been dreaming about? Memories and emotions collided as she tried to fit the jagged pieces together, but the remnants of her nightmare lodged deep in her psyche, just beyond her reach.

Breathe in, breathe out. You're okay.

But the words rang hollow when she glanced down and a flash of light caught her eye. A dagger—she was clenching the dagger she kept banded to her thigh at night. A clammy layer of sweat coated the handle, and her fingers had been squeezing the weapon for so long that they were achy and stiff.

She exhaled, blowing wisps of her rose-gold hair back, then dropped the dagger on the wooden nightstand with a clatter and stood.

Across the room, Haven met Demelza's stare. Demelza watched Haven as she padded across the floor, poured water from a clay pitcher into a cup, and downed it in one gulp.

A paring knife was clutched between Demelza's thick fingers.

If you see me trying to leave my room with a weapon, stab a sword through my heart. Demelza didn't have a sword tonight, so she chose to improvise. Good for her.

Demelza nodded to Haven and slid the weapon back under her pillow.

Goddess Above, is this my life now? Waiting for my lady's maid to murder me before I can kill my friends?

No, her dark magick was bound, evidenced by the searing fire radiating from her rune cuts. Her friends were safe. And this nightmare seemed different than the ones before.

Haven waited until Demelza's soft snores filled the room before grabbing her cloak and slipping out.

A quick check ensured Bell was all right. All it took was a simple sleeping runespell to incapacitate the two guards who stood outside his room, and she made a mental note to discuss that with the king in the morning—before she remembered she was Renfyre of House Volantis, not Haven Ashwood, Companion Guard to the prince.

With Bell's safety confirmed, Haven left the mortal apartments. A soft breeze carried the briny aroma of the sea mixed with the cloying perfume of jasmine and honeysuckle and the tang of baking bread.

Her stomach rumbled. Somewhere in the palace, bakers were already working to put together breakfast.

She nearly tripped over something—a thick arm of the Tree of Life. Several had crawled over the side of the balcony overnight and encircled the lower half of the mortal apartments. One particularly massive limb snaked up the wall toward her apartment window.

Nope—she would never, ever get used to a sentient, migrating tree.

Runelit lamps vined with jasmine and clematis spilled light into the courtyard. A few Solis were already awake—or had never fallen asleep—and they lounged on soft couches probably more comfortable than her bed in Penryth.

No one paid her a glance, which suited her just fine.

Her nightmare was muddled, jarring details slipping in and out of her memory. Screams. People fleeing. A thousand wings beating the sky. Streets running dark with blood.

As if the nightmare were replaying itself, she saw the ancient, horned knife inside her hand.

Saw the terrifying eye watching her.

It blinked. Whispering in the primordial language of evil.

She watched herself bring the knife down, powerless to stop from plunging it into an armored chest—but whose?

Bell's? No, whoever wore the armor was large, imposing. The nightmare slipped in and out of her vision and she grasped desperately at it. Scales of sleek black armor curved and tapered to a lithe waist. Bits of blood sprinkled the armor, some already dry, others still wet and gleaming.

There had been some type of battle, and now . . .

She blinked, focusing on the rest of the nightmare.

Wings—beautiful wings of onyx imbued with indigo and purple.

No.

Stolas. She couldn't see his face, but his voice whispered, "Do it, Beastie. If you ever cared about me, do it."

And then she plunged the wicked blade into his chest. Felt the armor give way like paper, felt the blade pierce flesh and bone. Felt his body sag against hers . . .

No.

She knew then . . . knew she couldn't kill him. It would destroy her.

A wild thought came, impulsive and reckless. She could go to him, find a way around the oath of silence. If anyone could break it, Stolas could. Then she would tell him. Would explain the horrible circumstances.

Stolas would know what to do.

The idea had barely appeared and she was sprinting toward the highest part of the palace where the Noctis stayed. They would have defenses, no doubt. But if she could sneak through them, if she could somehow reach Stolas . . .

The aviary would have the best view into the Noctis courtyard. Getting to the aviary required climbing several stories of drainage pipes up the royal apartments where most of the Sun Court slept.

She was surprised when she passed the window second from the top and discovered runelights still flickering from the dim apartment.

Her surprise grew as she recognized the occupant inside: Xandrian. Hunched over a desk facing the window, his face illuminated by the runecandles on the desk, all he had to do was look up and he would spot her.

Luckily, he was immersed in the papers and books in front of him, and she could study him without being noticed.

What interested him in those papers?

Her focus went to the fleshmarks dancing over his bare chest, and something caught her eye. Not a fleshmark—but a tattoo. From here, it was hard to make out all the details, but the marking looked like a serpent wrapped in battle with flames.

Deciding not to push her luck, she quietly pressed on before he could notice her spying. Thirty minutes later, she was perched on the glass rooftop over the aviary. Shadows limned the courtyard below where the Noctis were housed. Soldiers swarmed the area. They trained in darkness, making the shadows writhe like a living, breathing creature.

Twenty-foot walls framed the courtyard, gremwyrs posted atop the towers. Ravens lined the ramparts and rooftops, barely visible in the half-dark.

Was one of them Ravius?

She glanced back down at the Noctis, assuming what she witnessed was a simple training exercise for the soldiers . . . until she noticed how all the Noctis converged around one figure.

Whoever it was, they were creating the perfect distraction. Where would Ravenna keep Stolas? Assuming he was still a prisoner. She shifted on her feet, thighs aching from crouching low. An owl hooted in the aviary below and nearly sent her out of her skin.

Where could she enter? She had hoped the Noctis would be resting, but of course they were nocturnal creatures, at their best in the watery light of the moon.

Squinting, she searched the perimeter for a weak spot. But there were too many Shadowlings roaming about to slip in unnoticed anywhere.

Then there was that pesky glimmer in the air that hinted at a type of shield.

Runes. She kneaded her knuckles into her temples. *Soulwalking it is.*

Since her disastrous first attempt, Haven had practiced soulwalking short distances around Penryth, but that was with the aid of her dark magick.

Without it . . . she wasn't sure how long she could soulwalk, or how drained she would be afterwards.

Those were risks she had to take if it meant talking to Stolas.

THIRTY-NINE

Haven closed her eyes and counted backwards. Splitting from her body was always a bit jarring. Like falling out of your bed in the middle of the night and waking up right as you slammed into the floor. The air felt different, *colder*, a deep, penetrating chill. And it was hard getting used to feeling so insubstantial you might float away.

As soon as she fully parted from her flesh, she focused on the courtyard, her focus riveted to a section of the wall. Thinking of something else, anything else, might actually take her there. She learned that the hard way after her thoughts wandered to Renk and then she joined him in his bathroom as he *bathed*.

Below her, a war cry emerged from the Noctis soldiers as a training maneuver became particularly violent. Dark armor clanged so hard together she thought for sure the material would shatter. Wings flapped and teeth gnashed and magick erupted in chaotic bursts.

It was the sound nightmares were made from.

As much as she hated the idea of joining that writhing mass of creatures, she talked herself into it. She would be invisible, after all.

Focusing on a spot near a tower away from the training, she let her mind drift.

Once she was safely past the shield and inside the fenced yard, she let her focus shift to Stolas. She imagined his dark humor, the way his eyes turned silver the few rare times he wasn't angry, the way he scolded her for reading to him.

The wry half-smile that lit up his face right before he said something particularly snarky.

A heartbeat later, and she was somewhere else.

But instead of soulwalking inside the Noctis castle, her incorporeal form was thrust into the training soldiers. Noctis snarled and screeched around her; weapons clanged and dark magick sizzled the air. The demonic clamor was dizzying, the feel of their skeletal wings battering her soul like being shaken in a bag of stones.

And their dark magick—it scraped against her form, clawing, looking for a way in as her own bound dark magick welcomed it.

A gap appeared between two Noctis female soldiers and Haven darted for the empty space. She was about to say the words to return to her body when the cluster of Noctis surged backward, thrown by a wave of bright blue magick. As the space in the center cleared, Haven finally had a look at the figure the soldiers were fighting.

Stolas's wings flared out behind him as he drew to his full height. They were bigger than she remembered, massive in size and scale. Moonlight rippled over his sleek onyx feathers, each one longer than her arm and tinged indigo.

His face though . . . Goddess Above. There was something

almost animalistic in his fierce expression, lips bared and incisors catching the meager light. He wore a silver tunic and charcoal leather pants, no armor—as if a horde of Netherworld soldiers wasn't even a threat.

And his horns—the same jewelry adorned them, delicate silver capping the tips and spiraling down to cover a third of the shaft. Bluish fingers of light coiled around the metal, the same color as the runes covering the flesh of many of the Noctis. The ones with feathered wings.

The Seraphians. His people.

Could that similarity be important? Noctis weren't known to have runemarks, and Stolas had never worn adornments on his horns before.

Stolas's wings suddenly flared, sending the Noctis to their knees. Every single one. Their heads bowed. Leathery wings tucked into their backs in supplication. Even the Shadowlings scampering around the courtyard sank low in his presence.

Only Haven still stood. If not for her shock, she would have fled already.

But a terrible sickness glued her to the spot as she stared at Stolas. This wasn't a tortured prisoner. This was a vengeful king ready to take back his homeland. A dark, *powerful* king preparing to win a magickal trial—or wage all-out war.

Betrayal lanced through her. Betrayal and rage.

The soldiers bowed even lower, a few whining like dogs. Laughter echoed off the courtyard walls as Ravenna strode across the training ground and joined Stolas. Two beautiful, primordial monsters.

One with wings as soft as clouds; one with wings made of talons and bone.

And both primed for bloodshed.

Haven waited for Stolas to flinch in her presence. For a sign that he detested her, that she repulsed him.

That he'd somehow managed to hide a shred of his humanity from her.

Nothing—there was nothing in his dead, vacant expression except blind devotion. And then, horrifyingly slow, his attention drifted to where she stood vulnerable and perhaps . . . perhaps not as invisible as she imagined.

His eyes were predatory, twin pools of black ink. The only thing that distinguished his pupil was a ring of bright yellow—

Disgust propelled Haven back to her body. She entered violently like crashing into a coffin too small for her body. As soon as her spirit fully merged with her mortal flesh, she slumped over, struggling to breathe. Her heart slammed against her chest so hard she thought her ribs would crack. The fading stars above became a whirlpool of light.

She couldn't get his all-black eyes out of her head. The wild savagery inside them.

She was going to puke.

It was all she could do to roll on her side, glass painfully cool against her cheek, before the dry heaves started.

Thankfully her belly was empty, and nothing but saliva passed through her lips.

By the time the first slivers of gold pierced the sky and fingers of smoke spread over the wakening city, she had enough energy to climb down the metal rose trellis and drag herself back to the mortal apartments.

Damn you, Stolas. Damn you to the Netherworld.

There was no denying it now—Stolas had turned. Maybe it was the promise of his homeland or maybe Ravenna had finally, truly broken him.

Her hands ached as she dug her nails into her palms. He held out for so long—longer than any man ever could. He fought against Ravenna, he risked his life to help break the Curse, and he never asked for much in return except to keep his sister safe.

Her throat ached as she jogged down the seemingly never-ending stairs, in a rush to make it to the first practice in time. She mashed her thumbs into her eyelids, surprised by the wetness.

Stop being weak, Ashwood. That side of him, the prince who clung to humanity, even if he didn't admit it—that side is gone.

From this point on he was her enemy. Killing him would be a kindness, but she didn't feel kind right now. Her anguish had bled away to a darker, more jagged emotion. Rage.

A blinding rage that she had let him in.

Rage that she had cared about him.

Rage that, in the end, he had given up on himself.

Killing the Lord of the Netherworld was her destiny—and she hated him for it.

FORTY

The first training session had already started when Haven and Surai entered the arena.

Haven paused to take in the contestants and their training partners. They were grouped by nation, Surai explained, pointing out the Ashari and Asgardians spread across the lawn near an outcropping of snow-white cherry blossom trees. The two nations had been allies off and on over the centuries, she said, and they chatted in-between maneuvers, unlike the wild tribes from the collection of islands that made up Freya's Spear.

The tribes were grouped alone near the balcony railing—to keep them from starting fights, Surai commented, nose curled in disgust as she watched them.

"See, they fight even amongst themselves," she remarked as a skirmish broke out between two men from neighboring islands.

Surai halted as they passed a group of female contestants, a shadow passing over her face.

Haven didn't need Surai to explain this was the Morgani nation. The all-female group had sun-bleached hair braided intricately over their skulls, colored bands of gold and black and red over their eyes, and tall, athletic figures.

One particular warrior was almost the mirror image of Rook, only a few inches shorter with a rounder face. Surai stiffened beside Haven.

"That's Ember," Surai said in a choked voice. "Rook's younger sister."

Haven wanted to reach out and comfort her friend, but she remembered the Morgani's views on appearing weak and decided against it.

For her part, Surai appeared completely unfazed as she nodded to Ember.

Avaline Kallor stood quietly with a few other halflings from Lorwynfell. Haven tried not to stare at the beautiful half mortal half Noctis queen. Even though Avaline didn't know who Haven was, Haven still felt conspicuous. And when she passed, she averted the former Skeleton Queen's gaze.

The mortals were grouped near the three competitors from the Isle of Mist. Pale skinned and dark haired, with ancient symbols tattooed over every inch of their flesh, they looked straight out of one of Bell's books.

Haven joined Bell, who was dressed in a bone-white linen outfit that either looked ridiculous or amazing—she hadn't decided yet.

"Great morning for some swordplay," she remarked.

"Right," he quipped. "It's hot as the Netherworld, I've just learned my pants are see-through in the right light, and my stomach is on fire after drinking something Demelza brought to my room."

Haven chuckled. "I could have sworn I warned you not to

drink anything she makes."

Bell blinked against the angry sun, gagging in memory. "That stuff could kill a lorrack."

Voices drew Haven's stare to a marble mezzanine. All the foreign nations were in attendance. Most of the audience wore bored expressions as they waved silk fans over their faces. A few equally bored looking pages held umbrellas over their patrons.

Cressida and King Horace sat near the front, sipping fizzy flutes of hyacinth wine and nibbling small pink fruits. Eleeza and her father were there too, the side tables between their chairs filled with pastries.

Haven's stomach growled, and she cursed herself for missing breakfast.

The sovereign lounged beneath a shaded gold pavilion. It was one among many erected to house the Sun Court. Haven eyed the shade with jealousy; the sun had barely risen but already the air was thick and balmy, the cobblestones radiating heat.

The Sun Sovereign laughed at something Lysander said, and the court laughed with her. Even her poor concubines, who were gathered around her flowery throne, giggled, their chains tinkled in the morning air.

Lysander rose from his knees by the sovereign and announced the formal choosing of the finalists' mentors. Surai had explained last night that most finalists brought their own mentors to guide them during the trials, usually seasoned lightcasters who had been around long enough to witness a few tournaments themselves.

Haven bristled as Archeron left his place by the king's side and sauntered to stand by Bell. His long honey-gold hair was unkempt, as if he'd just woken up, his hard jaw lined with stubble. He didn't even glance at Bell as he leaned against a column and shut his eyes.

Even from here, she could smell the sickly-sweet tang of moonberry wine radiating from his person.

She glared at him until one emerald-green eye slid open.

Mess this up, her face said, *and I'll kill you myself.*

He scowled back at her, his anger so potent she could almost touch it boiling in the air between them.

Fighting the urge to roll her eyes, she looked away. He could stay mad if it made him feel better. He could drink himself stupid and stay perpetually hungover for all she cared. But his anger was pointless.

For better or worse, she was here and there was no turning back.

Lysander strolled through the courtyard, making the rounds from contestant to contestant. Each presented their mentor. Lysander looked to the sovereign who either nodded or shook her head at the choice.

So far, she had yet to deny a chosen mentor.

When Lysander reached Archeron and Bell, his eyes narrowed, and he let his disapproving gaze travel up and down Archeron before looking to the sovereign.

Without hesitation, she shook her head.

"I reject the mentor nomination from House Boteler and suggest a more fitting alternative," Lilith said. "My nephew, Xandrian, will take Archeron's place as Prince Bellamy's mentor."

King Horace slammed down his flute hard enough that if the glass had been ordinary blown glass, it would have shattered. But he didn't dare object. Not outwardly, at least.

Archeron refused to budge. "I know the prince," he said, his voice ringing across the open yard. His eyes were open and alert now, his arms no longer crossed over his chest but held out and ready. "I can be of greater help to him than my cousin who knows nothing of this mortal's weaknesses."

Xandrian strode from one of the court pavilions, hands in his pockets. Unlike Archeron, he was incredibly put together, every single blond hair in place, jaw newly shaved. He looked way too beautiful for this early in the morning.

"Aren't mortals weak in all areas of magick?" Xandrian countered, drawing chuckles from the audience.

"Being a mentor is beneath you, Xandrian," Archeron insisted, the muscles beneath his jaw twitching.

Haven glanced at the king, surprised to see his lips moving. Was he ordering Archeron to resist, despite the danger ignoring the sovereign's orders posed?

Either way, Archeron risked everything by arguing.

"Ah, perhaps the sovereign didn't make herself clear." Xandrian smiled, a glorious, cruel grin that didn't reach his eyes. "This isn't a choice, Halfbane. It's an order from your *queen*."

Queen, not mother.

Haven's heart sank as she watched Archeron reach for his sword. A murmur stirred the crowd. Across the courtyard, the sovereign went completely still, a flicker of curiosity brightening her face.

If Haven didn't intervene somehow this would turn bad, fast. She stepped forward. "I'll take him as my mentor."

Surai shot Haven a surprised look. They had already agreed Surai would be her mentor. But Surai's shock turned to understanding.

"There," Xandrian said, gesturing to Haven. "The House Volantis girl has taken a liking to you. Try not to get too attached, though. I'll wager fifty runestones your mortal doesn't even make it through the first trial."

For the first time since he'd arrived, Archeron grinned. "I'll take that bet." A new purpose flashed inside his eyes as he crossed to stand by her.

She might have said something to him, like *you're an idiot*, or *you're welcome*, when the sound of fluttering above caught her attention. Her breath hitched as she spotted the shadows darting across the cobblestones.

For a wild heartbeat, she thought the city was under attack. She took in the first Noctis streaking through the air and immediately went to create a shield to protect Bell and the others . . .

But, no, the Noctis were competitors too, even if they were unwanted. Her shoulders relaxed and she exhaled. The ground shook as the dark soldiers landed in soft thuds on the upper level courtyard just above theirs.

Ravenna and Stolas were the last to arrive.

The sovereign didn't even bother contesting Stolas's choice of mentor—Ravenna. The sovereign probably thought his decision didn't matter since Haven was supposed to kill him during the first trial.

Once Ravenna was appointed without incident, Lysander took his place at the sovereign's feet. If he were a dog his tail would be wagging.

There was something almost sad about the way he stared up at Lilith. The way he carefully smoothed out the train of her slippery golden dress when she stood, his eyes glossy with adoration.

The sovereign swept her gaze over the finalists. Did she linger over Archeron for a moment, or was that just Haven's imagination? It was hard to tell.

When her eyes fell over Stolas, she smiled, already so sure that he wouldn't be a threat. Then she threaded her long fingers together and said, "The Praetori Fiernum has been held every century for over seven thousand years. Only the strongest, brightest runecaster will ascend to the throne of the Nine. You have seven days before the first trial to train. May the fires of the

Nihl give you strength, and Freya's bounty give you courage."

With the speech over, the training began. An arena was set up on a huge floating disc over the city. Bridges connected to the arena from three different access points, and finalists began walking toward the disc.

Haven looked to Archeron. Their partnership wasn't ideal, but surely he could work through his anger to help her. Especially knowing what was at stake.

Holding out a hand, she said, "Ready to help me hone my magick, Sun Lord?"

His lips tugged into a wicked grin and then, without a word, he turned on his heels and began to leave.

Without thinking, she grabbed his arm, drawing a few curious glances from the other contestants. He was supposed to be a stranger and she a mortal who cowered beneath his beauty and power.

Screw that.

Angry heat burned her cheeks. "What is your deal?"

"Deal?" His eyes were hard as he glanced to her hand on his wrist and then back to her face. "No deal. I'm just feeling particularly parched."

"You're leaving me to train alone so you can find a *bar*?" Her incredulity spiked her voice a few octaves.

"Oh, you'll do fine on your own. Besides, you don't need me. You never listened to me before so why would you bother now?"

Fury made her speechless.

Walking backwards, he held her outraged stare. "You made this mess, you can clean it up yourself."

FORTY-ONE

Everyone watched Archeron as he strode away, including Avaline. The Skeleton Queen's gaze hardened as she looked at Haven, really looked at her, for the first time since she entered the courtyard.

"I can help you train," Surai said, rushing to her side.

Haven nodded, too furious to even mention Archeron's name. If she didn't need to feed Bell magick, she would have already chased Archeron down and kicked his ass.

Surai bit her lip, staring into the crowd where Archeron disappeared. "He'll come around. Give him time."

"It's fine. I don't need him anyway."

I don't need him.

She repeated the statement as she followed the others across a swaying wooden bridge to the floating disc. The arena was huge, a circular training ground with fields, forests, ponds, and sand pits. Xandrian led Bell to a marshy area where dark shapes flickered beneath the water.

Haven found a copse of trees near Bell and immediately started channeling her magick through his diverting runestone necklace. When needed, she sent magick surging down his blade. Erected a shield of water. She even lifted a stone and used it to crush one of the marshland Shadowlings that wrapped around his leg and tried to drag him under.

And all the while, she had to put on the appearance of training with Surai.

Haven sent Bell yet another blast of fiery magick. He let it thread between his fingertips, unapologetically showing off before sending the sphere streaking toward a Shadowling. But the Sun Lord just stood there watching Bell, one eyebrow arched, a look of supreme boredom on Xandrian's beautiful visage.

Occasionally Xandrian would send light magick dancing around Bell's head, but mainly he just watched him.

Watched him, for Runes sake.

Face still. Hardly blinking. As if trying to figure something out.

He knows.

As soon as the thought surfaced, Bell shoved it down. *Stay focused.*

It was hard enough to signal Haven for magick—a light tap between his pointer finger and thumb—without alerting Xandrian. Harder still, to coordinate the movement that followed afterwards.

Finally, tired of Xandrian's intense stare, Bell slogged out of the marsh, mud weighing down his boots, and faced the Sun Lord.

"Are you just going to watch me train?"

The Sun Lord shrugged, picking at some invisible speck of dust on his open tunic. "You seem to be doing just fine on your own."

"Then what's the point of having a mentor if you don't teach me anything?"

"Oh, did I not explain how this works to you?" Xandrian sank his hands into his pockets. "The sovereign wants me to spy on you, look for anything she can use against you. Didn't you know?"

His candor made Bell nearly lose his footing in the mud. "I thought the whole point of being a spy was keeping it a secret."

"This line of conversation bores me. Can you just go back to fighting the vile little creatures, and I'll go back to not caring?"

Bell marched over to the pack of weapons they were each handed upon entering the arena. He grabbed for the closest blade—a huge long sword. Using two hands to steady the weapon, Bell advanced on Xandrian.

Xandrian arched a pale eyebrow. "Now what are you going to do with that overly large thing, Prince?"

The sword wobbled in his hands. A burst of heat made him flinch as Haven sent fire whooshing down its beveled edge.

Not really what he was going for—he was as likely to burn himself as he was Xandrian—but he'd make it work.

"That's your first problem, Prince," the Sun Lord drawled, not even bothering to look at the sword. "You think bigger and flashier means better. But it's not the size that matters, it's how you use the blade."

The sword wavered in Bell's hands. Xandrian had an annoying way of making him feel small, incompetent.

"Fine," Bell muttered, dropping the long sword in the grass. "We'll just sit here and watch the clouds pass by. Oh, wait. The land of the never-ending sun doesn't have any."

When Bell turned back around, Xandrian was close enough

to touch. Bell stared at the double-bladed dagger in Xandrian's hand as his heart jolted.

"Here," Xandrian said, flipping the weapon so the two blades pointed away from Bell. "Try this. I think you'll enjoy this weapon much more than that barbaric thing."

He was right. The dagger's weight felt good in Bell's palm. His fingers nimble as they flexed around the jade handle in the middle. The blades curved out on either side.

Xandrian came up beside Bell and positioned his arm at an angle. His fingers were warm against Bell's flesh. "Like so. Keep your arm loose, elbow slightly bent. The trick is to slash like so around the belly." He made back and forth motions on an imaginary opponent. "After you master that, we can work on throwing."

"Will I have to fight other finalists in the tournament?" Haven came to mind. No way in the Netherworld would he fight her.

Xandrian lifted his shoulders in a cryptic shrug. "It's been known to happen. When you step through the magick portal and enter the tournament, there are no rules except survive. Although typically the other contestants are the least of your worries."

Bell tried to give the dagger back, but Xandrian shook his head. "Keep it. Get used to the weight. Practice wielding it in your spare time."

"Thanks." Bell accepted the twin sheaths from Xandrian. When both ends of the blade were covered, he ran a thumb over the stargazer lilies engraved across the ivory leather. "My father said knives are for cowards and women."

"First, this isn't a *knife*. It's a Hadrassian blade crafted from the finest metalsmiths in all the realm." Bell picked up sage, honey, and nectarine scents as Xandrian leaned in close. "Second, your father sounds like he lacks an imagination, among various other things. If he could see what I do with my blade . . ."

Bell retreated a step, his head spinning and skin flush. Did Xandrian know how entrancing his voice was, how sensual his words sounded?

Of course he did. That was the point. Overwhelm Bell with charm and beauty until Bell made a mistake. Revealed his secrets.

And, Goddess knew, he had *way* too many of those.

After that, Bell kept a safe distance from the Sun Lord.

FORTY-TWO

Every part of Haven was tired, nothing more so than her mind. Something about having to perform her own magick while coordinating Bell's all while their secret loomed over them both like a dark, damning shadow . . .

Two days. She and Bell had only been training two days and already she wanted to quit.

She sagged against the stone wall near her apartment. Demelza would be waiting with a hot bath and her horrible coffee, which was almost starting to grow on Haven. Almost.

How she would love to sink into that delicious warmth. Demelza would brush her hair and prattle over Haven.

But she knew once she entered her apartment and let the shields that had been keeping her safe down, they would be so much harder to erect again. And tonight was a dinner with the other finalists and the sovereign.

Haven needed every shred of her wits about her.

Instead of heading to her room, she switched directions and slipped down a narrow flight of stairs. Bell's apartment was on the fourth floor overlooking the west side of Effendier. His room had a gorgeous view of the Cliffs of Sandrian, a fact she was only a little jealous about.

As soon as his door swung open, she spotted a knife flying at her face. She cursed as she ducked low, the blade sinking into the wall behind her with a soft thud. The *marble* wall.

She whipped to face the intruder only to see Bell smiling sheepishly at her. "Sorry. But, hey, that's the first time the weapon actually stuck in the wall."

Her gaze went to the figure sitting beside Bell on a purple and gold brocade stool. Ashen-white hair like dirty snow was tangled into a crown of braids. Silver-blue eyes blinked from a heart-shaped face, widened to look young and innocent. Her wings were hidden—probably by magick—and she was dressed in one of Bell's outfits, a pair of baby blue pants and a white tunic with a high, ruffled collar.

"Nasira," Haven growled. "What are you doing here?"

"She was bored," Bell said conversationally, as if having the heir to the Noctis throne in his room was no big deal. When he saw the fury in her eyes, he amended, "No one saw her come in my window. I promise."

Haven retrieved the throwing knife from the wall, slammed the door shut, and tossed the light weapon in her hand. It was Hadrassian steel, beautifully made, the design's simplicity hiding its worth.

Hadrassian steel came from a hidden forge in the Ashari mountains, and it was made for one purpose: holding copious amounts of powerful magick. It was said the forge only produced weapons for royalty, and they were as rare as they were expensive.

More throwing knives were spread over a velvet red cloth beside a stunning jade-handled, doubled-edged dagger Haven would kill for.

"Who gave you those?" she demanded, ignoring Nasira's petulant frown. Veserackian throwing knives that could pierce stone were also incredibly rare and imbued with strong magick.

Somehow, in one day, Bell had stumbled upon a trove of weapons kings and queens would kill for.

"Xandrian." Bell tugged at his collar before opening the first two buttons. "The first he gave to me in the arena."

Haven remembered Bell wielding the impressive blade after failing to impress Xandrian with the long sword provided.

A good choice, she admitted begrudgingly.

Bell's slight figure struggled with the heavy swords the king's soldiers used, but his father had never allowed him to train with anything lighter.

She'd once snuck him a rapier to use in practice. When the king found out he had the weapon smashed—but not before he had a soldier lash Bell's delicate fingers with the slender blade as a reminder.

"And the others?" she asked.

"Sent over from Xandrian a few hours ago," Bell admitted, twirling one between his slender fingers.

Haven sighed. "You can keep the double-bladed beauty, but the others you have to send back."

"Why?"

"Think about it. If you wanted to know what someone was up to, what would you do? Send them a runespelled set of weapons that can track their movement? Maybe even let him see and hear what you do?"

Frowning, Bell looked down at the blade in his hand and then set it carefully with the others.

"Runes. I feel like an idiot."

Nasira circled the set of daggers like a dangerous animal she'd just discovered in their midst. Placing a hand over the gift, she chanted in an ancient language, the serpentine words whispering through the room.

After a minute, a greenish smoke surged from the knives and into her open palm.

She flashed her fanged teeth. "No more mirror spell. Thanks to me, our fun doesn't have to stop after all."

Nasira glared at Haven as if she'd been trying to ruin their party. Then she reached over, plucked a throwing blade from the pile, and flicked the weapon at Haven's head.

Before Haven could duck, the blade arrowed past her cheek, so close a strand of hair hanging by her face was severed.

Haven glared at Nasira, too angry to even know how to respond. "You missed, Noctis."

"No." Nasira thunked a bare foot on the table and leaned back, a glib smile brightening her face. "I never miss."

She was right; behind Haven, the knife had pinned a crawler to the door.

Right at that moment, Surai decided to enter the room. Her gaze narrowed on Nasira, one hand going to the katana at her waist. "What's *she* doing here?"

"Taking care of the pest problem," Nasira answered matter-of-factly. "I have no idea why they call this place the jewel of Solissia. The sun is an angry devil, the air is sopping wet, and the only thing to eat are cows and lizards. At least the light magick is plentiful."

Surai and Haven shared a look. She was hoping Nasira didn't know her brother was here, but how could she not?

"So they're safe to use now?" Bell asked, glancing at the knives. For once in his life, he actually looked interested in a weapon.

"Yes," said Nasira, hitting another crawler near the window. "No more watching us through his magickal mirror."

Alarm pulsed through Haven. "What if he saw Nasira?"

"Nethergates, you're such a killjoy," Nasira snarled. "My wings are hidden and I'm dressed like a common peasant." Bell cut his eyes at Nasira, obviously not enjoying the dig at his clothes. "And I'm supposed to be dead. No Solis in the world is *that* clever."

If they weren't discussing Xandrian, she would have agreed. But that gave her an idea . . .

"What if we used the other weapon, the ornate one, to spy on him? Is there a spell we can use to do that?"

Surai crossed the creamy-white tile floor and examined the dagger while Nasira clapped her hands together.

"Ooh, this is fun," Nasira said. "I know of a runespell we can use to inflict the same death last made by this blade on this too-clever Sun Lord. Poetic, bloody justice."

Haven shook her head. "I was thinking subtler magick to glean any information we can about the Sun Lord—not murder him. Killing isn't the answer to everything, Nasira."

Nasira tugged her lips into a pout. "Isn't it?"

Surai dropped to her knees beside the weapon, her hands hovering over the sleek dagger. "What if, instead of turning the death back on Xandrian, we use a spell to see who he last killed with the dagger?"

Nasira made a disappointed noise in the back of her throat before picking up the dagger. She placed it in the middle of the low coffee table and sent the blade spinning in a circle as she studied it. Then she dragged her long, curved nails around the moving blade, carving strange runes into the oak table.

Haven tried not to focus on the ease in which her talons burrowed through the varnished wood. Tried not to remember those claws penetrating her soft mortal flesh when they carved her runes and bound her dark magick.

When the final symbol was drawn, the mark flared to life, ghostly blue scribbles dancing around the weapon and casting blue light inside the steel.

Just as the mirror spell had been drawn from the blade, a memory was conjured. It started as dark smoke trickling from the edge and quickly filled the room. The far wall became an alleyway somewhere in what Haven assumed was the city below.

Her breath caught. The scene so vibrant, so real, she could smell the stench of cheap tavern beer wafting down the brick street, and hear the clop of horses' hooves in the distance.

Five figures coalesced from the smoke, pouring from both ends of the alleyway. Five Gold Shadows in their crisp purple and gold uniforms.

They closed in on something—no, someone.

A cloaked, hidden figure.

"You're trapped, heretic," the biggest Gold Shadow barked, the voice so real Haven actually looked to the door thinking someone had entered.

A younger Gold Shadow stepped closer. "Wait, I recognize him."

Fear permeated his voice.

The cloaked figure sighed and flipped back his hood, revealing his face. The smoky visage was highly detailed, right down to his pale blue eyes and a slight scar between his eyebrows.

Xandrian shook his head. "I wish you hadn't recognized me."

"Xandrian?" the big Gold Shadow said, his voice losing some of its authority. "But . . . how? Why?"

"Sorry, truly." He twirled his hand in the air. Ropes of water shot through the night, conjured from buckets and wells, the canals wending through the city, everywhere.

Before the others made a sound, the watery ties were wrapped around their necks, holding them in place. They were completely immobile, gagged and waiting at Xandrian's mercy.

They didn't have to wait long. With a quiet, horrible efficiency, the Sun Lord dispatched the Gold Shadows one by one, his gorgeous knife making quick work of them.

It all happened in less than a second.

When the final throat had been cut, the water ropes burst, dropping the men to the street and forming puddles of water around their inert bodies. It didn't take long for the water to turn red with blood.

The vision cut off abruptly, leaving Haven with more questions than answers and a cold pit in her gut.

Xandrian was terrifying, and it was obvious he wasn't working for the sovereign. But then who? Could it be the same person who wanted Bell dead?

One look at Bell, his normally dark skin drained of color and shallow breaths, confirmed he felt exactly the same way.

FORTY-THREE

Haven rushed through the corridor to her room, her hair—still wet from her bath—speckling the golden carpet runner with water.

Water. She would never look at it quite the same. Surai said Xandrian's skills with water weren't known, so he must have been hiding them. But to what end?

The sudden patter of nimble footfalls from behind made her whip around, her palm tingling with the promise of light magick.

Lysander stood a few feet away, the citrus and marine cologne he wore filling the narrow space. "Good day, Renfyre. Is there a place we can talk privately?"

Whatever he wanted, it was undoubtedly at the behest of the sovereign. Rolling her shoulders, she led him to her apartment. Demelza was busy sweeping the floor and humming loud enough that the entire courtyard below could probably hear her.

Waving off Demelza's instant coddling, Haven dispatched her

lady's maid to gather more supplies for her horrible coffee.

Once they were alone, and Lysander had done a thorough sweep of the rooms to check, she settled on the arm of the couch.

"The sovereign wants to give you this, Renfyre." He procured a tiny crystal vial a third full of an inky liquid. The stuff shimmered as if alive. A blown glass scorpion the same black color as the liquid topped the stopper. "Consider it a . . . gift."

Her pulse raced, the moisture from her mouth drying out in seconds. "Poison?"

"Indeed." Lysander stared at the vial with longing. "It's called Godsbane. The last of its kind in all the realm." His eyes were solemn as he handed the poison to her. "Take care it isn't wasted. What you hold in your hands could buy a kingdom five times over."

A tightness clenched her chest as she examined the glass vial, running her thumb over the multi-faceted surface. "I've never heard of this before."

"That's because it does not exist except in the books of old."

The vial grew heavier in her hand, the poison inside whispering of ancient, evil tales of monsters and gods. Gritting her teeth, she set the poison down on the nearest side table. "Where did you get this?"

"Plundered from Odin's treasures after his fall. It is said that he traded part of his horn for the potion, created by the Demon Lords of Neifgard from the venom of a giant scorpion."

Haven's breath caught. According to ancient myths, Neifgard was where Odin found his horde of demons to use in the Shadow War. It was one of the seven Realms of Other outside their own. Freya had come from Alfheim; Odin from Jotunheim.

Each realm housed gods of immense power, but wards kept them apart for the balance of each world.

Look at what happened when Freya and Odin found a way to enter Haven's realm. Two new races appeared: the Noctis and the Solis. War and strife had followed, and Freya's attempt to help the powerless mortals by gifting them magick caused a war that nearly consumed their world.

A sudden thought came to mind. "Is this the poison that felled Freya?"

Lysander's eyes brightened. "Clever girl. The poison was put onto a powerful dagger, the Godkiller, forged by the same Demon Lords who made the Godsbane. The dagger alone would have killed her. But, when Odin plunged the blade into his once beloved's chest, he wanted to ensure she would well and truly die." He grinned. "Love is fickle."

After that infamous battle, wounded and suffering from the poison, Freya found a mortal town somewhere high in the mountains. She hid there for months while she tried to heal, but in the end, the combination of poison and dark magick in the dagger was too much.

It's said her body slowly hardened until it became a statue, and that the statue was still there somewhere.

According to legend, at least. No one had ever discovered the town to prove that.

After the death of their beloved Goddess, the mortal kingdoms rallied together with the Solis and imprisoned Odin in the deepest bowels of the Netherworld. By killing Freya, Odin had sealed his own fate.

And by killing Stolas, Haven would do the same. She crossed her arms. "There must be another way."

Just having the poison that helped end the life of Freya in her room felt like a curse.

"Don't be stupid, girl. One single drop can incapacitate a god.

Think what it will do to the Lord of the Netherworld."

Girl? Haven dug her fingers into her thighs. She didn't want to think about what it would do to Stolas or *anyone*.

An image of all those soldiers training in the courtyard came to mind. Did Lilith suspect they were preparing for more than just the tournament? With Stolas gone, they would have no more claim to reside in Effendier.

"When?" she asked. She hated how breathy her voice sounded.

"Tonight at dinner you will be seated next to the Shade Lord. There will be a performance. Slip the Godsbane into his drink when he is distracted."

A horrible coldness had come over her, and she hugged herself tighter. "They'll know it was me as soon as it takes effect."

Lysander shook his head. "Godsbane is the perfect poison. Untraceable and completely odorless, it slowly trickles through the body. One doesn't feel any symptoms until hours later. And by then it's too late—they will die an unimaginable death, and rather quickly, if they're lucky."

By the way he was smiling, she wondered if he'd personally witnessed Godsbane used before. "He's the Lord of the Netherworld," she protested. "He'll have guards protecting him from harm."

Lysander shrugged. "From the Sun Court, maybe. But a plain mortal with minimal magick from a forgotten House?" He didn't even bother hiding his disdain as he swept his cold gaze over her. "The sovereign once told you beauty is a weapon, but so is being unremarkable."

Bastard. The real Renfyre had been remarkable, a fierce light that shone brighter than the sovereign ever could, even with her glamours and power.

As he moved to leave, she called out, "Why do you stay with

the sovereign? She treats you like filth and yet I see the adoring way you look at her. It's not an act like most of the others."

Lysander didn't even hesitate before saying, "I love her," as if that were the simplest answer in the world. And maybe it was.

Maybe love was the true poison. The one thing most people were powerless against. Just like with Freya, it killed you slowly until you were too far gone to resist.

If that were the case, Haven vowed to never fall under its spell.

FORTY-FOUR

"Are you really wearing that?" Bell asked as his gaze swept over Haven's black leather pants and gray tunic.

"What's wrong with my clothes?" she asked. They were walking in pairs down a spiral staircase as onlookers pointed and whispered. It was no secret the citizens of Solethenia laid bets on the contestants.

And it was no secret she was the long shot.

Bell took her hand, frowning at the dark stains beneath her nails. "You could have at least cleaned the charcoal from your fingers. Are you sketching again?"

She pulled her hand away and curled her fingers into her palm. "I wanted to capture the city."

These days, she only drew after a bad nightmare or when the weight of the Penrythian court became too much. But she didn't want him to start wondering why she was stressed, beyond the usual reasons.

"We can't all look as amazing as you do in their clothes," she added, hoping her teasing tone hid her nerves. Every few minutes she snuck her hand into her pocket where the Godsbane hid.

Truth was, looking beautiful tonight was the least of her worries.

"What, this old thing?" he asked, plucking at the hem of his silk vest. Golden stags were embroidered along the collar, and he wore nothing underneath, showing off his lean arms. A golden dahlia earring glinted from his ear.

He was even wearing cologne, a very Solissian thing, although Goddess knows where he found the stuff. Hopefully it wasn't another gift from Xandrian.

The banquet was held in the grandest room Haven had been in so far, which was saying a lot. The walls were creamy marble veined with gold, the arched ceiling adorned with murals and skylights that bathed the parquet floors in silver moonlight.

Bowls of runelight flickered from white stone tables, all with a view of the stage. But the best view was from the box seating carved into the walls above where the sovereign and her favorites watched.

Haven let her gaze wander to where the sovereign sat, dressed in an elaborate gown of black and gold. Their eyes met. The sovereign's mouth tightened, a little nod tilting her head forward and causing the diamonds inside her azerite crown to sparkle.

There will be a performance tonight. He will be distracted.

Haven clutched her belly; she was going to vomit.

"You okay?" Surai asked, coming up beside Haven. She glanced up at the sovereign, and her eyes narrowed.

"Fine," Haven promised, the lie catching in her throat. "Just tired."

Surai would join the other mortal courts at a table in the back in a few minutes. For that, Haven was grateful. Surai would definitely notice if Haven dropped something into Stolas's drink.

If only Haven could tell her . . .

Being magick-bound to silence was infuriating.

Surai looked unconvinced, but she nodded, squeezed Haven's hand, and left to join the mortal courts.

The finalists table was positioned in the very center of the hall with an unobstructed view of the stage. Attendants led them one by one to their places. When a young Solis girl with waist-length auburn hair guided Haven to her place at the table opposite from Bell, Haven's heart lodged in her throat.

And when she heard the final contestant being led to the seat next to hers, she could hardly breathe. The chair scraped back . . .

Surai didn't dare take her eyes off Haven. Something was off, she could feel it in her bones. Her mother, a scout like herself, swore they descended directly from an Ashari shaman who once foretold the future for the Ashari Emperor. Surai had always thought her mother embellished that part to make her father, a nobleman who lost his titles when he married her mother, feel better about his choice.

But she'd felt the same creeping darkness before Rook's tragic death, and now that cold heaviness permeated Surai's soul.

Something was wrong with her friend, something she couldn't help her with. Just like Rook, who bore the weight of her oncoming sacrifice alone, so did Haven.

Surai's eyes narrowed as she watched the Solis attendant lead the Shade Lord to his seat beside Haven. Haven stiffened, her body tensing, but she didn't seem surprised.

Above in her gilded throne, the sovereign watched it all, and Surai's unease gave way to full-fledged panic.

What tangled web had Haven gotten caught in? Surai should have never let the mortal girl come here. She was too inexperienced in the duplicitous ways of the Sun Court. If she were truly involved in some scheme with the sovereign, Surai feared Haven's fate was already sealed.

Not if I can help it. Surai pushed the silver plate piled with delicacies away and readied herself for whatever was to come. She would give her life for Haven without a second's thought.

Goddess willing, it wouldn't come to that.

Goddess willing.

FORTY-FIVE

Haven smelled Stolas first. The intoxicating scent of irises, blood mandarin, and musk. That annoying magnetism his presence always elicited infused the tiny bit of air between them as Stolas glided into his chair, and she fought her body's natural reaction to him. Keeping her breath calm and her heart steady.

He was dressed beautifully in a deep mist-gray tunic, the first two buttons opened to reveal opaline skin. His wavy bone-white hair was shorn at the sides and longer at the top, the tousled ends falling over one side of his forehead. The runelights strewn over the table guttered in his presence as his dark magick drew from their power, the soft glow throwing shadows along his razor-edged jawline and cliffed cheekbones.

And his wings—admittedly, her favorite part of him—were pulled tightly to his shoulder blades until they were half their normal mass. Even so, his chair was backless to accommodate their size.

From the corner of her eye, she studied his horns while his predatory gaze flicked over the other finalists. He wore those same silver caps. A faint blue light wafted from the metal.

If only she could remove one and study it . . .

She blinked, dragging her stare down to his kohl framed eyes, which were riveted to *her*.

She could almost hear the words leave his full lips. *Hello, Beastie.*

Instead, he arched an eyebrow and said in a lazy drawl, "Would you like to sketch them?"

"What?"

His wings flared slightly, the movement drawing out the myriad of colors inside the onyx feathers, and she fought the need to run a hand down the length of one.

"You mortals always stare," he replied in a sublime voice.

"No, but how . . ."

"Did I know you like to sketch?" he asked, and all her efforts at remaining calm came undone as she thought her heart would slam right through her ribs. *He knows it's me.* "There's a smudge right *there*."

And before she could so much as move to wipe it away, he reached up and ran his thumb over her cheek.

Slowly. So. Damn. Slowly.

The rough pad of his thumb halted at the edge of her lip. "There, now you are a bit closer to being considered presentable, Renfyre of House Volantis."

Then, as if he hadn't just *touched* her, he removed his hand and settled his focus on Bell.

A mixture of relief and disappointment crashed over her.

His disinterest is a good thing, she reminded herself. And yet every part of her wanted to talk to him.

No, that was a lie. She longed to bash him over the head with the crystal vase of white roses in the middle of the table and then scold him for ever joining with Ravenna.

"Prince Bellamy," Stolas said, his voice thick with some inside joke. "I am surprised to see you here."

Bell worried the gold buttons of his vest. "Why is that?"

Haven held her breath. Stolas was aware Bell was magick-barren. All it would take to get him disqualified—or worse—was a word.

"No particular reason. I just assumed you would have had your fill of queens and magick after Morgryth."

At the mention of the dark queen's name, a tremor rippled through Bell's face. But he refused to cower. "I might have assumed the same of you."

At that, a little smile curled Stolas's lips, but he said nothing more.

Thank the Goddess.

Haven smeared the sweat from her palms on her pants and tried not to think about how Stolas could smell fear as the performance began. She awaited his attempts to soulread her, terrified at what he would find if she couldn't repel him.

But he didn't even try to access her thoughts.

To him, she was just some ordinary mortal girl with dirty fingernails. Lysander was right. Sometimes being unremarkable was a weapon.

Confident in his disinterest, she slid into a calm facade, pretending to drink the moonberry liquor provided when the others did.

She forced herself to eat the countless entrees served by the attendants on little silver trays—truffle soup, steamed white fish and capers, escargot swimming in garlic butter, pickled vegetables.

She laughed at the jokes the Asgardian female on her left made. On the stage, the performers dazzled. The sovereign had procured artists from every nation. There were Ashari dancers with magickal ribbons, drummers from the tribal nations under Freya's Spear, and Asgardian singers who brought tears to Haven's eyes.

Through it all, Stolas barely held back a yawn. His eyes following each new performance with veiled boredom, the way a wolf with a full belly might watch a deer chew grass nearby.

Her hand kept slipping in and out of her pocket. The glass vial felt hot to the touch. The dark magick inside the Godsbane prickling her fingertips.

They were down to the last act. So far, he hadn't let his glass out of his sight. His pointer finger casually tapping the stem. His nails were neatly buffed and trimmed, no evidence of the slate-gray talons lurking beneath his fingertips.

Sweat snaked between her shoulder blades. The ache of not knowing when—or if—he would look away was killing her. She prayed silently that he would find something to distract him.

And, yet, when she finally caught a flicker of interest cross Stolas's visage, part of her felt sick with despair, and she prayed he would look away.

His gaze sharpened, and he went very still the way a cat does before it pounces as he turned to watch a Solis troupe of dancers enter the stage. Musicians took their places behind a curtain, their lutes and violins filling the air with a haunting melody.

It didn't take long to realize they were reenacting Freya's death in the dance. A male painted red and wearing thickset clay horns leapt around Freya, faster and faster. His membranous wings were made from real leather and adorned with talons, and if Haven hadn't seen real Golemite wings, she might have found them convincing.

Magick shot from his hands and spiraled to form a cage, trapping Freya. The crowd gasped as he lifted a dagger above Freya's heart and plunged it down.

Haven almost forgot what she was supposed to do as she watched the dance, captivated, hardly breathing. And when Freya lay dying at last on the floor, the troupe of dancers leaping and swirling around her, a chilling hush descended.

Another performer draped in feathered wings knelt beside the fallen Goddess. Lifting her carefully into his arms, he began carrying her to safety.

Haven's throat ached, anguish swelling her chest until she struggled to breathe. Never before had Freya's death affected her this way, but she'd never witnessed the tragic act replayed, either.

The death of the Goddess who once ruled over all of Solissia had been a huge blow to the realm.

When the nameless Noctis male set Freya down on a blanket of grass, a cloud of grief coalesced inside Haven's chest.

She knew what came next. Knew it and yet couldn't stop the flood of emotion charging through her.

A single violin played as Freya closed her eyes, her hands settling on her belly. Magick flickered over the performer's skin. Her tawny flesh darkening before their eyes. Turning to stone as they watched.

She grew still, so very still.

Haven couldn't look away. Just as Stolas couldn't.

The entire room was transfixed.

Now. It has to be now.

But something was happening. The dancer who played Freya moved her hands over her belly. Light flashed.

And then magick swept the prone Freya into the air, swirling her around and around so fast she became a blur. The music, too, moved faster and faster, the chords violently striking the air. Magickal flowers of light rushed the stage. Woodland animals appeared; rabbits, foxes, mountain lions, deer.

Stolas hadn't moved since the performance began, his unblinking gaze rooted to the scene. Head cocked slightly.

Mist rose from the stage, suddenly covering everything. The music stopped. And a female voice said, "Predators and prey, dark and light, sun and moon, day and night. One by one they fall to their knees as they worship their one true queen."

The mist cleared. The performers were gone. The animals, the flowers, everything just gone.

The only thing left was a tiny bundle wrapped in a green blanket.

A mewling noise rose from the piles of silky fabric. The kind a baby makes.

Now, a voice inside her ordered.

Pushing away the distracting emotions from the dance, Haven slipped the poison from her pocket. She held the vial beneath the table as she removed the dropper. Her hand was steady, her mind clear as she readjusted her grip to hide the dropper inside her hand.

One drop on her skin and she was dead.

One drop in Stolas's drink and her problems were over.

The Stolas you know is gone.

Keeping her eyes on the stage—and Stolas—she reached for a bowl of candied figs. She thought for sure he would hear the frantic beating of her heart. Smell the intoxicating mixture of fear and exhilaration coursing through her. Sense the way every muscle in her body clenched and shook.

But she was Renfyre of House Volantis. Unremarkable and

plain and incapable of poisoning the most powerful Shade Lord in existence.

Her hand passed over Stolas's drink.

One squeeze and the job was done.

She replaced the dropper, put the poison back into her pocket, and exhaled the breath she'd been holding.

The entire act took less than a second.

On cue, the sovereign stood and lifted her glass. "Let us raise our glasses to the finalists and their incredible magick."

Glasses lifted all over the room. Haven froze as she watched Stolas slip his long, deft fingers around the stem of his glass and begin to lift the drink. Watched as his full lips neared the rim.

He turned to her, his eyes like molten gold and brimming with dark amusement. "Cheers, *Beastie*."

As his nickname resonated inside her mind, something came over her, a wild and clawing panic.

Nonono—

Before she could think about the consequences, desperation whipsawed through her. Almost like watching another person, she saw her hand dart toward him. The glass shot from his fingers.

Light played off the glass as it tumbled through the air.

Rich, dark plum liquid sprayed the table.

A few drops dotted the Shade Lord's expensive tunic, and she held her breath, praying the poisoned wine wouldn't touch his flesh.

And then everything went quiet as the glass bounced across the parquet floor before finally shattering.

Silence.

Without looking, she was pretty sure the entire room was staring at her, but she only cared about one person.

Haven met the sovereign's gaze. The rage in her eyes sent cold trickling down Haven's spine.

Bell was staring open-mouthed at Haven, but she needed to leave before the destructive whirlwind of emotions raging inside her exploded.

"I'm . . ." She leapt to her feet, sending her chair tumbling back. "I have to go."

The heavy gaze of the entire theater seared her back as she fled.

FORTY-SIX

Haven didn't expect the Gold Shadows to come directly after her. She assumed the sovereign would wait to punish her, but the jingling footsteps ringing down the hallway behind her said otherwise. The Gold Shadows wore distinctive boots with metal buckles that made a light, barely audible chime.

When the soft footfalls were just around the corner, she ducked behind a set of curtains near a window and drew a simple cloaking spell. The Gold Shadows rushed past her, their labored breaths suggesting they'd been running for a while.

Lifting the heavy velvet an inch, she peered out at the fleeing figures.

There were five males and they were chasing someone.

Not me.

The sovereign wouldn't send that many soldiers after Haven because she would assume Haven wasn't a threat.

The soldiers split up, three going down one hallway, two the other. They moved with the quiet efficiency of all Solis, and she shuddered at the thought of an army of Gold Shadows, each soldier blindly loyal to the sovereign.

Dropping her cloaking spell, Haven released a breath and slipped from the curtains. She made it only a few feet before she spotted the performer who played Odin pressed into the shadows along the far corner. Gold and black wallpaper covered the walls, and the shadows were arranged to mimic the pattern, veiling his outline.

But once one looked, he was easy to spot. Thickset ram's horns crowned his head, his fake wings askew on his back.

Their eyes met and a trill of recognition went through her. The monk from the strange fountain. Fear lurked beneath his pompous grin, but when he saw her, his eyes lit up, and he tipped his head like he was still onstage.

Excited voices rang from close by. The man sank back into the wall, a veil of shadows layering over him once more. The magick wasn't strong; if any of the soldiers looked closely his way, they would spot him.

The first Gold Shadow rounded the corner followed quickly by the others. He stopped near Haven, his sword still out.

"Have you seen a man around here?" he asked. "He might be wearing horns and wings."

Haven laughed. In her periphery, she saw the monk watching her closely. "Horns and wings? If you're after the Noctis, you won't find them here."

"Not a Noctis, girl," the Gold Shadow growled. His upper lip flared in a sneer. "A heretic."

Heretic? Haven shook her head, doing her best to play dumb. "Sorry. No heretics here. Just me and you and them."

She nodded to the other soldiers who were casting furtive glances down either side of the hall.

The monk's magick was starting to fade. The shadows draining to reveal more and more of his features. All the Gold Shadows had to do was *look*. Really look.

But the Goddess must have been on his side because the Gold Shadow barked, "He must have escaped down the stairs," and they were gone.

Questions surfaced as Haven stared at the monk. Why did his play anger the sovereign? What about it, exactly, was heretical?

But before she could satisfy her curiosity, he surfaced from his cloak of shadows, tipped his horns to her again, and fled.

Surai waited for Haven outside her door. Bell joined her, his face pinched with the same worry that plagued Surai.

"What was that?" Bell asked, leaning against the door frame. His dark curls were unkempt, his eyes a little wild, giving him a raw beauty Surai had never noticed before.

Surai shook her head. "I don't know, but it cannot be good."

He rubbed his thumb over a red spot on his neck. "Only Haven could come to the Sun Court and instantly become embroiled in some dangerous plot."

As worried as Surai was, she found herself laughing. "The girl has a griffin's fearless spirit and a Pixie's knack for trouble."

Bell shook his head. "You have no idea. I don't know how Fenwick Castle survived her. Did I ever tell you she nearly burned down the west wing? Or that she once loosed a whole bucket full of rabid mice into Cressida's dressing room?" He let his head thump back against the door frame. "Only now, she's started a fire but I don't know where it is or how to put it out."

"Sometimes we have to let the people we love extinguish their own fires," Surai said, but the words felt hollow on her tongue.

Bell pinched the bridge of his nose. "Except, whatever she's gotten herself into, it's because of me, and I have to fight back this time. With or without magick, I have to fight."

For the first time, Surai truly understood what Haven saw in the prince, and she squeezed his arm. "We'll fight together, Prince. I think someday the world will learn you are much more formidable than you look."

Bell chuckled. "Thanks, I think."

FORTY-SEVEN

Archeron followed Haven at a distance, just far enough away that she wouldn't notice him. He watched her slink in the shadows of the royal stables where his mother's horses—only the finest Alpacian mares—were housed.

One of the mares whinnied softly.

After what happened at the banquet, he knew deep in his core that she was in trouble. There was no point talking to her, not with his anger still so fresh. Any conversation would only end in him yelling at her and Haven reacting badly.

Everything in his life was backward, but he was still coherent enough to know they both needed time before they could have a civil conversation.

Stubborn as a wronged siren, that one.

As if she could feel his thoughts, she paused, glancing back in his direction. He melded into the hanging carpet of ivy, employing a strong but simple veiling spell to hide his form.

After a moment, she frowned and then resumed her path.

What in the Goddess's name was she doing? Fury rose up in him, fueled by the moonberry liquor burning his veins. If only the fool had listened to him.

If only she had let him deal with everything.

Not that he was currently doing much. He knew coming home under the binds of the foolish mortal king would be hard—but he hadn't been prepared for the reality. Being here, in his home, forced to serve the king—no, not just serve but humiliate himself over and over, unable to stop the torture, unable to help himself . . .

Things had been so clear before he came here. Before they broke the Curse, even. When it was just him and Surai and Rook. When Bjorn had yet to betray them and Haven still looked at him with affection, not pity.

The way she looked at him now . . . the sorrow in her eyes when the king ordered and he obeyed—a loathsome puppet.

The thought made him physically ill.

She looks at you with such disgust, a voice whispered. He would have startled had the voice not been the same as the one from his dreams. The nightmares had started on the road as he searched for Bjorn. He couldn't remember when the voice first spoke to him, but now it whispered in his ear every night.

It spoke of shame and guilt, of rage . . . of justice.

And it promised him a day he could unleash his magick on the world, a day to destroy everyone who had hurt him. His mother, his sisters, the king and his entire sniveling court.

More, it whispered. *All of them. Every single one will be sorry.*

Had *it* just spoken or was he remembering its voice?

He jerked his head side to side, trying to dislodge the shadow of confusion he felt almost daily now as the voice grew louder until it was undeniable. Sometimes the voice sounded like his own, a twisted, broken version of himself.

Sometimes it was just a string of disembodied words so faint they could be his own thoughts.

But always, always, the voice returned.

Bile rose in Archeron's gut, a roiling mixture of rage and something else, something terrifying.

Almost instinctively, he found himself procuring the steel flask engraved with the Sun Court's sigil, a sun with flowering vines for rays. A gift from Rook and Surai. Drinking the liquid inside the flask felt like a mark against their friendship, a betrayal of the morals they once all clung to.

But Rook was dead, and Surai—well he saw the way she looked at him as he was forced to grovel and kneel before the king. Saw the disgust twisting her regal expression. And the judgement. She would have died by her own hand before suffering such a dishonor.

Shoving the flask to his lips, he downed the stinging liquid until his throat sucked air.

"Ah, that feeling when you get to the last drop."

Archeron rounded on the male presence, his body primed for offensive magick.

Magewick resolved from the nearby hedges, his wings hidden by magick. His slick black hair was pulled into a half-knot, the current Sun Court fashion, and he wore the light, airy clothes of the Solis.

He was trying to blend in. While Archeron had been following Haven, Magewick had been following him.

Once, there wasn't a creature in the world who could have snuck up on Archeron, and he swallowed down the fresh shame that cascaded over him.

Magewick pulled out a small flask of his own and offered it to

Archeron. "Would you like a drink of mine?"

Archeron snarled. "What do you want, Noctis?"

Magewick grinned. "Why do I have to want anything? Surely two friends can offer one another a drink on a night as fine as this?"

The Noctis watched Archeron with those feral eyes as Archeron circled him, searching the gardens for any sign of more Noctis. When Archeron was sure they were alone, he put his hand on his sword, in case the dangerous timbre of his tone hadn't been clear enough.

"You and your dark queen may have tricked your way into the tournament," Archeron growled, "but I'm not so easily fooled. Whatever you want, the answer is no."

Magewick tsked, his eyes going to the inch of blade Archeron exposed from the sheath. "Foolish Solis, it is not I that wants something from you, but *you* that wants something from me."

Archeron snorted. The idea was ridiculous—so ridiculous, in fact, that he was starting to wonder if Magewick was a distraction, and he flicked a quick glance in Haven's direction.

"What could you ever possibly offer me, Noctis?" Archeron grunted.

"How about freedom?"

Archeron stiffened as if he'd been impaled. *Freedom.* The word echoed through his mind, growing more powerful with every pass. *Freedom.*

A voice so soft it could be his own whispered, "You deserve to be free."

"What did you say?" Archeron demanded.

Magewick lifted his eyebrows, mock confusion on his hideous face. "I did not utter a word." Magewick took a step closer. "Are you hearing voices, Sun Lord? It's normal for those whose spirit is bound to dark magick, such as your king's ring, to begin losing themselves to the darkness. Especially after being enslaved for so very long, and the king taking such liberties."

Was such a thing true? Archeron knew little when it came to the dark arts the king used inside the ring that held him captive.

And yet, that would explain what was happening to him. Archeron's chest ached as he clenched his jaw and spit, "Leave, trickster, before I cleave your head from your body and give it to my mother as a gift."

"Ah, but is it my head or yours that will make her truly happy?"

Blinding fury surged through Archeron, and he yanked his sword from its sheath, the scrape of metal a balm to his rage. "If you want to keep your wings, I would not speak of such things, Noctis."

"Very well." Magewick turned to leave. "But there will be a day when you come to me broken and begging, Solis. When the time comes, remember this very moment."

"Never," Archeron roared, sending Magewick scuttling into the shadows where he belonged.

No matter how bad things became, he would never make a bargain with the Noctis. Never.

FORTY-EIGHT

A headache nipped at Haven's skull as she entered the training arena, prepared for yet another day of sparring without her mentor. She blamed the blasted sun, although going to bed a few hours before dawn didn't help either.

Runes, she hated the need for sleep. Mortals lives were already so short compared to Solis that spending six hours a night sleeping seemed unfair.

She yawned as she recalled the hours she wasted searching for a place to hide the Godsbane, and then the countless time she spent arguing with Demelza about coming in so late.

Unsurprisingly, Lysander paid a visit shortly after to collect the Godsbane. The story she concocted—that she panicked and threw the rare poison into the sea—didn't exactly make him happy.

Then again, he was already so furious at her failed assassination that there was little she could do to make him any angrier.

After that, she'd wanted to throw herself in bed and sleep away her growing list of troubles. Instead, she had to wake Surai to recarve her binding runes, an excruciating ordeal. Each time they were redrawn the pain was worse, as if her body was protesting the binding of her dark magick.

All in all, a crappy night. And she hadn't even had time for coffee this morning.

But at least she felt a bit safer with the Godsbane hidden. She'd found a cave beneath one of the waterfalls cascading through the city to hide the foul stuff. She still wasn't quite sure how she discovered the cavern or the tunnels leading back into the city, but it felt right.

Sweat trickled down her forehead as she bounded over to her spot near the clump of pink cherry blossom trees opposite Bell. When she spotted Archeron leaning against the trunk of a bowed sapling, she slowed.

"You're late," he said. His clenched jaw said he hadn't quite forgiven her yet, but he was *here*. That was a giant step toward reconciliation.

"So are you," she growled, settling into her stance as she readied herself for whatever he was about to throw at her. By the angry glint in his eye, it could be an orb of magick . . . or the sharpened blade of an axe. "By, like, three days."

"Better late than never," he drawled, tucking a strand of golden hair behind his ear, the peacock.

They fell into a routine of defensive maneuvers, and Haven practiced using all forms of magick. But whenever it came time to speak the ancient language, Haven was always a second too slow.

It didn't help that she had to focus on Bell and simultaneously feed him the right magick. Xandrian was working him harder than ever today. They had moved away from the water and were practicing leaping over a ravine.

From here, Haven couldn't see how deep it was, but the width was at least twenty feet.

"Quicker," Archeron demanded, his gravelly voice making her headache worse.

"Burstadi!" she cried, and the spear hurling toward her face shattered.

She barely had time to conjure the raw wind magick behind Bell as he leapt across the ravine. For a heart-stopping moment, he faltered, sinking in the air, before the wind buoyed him up again and across to the other side.

That wasn't going to work. She needed something better. A strength spell that allowed him to leap farther.

No, that wouldn't be enough, either. The distance was too great.

Archeron pulled out his sword and arced it toward her. She was so intent on solving Bell's problem that she barely had time to jump out of the way. Steel flashed.

Cursing, she ducked, the blade clipping the top of her hair. The ground slammed into her face, the dry underbrush of the arena scratching her bare skin.

Runes, she was so not in the mood for this right now.

As she leapt to her feet, she caught a flash of dark wings in the distance. Stolas was high above the arena, fighting Ravenna in the air. Blue shocks of dark magick shivered between them. The sight was mesmerizing.

It also gave her an idea. The next time Bell went to jump the ravine, Haven drew a quick rune against her forearm, making a series of curving slashes.

She held her breath as he jumped, totally trusting that she would keep him safe. He dipped in the air, arms flailing, and then wings of pure white sprouted from his back. It was all she could do not to whoop with joy as the wings carried him over the chasm to safety.

Archeron glared at her. "Stop showing off."

She dodged another round of attacks, emboldened by her pride. She gave Bell wings. *Wings*, for rune's sake.

With that problem solved, she could focus more on her own safety. And despite Archeron's lingering annoyance—and the lingering scent of moonberry liquor on his breath—he took the training seriously.

"Stop smiling," he growled after she set a sword on fire and nearly impaled him with it.

"Anything I *can* do?" she breathed, lunging toward him.

He danced away from her attack, drawing her in, and then slammed a wave of bright, fiery flames into her face.

"Yeah, stop falling for my tricks. I've used that same one on you three times already."

"Well, I'm a little distracted keeping someone else alive." She gestured with a look toward Bell. "So maybe you can give me a break?"

She fell back, hand high and ready to defend another surge of magick. But, apparently, he was only going to attack her with words, now, because he continued, "Want a break? Leave. *Today.*"

Haven exhaled. She was too tired to deal with this right now. "I can't leave; I belong to your mother."

"She can't have you," Archeron snarled, closing the distance between them. "Not you, do you understand?"

There was something in his voice that scared her. "Archeron, if I leave—"

"Bell will lose, and she will own him—not *you*."

"I can't do that."

"Don't be stupid, Little Mortal. You have no idea what she's capable of. Or maybe you do. What happened last night with the Shade Lord?"

So he knew about that. She wasn't sure he'd seen, but of course he had. Frustration welled inside her chest. Not just over her predicament, but because she was bound to silence over her deal with the sovereign.

And now—now there was no telling how or when the sovereign would strike at Haven for disobeying her orders.

"What did he say to you?" Archeron asked, his eyes gleaming. "Right before you knocked his glass away, he said something that made you react. What was it? Something personal?"

The jealousy in his voice was made all the more disturbing by the truth behind it. If Archeron knew of Stolas's nickname for her . . . she'd never given the name a second thought.

Not until last night when he'd spoken those words and made her lose total control over her actions.

That went way beyond personal and into dangerous territory.

Before she could find an answer, a horn blasted. At the same time, the magickal illusion began bleeding away from the arena. The mountains and forests and lakes they trained within disappearing in front of their eyes.

Archeron's stiffness was the first indication that the Sun Sovereign was near, and Haven turned to see her and Lysander strolling through the contestants. White roses formed a path at her bare feet, the crown at her head glittering like a thousand little suns.

Everyone bowed—everyone but Stolas and Ravenna.

"I have come with wondrous news," the sovereign said, casting her gaze over the contestants. "Today is such a glorious day that I have decided we will do the first trial."

Haven inhaled sharply. She and Bell weren't ready. They needed a few more days to coordinate the gestures and signs that went with their magickal act.

Behind her, Archeron cursed under his breath.

"I know you were supposed to have a few more days of training before the first trial," the sovereign continued, "but after the lackluster performances last night, I think we are all ready for more entertainment."

It was impossible to miss the way the sovereign slid her vengeful gaze to Haven.

Archeron cursed again, this time louder. "I don't know what you did to piss off my mother, but if Stolas has anything to do with it, he will regret ever making that vile bargain with you."

After that, things happened very quickly. The mentors were shuffled to a viewing area overlooking the arena, and the finalists were lined up. Then the sovereign created great swirling portals, one for each contestant.

Haven looked at Bell beside her, hoping his close proximity in the arena meant he would be near when they came out the other side—wherever that led.

Lysander stepped forward. "For the first trial, the sovereign has chosen the decimated bogs of Verymeer."

Bell's face darkened. "Verymeer was an island in Freya's Spear that was overtaken by one of Odin's monsters during his last reign," Bell explained. "They say the creature . . ." Bell released a breath. "They say the creature is a bog crawler, and big enough to wrap around the entire island."

Our first trial involves a giant monster. Fabulous.

"To win," Lysander continued, "each contestant must collect fifty runestones, make it across the bog, and exit through the awaiting portal. You are allowed one weapon. The first twenty finalists to finish their tasks and re-enter the arena will go on to the next trial." He smiled. "Luck of the Goddess, everyone."

Haven barely had time to grab a long sword before someone blew a horn and the contestants began jumping through the portals. Each time someone entered the fiery rings, the air crackled.

"Meet you on the other side," Haven called before taking the leap. A bright flash exploded all around her and then darkness.

FORTY-NINE

The bog's stench assaulted Haven's senses. Her eyes stung; her nasal passages burned. A rocky slab just wide enough for two people held firm beneath her feet. Far below, the tarry bog bubbled and oozed, the gooey black liquid stretching to the murky horizon.

Steadying her feet, she scanned the misty air, tinged yellow by the sulfurous gases that permeated the place. In the distance, she caught sight of other contestants doing the same.

Where was Bell? Her heart clenched as she pivoted in a circle, searching for that familiar face.

There! He wobbled on top of a tall protrusion of rock, throwing out his hands to steady himself.

Relief crashed through her. He was close. So far, so good.

What were they supposed to do now? Squinting, she peered through the layers of rancid fog and mist. At least thirty feet away, another slab rose slowly from the ground, black tar coating its surface.

As the pedestal rose, hers began to drop.

Her stomach lurched into her throat. She threw her arms out for balance as understanding dawned. They had to find a way to the rising rocks ahead before theirs sank. Only, there weren't enough replacement slabs.

All across the bog, contestants began to figure that out too.

An Ashari male was the first to cross. He had an ember-wand, basically a long, eternally lit match, and he quickly scrawled a rune into the air. As soon as he was finished, a small wyvern composed entirely of smoke materialized and swooped him onto its back.

The wyvern screeched as it glided across the bog.

They made it halfway to the rising slab ahead before a great roar sounded below. The magickal wyvern flapped its smoky wings harder, the rider yelling something Haven couldn't hear but imagined was similar to *hurry up*.

But it was all for nothing. Something shot from the bog, rising lightning quick from the tarry waters, and snatched the magickal wyvern and rider from the air. The smoke wyvern broke apart at first contact, leaving the Ashari male helpless.

The crunch of bones seemed to reverberate through the air, amplified so that every snap of bone, every tear of flesh was heard by every single contestant.

Haven clapped a hand over her mouth. The monster was some type of horrifying mash between a centipede and a worm, only it had grown to the circumference of five men. There were no eyes she could see, only a yawning mouth of serrated teeth set in circular rows. Barbed red feet surrounded its squirming body.

The Ashari contestant screamed as the bog crawler's mouth shuddered closed.

The attack was over in a few seconds.

Goddess Above.

Feelers lifted from the crawler's formless face, tasting the air. Then it sank back into the bog with a resounding crash that rocked the too-small piece of ground Haven stood on.

Haven didn't have time to think. Already contestants were leaving their perches, the tang of magick cutting through the sulfurous stench. Across the bog, she caught sight of Stolas. Envy coursed through her at the sight of his glorious wings lifting him into the air.

That envy transformed into fury as he looked her way and *winked.*

Cheater. He still had to stop at every rock to grab a runestone, but his wings gave him an advantage.

Stop complaining and figure this out, Ashwood.

Whirling to face Bell, she drew the flying rune across her forearm again, sending the magick sizzling across the space to Bell.

She could only pray the magickal wings would lift him high enough to avoid the bog crawler.

Only once she spotted the golden flare of wings pulsing across his back did she start thinking about what she would do. Of course, she could replicate the wings on herself, but a wing spell was incredibly complex, beyond the pittance of magick most mortals possessed.

Two mortals who could pull it off would be suspicious, especially if the wings looked exactly the same.

Everyone's magick manifested spells differently; Surai's wing spell might produce dazzling wings of silver. Archeron's might look black as the bog below.

If both their wings were mirror images . . .

No, she had to do something different. And fast. Already, her slab had sunk nearly half its height, the oily waters too close for her comfort. Something churned below the surface. Something huge and impossibly fast.

If only she could jump that far. Maybe she *could* with the right wind.

With the word for wind on the tip of her tongue, she crouched down and then leapt.

She didn't make it far before she was falling.

"Ventus!" she yelled. The moment the word finished passing through her lips, a violent gust of wind slammed into her, thrusting her body forward. She was already falling, so her momentum dragged her down as she arced across the bog.

Thankfully the rock she jumped to was still lower than the previous slab, and she just barely made it. The rock face slammed into her chest. She scrambled for a handhold with sweat-slick hands, her adrenaline fueling her muscles as she threw herself on top of the pedestal.

The impact stirred something from below. The creature slammed against the outcropping she stood on so hard she nearly rolled off. She leapt to her feet. A flash drew her attention to the first runestone, a pearl.

She grabbed it moments before it tumbled into the bog, tossed the stone into her pocket, and looked to Bell.

He waved at her without making a sound, his movements careful and small. He noticed the same thing she had. The creature was drawn to the wyvern's screeching. She'd bet her favorite hat it wasn't the *sound* that drew the monster—it was the vibrations.

Ready? she mouthed.

He gave a tiny nod.

The wing spell only lasted for as long as Bell stayed in the air. If she could have drawn the rune into his flesh with pigments infused with iron or even carved it into his flesh, she could have given him wings for days.

Instead, she had to keep redrawing the rune. Once again, she waited until she watched his wings carry him to the next slab across the way. Then she went to conjure the wind spell . . . and hesitated.

The wind spell was messy and violent. Last time, the impact had drawn the creature to the rock.

She couldn't take that risk again.

She needed something else, a spell that allowed her to quietly and softly land on the next available slab. Preferably soon, before the current outcropping she stood on sank any farther into the bog.

Ice—she was good with ice. What if she made an icy path from this perch to the next one? But the path would be slick and, if she didn't slip to her death, it would take precious seconds to walk across.

A sudden idea came to mind. What if she drew the rock beneath her feet higher into the air and then made the ice path? Instead of walking across it, she could slide down to the next slab, all the while the bog crawler would focus on the rock she just left.

Worth a try.

Sweat slicked her palms as she readied her mind for what came next. She would have to be quick. The moment the slab started to rise, the crawler would come.

Let it. She could do this.

Steeling herself with a breath, she pictured the rock she stood on in her mind and then sent it sprouting toward the murky, sunless sky. The momentum sent her into a crouch.

Almost high enough . . .

Right as the dark water parted below and the crawler broke the surface, she sent a path of ice surging across to the next rock. It crackled as it formed, a light popping noise. Before the crawler could even get close, she dropped to her butt and slid down the ice to the next runestone.

The pearl went into her pocket. Behind her, the crawler's mouth snapped over the spot where she'd been only a few seconds before. Its slimy body streaked black with mud as it writhed around the slab, chunks of ice splashing to the bog below.

Not too bright, are you dummy? She dusted off her hands. She needed to perfect the timing, but it worked.

Bell cheered silently from across the way. After grinning back at him, she repeated the process.

Wings. Rise. Ice. Repeat.

They picked up a rhythm. Her confidence grew.

Soon the crawler tired of her empty rocks and began hunting others. Screams followed. The sounds of churning water and frantic magick and desperate prayers swelled the air.

Haven blocked out anything that didn't have to do with her or Bell. She couldn't afford pity or emotions to cloud her judgement. They were gaining speed. She lost count of the runestones she collected. Lost count of the shrieks and pleas.

Still, she knew one thing: they were close.

They wouldn't be the first to enter the arena. That wasn't possible when she had to perform magick for both of them.

But they could make the first twenty. She felt confident they would get there in time.

A glowing blue ring of light materialized up ahead just above a huge outcropping of rock, the last destination.

Two more jumps.

They were so close she could taste it.

She watched Bell flutter softly down to the last rock before the portal. Quickly Haven sent a burst of magick to lift her pedestal. Icy magick shot from her fingers, the air around her cooling.

She jumped a half-second before the ice path touched the other rock.

She was sliding down the ice, grinning like a lunatic, when the magickal ice stopped.

Just . . . stopped.

Crackling filled the air as the end began to break away, chunks of ice falling to the bog with loud splashes.

No. She tried to conjure the magick again. Nothing.

Ten feet separated the end of the path and the next slab. Now twelve. Pieces kept shattering.

If she could just stand she might be able to jump . . .

She was going too fast. The ice too slick to get a foothold. Her insides twisted as she readied her mind for what came next. She was going to fall. The bog crawler would be on her in seconds.

That reality gave way to raw anger as she realized someone had to be actively fighting her magick.

Haven glanced to her left just in time to see Avaline grinning, her magick seeping from her fingertips in snakes of white.

Of course, she thought dully. She should have expected something like this.

A roaring sound drew Haven's focus forward again. What she saw made her mind go blank with instinctual fear.

The crawler must have sensed the falling pieces of ice, and it waited at the end of the path, its quivering mouth stretched wide. Scraps of clothing and flesh hung from its many teeth—hundreds and hundreds of serrated blades made for shredding its victim in seconds.

And she was headed straight for it.

FIFTY

Bell waited for Haven to do another wing spell so he could fly to the final pedestal where the portal shimmered, the blue glow flickering between swathes of smoke. Part of him even regretted that this would be his last flight.

The magickal wings were growing on him.

Maybe later, if Haven had time, they could both use this spell to fly over the city and—

An enormous explosion rocked the air as something shot from the dark waters below. By the time he turned around, Haven was already plummeting toward the broken shaft of ice.

Oh, no.

Shock froze his limbs as he watched her slide straight toward the hideous creature's mouth, feet kicking helplessly against air.

Dread spiked through him. Dread and his usual feeling of frustration at being completely unable to help her.

The moment before she crashed into the cavern of teeth, she

whipped her sword from the sheath swinging at her side and plunged the blade into the ice in front of her to stop her descent.

Her body halted inches from the crawler's expectant mouth, the momentum throwing her against her sword with a grunt, her rose-gold hair flying out in front of her.

Before the crawler could realize what had happened, Haven jerked to her feet, yanked the sword from the path of ice, and leapt straight into the air, a war cry spilling from her bared lips.

Jump away from the monster, Haven.

Away.

But she was Haven, and she never ran from a fight. He cringed as she landed on the thing's head, spread out her legs for balance, and sank the blade deep into the quivering black flesh.

An enraged screech echoed through the bog as the creature bucked wildly, jerking its head side to side as it tried to knock her loose. She held firm to the sword. Her hands clenched in a death grip around the handle.

She couldn't release her hold without falling, but without her hands free to perform magick, she was reliant on her verbal spells. Which weren't exactly great.

For a heart-stopping moment, she freed one hand. Bright bursts lit the dingy air as she managed to hit the thing with magick. But she was too busy trying to hold on to properly weaponize her powers and the attacks didn't seem to faze the beast.

He needed to distract it somehow.

The creature suddenly dropped to the bog and began rubbing the back of its head against the nearest stone, trying to scrape her off.

She cried out, the pain flickering across her expression turning to determination as she twisted the blade deeper.

It was all she could do to hold on and avoid being slammed

against the rock.

Help her, idiot.

There was little he could do. He had no magick and only Xandrian's double-bladed dagger, which now felt small and inept. But he wouldn't stand by while his best friend fought for her life.

Saying a quick prayer, Bell did the only thing he could do. He jumped from his perfectly safe rock and plunged to the bog. Warm, fetid waters swallowed him. His feet hit mud and he shoved to the surface. The bog here was shallow, the brackish liquid bubbling around his chest.

A bit got into his mouth and the acrid, foul taste nearly dredged up the sticky buns he had for breakfast.

The crawler was only feet away. Black goo coated its thick body, its slimy skin crawling with little red feet that were barbed at the end. Gathering his strength, Bell threw himself at the closest portion, but the skin was too slippery to get a good hold.

Bell yanked Xandrian's beloved dagger from his waistband. Muddy flecks of bog water darkened the jade handle. Shadeling's shadow, the Sun Lord was going to be furious.

Tightening his grip on the middle section of the handle, Bell sank one of the twin blades deep into the blubbery flesh.

A screeching sound pierced the bog, and then the crawler shot across the water. Bell held on to the dagger, using it like a climbing axe as he swung and leapt, swung and leapt. He was gaining ground.

All at once, the crawler halted, sending Bell careening across its body. Spindly red legs caught him in their grip. They wrapped around his arms, his ankles, his neck.

Just like that, he was trapped.

The crawler's ugly head peered down at Bell. He nearly shrieked as the mouth split wide open, row upon row of teeth glinting as they closed in. The jagged tusks were positioned in concentric rows that grew smaller and smaller, covering every portion of the red mucosa.

It was a perfect killing machine.

His flesh shivered as he braced himself for death. A very painful, very gruesome death.

Haven met his eyes. She was smiling—*smiling*—the grin wild and somewhat deranged. Lifting her hand, she coaxed a pulsing orange orb to life over her palm.

"Haven!" he yelled as the crawler drew closer. Feet became inches. "What the bloody Netherworld are you waiting for?"

"Hold on!" she called as the magickal sphere surged outward, growing bigger. "Almost ready."

Bell flinched as some sort of gooey substance splattered his face. The creature's decaying breath washed over him.

He shut his eyes.

Silence. As if the entire world had been paused. And then an explosion rocked the bog. Bright red light seared across his eyelids. Then warmth and wetness hit him from all sides as . . .

Runes. Tell me I'm not covered in crawler guts.

His eyes snapped open to see Haven bent over a mound of black, oozing goo. "Found it," she called cheerily as she yanked out her sword, sending bits of crawler flesh sprinkling Bell's face.

Yep. Covered in crawler guts.

Bell wiped his sleeve over his face only to smear more disgusting material on his cheeks. "What happened?"

"Avaline happened," Haven growled. "I don't know how she knows it's me, but she does. Or maybe the sovereign ordered her to kill me. It's a toss-up, really."

Bell raised his eyebrows. He wasn't even going to broach the latter option. Haven had told him about Archeron's fiancée, but he hadn't realized she was here. "I thought she was okay with you and Archeron being together?"

"Apparently not." Haven yanked her bog-drenched hair over her shoulder and then stumbled toward him, her boots sinking in the pile of guts. "It doesn't matter, we're not, you know, together anymore. Not that we ever really were." A shadow of pain flickered over her face, but she chased the emotion away and held out her hand. "Get up. This is personal now. I want to see her face when we walk through that portal still alive."

FIFTY-ONE

They weren't going to make it. Surai had been staring at the flaming portal for so long, waiting for them to exit, that whenever she allowed herself to blink, the blue ring engraved into her eyelids. She was seated next to Archeron with the rest of the mortal court high in the viewing balcony above the arena. The limbs from the Donatus Atrea wound above them, forming a floral canopy that provided shade and scented the air.

She glared down at the arena. Every contestant that came through was lauded with cheers and applause.

So far, nineteen had made it back. There was only one spot remaining. Which meant, whomever walked through next was the final contestant remaining in the tournament.

Whatever happened, either Bell or Haven was out.

She tugged on the jade and amber pants that flowed loosely around her thighs, leaving sweat marks on the airy silk. Something was wrong. And by the way Avaline had walked through the portal with a cunning look in her dark eyes, the half Noctis queen was probably involved.

"If Avaline hurt Haven," Surai growled, low enough that the king and his consorts couldn't hear, "I'll skin her alive, fiancée or not."

Archeron cut his eyes at her. Worry lined his forehead, the divot between his thick eyebrows deepening with every minute. "She wouldn't. Not over me. She doesn't care who I love, you know that."

His voice couldn't hide his unease.

"Then someone else ordered it," Surai insisted.

"You're jumping to conclusions. We don't know—"

"I do know," Surai interrupted, daring him to argue.

Archeron ran two fingers over his jaw as he focused back on the portal. "She shouldn't have come to Effendier."

"But she did, and now you have to forgive her, Archeron. Or at least, accept that she's here."

He shook his head. "If only she had listened, she would never have seen me like . . . this."

Surai frowned, her gaze sliding from Archeron to the king. Being in Solethenia made the king act even more depraved, as if humiliating the sovereign's son in front of her court made him feel more powerful.

Since arriving here, Archeron's torment had only gotten worse.

A few minutes ago, she'd watched as the king *lended* Archeron out to a mortal nobleman to help the nobleman's daughter find a missing ribbon. Afterwards, when the girl said she found Archeron beautiful, the king forced Archeron to kneel down and kiss her foot, and then the king promised Archeron would dance with her at the upcoming ball.

All of it—from the blatant disrespect to the pleasure the king took in Archeron's humiliation—made Surai's blood boil.

The mortal king needed someone to remind him how to behave . . .

Still, she couldn't very well threaten a king, even one as incompetent as King Boteler. Not without only making things worse.

"As soon as this is over," Surai promised, "we will leave this place and—"

"And what, Surai? I'll go back to fetching him wine and being groped by his mistress in Penryth? I'd rather run his heart through with a blade and suffer eternal damnation than return to that horrible little kingdom."

She startled at the barely bridled fury in his voice.

"Archeron, as much as I would love to see that happen, you know it cannot."

"I know," he growled. "Why else do you think I'm still a slave? Because I enjoy the absolute humiliation of entertaining a king whom I could kill with a single word?"

She stared at him, trying and failing to think of words that might calm him.

"I'm sorry," he said at last. "It's just . . . I've dreamt about coming home every day for years. How cruel is fate that when I finally see my homeland again, it's as a slave to the king responsible for murdering my soulbrother?"

Worry bubbled up inside her. Never had she seen Archeron like this. Even after Remurian's death, when he was drowning in grief and the all-consuming need for vengeance, he was still Archeron. Wounded and grieving, sure—but he was still himself.

This seemed different. Like something inside him had changed.

She pushed the thought away. Archeron was one of the greatest Sun Lords of the realm, and he would find himself again.

A murmur rippled through the balcony, and she turned her

attention to the arena. Someone was coming through the portal.

The pale blue ring pulsed and darkened as a shadow silhouetted the inside of the portal. Surai leaned forward but the figure that appeared was unrecognizable. Mud and slime covered the staggering form, the only thing not black a pair of bright blue eyes the exact color of the sky above.

Prince Bell.

And right behind him, cursing like a Tunisian sailor, was Haven. Every part of her coated in varying shades of black and brown. She shook off her boots as if, out of everything that was bathed in disgusting . . . whatever that was, her boots were the only thing she cared about.

The tension bled from Surai's shoulders. No matter what happened now, at least her friend was alive. Limping and pissed and out of the tournament, but alive.

Surai glanced over at Avaline in time to see the skin around her mouth pucker, her displeasure obvious.

The sovereign strolled over to the finalists, many muddy and speckled with blood, some hunched over breathing hard. A gown made of white orchid petals clung to her figure, more orchids strewn in her flowing gold hair. The smile that found her face was two shades too bright and didn't reach her eyes.

"Prince Bellamy, you are the last of the contestants to make it to the next trial. Congratulations."

Bell looked stricken, and he shot a panicked look at Haven. "Have all the runestones been counted?"

That's right. The finalists needed fifty runestones to qualify.

Surai hardly blinked as she watched Lysander count the runestones from each contestant. Her heart seemed to drop a little more as each finalist came up with the right amount.

This was a formality.

No one would go through all that trouble and forget to grab all the stones.

The second to last finalist stepped forward. A willowy male from the Isle of Mist, he spread his palms wide, revealing a pile of pearls, the glowing runes on them visible even from here.

As Lysander began to count, Surai caught a flash of movement from the finalist next to him, and she froze.

Stolas. What had he done? It couldn't have been more than a sly twitch of his hand, but it stuck out in her mind.

Her heart raced. Beside her, Archeron placed his large hands on the marble railing and leaned forward. Whatever problems existed between Archeron and Haven, he still cared deeply for her.

Lysander counted the runestones again, including Haven's this time. Then he stepped back, his brow lowered, lips wrangled into a perplexed expression. "It appears this contestant is lacking one runestone and will not advance. Renfyre of House Volantis, congratulations, you are still in the tournament."

Surai reached over and squeezed Archeron's hand. "She made it. The fool made it."

Instead of smiling, Archeron was frowning, his gaze not on Haven at all—but the Lord of the Netherworld. Sweat darkened the honey-gold hair of Archeron's temples to wheat.

Beneath his grip, the marble banister cracked and groaned. If he squeezed any harder the entire thing would give way.

"Sun Lord," the king called, snapping his fingers. "Cressida and her ladies are bored. Entertain them, please."

The king hardly seemed to notice the black look Archeron gave him as he glanced over his shoulder, and Surai had to sit on her hands to keep from launching herself at the foolish king.

"What shall I do now, my liege?" Archeron asked, his voice terrifyingly emotionless. "I am afraid I will bore them with the same magick tricks as last time."

Last time? Surai was appalled.

The king waved his hands, greasy from the half-chewed pheasant leg on his plate. "You'll think of something."

The king's mistress ran her tongue along her upper lip as she stared at Archeron while her friends laughed beside her. "Don't be afraid, Sun Lord. We don't bite . . . unless you want us to."

She patted her lap like Archeron was a puppy to be coaxed and petted, and Surai fought off the stab of rage that pierced her chest.

The thought of him suffering all these years under such treatment, the idea of her friend and brother-in-arms, the most loyal and brave Solis she knew, being treated like a male whore, a toy to be passed around, made her physically ill.

She had to find a way to free him. Had to—before it broke him.

Jumping to her feet, she stalked away from the situation before her urge for violence loosed itself on the king's witch of a mistress.

She did, however, allow her elbow to accidentally bump into the chilled flagon of nectarine wine as she passed, knocking the entire contents into Cressida's lap.

Surai could only pray that someday it would be Cressida's blood—not wine—soaking her dress, and that Archeron would be free of this mockery before it destroyed him.

FIFTY-TWO

Three baths—it had taken three steaming hot baths to clean the muck and guts from Haven's hair and skin. Technically four if she counted jumping into the canal first.

Afterward, Demelza had relished the job of scraping the tarry bog water from her arms with the rough sponges the Solis used for exfoliation. The woman sang to Haven as she used a combination of combs and her fingers to dislodge the chunks of crawler from Haven's poor hair.

That was hours ago and her flesh was still tender. Haven rubbed her arms as she stared into the city. Demelza, Bell, Surai, and Haven were taking a gondola through the canals to the theater district where a festival raged. The sound of wild, exotic music and revelry drifted down the high walls of the canal and over the slow-moving azure water.

Bell leaned over the hull, gripping the red petal-shaped side so hard his knuckles turned snow-white. The gondolas were crafted to resemble flowers, this particular boat a blooming rose.

"Yep, I hate all boats," he moaned.

Demelza scoffed at him. "Do not be such a weakling. Water is good, it wards off demons."

Haven would have rolled her eyes if she hadn't seen real demons with her own eyes. Now she would take anything she could get as protection.

A groan left his lips. "I'd take demons over this misery."

Haven laughed. "It will be worth it, I promise."

After this morning, they all desperately needed *something*. The first trial had nearly ended in disaster, and if the sovereign didn't have Haven killed in the next few days—a possibility—the second trial promised to be even harder than the first.

"Did you know," Haven offered, trying to lift his spirits, "that, according to this pamphlet, the festival of lights started after Freya died as a way to celebrate her ascension to the Nihl?"

She waved the light blue paper in front of his face.

Bell perked up. Nothing intrigued him more than random, pointless facts from history. "What do the colors of the lanterns we release signify?"

"I don't know." She shrugged. "I haven't gotten that far."

Bell snatched the pamphlet from her hand. "Here, let me. I've been practicing my Solissian."

Haven smiled as Bell read aloud more about the festival. How the runelight colors they released both in the water and the air signified three things: Freya's unconditional love for the Solis and mortals; her prowess in battle; and her infinite wisdom.

Haven tuned the rest out. All she truly cared about was that the festival was the perfect place to lose the sovereign's spies.

Haven glanced back at the honeysuckle boat drifting behind them, shooting ripples over the water tinged pink and tangerine with the setting sun. The two female Solis had been following them ever since they left the palace.

Did the sovereign have all the contestants followed, or were she and Bell simply special?

They made it to the celebration just as the last bit of light bled from the city. A whirlwind of music and bodies and scents engulfed them. Colorful swaths of revealing fabric adorned the crowd. Their hair was braided and strung with metallic runebeads, and they waved gold and purple streamers.

A heady scent permeated the streets. An intoxicating mixture of magnolia tea, the clove incense used in the nearby cathedrals, and the popular fried crepes slathered in powdered sugar and honey that most vendors sold.

As the others all snatched streamers from a bucket, Surai turned to Haven, her eyes solemn. "Are you sure you can't stay? I could get word to Archeron? Perhaps if you met outside the confines of the court, he would be more amenable?"

Haven shook her head, fighting off the stab of pain that came with thinking about the Sun Lord. "Archeron was clear. He'll never forgive me. And to be honest, I'm tired of apologizing when I haven't done anything wrong."

The corners of Surai's eyes wrinkled, something that only happened when she was deeply worried.

What was Haven missing?

"This place . . ." Surai blew out a breath. "Archeron isn't himself right now, Haven. He needs us more than he would ever admit. He needs *you*. Bjorn was right; you are the only thing in years capable of piercing the dark fog of tragedy that surrounds Archeron."

Haven stiffened. "What do you mean, Bjorn was right?"

Surai blinked, the shame from accidentally saying the name of the Solis responsible for her mate's death written all over her. "He was the first one who noticed Archeron's affinity for you. Truly, the cursed seer probably knew how Archeron felt about you before Archeron did." She tossed her sleek black hair away from her face. "Anyway, forget the cursed seer—may the Shadeling take his soul. My point is, Archeron is acting this way because the thought of losing you, the only thing that's brought light to his life in decades . . . he's terrified if his mother found out, she would kill you just to punish him."

Haven rolled out her shoulders. She wanted things to be right between her and Archeron. Above all else, he was her friend. And not having him by her side now, when she needed him most, was painful.

And a part of her yearned to stay with her friends. She needed a night to relax, and it felt like ages since she and Bell had a proper good time together.

Still, she couldn't ignore her nagging curiosity over the heretical performer from dinner the other night. Nor could she shake the suspicion that the performance had been—in part—for her.

She wouldn't find a better night to lose the spies than tonight.

She swore to give Archeron another chance, made Surai promise to look after Bell, and then slipped through the crowd as her friends went the opposite direction in search of lanterns to purchase.

The city was a maze of rivers, vendor tents set up for the festival, and stores open late. The streets were crowded, barely passable. The crackle of the simple magick most citizens possessed— enough to do parlor tricks, but nothing compared to the Sun Lords in court—swept over her skin.

As she left the main part of the city, the sounds of the celebration lessened, the faint prickle of magick softening.

By the time she found her way to the small monastery off the beaten path, the one with the strange fountain of Freya, the moon peaked just above the tallest point of the palace.

At least here, the city was quiet. Not a single person in sight.

She stopped at the fountain to admire the statue again. Little candles of runelight floated in the water, casting pools of shadow over Freya and the mysterious Seraphian Noctis, Varyssian.

Immediately she sensed she wasn't alone. From behind, a man said, "I wondered when you would come back."

The voice wasn't aggressive or imposing. If anything, it was calming.

But her heart raced anyway, and she slapped a hand over the pulse jumping in her wrist as she turned. "Maybe I got lost, ended up here by mistake."

The performer who played Odin, the one they called a heretic and was chased by the Gold Shadows, shook his head. "No, *she* called you here."

She swallowed. This was silly. Why was she even here? "Who?"

"If you don't know the answer to that, you soon will." He smiled, a benevolent, uncomplicated smile. The kind she hadn't seen in a while. Not since coming here, at least. "Come, take some hot fermented milk thistle."

"I'd rather not." She dug her toe into a loose cobblestone. "The Gold Shadows, how have they not tracked you here yet?"

"The city is vast, and there are many places one may hide, when needed."

"I found you on my first try," Haven pointed out, unable to keep the smugness from her voice.

"Perhaps she told me you were coming," he answered.

The idea that he knew she was coming—no. He was messing with her, trying to get inside her head.

"Sorry, this was a mistake." She turned to leave. Turned . . . and then pivoted back to face him. "Why did they call you a heretic?"

The monk, or performer, or whatever he was heaved a weary sigh. "They are scared of the truth."

"What truth?"

"The one that will set us all free."

And . . . just like that, she understood. He was mad. Out of his mind. That explained it. Of course he was. Anyone who defied the sovereign just for a bizarre performance had to be.

She had been foolish for coming here. Whatever nagging feeling led her here was replaced with skepticism.

"Whatever you say," she quipped, leaning forward to pluck a floating lantern from the water. "Mind if I take this to release?"

"Take more," he insisted pleasantly. "One for each of her children."

Haven knew she shouldn't ask—who knows what a madman would say—but she couldn't help her curiosity. "What *children*?"

"The colors of the runelight. Over time, they've forgotten what the colors signify. The gold flame is for the Solis and the blue flame is for the Noctis."

"And the last one?" Haven probed, peering down at the strange almost purple light. If she focused hard enough, she saw it flicker from gold to blue and back, like it was both colors at the same time.

Instead of answering, he stared at her for a breath, seeming to contemplate something. Then he dug into the pocket of his heavy brown robe and pulled out a scroll. "Take this. Read it. When you're done, come back."

"Where?" she asked, ignoring his offering. "Here, or the hundred other places you claim to hide?"

"Wherever you choose, I will be waiting for you."

His smooth talk was starting to grate on her nerves. She eyed the scroll like it was a serpent about to strike. "What is it?"

He waggled the paper at her. "Read it and see."

"Fine." She took the scroll, surprised by how light the thick, yellowed papers felt, and stormed off, annoyed that she wasted time coming here. She didn't even bother reading it.

It wasn't until much later that she realized the only way he could have the scroll in his pocket ahead of time was if he was telling the truth.

He'd been expecting her.

Of course, he could keep pamphlets in his pockets for any of the straggling tourists who were naive enough to believe that lie. Whatever the scrolls said, they undoubtedly ended in a plea for money.

Still, when Haven passed by a trash barrel near a floral storefront, she didn't throw the papers away as planned.

She would read them later, and then, when they turned out to be the scam she suspected, she'd forget all about the mad heretic.

FIFTY-THREE

The thought of going back to the festival with all those people was exhausting, but Haven still wanted to watch the lantern release at midnight.

After a few minutes of deliberation, she found herself climbing the side of the Solaris Cathedral, the largest and most famous of all the places of worship built for Freya. The ornate stonework made most of the climb easy, although there were a few areas that were tricky.

When she reached the copper dome that crowned the sanctuary, the city sprawling hundreds of feet below, she scrambled to the top, plopped down, and retrieved the bag of meat pies she bought from a vendor. She wasn't exactly sure what type of meat they were, but it couldn't be worse than what she ate in Spirefall.

She sighed as she lifted the first pie. The flaky pastry was warm and fell apart at the slightest touch, sending steam infused with saffron, cumin, and clove cascading over her face.

"Oh, sweet Goddess Above," she moaned as she polished off the first pie. "Whatever you are, you're amazing."

Do you always talk dirty to your food? said a voice inside her head, the arrogant brogue familiar.

Ravius! He hopped over to her lap and began pecking at flakes, as if he hadn't betrayed her and disappeared without a word.

Her happiness at hearing his voice was fleeting, replaced by supreme annoyance. "Scat!" she snarled, swatting him away. "I don't share my food with traitors."

Ravius stopped a few inches out of her reach. He had the audacity to look wounded, the jerk.

"He didn't betray you."

As the velvety male voice swept across the roof and recognition set in, Haven's breath hitched. Only this time there was no initial happiness, only alarm followed quickly by a spike of fear.

Stolas perched high above on the gilt spire, a domineering cutout of horns and wings against the stars.

She didn't know what frustrated her more: The pulse of fear she felt as she made out the feral glint in his eyes or the tug of familiarity she felt in the wicked crook of his lips.

Then again, one could get used to a wolf if around one enough, but that didn't mean it wasn't a wolf.

"A wolf?" Stolas purred, cocking his head at her. "And here I was thinking I inspired something more regal like a dire hawk or a mountain dragon."

Runes. She threw up her mental blocks, waiting until she felt the heavy dullness around her mind that meant her thoughts were protected before relaxing again.

There were too many things she was hiding from him.

"Don't bother with your mental walls; I already know everything I need to know."

She bristled, annoyed by his ability to read her without even needing to access her mind. "Like what?"

"Like the blasphemous runes that snake down your spine."

The wounds that bound her darkness throbbed in reply. They were healing faster every day. She needed to find Surai soon to reopen them, as much as that was going to freaking hurt.

"What I don't know is . . . why," he continued, his tone dangerously soft. "Was it for your Sun Lord?"

A dark emotion bordering on rage shadowed his face, and she felt a chill go through her.

"I don't need to justify my actions to you." His eyes flashed, his disapproval fueling her anger. "You don't get to do that," she seethed. "Disappear from my life and then reappear, totally changed, and scold me for my decisions. I was tired of the constant worry that I would hurt my friends, so I bound my dark magick."

A wry expression transformed his face. "In my experience, one doesn't need dark magick to hurt others. You only need to be alive."

She startled as he began to wind down the side of the spire in graceful, too-fast movements. A simple yet elegant black tunic embroidered with silver blended into dark leather pants. The moonlight made his tousled white hair and pearlescent skin seem to glow from within.

He settled beside her without a word, and she tried not to focus on how easily he could kill her, if he wanted—or how soft his feathers were as they brushed her arm.

"You have an answer for everything," she scoffed, frowning to hide the unease his presence conjured.

"Not everything. For instance, why you poisoned me. I have an idea, but not a conclusive answer."

Her pulse spiked, but there was no use denying the obvious.

"*Almost* poisoned you. But I didn't, remember?"

He arched an ash-colored eyebrow. "I do. Vividly. I was there."

"What gave it away?"

"Besides you slapping the glass from my hand?" An amused grin found his face, as if he were reliving the moment—and enjoying it. "Do you think that's the first time I've encountered Godsbane?"

Exhaling, she dropped the second meat pie onto the paper bag and wiped off her hands. Ravius immediately pounced on it. "So you knew even before I stopped you?"

"Beastie, I knew the moment the sovereign sat you next to me, which also hints at her involvement." He turned to face Haven, his eyes a little too teasing for someone discussing his own near-assassination. "Did you know, the demonic version of dark magick inside Godsbane gives off a very specific . . . vibration."

"No, I . . ." She didn't finish that statement because she was starting to feel like the worst assassin in the history of ever.

"Right after Morgryth murdered my parents and took me prisoner," Stolas said matter-of-factly, "back when Godsbane wasn't so rare and Morgryth was just discovering her talent for creating infinite ways to torture me, the vile poison was part of my regimen of pain." His focus hovered on some distant point in the horizon only he could see. "She started slowly. A drop here, two there. Honestly, I think she was curious how much I could take without dying. Turns out, a lot."

"I thought it could kill gods?" He grinned at that, so she quickly amended, "Not that you're a god."

"Of course not," he teased. "I only look the part."

She rolled her eyes.

"The ancient magick that binds me as the Netherworld's master is tricky. It works to keep me alive because it needs me. Even that entire bottle wouldn't end my suffering. I know because I've tried myself. The effects are excruciating, but I wake up still very much alive and still very much bound to my own personal hell."

"So then you can never die?"

"It would take the most powerful weapon in the realm to kill me, and then—only then—would the curse binding me to the Netherworld be broken."

"You should probably inform the sovereign of that fact."

A dark chuckle. "You really think she doesn't know?"

Oh—oh. Runes. Haven felt so incredibly stupid. "Then why put me through a fool's errand?"

"What do you think would happen if you'd been caught *trying* to poison me? The girl Prince Bellamy got into the tournament?"

As the full truth hit, she sucked in a breath of air and then slowly let it out again. "It would look like Bell had something to do with it."

Groaning at her foolishness, she let her head drop back against the stone base of the spire. On her second day in the Sun Court, she'd nearly fallen into the sovereign's trap.

And no one would have believed her when she claimed it wasn't Bell who ordered the assassination attempt. Bell had been taken by the Shade Lord and tortured by Ravenna.

To the outside world, he had every reason to want Stolas dead.

"And?" he pressed.

She felt like they were in her meadowscape training all over again, only this time, instead of magick, she was trying to master courtly intrigue . . . and failing miserably.

"And . . ." she began, trying to get inside the sovereign's head. To see what she could gain from the trick. "The sovereign would benevolently overlook Bell's role in the assassination attempt, ensuring the most powerful mortal king owes her. She would kill me, of course, the idiot assassin who thought she could off the Lord of the Netherworld. And five years from now or a hundred, she would collect that favor."

"Now you see. In the Sun Court, nothing is as it seems."

"Even you?" she asked softly.

He pinned her with his heavy gaze. "Especially me."

Their eyes connected long enough for her to feel heat spring to her cheeks, and she focused on her third meat pie instead, taking an angry bite. Crumbs littered her shirt as she glanced down at the city. "Then why play along?"

He shrugged. "I was curious to see how far you would go. After all, you did *think* it would end my life."

His smug tone made her want to both punch him and apologize, but she sagely chose the latter. "I'm sorry. For almost—but not—poisoning you."

"I imagine in your world that passes as an apology, so I will accept it."

An annoyed sound convulsed her throat.

"I also imagine," he continued, slowly, dragging this whole apology thing out because he was a sadistic jerk, "that she used something you hold dear as leverage. Perhaps that wide-eyed prince you keep insisting on saving? Is that why you're here?"

"You wouldn't understand."

"And my sister? I felt her presence the minute I arrived. Just tell me she's safe."

"She is, relatively speaking." Haven exhaled. "It's the citizens of Solethenia I'm worried about."

His lips were quirked at the corners as if he found all of this amusing. Yet, despite the frustration she felt, she had the misfortune of wondering, just for a moment, what those lips would feel like to kiss.

Would Stolas use them like he did his words, weapons to disarm and wound and distract, depending on his mood?

More unwanted questions followed.

How many other lips had they touched? How many hearts had they broken? How many promises and lies had they spewed?

For the first time ever, instead of seeing Stolas as a monster without wants or desires, she recognized him for what he was: a powerful male imprisoned in the prime of his life.

She tried to imagine him as a young prince in this city, reading poetry and strolling around with that arrogant I-rule-the-world demeanor she used to despise. Tried to imagine him courting girls and struggling with untying corsets.

Only, that was too normal, and Stolas was anything but normal, even as a young, smarmy prince.

She let her gaze wander to his horns, the silver caps still there. Soft strands of blue light fluttered around the metal adornments. How she wanted to ask Stolas about them.

How, suddenly, she wanted to ask him a *thousand* questions.

But one question superseded all the rest. "Stolas," she said, holding his gaze despite the strange intimacy that came with it. "I need to know if you've sided with Ravenna."

There. She'd said it. The wyvern in the room. The one thing that would make all of this right. Because if he said no, if he looked her in the eyes and promised he was still her friend, still working for some greater cause, she would believe him.

He had never lied to her . . . that she knew of. Never.

"You nearly poisoned me for someone you love," he said softly. "Do you imagine me incapable of the same?"

Was that his cryptic way of saying yes? That she had some leverage over him the way the sovereign did over Haven? Besides Nasira, who could Ravenna threaten to make Stolas turn so fully to her side?

All the questions were giving her a headache. New tactic. "We both, obviously, will do what we have to for those we care about," she said. She was still looking into his eyes, willing him to confide in her. "But I need to know, Stolas. Can I trust you?"

Shadows caught in the hollows of his cheekbones as he held her gaze, and she was reminded just how beautiful he was. Especially beneath the stars, the delicate light of the moon pooling inside his silver irises and turning his ivory flesh luminescent.

His refusal to look away made her all the more hopeful that he would reassure her somehow. She didn't want to give him up.

In a strange way, he'd been the only constant in her life since Bell was taken what felt like years ago.

She tensed as he brought his hand to her face, his fingers cool beneath her chin, and lifted so that she couldn't look away.

"Beastie, you are a mortal and I a Noctis, therefore you should never trust me."

Her heart sank. She tugged her chin from his grasp and glanced over the city before he could see the utter disappointment in her face.

"So we're to be enemies?" she breathed, finding the idea foreign, despite everything.

"I prefer soldiers on opposite sides of the battlefield."

The ease of his answer compared to her conflicting emotions angered her. "Soldiers on opposite sides kill one another," she reminded him. "If it comes to that, if the sovereign finds a weapon capable of ending your life, am I supposed to wield it against you?"

He loosed a mournful laugh. "I know my life must seem glamorous with the unending torment, week-long torture sessions, and absolute enslavement and humiliation at the hands of my parents' murderer, so let me be clear. If you have the opportunity to finally end my eternal misery, take it."

The implication in his words pierced her heart. How many times had he tried to kill himself? Tried to end his misery and suffering?

"Until then," he continued, tugging on an errant strand of his wavy pale hair. "We could pretend to be normal for once and do something . . . trivial."

"What do you have in mind?"

What more could there be between them when he had just basically declared they were enemies, both employed by opposite tyrants?

Perhaps, like her, a part of him was lonely. She was a constant in his life the same way he was in hers.

In fact, sitting here with Stolas was the first time since she'd arrived that she felt able to truly breathe.

To be herself. Whoever and whatever that was.

Without a word, he drew a small paper lantern shaped like a peony from his pocket and lit the wick with magick. Haven did the same with hers. The flames guttered in the wind so he spread his wings, protecting the magickal fires until they grew strong enough to withstand the breeze.

Far below, a thousand runeflames choked the air and swelled the rivers until the fires joined into one single beast, a living embodiment of the city, so brilliant it lit up the entire sky.

All that magick created a perfume of cinnamon and roses that, when mixed with the briny, floral scent of Solethenia, made something wholly strange and wonderful.

Stolas nodded to the magnolia orchid in her hand. "You are supposed to make a wish before you release it."

Haven closed her eyes. She was about to wish that Bell would win the tournament and become king of the Nine when Stolas said, "No, Beastie. You must wish something for yourself and only yourself."

Her throat was dry as she swallowed, suddenly uncomfortable. Wishing good for others was easy, but for herself?

I wish . . . what? What do I want?

There was only one thing in all the world that she had ever truly desired . . .

I wish to discover the truth about my family.

"Done?" he asked quietly.

She realized his wings were still wrapped protectively around them, the feathers close enough she could lean back an inch and feel their silky-soft filaments against her cheek.

She nodded. "What did you wish for?"

He tilted his head to the stars, a faint grin curving his lips. "The impossible."

Then they sent their lanterns into the air to join the others, watching the sky in silence, long past when the fires had burned out and the shadows had reclaimed the night.

FIFTY-FOUR

There were twenty finalists at the training field, when only yesterday, there had been over fifty. Instead of the illusion of forests and mountains and lakes, the arena had been left as is: a long stretch of marble encircled by heavy railings.

Haven and Bell had arrived a few minutes early so they could go over a new maneuver Xandrian showed Bell last night.

She eyed the prince, his tired eyes, wrinkled clothes, and too-big smile. "And, what did you say happened again after the festival ended?"

Translation: how did you meet up with Xandrian?

Surai clapped Bell on the shoulder. "Your innocent friend here talked me into entering one of the *residences* on Hyacinth Street."

Haven flicked up her eyebrows. "Wait—aren't those known for—"

"Shh." Bell pressed a finger over Haven's lips. "Your friend here promised we wouldn't talk about that part of the night. There are

380

things that transpired that I will never be able to scrub from my mind. Ungodly, unnatural things."

Haven took in his bright red cheeks and burst out laughing.

The Meadow District had streets all named after flowers. Hyacinth Street in particular was known around the world for its eclectic herbal shops, colorful residents, and occasional orgies. If the bards were to be taken seriously, kings and noblemen from every nation attended the lavish, week-long affairs.

"I love the smell of hyacinth in the morning," Surai said, rolling her eyes. "That's the code phrase to enter. Don't ask me how I know that."

"And . . .?" Haven pressed, cutting her eyes at Bell. No way was she going to let him off that easy.

"And," Surai answered, "we decided Hyacinth Street and what it offered was *not* what we wanted—"

"At *all*," Bell offered, interrupting Surai. "I might have seen my father and Cressida there, I don't know. It's all a bit hazy."

"The incense is infused with spells," Surai added. "Love spells, lust spells, euphoria spells. We're lucky we got out with all our clothes on."

Bell rubbed his temples. "Don't remind me."

"And, then, somehow, we ended up at a tea shop on Wisteria Lane having magnolia tea with Xandrian," Surai finished, cutting her lavender eyes at Bell as if she didn't know which was worse: orgies or the gorgeous Sun Lord. "But don't worry," she added quickly. "I didn't leave them alone."

Alarm prickled across Haven's skin. "What did Xandrian want?"

"Nothing, really," Bell said, but the way he kept pressing his lips together—his nervous tell—said otherwise.

Xandrian finding Bell last night couldn't be a coincidence.

"Did he ask any questions?"

"No," Surai insisted. "It was boring. Small talk mostly. I nearly fell asleep. At one point, Xandrian joked about Bell showing him his chest tattoo—"

"He doesn't have a tattoo," Haven interjected.

"I know," Surai answered, frowning. "Bell pointed that out, all too happy to unbutton his shirt and show Xandrian his birthmark."

Surai shot Bell a withering gaze, and Bell threw up his hands. "What? He asked."

Haven narrowed her eyes. "I thought you said he didn't *ask* any questions."

Surai shook her head. "That wasn't a question. That was a spoiled Sun Lord who wanted to see how far he could undress a naive mortal. At that point, I decided it best we leave before the prince took off his pants too."

Something felt off about the entire interaction, but Haven couldn't place what, exactly. Tucking the story away to examine later, she retrieved a long sword and an axe from the pile of weapons offered to contestants and shifted each in her hand, testing the weight.

She chose both.

As they walked to an empty spot by the balcony, she glanced over her shoulder at Surai. "Nothing about Xandrian is boring."

She nodded. "I'll agree to that."

Haven whipped around and nearly bumped into the grinning Sun Lord. Unlike Bell, Xandrian looked rested and fresh. The top half of his sleek blond hair was pulled into a top knot, the rest falling artfully around his shoulders.

His icy blue eyes skipped over her to Bell. Something flashed inside them, and the corners of his wicked mouth flicked up.

What the Netherworld was that?

Haven couldn't help but notice the way Bell brushed a hand through his hair and looked away.

Oh no.

No. No. *NO.*

Xandrian was toying with Bell, and Bell was too innocent to understand that Sun Lords like Xandrian used sex and attraction as weapons. Perhaps Xandrian thought he could seduce Bell and gain valuable information on the mortal kingdom. Perhaps Xandrian had a bet going with those horrible, preening friends always hanging on his arm.

Or perhaps he was simply bored and Bell, with his sweet, trusting nature, made an easy mark.

But no way in the Netherworld would she let Xandrian hurt Bell. Not when he was just starting to heal from Renault's death.

As if Xandrian heard her thoughts and was taunting her, he insisted on joining them as they practiced the maneuver.

It was a gateway spell similar to creating a portal, called threading. If used fast enough, the spell could transport the lightcaster seemingly through thin air, threading them from one point to another.

The problem was the spell took the lightcaster between the fabric of this realm and the Realms of Other. If done incorrectly, the lightcaster could be trapped in another realm.

And it took years of practicing and high-level skills to puncture the realms and skip between planes.

Years Haven didn't have. After a century of practice, she might be able to conjure the magick needed to pierce the plane with her mind, but until then, she needed to use runes and verbal spells. Only she was horrible at making the correct rune, she couldn't pronounce the word correctly to save her life, and trying to do either one fast enough to thread any distance was beyond her capabilities—which meant Bell sucked at the spell too.

"Don't worry," Xandrian assured them. "Threading takes a millennium to truly master. This is a complete and utter waste of time."

"Then why help?" Haven hissed.

"Because it's . . . entertaining?" He bared his perfect teeth in a grin and she imagined knocking each perfect white pearl out with the butt of her sword.

"As always, Xandrian," Surai growled as, perhaps sensing Haven's anger, she put herself between Xandrian and Haven. "Your company is a pleasure."

Xandrian winked at Surai before turning his proud gaze on Haven. "That was an impressive showing between you two yesterday. And that wing spell . . . I'm just glad Prince Bellamy practiced it before the trial."

Haven narrowed her eyes. "How fortuitous."

It came to her that Xandrian creating a ravine that forced Bell to practice the wing spell probably wasn't a coincidence.

That didn't mean he was their friend, though, or even rooting for Bell to win. There had to be something behind his motives.

Xandrian gave a curt bow, his fist pressed into his heart, and then he led Bell off to train.

Surai seemed about to say something, and by the downturn of her mouth, it was likely scolding Haven for something, when her gaze suddenly darted behind Haven.

Haven followed her stare to the athletic girl bounding toward them, and for a breath, Haven's heart clenched.

Rook! A wild shock of joy swelled Haven's chest—but no, it *couldn't* be Rook. And now that she looked, really looked, she saw it was Rook's sister, Ember.

All the same, the irrational hope and following disappointment settled deep in Haven's core. And she could tell by the stricken look on Surai's face that she had mistakenly thought the same thing.

Haven thought Ember and her mentor, an older Morgani female who stood a foot taller than all of them, would pass by, but they stopped a few feet away.

Haven studied Rook's youngest—and according to Surai, favorite—sister. Kohl smudges shadowed her deep brown eyes, the moss-green band that ran from temple to temple drawing out the amber flecks inside the brown. Unlike Rook's tawny, sun-bronzed skin, she was fairer with a dusting of taupe freckles.

Surai had once told Haven the Morgani were allowed to color their eye band red only after one hundred kills in battle. Yet, the fierceness in Ember's face made it hard to believe she hadn't already accomplished that feat.

Ember nodded to Haven. "Well done yesterday. It took guts to go after a bog crawler." Ember slowly settled her gaze on Surai, and Haven felt her friend go stiff. "Surai, thank you for bringing Rook's body back. She was interred in the Elysian crypts with her ancestors. My mother held a big ceremony for her and everything, the daughter mighty enough to break the Curse. I thought you might like to know."

Surai tilted her head, her dark hair bobbing around her chin as she found the Morgani Queen high up in the balcony, surrounded by Morgani female guards. "You know talking to me is forbidden. You shouldn't risk your mother's wrath."

"Rook is gone so the oath of silence against you is broken. Besides, Rook isn't the only one who can defy my mother."

Surai's face remained emotionless as she watched Ember and her mentor leave, the apathetic mask she'd donned since the moment she spotted Ember perfectly crafted.

But, as practiced as she must have been at not letting Rook's family see her hurting, when Surai looked to Haven, a deep well of emotion glinted in her lavender eyes. "Those are the first words her sister has ever said to me. Rook desperately wanted us to be friends, but . . ." Drawing in a breath, Surai squared to face Haven. "Enough emotions. Time to train. And since Archeron isn't here—"

"Telling lies about me, Surai?" Archeron drawled, loping across the arena to join them. Haven's muscles automatically stiffened as she prepared for his usual hostile attitude, but he surprised her with a wide, beautiful smile.

Her insides warmed, thawing some of her ill temper toward him. Goddess Above, she'd missed that smile.

Surai's shocked face mirrored Haven's as the Solis girl stared open-mouthed at Archeron. Then she flashed Haven a thumbs up and bounded off, probably to find some decent coffee.

Living in Penryth had made Surai quite the addict.

Without a word, Archeron began a light swordplay warm up and they settled into a comfortable back and forth. Part of her was afraid to speak first. Afraid the moment she did, his anger would come surging back.

The warm-up moved to a quick series of lunging, feinting, and parrying, and soon sweat pasted Haven's fresh tunic to her arms and chest.

Archeron noticed, too, his eyes tracing the exposed curves. Unapologetic.

"Have you never seen breasts before?" she teased, trying to hide the edge in her voice, the one that belied the hurt from their estrangement.

"Plenty," he countered. "I'm only staring because you forgot to button the top of your tunic and, well, it's distracting."

A quick glance down confirmed the opposite; the gold buttons with dahlias on the face were very much still—

She sidestepped the fiery orb he tossed at her a half-second before it would have knocked her on her ass. "Cheater!"

"There is no cheating in magick," he amended.

A laugh spilled from her throat as she opened the top three buttons of her blouse, the air wonderfully cool against her sweaty chest. "You're right. There isn't."

His smile faltered, his stare lingering exactly where she wanted it.

Grinning, she lunged into a quick volley of attacks that sent him falling back. After that, they fell into a rhythm of maneuvers, and when practice was over, it was as if they had never argued.

The next day, it was the same. And the day after.

On the fifth day, it was as if they'd never missed a beat, and she watched him as he explained some offensive spell. Even sopped in sweat, his face serious, almost studious, he was beautiful. A god among gods.

Runes, she'd missed this part of them. The playful back and forth. The simple acknowledgement of their attraction. And yet . . .

She snuck a glance toward the east side of the arena where Stolas and Ravenna trained. Last night, she'd dreamt of him. For some reason she couldn't recall, she was trying to get to him, and he to her. But there was a monster between them, a horrible beast of shadows and claws and the most terrifying red eyes—

No. She ripped her gaze back to the beautiful Sun Lord in front of her.

Stop thinking about Stolas. Focus on Archeron.

Archeron was simple. Easy. He was a friend, a loyal companion, and he could be her lover—she saw that with such sudden clarity.

He would be a great lover.

Goddess Above and everything holy, that was *beyond* clear. She blushed just thinking about what they would do to each other when finally alone.

As if reading her thoughts, Archeron sheathed his sword between his shoulder blades and cleared his throat. "So, any plans tonight?"

Haven blinked. "Plans? Beyond watching Demelza and Surai argue over the best way to prepare coffee?"

"I ask because, well there's this place in the Asgardian district, a . . . they serve food, and I thought . . ."

Haven had never seen Archeron this nervous, and it took everything she had to hide her smile as he continued.

"If you are hungry later, and you aren't doing anything, would you like to join me?"

For a heartbeat, she hesitated. The past five days had nearly made her forget the hurt his anger had caused—but it was still there. Lurking behind every smile, every laugh.

He had hurt her. More importantly, he abandoned her when she needed him most.

And yet . . . she understood his anger. And she wasn't naive enough to think being in a relationship meant getting along all the time.

She stared innocently at him. "Is this your way of apologizing?"

His grin was devastating. "This is me offering us both a new start."

"Huh." She pretended to ponder the idea. "I will think about it."

He swallowed. "Well, if you decide to join me, I'll be waiting outside your apartments at dusk. No later. They don't take reservations and we won't get a seat if we go after dark."

"Noted." She smiled sweetly. "Anything special I should wear? I mean, if I go."

Grunting, he raked his gaze down her form. "I'm not sure *what* you wear will matter much later."

Her toes practically curled as she watched him stroll away, his swagger very much indicating he knew she was staring at his ass. *See*, she thought. Archeron is easy. Uncomplicated. Predictable. With Archeron she could have fun.

On the other hand . . .

Across the arena, she lifted her gaze to Stolas—only to discover the Lord of the Netherworld already staring at her. He was clad in dark pants, his shirt stripped off to reveal cords of muscle writhing beneath his flesh. The wings shading his body looked almost blue in this light, and they flared as if they could feel her appraisal.

Unlike Haven and even Archeron, not a drop of sweat soiled his body.

He smiled, a wicked thing, and she responded with a grin of her own.

Now *that* was complicated. A soldier staring at another soldier across the battlefield, knowing there might come a time when they had to fight to the death.

With a curt nod, she cut across the arena toward the hydration tents, ignoring his lingering gaze. She needed to do something that should have happened a long time ago.

FIFTY-FIVE

Haven found Avaline beneath one of the cooling tents used by finalists alongside two members of her court, also halflings by their small wings and dark hair. In fact, early on, it was informally established that this was the Noctis tent, and the Solis and mortals wouldn't step foot inside.

Good. They wouldn't be expecting her then.

Haven paused just outside the entrance, sizing Avaline up. She looked admittedly striking in a long charcoal skirt slit up the side to show off long, lean legs. A matching charcoal breastplate covered her torso, her unbound onyx hair cascading to the sword belt at her waist.

One of her friends was busy combing dust and bits of debris from Avaline's dark gray feathers while they all laughed.

None of them noticed the surge of light magick Haven cast until it was too late. It slammed into the three halflings, binding their arms and wings on impact.

Haven lifted her hand, palm up, and Avaline jerked five feet into the air.

The entire tent went silent as Haven prowled toward Avaline. The Skeleton Queen's eyes were livid, her teeth bared, a look of rage twisting her beautiful face into something ugly.

This could end very badly.

"Be very careful what you do next, mortal," Avaline said, her voice surprisingly soft.

"I just thought, since you tried to kill me in the first trial, that it was time we finally spoke."

Avaline laughed. "That's what this is about?" She glanced around at the others in the tent, then said, "Leave."

Haven unbound the three halflings, her pulse slowing as the tent emptied. None of the other occupants even hesitated before complying, which meant they either didn't see Haven as a threat or were too terrified of Avaline to argue.

Neither of those options were good.

Haven dropped the queen a few inches, teasing her with the possibility. "If I release you, will you behave?"

Avaline tilted her head at Haven, the gesture disturbingly animalistic. "Do it and see."

Haven pinned Avaline with an unflinching stare. "Do something stupid and I'll make it so you never fly again."

Jaw clenched, Haven slowly lowered Avaline to the ground. As soon as Haven unbound the queen, she flared her wings to their full wingspan, the movement sending metal cups flying and the tent flaps fluttering out.

Avaline cracked her neck, her eyes never leaving Haven's. "There are no rules inside the trials. What I did was fair."

"And it has nothing to do with Archeron and me?"

Her eyelashes fluttered in surprise. "You are the mortal he has fallen for?" She laughed. "To be honest, I expected . . . more. The most beautiful women in all the realm have been trying to enchant him for thousands of years, and he falls for *you*?"

Haven bristled, but she did look completely different to Avaline, so she decided not to take that personally. "That's why I'm here. You are bound to him, and he to you. If you don't want me to continue . . . whatever it is we're doing, I'll stop."

Avaline laughed again, her head falling back and pale throat bobbing. "Oh, Shadeling Below, you are hilarious. I could care less who he fucks." She looked Haven up and down as if she still found it unbelievable that Archeron could consider her attractive. "I do, however," she continued, "care very much that he knows which side he's on."

"Side? What side?"

"Stupid mortal, there are always opposing forces at play, and there are *always* sides. Mortals have a tendency to end up on the wrong side, meaning you complicate things. So sleep with him all you want, but do not meddle in things you do not understand or try to force some false sense of convoluted morality on him."

"If you haven't noticed, I can't force *anything* on him. He's the most stubborn person I've ever met."

The sharpness of her features softened, and Haven wondered for the first time how much Avaline actually cared for Archeron. "Typical mortal, you are blind. Halfbane loves deeply, and he is influenced by those he cares about. That's what makes you potentially . . . dangerous."

Haven was willing to bet that if Avaline thought Haven truly was dangerous, she wouldn't hesitate to murder her. And it probably wouldn't look accidental like the ice breaking on her spell.

"So why try to make me lose in the trial?" Haven persisted.

"That wasn't personal." Avaline laughed again, and Haven

could see how one could find Avaline charming, when she wasn't being murderous. "The sovereign ordered it." Avaline winked. "Welcome to the Sun Court, mortal. Where every friend is a potential enemy, every honeyed word drips with lies, and every too-sweet smile hides a poisoned dagger."

As Avaline strolled away, the light wind ruffling her soft gray feathers, Haven called out, "I don't care who orders it. The next time you attack me, I'm taking it personally."

"Good for you," Avaline said without looking back.

FIFTY-SIX

After a long nap and an even longer bath, Haven started the painful process of finding appropriate attire for tonight. She stared at the few gowns she'd brought from Penryth, suddenly hating every single one.

Archeron had never seen her in anything but riding attire. The thought of wearing something just for him . . .

She should have been excited by the prospect, but—now that she'd had time to think about it, something kept nagging at her. A reservation about tonight she couldn't quite articulate.

After days of suffering under Archeron's anger, she'd been so relieved when he suddenly turned on the charm again that she hardly questioned if she wanted their relationship to continue.

Of course she did. How could she not? Especially after everything he'd done for her.

Stop overthinking things. Tonight is just for fun. You need this.

She ran a hand down a crimson velvet dress before dismissing it. She was just nervous after their fight, that was all.

By the time Bell arrived, she'd given up on both dresses and was dead set on her usual leather pants and tunic.

Bell and Surai insisted she at least throw on a fresh silk top that wasn't riddled with stains. The wounds winding down her spine were breaking open, the blood seeping through her bandages and into her shirts.

Demelza's solution was a type of rust colored moss that was supposed to stifle bleeding. Whether it did or not, it smelled horrible, and even after Surai dabbed her own collection of tuberose and mountain honeysuckle perfume oil along Haven's neck, the musty stench clung to her nose.

It was strange looking into a mirror and seeing a stranger before the illusion fell away, but when it did, she studied her true reflection. Like always, her focus went to her runemarks. Her flesh had darkened beneath the relentless sun and the graceful swirls seemed to glow against her flesh.

"Where's he taking you?" Surai asked as she plucked the jasmine from their windowsill, broke off a stem, and settled the pale yellow flower in the elaborate tangle of braids Demelza had created.

Haven shrugged and released a breath. "I don't know. He said some little restaurant in the Asgardian district."

"Rafoli's?" she squealed, clapping her hands together. "That place is amazing. Try the black truffle soup, fried oysters, and bouillabaisse. Oh, and if you don't get the sticky kumquat pudding we can no longer be friends."

Haven laughed. "Sure you don't want to come? Archeron won't mind."

She snorted. "He would definitely mind. I'm just glad, you know, you guys are okay and that he's . . . better."

"Better?"

"More adjusted to being home and everything."

Haven tossed her hair over her shoulder as she crossed to the door. "I'm sure after I order one of everything on the menu he's going to be less adjusted."

It was Surai's turn to laugh. "Don't forget to bring your friends something too."

Haven grinned. "Of course."

It was still early in the day, a few hours of sunlight left, so Haven set out toward the library first. When the monk gave her the scroll yesterday, he'd forgotten to mention it was written in another language. She just wasn't sure which one yet.

Hopefully someone at the library could help her.

The library was nearly empty, only a handful of patrons scattered along its winding, shaded balconies overlooking the city. Inside, she found a librarian restocking books in the maps section. Haven guessed by her mahogany skin and sharp, angular runes the slim, older woman was Asgardian.

Kind brown eyes appraised Haven. "I am Riella, how may I assist you today?" the Asgardian said in perfect mortal tongue.

Carefully, Haven retrieved the scrolls from the small pack she carried and unfurled the thin, brittle paper. There must have been a preservation spell involved because the entire thing felt one tug away from crumbling to dust.

Haven cringed, expecting the librarian to tell her the writing was a scam, some tourist trap.

"Hmm." Riella frowned at the paper, one hand reaching out as if to touch the item. As she took in the strange hieroglyphs engraved into the vellum, her demeanor changed.

She inhaled sharply and removed her hand. "This is demon tongue, most likely Serakki, common language of the Demon Lords. Where did you find this?"

Haven shoved the scroll back into her pack. Instinct told her to lie. "An old relic passed down from my . . . grandfather."

"Well, you will struggle to find anyone who can translate Serakki. The ancient demon language was banned after Odin's final imprisonment, when the nations purged everything that came from the Demon Lords' realm, including literature."

Crazy old monk. Why give her something she couldn't read?

Haven shifted on her feet. The wounds binding her dark magick throbbed, making her more irritable than usual. Still . . . her curiosity was piqued.

Surely someone could translate.

"What about the"—Haven lowered her voice—"Noctis?"

Even though the library was practically deserted, she felt the need to whisper the word.

Riella frowned again. "Perhaps, the Seraphians . . . out of all the kingdoms, they consorted most with the Demon Lords— but, no." She shook her head, a pitying look crossing her face. "Sending an innocent young mortal like you to trade favors with a Noctis would be a terrible mistake."

Haven refrained from correcting the kind librarian. Haven was two of those things she claimed—young and mortal—but innocent? Whatever innocence she possessed had been stripped away slowly. First when she was stolen, then used by Damius, and finally when she faced down Morgryth.

By the time the Curse was broken, any trace of innocence clinging from her youth had been destroyed.

"Please," Riella added, "you would be better off burning the scroll than bargaining with a Noctis. They are hideously clever creatures that trade in lies and pain."

Haven grinned. She knew of a Noctis in particular who would take great offense to that.

It took five minutes to craft a note to Stolas, and four times that long to lure Ravius with a ruby-encrusted dahlia brooch, a present from Bell years ago. Another thirty minutes passed as she climbed to her hidden spot on top of the aviary.

Meeting with Stolas, in the open, meant questions she didn't care to answer.

Ravius arrived first. His claws prickled her shoulder as he landed.

Where is my reward? the greedy little beast asked.

She shooed him off her shoulder, ignoring his squawk of protest. *Where is my Shade Lord?*

As if in answer, a tug of familiarity pulled at her core as she felt a presence enter her space.

There you are, Stolas.

FIFTY-SEVEN

That familiar prickling heaviness sifted over Haven's skin, a caress of dark magick reaching out for hers. Only this time, her dark magick, bound as it was, burned like molten fire down her spine at the contact as it struggled to escape.

Pissed—her imprisoned magick was so very pissed. It was growing stronger with every second her skin mended itself, which was happening earlier and earlier each day. As if her light magick was eager to be joined again with the dark—an idea that made no sense.

Beneath the thick paned glass, the falcons shrieked in alarm. They felt him too.

"Are you always going to sneak up behind me?" she asked, pivoting to face him. One hand still rested on the small sphere of iron-reinforced glass that rose from the middle of the domed enclosure.

Stolas chuckled. "Are you always going to refer to me as 'your

399

Shade Lord'?"

At the sight of him, her heart ratcheted into a wild cadence. A raw savageness clung to him, as if he had been training hard recently, his eyes sharp and cruel. A leather tie bound his pale hair back from his handsome face, and clothes so black they swallowed the light clung to his predatory body.

The way he moved, the inhuman quickness and grace . . .

His eyes—silver and ringed with gold—twinkled. "Perhaps," he added, "I was ensuring this wasn't some sort of trap."

She bristled at the cutting edge of his voice. "What do I have to do to make you forget I nearly poisoned you?"

A roguish smile. "A few things come to mind."

She cringed at his innuendo—and the flutter her heart gave at the thought. And when his grin deepened—

He was reading her thoughts even now.

This was a bad idea. He was toying with her.

Gritting her teeth, she glanced at the sun sinking lower by the second, its pinkish-gold rays gilding the chapels and rivers below. "You kept me waiting on purpose."

Prick. Soulread that.

"Perhaps I enjoyed watching you wait. The way you played with your hair and unconsciously hummed to yourself as your impatience grew. Has anyone ever told you that you're adorable when you're frustrated?"

Against her will, heat bubbled beneath her cheeks. Runes, she hated letting him know he got to her.

Tucking his wings into his body, he crossed the roof and settled beside her, his black leather boots quiet against the glass.

"I sent Ravius with that note an hour ago." Haven flicked her focus to the east where the Asgardian District nestled, runelight twinkling from the smoky-gray painted restaurants. One of those was Rafoli's.

"Yes, a strangely worded note about wings that can't fly and sky you can't reach." He chuckled. "You are atrocious at riddles."

"And yet, you found me."

He met her stare, grinning. "When needed, I can find you anywhere, Beastie. Especially now that"—he sniffed the air— "you reek of shade moss. But it's the other scent that interests me. You're wearing perfume." He inhaled again, his lips twisting into a vicious grin. "The cheap brand the prostitutes near the port favor. I doubt your Sun Lord will mind."

So that's why he made her wait. Haven rolled her eyes. He was trying to unsettle her, or piss her off—or both. And it was working.

Her temper flared. "I was trying to be secretive in case . . . well I imagine your wife would be pissed if she knew we were meeting."

"Don't," he growled, an emotion close to hurt glittering inside his eyes. "Don't use that word. She may call me her husband in public, she may have forced me to attend the crude Golemite ceremony that bound us, but when I take a wife, she will be chosen by me—and my equal in every capacity."

Haven swallowed hard, immediately regretting her words. Especially knowing how he felt about Ravenna—even now.

How could she have ever thought he would willingly join that witch's side?

The entire world viewed him as husband to Ravenna, complicit in her madness—but Haven knew the truth because he had shared it with her. Had trusted her enough to be vulnerable in her presence.

"Sorry," Haven said. "Low blow." He might enjoy needling her, and she him, but some things were off limits.

"You are forgiven, Beastie, as always."

There was a light in his eyes that made her nearly forget his mercurial mood, and she toyed with the jasmine in her hair as a thought came to her. "Wait. You said, 'when I take a wife.'"

Just like that, the light vanished. "Slip of the tongue. Now, what do you need? Ask and it's yours."

For a price?

Settling against the enclosure at her back, she retrieved the scroll. His long fingers were delicate as they spread the paper. As he read, perhaps unknowingly, his teeth captured his full lower lip and his wings twitched, the wind rippling over the gorgeous tapestry of feathers.

She watched his teeth needle his lip back and forth. The little gesture made him seem so . . . mortal.

Bell did the same thing whenever poring over boring historical documents, sometimes to the point of chewing his lip raw.

Stolas handed the scroll back. "Where did you get this?"

"Can you read it?"

His focus shifted to the city below. His jaw set.

The silence stretched long enough she thought he was going to refuse—but then he said, "My mother entertained the Demon Lords once a year—when they were still allowed to come to our world. She used to trade with them for their dark artifacts and magick-imbued weapons and, on rare occasions, ancient spells. Once she even traded for a demon, a worlack, to guard outside my and Nasira's room at night."

"A demon guarded your room?" What kind of mother would trust a demon around her children?

He smiled at the memory. "I ended up slaying the worlack after it slaughtered a maid who heard me crying one night and tried to come to my aid. She was barely older than me. By the time the worlack finished with her, there was nothing left but a shard of her femur. And by the time I finished with the demon, there was nothing left of him but smears of pitch-black blood." Another grim smile. "My mother was furious when she saw her grand hallway mired in demon gore."

Correction, Haven thought. It was the demon who should have been protected from Stolas, not the other way around.

Still, she shuddered, remembering the demon that nearly killed Bell. "How old were you?"

"In mortal years, twelve."

She tried and failed to imagine him at the age. Children belied an innocence that Stolas had probably never possessed. "What did your mother trade for the items?"

A dark shadow fell over his edged features, now veiled in shadows from the setting sun. "Slaves. Mostly prisoners of the Shadow War."

The Shadow War—which meant some of those prisoners would have been mortal. Another shudder, this one deep and violent, wracked her core. "That's horrible."

Still looking out into the city, he shrugged, even as one corner of his lip twitched. "All the kingdoms did the same. It's the only thing the Demon Lords would trade for. Some like the old Sun Sovereign, King Aramos, tried to resist, but the ancient spells and runes the Demon Lords could offer were too powerful."

"Powerful but dangerous." Powerrunes like the one Haven gave Bell came from the Demon Lords, runes that harnessed raw, unpredictable power.

Stolas nodded, some of his snowy hair slipping over his forehead. "By the time we understood the consequences of the archaic blood magick, it was too late. Demons infiltrated our lands, answering to only one master."

"The Shadeling." Even saying the name aloud felt wrong

somehow, like she might accidentally conjure the fallen god.

Dusk tinged the air, a delicate watery gold that faded with her every breath and drew out the tawny rings inside Stolas's eyes. Eyes that were now staring at her in a way that trapped the breath in her lungs. "Where did you get this?"

She shook her head. "Can you read it or not?"

Still holding her stare, he said, "The Demon Lords often required written contracts signed in blood, so my mother ensured Nasira and I were both capable of reading and writing Serraki. I can translate this for you, but you may not like what it says."

"So you already read it?"

"No. Translating the glyphs will take an enormous amount of effort and time." A cryptic smile played off his lips. "But by the first two glyphs alone, I have a hunch what this scroll is."

Not says, but *is*. "What?"

"Have you heard of a blood augur?"

She shook her head.

"Demon Lords used them to divine the future much like the Solis use seers."

Her fingers flexed over the scroll as she peered down at it. "So what is this? Some sort of prophecy?"

He tsked. "All good things come to those who wait."

"Not in my experience." She snorted, wrapping her arms over her chest as the temperature began to drop. Below in the Noctis quarters, figures swarmed the courtyard, night drawing them out like a snake charmer's whistle.

Night. *Oh, no.* Dusk had already come and gone. She thrust the scroll at him. "Take this. I need to hurry back to my apartment."

He slipped the scroll into a pocket. In the darkness, his irises glowed softly. "You haven't asked what I want in return."

"That's because you haven't told me," she snapped, in a rush to shimmy down the aviary toward the stairs.

Wait, Archeron. Please.

"There is nothing I need currently, but when I think of it, I'll let you know."

She glared at him. Of course he would leave a bargain open ended. "Fine, but—I have the right to refuse if it puts me or anyone I love in danger."

"Of course."

Before she could take another step to the side of the aviary, he slid behind her and scooped her into his arms. She nearly gasped as they lifted into the air, his wings spreading to their full length.

Bastard.

"Put me down," she snarled, squirming against his hard, muscled flesh even as . . . inexplicably, her body rejoiced at the contact.

The feeling of absolute safety in his arms was strangely intoxicating—and an irony considering *who* he was. But her body didn't care, and she blushed as warmth crept down her middle.

Goddess Above . . . "Put me down," she ordered, worried he would sense her unexpected desire.

Amusement made his voice lilting as he said, "Are you sure? I've seen how slow you are at conjuring a simple wing spell. If I let go . . ."

She turned in his arms, ready to rake her nails down his chest—only the flash of excitement in his eyes said he might enjoy that too much.

"You did say you were in a hurry," he reminded her, the smarmy, smug, pompous bastard.

A few seconds later, they were in the courtyard in front of her apartment. Stolas landed silently. His teasing might have been rough, but his touch was gentle as he lowered her to her feet.

The moment her boots scuffed the uneven cobblestones, she wrenched from his arms, her gaze scouring first the doorway to her apartment building and then the garden.

Her heart fell. Archeron hadn't waited.

As Stolas took in her expression, he instinctively moved toward her, his voice lacking any of its usual biting sarcasm. "What's wrong?"

"Nothing—I just, I think I hurt a friend." When she realized she had moved *into* his touch instead of away from it, she darted to the door. "I'm fine. Let me know when you finish the text."

"See you tomorrow bright and early," Stolas called.

Right, the second trial was tomorrow. She desperately needed a good night's sleep, but she knew she would never rest until she smoothed things over with Archeron.

So she searched for him. She went to the restaurant just in case he'd gone there to wait for her. She visited the small room he shared adjacent to the king's in the mortal wing of the palace. When all else failed, she wandered the corridors of the palace, praying she would run into him somehow.

Until, finally, when the first pink whispers of dawn streaked the night sky, she wearily climbed the steps to her room, defeated. She couldn't shake the shadow that fell over her, and she resolved, somehow, *somehow*, to make this right.

FIFTY-EIGHT

She isn't coming. The thought repeated every few minutes as Archeron waited in the darkness like a fool, the prized pink begonias he'd picked from the royal gardens—the ones he'd risked punishment for stealing—drooping at his side.

He had done everything to prepare for tonight, including bargaining with the mortal king to secure a night of freedom. Everything had been planned. The food—Haven would love it— perhaps dancing afterwards—Haven would probably hate that— and then he would have taken her to the room he rented, the one he sold the last of his stash of runestones to pay for, the one with the huge king-sized bed and stunning view of the ocean . . .

She isn't coming.

A wave of embarrassment crashed over him, and he retreated from her front door until partially hidden by the thick tangle of clematis and wisteria blanketing the pavilion wall.

A male standing with flowers in hand, waiting in darkness—

anyone who passed would guess at his humiliation.

So this was what it felt like. How many times in his youth had he done the very same to expectant females? How many promises had he made only to break them later when something better came along?

No. This was Haven. They had fought, sure, but she would never stand him up.

Minutes passed. His shame deepened until it became a hideous beast wrapped around his neck, as real as the pathetic flowers in his hand. His mind warred with itself.

He should wait.

He should go.

She was held up.

He was a fool for waiting.

She was always late.

She was with another male, laughing at him.

She would never . . . never . . .

A growl exploded in his chest as he recalled with perfect clarity the way she looked at Stolas after he whispered to her a week ago. The primal urge to find her exploded inside him, overtaking his senses.

No. She would never lower herself enough to cavort with the Lord of the Netherworld. Just the thought repulsed him.

The dark flash of wings drew his gaze to the courtyard in front of her apartment. As he made out the Noctis male so close to the mortal apartments, instinct had him dropping the begonias and then reaching for his sword.

Reaching . . . and then stilling as he made out first Stolas and then the female in his arms.

He didn't recognize her—not at first. The illusion that dulled her features and hair was too strong. Then, as if his nightmares were coming to life, he caught her unmistakable scent.

Haven.

Wrapped around the usual notes of sweat and her preferred jasmine soap was the Shade Lord's scent, along with the telltale mark of excitement and . . . his insides contracted as he picked up the faint scent of desire.

No. He hated himself for even thinking such a thing.

And yet—mortal women put off a particular pheromone when they were attracted to a male. After years spent in a court of mortal females who didn't even bother to hide their lust for him, he knew the aroma well.

No, she would never.

Revulsion twisted his gut. His mouth was bone-dry, his heart beating thunderously in his chest as he watched Stolas draw close to Haven.

Watched Haven lean *into* him the way he'd imagined she would tonight in his bed—

Goddess, no.

Rage—a blinding rage so visceral he thought he'd blacked out—burst inside his head. Pain roared through him as if the betrayal was a poison spreading through his veins.

Even now, knowing she stood him up, he might have given her the benefit of the doubt. But not after he saw the way she looked at Stolas—and the way Stolas looked at her.

Not after physically detecting her desire for the vile Shade Lord.

How long had it been going on? How long had they been laughing at him? Because of her, he endeavored to help the son of his enemy. Because of her he had held onto hope.

Because of her, he had given up *everything*.

He couldn't breathe, couldn't calm his heart. He wanted to smash something. Wanted to destroy everything around him.

Calm down. This was not him. He didn't lose control.

He needed to talk to her, at least. What if he was overreacting? There had to be an explanation.

She thinks you are nothing, the voice inside his head whispered. *She will just manipulate you again.*

"No," Archeron snarled.

They laugh at you while they fuck.

He was losing his mind.

How could anyone love you when you grovel at the king's feet like a dog? When you long after a mortal girl who laughs at you.

No.

She loathes you.

No, stop—

She teases you. Toys with you. She doesn't respect you. If she did, she would have obeyed when you forbade her to come here.

He tried to stop the torrent of words but they kept coming, drowning him with their accusations until he didn't know what was true and what was in his head.

The king did this to you. Your mother did this to you. Haven did this to you. They deserve to be punished.

"Show yourself," Archeron growled as he pivoted in circles searching for the source. A shadow flickered and he prowled through the garden after it.

He. Was. Losing. His. Mind.

More shadows converged. They pooled in the air around him, shifting whenever he tried to look directly at one.

And then he focused on a figure in the distance, and the darkness resolved into a face.

Magewick.

At the sight of the Noctis, Archeron drew his sword. Even without full control of his mind, he could still remember how to kill a man.

Magewick drew up beside the Sun Lord, dark shadows flickering where his wings would be. "Ready for me to help you yet, Sun Lord?"

Archeron's sword swept through the air. Disappointment hit when the blade cut smoke instead of flesh and blood.

"I'll never bargain with you," Archeron snarled, hacking wildly at the shadows.

"Soon," Magewick promised before his illusion faded into nothing.

Archeron kept chopping at that nebulous darkness until his shoulder burned and his vision blurred.

FIFTY-NINE

Haven stood in a circle with the rest of the finalists inside the arena, but her gaze kept wandering to the balcony above, searching for a particular Sun Lord's face.

There. Archeron sat next to the king. Unlike the rest of the audience who stared into the arena, undoubtedly taking bets on which contestants would make it back through the portal, he stared at something on the horizon.

Her pulse raced as she tried to read his face, his posture, something—but he was a blank slate. As she watched, the king gave him an order. His expression was emotionless as he leaned over and began helping Cressida with her cloak.

Pushing aside her anger, she focused on the twinge of unease. Something was wrong. Something that couldn't be explained by her absence last night.

For all she knew, he was the one who stood her up.

What had changed?

If only she could have talked with him this morning. She left early before the trial and went to his room again. But his attendant said he hadn't returned home last night. She'd left an apology note for him, but there was no way to tell if he'd gotten it.

She tried not to dwell on that now as she mentally prepared for the second trial.

Surely if she explained how it was a careless mistake, he would understand.

Stop. None of this matters right now. Haven bit the inside of her cheek until the coppery tang of blood stung her mouth.

Focus, Ashwood.

In a few minutes, she would need every ounce of strength she possessed to keep herself and Bell alive—no, not just alive. She needed them both to win this trial.

Goddess save us.

Tilting her head to face the sun, she focused on her breathing as everything else faded away. Rare clouds streaked the faded turquoise sky. The arena had been moved to one of the balconies on the far west side, and the topaz sea glittered below, dotted with the white sails of ships.

She drank in the beautiful view as she willed her heart to slow, her mind to calm. *You can do this. You're mentally stronger than every single person here.*

Her eyes trailed the metallic runemarks mapping her flesh. She was made for this. Literally. A clawing sensation scraped down her spine as the dark magick imprisoned inside her tested its cage. Pain lanced down her back, but the binding held.

I can do this without you.

She swore she felt the darkness snarl in frustration, the growl reverberating through her bones.

Murmurs drew Haven's attention back to the center of the

arena where the sovereign stood, poised to speak. The metallic fabric of her slinky silver dress pooled inside Lysander's slim fingers as he held the train. Archeron's seven sisters—lounged under a pavilion at the far end of the arena—wore similar metallic dresses that glittered sharply beneath the sun.

Attendants began passing around small nets—large enough for perhaps six medium sized fish. Haven strapped hers to the waistband of her pants.

The sovereign swept her harsh stare over the finalists, her eyes heavy-lidded against the morning light. "Welcome to the second trial in the Praetori Fiernum. For this task, you are traveling to the waters outside the Isle of Mist. Beneath that tranquil sea lies the sunken palace of a king of old. Inside the castle are five giant clams, each containing a rare magickal pearl. But beware, the rare jewels belong to a sea witch that lurks deep within the underwater ruin."

Sea witch. Where had she heard that name?

One of Bell's stories repeated in her mind. Sirens who fell in love with mortal men were cursed by their sisters, banished to a dark existence. Only, there was something else.

Her blood chilled. Part of the curse . . . they were inflicted with an insatiable need for human flesh. If the illustrations were accurate, they became infested with thick black tentacles that eventually grew large enough to take down full size warships.

Haven glanced over the twenty finalists.

Twenty.

And there are only five pearls.

Haven managed to hide her panic as she met Bell's nervous stare. There were twenty finalists left and only five spots available for the final trial.

Two of those spots had to go to Bell and herself.

No—not *go*. No one was going to *give* the spots to her. She had to *take* them by whatever means necessary.

She ripped off her boots and other accouterments as the other contestants did the same. A solemn quiet had fallen over the arena. If the last trial was any indication, not everyone would make it back alive.

That will not be Bell and me. We're going to win by any means necessary.

She glanced through the crowd and caught Stolas watching her with a feline smirk. He was thinking the very same thing.

Hope you can swim, he mouthed.

Making a crude gesture, she mouthed back, *hope you enjoy wet feathers.*

Then the portals were in front of them. Without wasting a moment, Haven leapt through the spinning oval of blue fire into darkness.

SIXTY

Rain lashed at Haven's face and neck where she stood atop a sheer cliff overlooking the sea. A light tropical storm passed over the azure water, the dark clouds an island in a sea of otherwise perfect blue skies.

Good. I got the wet part over with.

Light flashed all around her as contestants burst through their portals. The bizarre scent of burnt hair and aloe she'd come to recognize came from the portals filled the air.

Waves crashed against the cliff's edge a hundred feet below.

She barely had time to find Bell before the finalists began jumping. Stolas was first. His wings magicked away as he dove straight into the choppy water below.

Runes. What spells would she need underwater? They would definitely require something to help them sink—

"Fill your net with rocks," Haven ordered Bell. When three fist sized rocks hung at her waist, she focused on what magick to use.

More contestants jumped. Rook's sister, Ember, grinned at Haven before she took a running leap off the cliff, somersaulting through the air toward the azure waters.

They were the only ones left.

There was no time to warn Bell. With a quick rune traced into her arm, she sent him a mimic spell and then thought of a fish.

His lips spread wide as he gasped for air, his hands jerking to his neck. When he felt the three gills on either side, he threw a panicked glance her way.

Sorry, she mouthed just as a sheer red webbing formed between his fingers. He glanced down, wiggling his webbed toes.

Her turn. She uttered another spell and a bubble slowly formed over her head. Once the bubble was fully formed, the world outside blurred slightly, like looking through a smudged window.

Better than drowning.

There was nothing left to do but jump. They shared a look and then threw themselves over the side. It felt like minutes before she hit the churning waters below. She dove but immediately realized her mistake; even with the rocks, the air bubble around her head made diving impossible.

They were losing time.

Surfacing, she burst the bubble and cast a longevity spell. At the same time, she sucked in air until her lungs ached.

The longevity spell amplified the object or action a hundredfold, meaning her breath would last for a while . . . unlike the time she almost became selkie dinner.

Hopefully it was long enough.

It had to be or she would die.

Correction, they would probably both die.

Happy thoughts, Ashwood.

As soon as she submerged, she lit an orb of magick, golden

light spearing the dark. Bell's webbed hands and feet made him fast, but she was a good swimmer and she kept pace. Her hair clouded around her head, the rose-gold color vibrant against the dark blue water.

She almost missed the urge to draw in air, and a part of her kept waiting for the instinct to breathe to kick in.

After what felt like countless minutes clawing and kicking deeper into the ocean, the seafloor rose to meet them. Their bare feet kicked up clouds of sand. They surged forward until the jagged edge of a stone wall appeared.

Throwing more orbs of light, she watched the structure grow into a grand staircase that led to massive double wrought iron doors. Shaped like seahorses and shells, they must have once been beautiful, but now barnacles and rust crusted the door.

They pushed through a fallen portion of the front facade. High above, a chandelier hung from the domed ceiling, suspended in time. Once luxurious furniture revealed from the gloom, covered in inches of sand and silt.

Schools of small silver fish darted through everything.

The deeper they penetrated, the more her body rebelled at what it felt inside these depths. There was a wrongness, as if the water itself was ruined. Even the kelp that had grown here was black, the slender plants dragging over their flesh like the claws of some immortal beast.

A stairwell appeared. They could either go up or down. Her heart sank as Bell pointed toward the darkness below.

Yes, let's go into that ominous, dark hole. I'm sure there's nothing scary down there.

But Haven knew what Bell was doing. Sea witches were supposed to make their homes in underwater caves—which meant sea witches felt comfortable in deep, dark, hidden places.

That's where the pearls would be kept.

Every stairwell they encountered took them deeper into that watery grave. Haven's heart slammed against her breastbone. Her ears popped. Every twinge of her lungs made her afraid her oxygen was running out.

One could panic here very easily. And panic underwater meant death.

As Haven swam past a grand piano and turned the corner, faint purple light spilled down the underwater hallway. Paintings lined the wall, the canvases deteriorated so that the subjects inside the frame looked like twisted monsters.

She extinguished her orbs and followed the strange light, Bell right behind her. It ended in a huge dining room. As Haven took in the frayed tapestries hanging from the walls, the whimsical chandelier made to look like coral, and long mahogany dining table, she imagined the parties that must have once been held here.

It took a moment to determine where the light came from. The clams. Giant mauve clams that barely fit atop the table. Four were closed. One was open, the pearls already missing from the pink inside.

The one in the middle had been pried open a crack. Just large enough to spot a pearl the size of a grapefruit inside. A magickal violet glow emanated from the misshapen jewel.

Haven startled as she spotted a silhouette kneeling in front of the clam—Ember. Some of her blonde braids had slipped free and they floated around her head like bleached seaweed.

The girl put a finger to her lips and nodded toward the far end of the huge dining hall.

As Haven took in the massive nest of slippery black tentacles, each one easily the girth of her thigh and lined with gray suckers, she nearly gasped water into her lungs. The nest of tentacles ended in the upper torso of a woman. Only the curse had turned her flesh wrinkled and ashen, and a monstrous face hovered above sunken ribs, deep purple gills, and shriveled breasts.

Thank the Goddess, the sea witch was asleep.

Sirens were notoriously beautiful, and Haven understood why the sea witch hid beneath the waters. She was ashamed of her hideous face and monstrous body. Ashamed, and angry.

Best not to wake her up then.

Haven nodded to Ember, who held a long bar and was prying open the clam, and floated to the first unopened shell. Bell took his place beside her.

They needed a tool to pry the shell open. Ember's appeared to be a piece of wrought iron taken from a stairwell. If Haven left the room to search for something, she took the risk that someone else would claim the pearl.

Think. What opening spells do you know?

She drew what she thought was the right rune on the outside of the clam, the exterior rough beneath her fingertips, but instead of opening, the clam began to float.

Runes. She undid the spell before the clam could drift away. Her pulse roared in her head. Soon the others would discover them. Desperate, she brandished the knife she carried, but it wasn't long enough to get proper leverage.

A surge of light.

Haven swung around. Ember's clam was fully open, the light from the pearl illuminating all the way to the rafters in the ceiling.

Ember grinned as she tossed the wrought iron bar through the water to Haven.

If they weren't in a rush, Haven would have kissed the girl. Flexing her fingers around the bar, she sank the end deep into the crack where the two edges met and heaved. Her clam opened for her, the pearl inside giving off a buttery golden glow.

That was easy.

Haven handed the bar to Bell, watched him snag his pearl, and was just about to grab hers when a whoosh of water rushed over her, sending her tumbling back. She looked to see what caused the disturbance, and her heart fell.

Ember's clam had slammed shut. She probably touched the inside as she reached for the pearl. Somehow she'd managed to get the jewel inside her net sack, but her leg was trapped between the two sides of the clam's shell.

Her leg was probably broken.

Don't help her, Haven thought. *We can't afford to lose this.*

And yet . . . Haven slumped against the outside of the shell. A year ago, risking her life to save a stranger wouldn't have crossed her mind.

Except, Ember wasn't a stranger. She was Rook's sister. Which meant Ember was family, in a way.

And if Surai knew Haven left her partner's youngest sister to die . . .

Runes. The pearl went into the net at her waist, and then she swam over, bracing a foot in the crack while Bell jammed the bar between the edges. Haven grabbed the end of the bar and they both slammed their weight into the thing.

A puff of air slipped from Ember's lips as she freed her leg. A quick inspection showed a shard of bone poking through the skin.

Alarm spiked through Haven.

Already, the blood spread through the water, darkening it.

Blood.

What did a sea witch crave more than anything else?

Haven reached for her knife, but it was too late. A tentacle slammed into her, sending her spinning sideways. And then a serpentine arm snaked around her chest, pinning her arms uselessly against her body.

SIXTY-ONE

Haven thrashed but the tentacle only squeezed harder. The pressure was unbelievable. Her ribs groaned. The precious air in her lungs tried to spew out her mouth. Shadows nibbled her vision.

A melodic underwater laugh warbled through the room as the sea witch drew herself up on her tentacles, using them like spider legs. Hair the color of pearls undulated around her hideous face, the only thing left of her still beautiful.

Massive black eyes drank Haven in, a terrible, endless hunger glittering in their depths.

Her mouth was a wrinkled pit, and it gaped to reveal shark-like teeth. "Three little fishies caught in my net. Who shall I devour first?"

Her ravenous gaze drifted to Bell. He and Ember were caught in giant slippery tentacles and suspended across from Haven, their arms also trapped to their sides. Both squirmed, trying to break free.

"Sweet Prince," the sea witch sang, her melodic voice worming into Haven's bones. "Do you think I am pretty?"

As the sea witch toyed with them, Haven ran through her list of spells, but adrenaline fogged her mind. She fought, jerking her arms and bucking. If she could just create enough space between the tentacle and her body—

Her left arm slipped free.

Haven reached across to her right side. Hope shot through her as her fingertips brushed the cool handle of her knife. She hadn't trained with her non-dominant hand in years, and her grip felt wrong.

Don't overcomplicate this. Stab, slash, repeat. Easy.

Stilling her mind, she slammed the blade into the black flesh constricting her chest. Dark, inky liquid poured from the wound as she quickly sawed back and forth, trying to sever the appendage.

But muscle waited beneath the slick skin—and muscle was hard to cut.

A screech of pain echoed through the water. Haven's head jerked back as the sea witch slammed her into the wall, headfirst. Her knife slipped from her hand. Pain shot down her spine and burst behind her eyes.

She groaned, spilling some of her precious air into the water.

Magick pulsed inside her palm. Even half conscious, Haven had somehow formed an offensive orb. She flung the fiery projectile at the witch, only to watch the orb shrink and die.

Again and again she tried. Her attempts pulsing light across the room.

Ember did the same, her magick searing the water as it streamed from her trapped hands.

Each time, the golden magick fizzled out.

Dark magick. The witch was cursed with dark magick. Any light magick would be devoured in her lair.

One of Ember's attempts singed the tentacle holding her, and the sea witch roared. As she flung them around, Bell and Haven passed close enough to touch.

Something flashed from his hand.

The double-edged Hadrassian blade. Somehow—somehow he'd managed to free it from his waistband, and now it lay inert in his trapped hand.

Their eyes met. Their hands brushed.

The dagger handle was hard and wonderful inside her palm.

She glanced down at the tentacle around her. Her attack from earlier had left a gaping wound, deeper than she'd hoped.

"Should I let you watch while I devour your friends?" the sea witch asked Bell, one of her free tentacles caressing his cheek. "Perhaps I will mount your head on the wall when I am through with you. Such a pretty, pretty face."

Right before Haven brought the dagger down on the arm holding her, the sea witch flicked those horrible black eyes to Haven. Her focus slid to the new dagger in Haven's hand.

Before the sea witch could react, Haven sliced the perfectly honed Hadrassian steel through the muscular tentacle, severing it in one go.

Another roar of pain, but this one sounded different. She cradled the injured tentacle to her body as fiery light rippled from the wound. Glowing veins appeared over her flesh, growing larger, surging like molten lava about to burst from her skin.

What in the Netherworld?

She'd ask Bell about that later. After they escaped the water.

Bell grabbed Ember under one arm, and Haven took the other side. Together they kicked for the hallway, the enraged screams of the sea witch right behind them.

Ten minutes passed. The twinge in Haven's lungs became an inferno. She needed oxygen and soon. The last stairwell appeared. When they emerged, shafts of watery light poured over them.

They dumped the rocks from their nets and began their final ascent.

Every kick was torture. Haven's arms burned, her thighs ached. Walking was going to be an effort. And the pearl hanging from her body threatened to drag her back under—along with Ember.

Halfway up, Ember wrenched from their grip, insisting on swimming the rest of the way herself. Pain wrangled her face with each thrust of her injured leg, but she pushed through it, the stubborn girl.

Rook would have been so proud.

Haven knew the sea witch was injured, but she didn't relax until they were on top of the cliff once more, thanks to a wing spell. Ember was too overwhelmed with pain to notice the signature wingmark was the same.

As they neared the portal, wet and holding each other up, Ember limped ahead.

Haven turned to Bell. "What happened back there?"

Bell's grin brightened his entire face. "The night blooming rose thorn extract from Spirefall? Apparently it grows on a tiny island near Effendier. I had our young *friend* scour everywhere for it."

Friend? Oh—*oh*. The winged she-devil. Friend seemed like the last word to describe Nasira, but Haven was too tired to belabor the point. "I don't remember it being that powerful."

Bell cleared his throat. "Xandrian gave me a book on poisons, which helped me discover a way to increase its potency."

Xandrian's name clanged through her. She didn't like that Bell was consorting with him anymore than she liked him hanging out with Nasira.

How many things had Xandrian given Bell now?

First an obscenely rare and expensive dagger and now a book?

"Well, whatever the Netherworld it is," Haven remarked, "I'd like some, please."

The heat from the portals sizzled over their wet skin. Because they weren't sure how many contestants had already passed, Ember insisted Bell enter the portal first.

"I would have died if you hadn't helped me," she added. "It's only fair."

Haven watched Bell disappear inside the light blue flames. Then she and Ember entered their portals simultaneously and found a cheering crowd waiting.

SIXTY-TWO

Stolas was waiting on the other side.

Surprise, surprise.

Lounged on a couch, his body casually leaned back and legs spread wide, he looked as if he'd won without an ounce of effort. His impressive wings were tucked into his back, and—much to Haven's annoyance—perfectly dry.

Ravius perched on Stolas's shoulder, looking for all the world like he'd survived the second trial, not Stolas.

Stolas's bored gaze crashed into Haven's and something passed between them.

He was happy she made it.

One side of his lips ticked up, and then he winked, the bastard. Fire shot down her middle, warming her from the inside out.

She dragged her eyes away before he could observe her reaction.

Above, their respective courts roared from the balconies. Streamers danced through the air, and some of the fans sang their

428

nation's anthems in languages Haven could only guess at.

A few minutes later, Avaline sprinted through the portal. Unlike Stolas, she was breathing hard, her wet wings dragging limply across the stone floor. But the last pearl glinted from her netting, meaning she was the final contestant to move on.

Avaline brushed by Haven as she passed. "Thanks for taking out the sea witch. I owe you one."

Haven wanted to smash the smug look from her face, but she smiled sweetly. "You're welcome. Figured you might need the help, and any friend of Archeron's is a friend of mine."

At the mention of Archeron, Avaline's eyes flashed, but she tamped down her rage with a cloying smile of her own.

Afterward, the five finalists were taken to the courtyard where a celebratory feast awaited. Tables shaded by large canopies were set up, and attendants walked around with silver trays passing out drinks. Mentors, family, and select members of each finalist's court were allowed to join the celebration.

After a night of searching for Archeron and worrying about the trial, Haven was tired. More than anything, she wanted to get out of her wet clothes and into a steaming-hot bath and then take a two-day nap piled beneath a mound of covers. Actually, she wanted to fall asleep *in* the bath while Demelza brushed her hair and fed her pastries.

But Bell needed this. Especially if, in less than a week, he would become King of the Nine. Mingling with the important mortals of their court would ensure he already had alliances formed when he began his duties.

She blew out a breath, and tucked her wet hair out of her eyes. *They were so close.* If she could endure a man-eating sea witch, what were a few power-hungry nobles?

So instead of sneaking away, she forced herself to grab a flute of moonberry liquor—watered down for the mortals, thank the Goddess—and find a shaded area on the palace wall to lean against.

From her vantage point, she watched Bell beam as his father clapped him on the shoulder, proudly bragging to anyone who would listen about his magickal capabilities.

Eleeza and her father were among the crowd, and Haven couldn't help but notice the way Eleeza looked at Bell—as if he had just broken the Curse all over again.

Although there was something in the princess's look that reminded Haven of the sea witch's starved gaze.

Poor girl. It was cruel to let her think Bell would ever marry her.

The angry sun dragged across the pale blue sky. Haven grabbed—and downed—another drink. Then a third. This was going to take a while.

She was flush against the wall, eyes slitted against the brightness, when she felt the tingle of dark magick prickle her skin.

"Stolas," she said without looking his way.

"You look as if you're having the time of your life," he remarked dryly as he joined her in the shade.

"What can I say? I'm never more in my element than when surrounded by conniving politicians and entitled royals."

Stolas chuckled before turning his attention to Bell. "The prince seems perfectly in his element."

Haven watched as Bell talked animatedly with a nobleman from somewhere in the recovering mortal lands of the north. "He loves people, and he sees the good in them when you and I see their every fault."

Stolas was quiet for a few breaths. "Have you thought through what will happen if he wins, Beastie?"

"*When* he wins," Haven corrected. "And it will take time for him to adjust to his new role, but when he does . . ."

"No. I mean, when you lose and the sovereign claims you for the rest of your mortal life."

She swallowed, the moonberry liquor suddenly warm and queasy in her belly. "I could ask the same of you."

"A mortal lifetime is nothing to me."

"I'll figure something out."

In her periphery, she caught his stare, but she kept her eyes on Bell. Afraid that if she looked at the Shade Lord, he would see the twinge of panic she felt.

Her shoulders relaxed as he turned to leave, but then he hesitated.

Silken fingers of his power brushed over her arm, so lightly it could have been the breeze. "You take care of everyone, but who takes care of you?"

As soon as he was gone, she relaxed. She wouldn't let him get in her head. Not when they were so close to their goal.

Luckily, Surai and Demelza found Haven, instantly brightening her spirits. They were arguing over whether demons could swim. At some point the conversation turned to the ball the night before the final trial. Demelza thought Haven should wear her hair up while Surai insisted she wear it down.

Runes, these two would argue whether the sky was blue.

Haven skipped a bored gaze over the partygoers—her eyes settling on Xandrian. As soon as Bell saw him arrive, he broke away from his adoring crowd and went to the Sun Lord. Haven tried hard not to scowl as the two found a quiet corner and fell into conversation.

But more troubling than Bell's newfound friendship with Xandrian was another Sun Lord. The one that, as her mentor, was supposed to be here for her.

No. She pushed thoughts of him aside. If Archeron wanted to be pissed at her over a misunderstanding, if he chose not to even let her explain about the other night, then maybe her doubts had been well placed.

Maybe Archeron hadn't been simple after all. Maybe a relationship would only make her already complicated life impossible to figure out.

Strangely, a part of her felt relieved. Being with a man promised to someone else weighed on her. Archeron had given up everything for her—and she knew deep in her heart that's why she kept trying to make it work.

Perhaps Stolas was right. She needed to take care of herself so she could focus on *why* she came here—to save Bell. Not just save him, but finally give him a role that could change the lives of mortals for the better.

As Ruler of the Nine, Bell would have authority over all of the mortal realms, the pact sealed in magick and unbreakable. He would leave a lasting impact on the entire realm.

That was worth sacrificing everything for—her love life and her freedom.

Determined now to end things with Archeron, Haven waited for him to show up to training the next morning. The carefully thought out words were poised on her tongue, ready to be delivered. Although she feared that when he appeared finally and she took in his face, the words would become jumbled and wrong.

He saved her from that humiliation when he didn't bother to show up that morning or the two mornings that followed.

Haven spent her days training with Surai, drinking tea at the library with Bell, and trying to find moments to speak to Archeron. But he was tied to the king, always gone on some errand or busy entertaining Cressida and her friends.

She left him notes but they went unanswered. Had Surai plead on her behalf for a meeting to no avail.

It was as if, overnight, their friendship vanished. The bond between them, the one forged from bloodshed and loss, gone as if it never existed.

This wasn't like before when he was mad but still acknowledged her. This was different. As if she had done something to irreparably damage their relationship forever.

On the fourth day, after he didn't show up to train her, she holed up in her room, furious. If he wanted to destroy their entire friendship over a missed date, fine. The stubborn, pig-headed peacock.

Demelza appeared with her usual offerings of horrible coffee and coddling, and Haven accepted both.

"Why so grouchy?" Demelza asked as she brushed out Haven's hair. Haven had gotten used to the daily ritual, found it . . . pleasant, even. Haven squirmed on the bed and was rewarded with a quick tug of her hair. "Stay still!"

"Maybe I'm grouchy because you keep yanking chunks of my hair out," Haven snarled.

"Hmm. Or perhaps it has to do with a boy?"

Calling Archeron a boy seemed wrong, but she didn't correct her lady's maid. "Maybe."

"Did he hurt you or did you wound him?"

Haven blew out a breath. "Both?"

Demelza chuckled. "That is usually the way of these things. Love is messy."

"It's not . . . love."

"Ah. Pleasure."

A blush swept over Haven's cheeks. Yes—so much *yes*.

"No, I—maybe." She had never truly analyzed her feelings for Archeron beyond wanting to make love to him—that was the point. Nothing complicated.

Except things *had* become complicated, and now . . .

Demelza tsked. "You are young. Pleasure with men you do not love is nice—if you are being safe." Demelza tugged her hair again, hard, to drive home that point. "When you love a man, you will know. There is no mistaking it."

Haven was about to find a way to distract herself from the entire awkward ordeal when a shadow fluttered over the windowsill and Ravius entered. He landed on the back of a wooden chair, eyed Demelza carefully, and then dropped a note on the dining table.

Tell that witch that if she dares to touch a feather on my beautiful body, Ravius said, *I will have my master rain down Netherfire on her miserable head.*

Knowing only one person would send Ravius with a note, Haven scrambled for the paper. "Demelza, he said you look pretty today."

Demelza let loose a string of curses, but she didn't go after the poor bird with a broom, so that was something.

When the note was in Haven's hand, she excused herself to the bathroom to read it.

Need cheering up? Meet me at the museum.

She wasn't sure what to expect from Stolas, but not that. Annoyed, she found a set of stationery in the desk by the window and scribbled back, *No.*

Ravius was barely out the window with the note before he came back with another one.

It might be fun.

"No," she muttered, penning a quick reply. "It won't be."

Ravius took the letter and, once again, returned swiftly.

She read the letter with narrowed eyes. *I could demand you accompany me. You still owe me a favor.*

Crumbling the paper in her hand, she marched to the window and went to throw the letter out—

Stolas entered the window, a devilish grin on his face. "Hi. Is that for me?"

Shock and anger made her throw the crumpled up ball into his face. It landed square on his regal nose and bounced to the floor.

For a wild heartbeat, as the realization that she just hit the Lord of the Netherworld in the face registered, she tensed, ready for anything.

Stolas arced an elegant eyebrow. "Am I to assume, then, that's your refusal?"

"Shouldn't you be translating my scroll?" Haven snapped.

"I was trying to, but I can feel your sour mood all the way from the roof of the palace."

"I'm not in a sour mood," she countered sharply, "and I don't appreciate you spying on my emotions."

"It's not spying when you fling them at me."

Bastard! If there was anything substantial close by she would have hurled it at his smarmy face.

Behind Haven, curses and prayers filled the room as Demelza rushed around, probably looking for a weapon.

His feral gaze slid to Demelza. Amusement tinged his voice as he said, "I will not force you to go. Stay here, by all means. She seems like lovely company."

Haven looked from Demelza to Stolas. She had been wanting to visit the museum, and considering it was the most famous in the realm, Bell would probably never let her live it down if she didn't.

Still . . .

"How long will it take to get there?" she asked warily. She was meeting Bell later at the library café.

"So that's a yes?" Stolas purred.

"Fine, but—"

Haven's words cut off as Stolas lifted her into his arms and swept them into the sky. They shot into the city, Demelza's screech of surprise growing fainter until all Haven could hear was Stolas's massive wings beating the air and the rush of her heart inside her skull.

SIXTY-THREE

At least this time, Stolas didn't carry Haven like a child, instead holding her from behind, his arms shackled around her waist. That was almost worse because it required his body to be pressed intimately against hers.

Again that physical reaction sizzled between them.

"What if someone sees us?" she asked.

She gasped as his lips brushed over her jaw. "I used a cloaking spell," he murmured, his smug voice hinting he felt her shiver as his breath stroked the inside of her ear. "This will be our little secret."

Ignoring the tingle of warmth that spread through her middle, she focused on the city below. The museum was near the theater district where the festival of lights was held.

Which meant it was on the other side of the city, far away from the palace. As they passed over stunning cathedrals with domed copper roofs, intricate mosaic tiles, and spires so tall Haven could almost touch their pointed gold tips, everything else bled away.

From here she could see residents strolling through the markets, gondola's gliding down the rivers, and the larger seafaring boats drifting down the canal.

Bell had showed her a map of the city the other day, pointing out the massive Heronia museum, a collection of interconnecting structures of white marble and glass ensconced in the side of a mountain. According to legend, the ancient museum was built by the first Sun Sovereign, King Annapoli, for his mistress.

As much as Haven hated to admit it, traveling here any other way would have taken hours to cross the city.

"Beautiful, isn't it?" Stolas remarked, his breath rushing over the shell of her ear. "I never tire of this view."

Her stomach dropped as they descended. She thought Stolas would make for the entrance, but he set them down on a rooftop garden connected to the largest structure, a circular building made entirely of glass.

For a moment, they stood locked together on the lawn. His long arms heavy around her waist, the feathers of his wings fluttering softly in the breeze as they canopied them.

Haven was the first to pull away. She scoured the side of the building for a public entrance. "What, are we breaking in?"

Stolas laughed. "Would that excite you? Because we can, if you prefer. Although I very much would like to use the door."

He waved his arm toward a section of red and green ivy, and a steel door appeared.

"How do you know of a secret entrance to a Solis museum?" Haven asked as she ducked beneath his arm—holding open the door in the guise of a gentleman—and went inside.

"First, it's not a Solis anything. The museum belongs to the realm and all the nations. They put it in Solethenia because, once, when there was peace, this city was considered nationless. Second, and more importantly, my mother was the largest donor. This wing is named after her, Corinth Hall."

They were at the top of a floating set of winding stairs, and Haven practically skipped down the hovering iron steps. Corinth? The name hardly filled the image in her mind of Stolas's mother, the former Empress of the Noctis.

It sounded so . . . normal. Sweet, even.

At the bottom of the steps, large oil paintings lined the walls. So many that Haven wasn't sure which to look at first. She let her eyes drift over the canvases, drinking in the rich colors and masterful use of light.

"These are from the whimsical era after the Shadow War. Most are by an Asgardian male named Dracoy who pioneered infusing magick into paintings."

Haven's eye caught on a gorgeous woman with large, soulful brown eyes and beautiful copper hair that draped over her naked body, doing very little to hide anything.

As Haven watched, entranced by the sheer skill it took to capture her cryptic smile, she began to change. Her brown eyes turned black, her half-smile twisted into a menacing sneer replete with an underbite of tusk-like fangs dripping blood, and ram's horns grew from her head.

Her naked flesh, once pale and youthful, turned gray, wrinkled, and pocked.

Haven flinched, the demonic image horrifying after such beauty. "What was that?"

Stolas stared at the painting, admiration in his face. "Dracoy wasn't just a master artist, but he dabbled in science and demon hunting. He was the first to discover that demons could possess bodies, and much of his work is dedicated to that subject."

He was right. The rest of the paintings depicted similar subjects, many with their blood mage's marks tattooed on their bodies—usually the nape of their necks, like with the demon vessel that attacked Bell.

"Is this entire wing dedicated to demon art?" Haven asked.

Stolas scoffed. "*Demon art*? Did your tutors not teach you the art histories?"

Haven rolled her eyes. "No, the king doesn't see art as something worth studying."

"If we had time, I would remedy that."

Haven swallowed, caught off guard by the intensity of his voice, and she strode down the hallway, if only to create space between them—and nearly jumped back when she encountered the life-sized bronze sculpture of a half-demon half-man with hooves and two heads.

Goddess Above, this place would give Demelza a heart attack.

Thinking of Demelza reminded Haven that her lady's maid would probably be worried about her. It wasn't every day the Lord of the Netherworld flew in your window and took you away.

Except, as Haven glanced over Stolas, he didn't seem like the Shade Lord everyone feared. The harsh lines of his face had softened, the cruel semi-permanent sneer he wore like a mask evaporating beneath the shafts of sunlight that poured from the glass ceiling.

In fact, he seemed the most relaxed she'd ever seen him.

"Come," he said, leading her through a set of heavy metal doors to another gallery. "This is only the beginning, and we have so much to take in. Normally I would recommend spending a week here to see everything, but time is short."

A *week*.

And he was right. Each new room held works of art that stole her breath and sent her pulse crashing dizzily through her veins. The idea that people could craft such wonderful creations—colorful blown glass made into huge flowers that took up entire rooms; life-sized hour glasses and sundials carved from azerite; busts of famous figures in history, from kings and queens to heroes and gods; abstract paintings that, when looked at long enough, uncovered the viewer's hidden desires.

Afraid of what they would reveal, Haven made sure to pass by those quickly.

When they entered a marble room with a landscape painting that took up the entire wall, Haven hesitated, her gaze clinging to the pastoral setting. Verdant, plush grass filled the canvas, a stone bridge arcing over a winding stream. An ancient forest of tall trees rose beyond, layered with mist.

It seemed so real, right down to the ripples in the water and the green-and-yellow shelled turtles sunning themselves on the rocks. And the light . . . the light sifted through the air, layers of gold trickling from the dense canopy of clouds.

She was so lost in the strange painting that she didn't notice Stolas reaching for her hand until it was too late. His fingers flexed around her wrist, his touch gentle but firm, and he pulled her toward the painting.

No, not toward the painting. *Into* the painting.

They entered the canvas, literally, and suddenly they were enveloped by that rich landscape, the burbling river only a few feet away. A cool breeze fluttered Haven's hair, infused with the smells of mud, rotted leaves, and pine. Silver fish flashed just below the stream's clear surface, and Haven squeaked with surprise as a rust-colored mother fox pawed at the fish while her kit swatted her swishing black tail.

"Where are we?" Haven whispered, afraid to scare away the

animals, even though they seemed entirely unaware of their presence.

"Inside what's called an oilscape, a tiny fold in the realm created by strong magick." He loosed a near-silent breath, his eyes following something in the forest beyond. "See, just there?"

He nodded his head toward one of those giant trees, and Haven gasped as the biggest stag she'd ever seen appeared from the mist. His ears flicked back and forth as he listened to something before he strolled to the river and drank.

"You knew he was coming?" she asked, unable to look away from the majestic creature.

"Yes, the same thing happens every day. If we had come an hour later, we would see a giant brown bear foraging beneath that rotted stump just ahead." His eyes were on the stag, but they were distant and unfocused, as if he was looking through the animal to something in the distance.

It came to her then. The details. The magickal feeling imbued in the very earth. "You know this place? It's real?"

"This is the land just outside my mother's childhood home somewhere deep in the wild forests of Shadoria. She wasn't royalty, she wasn't even from noble stock. But my father was marching with his army one day and he spotted her from the bridge, bathing in the river. He was smitten from that moment forward, and eventually she became his queen."

Haven breathed in the air, thick with magick, and tried to imagine his mother here. What had she been like?

And then something else occurred to Haven, and she took in the world with new eyes. "She created this oilscape?"

"She was a prolific artist, but this piece is the only artwork of hers that survived. It was her favorite. When she first became queen, she used to escape inside this gilded frame. Just hide for days on end. Sometimes she brought me and I would fish and hunt in the woods while she just sat there on the edge of the bridge, singing. Sometimes she would hunt with me."

A chill passed over Haven as she imagined Stolas and his mother hunting.

"What was she escaping from?" Haven asked, carefully, wary of the change in his voice. The raw, barely hidden anguish.

"My father loved my mother deeply, more than I've ever witnessed a Noctis male love a female—but when he chose her as his mate, he sealed her fate. By ancient law, the Seraphians are ruled by an Empress, and she was forced to take on that role. She was an admirable ruler, strong and commanding, fiercely loyal to our people . . . but sometimes—sometimes I think she would have been happier here."

Haven toed the plush grass. "How did the painting end up in the museum?"

"After Morgryth killed my mother, I lost my mind for a time. This was before they bound me to the Netherworld as its lord, before Nasira escaped even. I somehow got away from my guards and rushed to the oilscape. In my grief, I thought my mother had somehow hidden her soul here before she died. But I was a fool, a scared boy who couldn't face life on my own. She wasn't inside. I didn't have much time, and my magick wasn't what it is now, but I managed to thread it here." He raked a hand through his hair—the color of bleached stones in the watery light—and met her eyes. "This was the one thing I loved that Morgryth couldn't take from me."

"And Nasira," Haven reminded him, again carefully—her instincts warned her Stolas was on the edge. Despite what Stolas said, his mother's essence whispered from every blade of grass, every errant breeze.

This place affected him deeply.

Stolas laughed, a soft, bitter sound. "That remains to be seen. My sister was scarred by what she saw in Morgryth's court. Witnessing our parents' deaths at that age was enough, but there was so much depravity and I couldn't shield her from it all. Seraphians are predatory by nature, but we are civilized monsters, unlike the Golemites." A dark grin curved his lips, but it didn't reach his eyes. "I thought perhaps, being around you, your friends—I thought that might set another example."

Haven had no words. She'd certainly never thought of herself as a role model. Then again, they were talking about Nasira.

A sudden breeze sent dead leaves rustling near the forest. Flicking up his nine-point rack, the stag bolted into the woods, his hooves ripping up chunks of grass.

Stolas jolted from his trance and took her hand again. "Come. There is more to see."

After they left the oilscape, Haven couldn't imagine anything could top what she just experienced—not until she walked into the last room on this floor. Instead of glass like the first chamber with the paintings, this one had skylights positioned to illuminate the paintings at certain times of the day.

Currently, only one painting was highlighted. The largest one in the room, it would have drawn Haven's attention without the light. A family of Solis stood admiring the artwork, the parents whispering to their children in hushed, reverent tones. Plush red ropes cordoned off the painting, preventing the family from getting too close.

The cloaking spell must have hidden Haven and Stolas because the guests didn't spare them a glance.

They waited until the group left and then approached. Every step closer to the artwork made her more aware of the wounds at her back. The dark magick inside her clawed to get out. Throbbing against her flesh. Tearing at the deep scabs ridging her spine.

"The killing hour," Stolas murmured as he appraised the canvas. "Every day a few minutes before sunset, the light falls on this work of art."

The killing hour. The time when supposedly Odin stabbed Freya during battle with his poisoned blade, sealing her fate forever.

A pit of dread opened inside Haven as she took in the graphic scene of warring gods. The painting was split into halves, the right side dark and stormy, the great and terrible Odin surrounded by his army of demons, Noctis, and Shadowlings.

On the left, bathed in sunlight, were the mortals and the Solis led by Freya wearing luminescent golden armor. Odin, clad in spider-black chain mail, held Freya in an embrace that could almost be considered affectionate—if not for the dagger piercing her breastplate.

The frame itself was magnificent, heavy ash wood carved into all manner of creatures, and a silver plaque at the bottom read, *The Godkiller.*

"Beastie, you are looking at the most famous painting in the entire realm," Stolas murmured, his voice filled with rare awe.

Haven couldn't tear her gaze away from the horrible image even as her mind and body recoiled from it.

Her trapped magick purred, sliding around inside her, scraping against her ribcage like some awakening beast.

Clutching her side, she said, "What happened to the dagger?"

Stolas shifted his intense focus to her. "After the fall of Odin, the Solis nations had the Godkiller cursed and then locked away in the vaults beneath the city."

"So it's here?" Haven asked, surprised by how breathless she sounded. "Why not destroy it?"

Stolas chuckled. "I thought I taught you better. You cannot destroy something that powerful, and Demon Lord magick is especially tricky. So they locked the weapon beneath the vaults, and as an extra precaution, placed a curse on the blade that prevents Solis or Noctis from wielding it."

Not enough, she thought. *It's not nearly.*

A shiver passed over Haven, but she couldn't explain why the dagger had such an effect.

At least, not until she leapt over the ropes that were supposed to keep visitors from touching the painting and peered closely at the depraved weapon, drawn by something she couldn't articulate.

As she took in the highly-detailed dagger, dread spiked through her heart—dread and blinding terror.

Her blood went cold. Her lungs shrank until every breath was an effort.

She had seen this particular weapon before. The horns and fiery red eye, the slashed pupil. They were unmistakable.

The knife from her dreams, the one she plunged over and over into her friends' bodies, the one tied to the revolting presence—

That was the Godkiller responsible for murdering Freya.

No.

She stumbled back, nearly knocking over the ropes, the world tilting around her. Stolas caught her with his usual grace, but his face was anything but casual as he breathed, "What's the matter?"

Haven shook her head, breaking from his grasp. She couldn't let him know . . . couldn't let anyone know the truth. "Nothing, I—it's time to leave. I need to meet Bell and Demelza will be worried about me."

For a long, stretched out second, Stolas just stared at her, his eyes flickering a soft steely blue. She'd never seen that color before.

If she had to guess, she'd say grayish-blue meant worry. But worry didn't even begin to match the panic and disgust blazing through her.

Stolas didn't press her as they left.

He hardly said a word as he took her in his arms and lifted into the dusky sky, tinged scarlet with hints of gold. And maybe it was her imagination, but his hold seemed a bit tighter, more protective.

Not that it mattered. If Haven was dreaming about the most powerful weapon in the realm then even the Lord of the Netherworld couldn't protect her from the monster that haunted her dreams.

Herself.

SIXTY-FOUR

Haven gaped at the floor-length bedroom mirror illuminated with runelights, sure some magick was at play here.

"That can't be me," she breathed, staring at her reflection. The girl staring back at her wore a sleeveless champagne gown encrusted with pink morganite and gold dust, the thin silk clinging to every curve she possessed. A ruby inlaid dragon jewel pinned one side of her rose gold hair away from her face, forcing the wavy locks to tumble down her bare shoulder.

Her exposed skin—and there was a lot of it—rippled and danced as her fleshmarks made themselves known. Her marks were different than the tattoos engraved into the Solis flesh. The lines more delicate, the swirls and curves more pronounced.

And sometimes she could swear her marks changed . . .

"Runes, it looks even better on you than I imagined," Bell breathed. He was standing behind her looking gorgeous himself in a black jacket that showed off his wide shoulders and trim waist. Dahlia cufflinks sparkled from his wrists, and another dahlia encrusted with diamonds was pinned to his jacket. "What do you think?"

She traced her gaze first over the thin fabric hugging her hips and then down the slit in the center that stopped just above her belly button before cutting her eyes at him in the mirror. "I think I could have a job at Love Row in the city."

Love Row was where the madams and their girls sold their bodies. In Solethenia, it wasn't a bad profession, and many of the more notable prostitutes were stars in their own right.

Still.

Bell looked to Nasira who was sitting cross-legged on the bed, her pale hair disheveled and wings tucked tight to her body. She'd been visiting more and more lately. If Haven didn't know better, she would have thought Nasira was lonely.

Against Haven's wishes, Bell had promised Nasira she could sleep in his room. He'd ordered mini cakes from a bakery and special sugared candies for the occasion.

"Nasira, tell her she looks gorgeous," Bell said.

A sticky-sweet smile brightened Nasira's face. "You look practically good enough to eat."

Haven shot Nasira a scowl, but at least the girl finally seemed in good spirits. All things considered, Stolas's sister was faring well at the cliffs. Whatever she was eating, it had filled out her cheeks and body. Or perhaps it was simply the newfound freedom that accounted for her health.

Even monsters hated cages.

Surai entered the room wearing a deep emerald green gown with an open back, revealing the intricate fleshmarks mapping her shoulder blades down to her tailbone. Her sleek black hair, just long enough now to pull back in a small bun, was held together by two pearl-inlaid hairpins that would act as weapons in a pinch.

Surai's gaze went to Haven and the Solis girl let out a low whistle.

Haven rolled her eyes. "Why does Surai get the gown that covers her chest?"

Bell grinned. "Because it shows off her elegant back. Every dress should highlight one feature, and since your poor back is currently a mess of scabs . . ."

"Right, we get to parade my poor breasts around instead." Haven twisted, her wounds protesting with the movement. If not for the ball, she would have already had Surai recut the runes that bound her dark magick—but she was afraid of getting blood on the dress.

And Bell had undoubtedly spent a fortune on the thing.

"At least you can hide your face," Nasira pointed out as she stroked the three bejeweled masks on the bed. Apparently, it was tradition to wear masks during every Gathering of Flames ball.

For a night, every guest was nationless, stripped of their cultural identities and prejudices. The Noctis would magick away their horns and wings, the Solis would use spells to darken their hair, the mortals would be just as exquisitely beautiful as the others, and everyone would get along.

Hopefully.

Demelza came up beside Haven carrying something—a dove brooch. It was a simple thing, made entirely of gold and devoid of any jewels. Yet, for someone like Demelza, it would be worth a fortune.

Haven watched quietly as Demelza pinned the dove to Haven's dress just above her heart. "For protection, m'lady," Demelza said quickly, not letting Haven have a chance to refuse. "This was my daughter's and now it is yours."

An ache opened inside Haven's chest, words failing her. Demelza never talked of her daughter who died under the Curse's reign.

Too much—this was too much. But Haven couldn't refuse such a precious gift, so she squeezed Demelza's hand and said, "Thank you, Demelza. I'll cherish it always."

The ball was held in the largest hall on the highest floor of the palace. The walls opened up into balconies on three sides letting in the soft night breeze and heady scent of wisteria and honeysuckle. As Haven entered beside Surai and Bell, she tugged at the mask covering the upper half of her face. Made from porcelain, it was shaped and painted into the head of a stag complete with azerite antlers.

Bell's, on the other hand, was a blue and yellow butterfly mask, while Surai's was the face of a raven. That certainly wouldn't make her popular at the ball—not that the Solis warrior seemed to care.

As they strolled to a table filled with drinks, Haven looked around, trying to recognize someone—anyone—from the veiled guests. But the masks and the magick and the opulent outfits worked to disguise almost everyone.

It was disconcerting, being unable to distinguish friend from foe, and Haven toyed with the stem of her glass, unable to hide her unease.

"Stop fidgeting," Bell ordered, stilling her thumb over her drink. "You look beautiful tonight, *Ren*, the most beautiful woman in all the realm, and you deserve happiness."

Haven snorted. "All the realm seems a bit much, but go on.

Flattery will get you everywhere."

Across the room, Haven caught what had to be Eleeza watching them. A mask shaped like a tabby cat's face—orange striped, with whiskers made of spun glass—hid her expression, but Haven didn't need to see Eleeza's face to know the girl wanted desperately to dance with Bell.

Haven jerked her head in Eleeza's direction. "Put her out of her misery and ask her to dance, Bell."

"That would be a cruelty, giving her false hope like that." He flashed a handsome grin. "But there is one girl I'd like a dance with."

"No," Haven protested, retreating a step. "We both need our feet working and in good condition for tomorrow."

"We are inside one of the most famous ballrooms in the entire world, in a place where magick is hewn into every wall, every flower and crevice. And one day we will tell our children how we danced with Sun Lords and Shade Lords and queens, the two most beautiful people in the room." Bell swept into a low bow. "Remember, you cannot refuse a prince."

Haven laughed at that, but Bell was persistent, and he pulled her into the thin crowd already dancing, their shoes squeaking over the sun and moon mosaic at the center of the room.

"Aren't you in a lovely mood?" Haven teased.

Bell flashed a hesitant smile. "What would you say if I told you I was happy again? Truly happy? Despite what happens tomorrow, despite what my future holds?"

Haven's fingers flexed over his arm as he swept her over the dance floor. She had a tendency to lead, not follow, which made her a very poor dance partner. "I would say that's wonderful, Bell."

Light and shadows crafted by the thousands of runelights above swirled at their feet. Bell's hand was firm against hers as he dipped Haven, her hair spilling low enough to nearly touch the tiled floor.

Memories of dancing together at banquets in Penryth came to mind. She'd been terrible then, too, Bell's skills not good enough to compensate for her inadequacies. Cressida and his father always tried to make Bell dance with the daughters of the visiting lords, but he always chose Haven. And when no one was looking, they would sneak away to the library or the kitchen or the gardens. Anywhere they could be alone.

Because once upon a time, she was all he needed.

Surfacing from her memory, she focused on his face, alarmed as she took in his faltering smile.

"You're happy for me then?" he said.

Her footwork slowed, nearly tripping him. "Of course I'm happy that you're happy."

His fingers tightened around hers. "And . . . if I told you the reason for that was a certain someone?"

Haven blinked.

"I know," Bell continued, picking up the pace, "that I will never be able to replace Renault. But I think I'm finally ready to open my heart again."

Haven wanted so badly to celebrate this new revelation. Except, if her suspicion about *who* he was referring to was right . . .

It couldn't be, but who else?

She let him spin her around a few turns as she tried to clear her head.

Finally, when the music slowed, she met his anxious gaze. "Is this certain someone impossibly good looking and also incredibly dangerous?" Her foot collided with his, and he winced as she disentangled their feet. "Because," she continued carefully, "if that were true, I would have to tell you that I don't approve."

Bell couldn't hide his disappointment, and his gaze collapsed to the floor. "I'm not asking for your approval."

"Then what are you asking?"

"For you to support me the way I did you with Archeron . . . when you told me there was something between you and the Solis who murdered my brother, it felt like a betrayal, Haven. Still, I supported you, I tried to understand."

"That's different, Bell. He helped save you—"

"And Stolas?" His mouth was firm beneath his butterfly mask.

Heat flared across her cheeks. "What does Stolas have to do with this?"

"You are in love with the Lord of the Netherworld and yet I can't find a shred of happiness with Xandrian?"

She scoffed. "In love? With Stolas? Are you mad?"

He shook his head, a bitter laugh spewing from his lips. "You share his dreams, you talk about him constantly. Just yesterday, he came into your window and stole you away, and you came back glowing. Demelza was worried sick."

"I didn't—first, he didn't steal me away. And that meant nothing."

His eyes became pleading as he pulled her close. "I know you better than anyone. I don't understand what happened to make you fall for him, what dark spells he used to bewitch you, but you have. You care for a monster, Haven. A monster who kidnapped me on my runeday. A monster whose sole purpose is to torture and punish. And if you don't love him yet, you will."

Her heart was beating rapidly. Her breathing shallow.

"You don't know Stolas," she protested, wishing there was a way to make Bell understand something that even she couldn't make sense of.

He stopped right there on the dance floor as bodies whirled

around them, his nostrils flaring. "And you don't know Xandrian—"

"I know he's cunning and I know he's hiding something, Bell." She retreated a step. "And are you forgetting the vision we saw? The one where he *murdered* six Gold Shadows in the street?"

"Shh," Bell seethed. "Are you trying to get him killed?"

"No. I'm trying to keep you alive."

"Maybe I'm tired of you constantly saving me. Have you ever thought of that?"

She gaped at him. Where was this coming from? "Yes, I'm sorry to inconvenience you by trying to keep you alive. It must be a real hardship."

"Don't. You know what I mean. It goes beyond your oath, beyond your job—if that's what this is anymore. You continue sacrificing everything for me, but I don't want you to. Can't you see that? If I am to be the prince my kingdom needs, you have to stop protecting me from every mistake."

His words cut deep.

Walk away. In a few hours, this will all blow over.

Her heart ached to stop this madness, and she tried to swallow the angry rebuttal rising in her throat—tried and failed.

"How can you be so ungrateful?" she seethed. "People died so that you could live. People I care about. Archeron gave up his freedom, I died, Surai lost her mate, even Stolas gave up everything so that you could live." *Stop. Don't say another word.* Angry tears stung her eyes, but it wasn't enough. "The prince your kingdom needs? All I see is a spoiled boy who loves being adored."

He flinched, and she felt like puking. It was too much—it cut too close to the truth. Just as she felt the crushing guilt of what Archeron gave up to save her nearly every day, Bell would have felt something similar.

"Right." Hurt made his voice sound raw, almost hoarse. "You know, I get it now. Why you can't let me go. Without me, the poor, helpless prince, you have no idea who you are or where you belong, and you're too afraid to figure that out."

"Bell—"

Behind his beautiful mask, his normally kind blue eyes were unrecognizably cold. "I release you from your oath to me. I'm no longer your burden to bear."

Her hands shook at her sides. All the horrible words hung between them, choking the air. She wanted to say the oath didn't matter, she would always be loyal to him. She wanted to say so many things, but her anger drove away all the words but one.

"Done."

SIXTY-FIVE

Bell's words clanged through Haven as she fled.

I release you from your oath to me.

Ripping off a heel, she flung the shoe into the crowd, not caring who she hit as she darted toward the night sky peeking from the balcony. The second heel went sailing through the air—and skidded to a halt next to a group of three Noctis.

Her focus immediately shot to the largest and most dangerous Noctis in the middle. Stolas. His eyes twinkled with their usual amusement. But beneath the mirth, something else lingered in his black gaze as he drank her in. Devouring every inch of her with his eyes.

A villainous grin curved his jaw, and he dragged his focus up her bared throat to her lips before folding into a low, ostentatious bow.

His horns and wings had been magicked away for the night. Crafted from the deepest black, his jacket was fitted expertly to his muscular form. His silver shirt was casually open at the top, showing off a smooth, chiseled chest. Moonlight glinted off his mask, two obsidian wings that flared out on the sides and were centered by three rather large rubies.

The other two wore similar masks and attire. A female and male, they regarded Haven curiously.

Behind them, Solis and Noctis women danced together, the wisps of fabric they wore barely enough to be called dresses. Haven couldn't help but notice how they stared wantonly at the two Noctis males—Stolas, in particular.

"Delphine, Bane, meet Renfyre of House Volantis," Stolas drawled, taking a sip from his wine.

The two gave curt nods, and that's when Haven noticed their similarities. Both had cloud-white hair with widow's peaks, dimples, strange silver eyes, and the same half-smile.

Siblings? No—twins. Seraphian twins. Their wings hidden much like Stolas's.

Stop. She wouldn't get pulled into Stolas's orbit. Not right now with Bell's accusation still echoing in her mind.

If you don't love him yet, you will soon.

Jerking her chin in response, she muttered, "Pleasure," and then flashed Stolas an unmistakable look. *Leave me alone.*

The marble floor was cool against her bare feet as she stormed to the other side of the balcony—as far from Stolas and his friends as possible. She leaned over the marble railing and looked down at the waves breaking themselves over the dark cliffs far below.

Inside she felt the same. Like a thousand emotions breaking against her heart over and over.

I release you from your oath to me.

Bell didn't want her around. Somehow, she made him feel less than. Not good enough.

That had never been her intention. Never.

A light sea breeze blew over her bare skin, and she cursed her stupid, barely-there dress as gooseflesh ridged her arms. It didn't help that Bell had chosen this dress, and wearing it reminded her of how happy he had been when he saw her in it.

Or maybe it was that now her wounds were nearly healed, her dark magick clawed beneath her skin, searching for a way out.

As they danced, she hadn't noticed it, but now . . .

Sucking in a breath, she gripped the marble banister of the balcony, hard, as another pulse of the impatient magick reverberated through her body.

She should have had Surai draw the runes before they left, the dress be damned.

She needed to find Surai and have her recarve the runes, but currently, Surai was deep in conversation with Rook's sister, Ember, on the other side of the balcony.

Haven refused to be the one to take away that closure. She could wait another hour. She could endure the discomfort for that long, at least.

An attendant holding a silver tray brimming with glasses of dark wine stopped to offer her a drink—then saw her scowl and quickly moved on.

An Ashari male who stunk of moonberry liquor slid beside her, a salacious smile on his drunk face. He barely reached for her before she sent him reeling back, practically falling on his ass as her magick twisted his bones, threatening to break them if he tried again.

Turning quietly back to face the sea, she ignored his pain-filled curses.

Anyone that tried to talk to her fared the same. Mostly males who wanted to dance, or perhaps thought, as a mortal, she would have already been drunk on the strong liquor, enough to take to bed.

A few unlucky souls even tried to use their magick against her. Every single one left writhing in pain.

A figure caught her attention to her right. He was prowling toward her, and she prepared to send him away like the others . . . until she recognized that swagger, like he owned every inch of the world, the power roiling just beneath the surface of those elegant, gliding movements.

Stolas.

A flicker of heat sparked inside her chest. She recognized that too—recognized the emotion and hated herself for it.

It means nothing.

Inside his mask, his eyes glowed silver, those yellow rings around his irises as bright as the stars above. And when they looked at her, once again taking in her dress, her hair, her face, they darkened to pewter.

His appraising stare wasn't like Archeron's—unapologetic, taking what it wanted. He drank her in slowly, methodically, gauging her reaction as he did.

It reminded her so very much of the reverent way he admired the paintings. Devouring every single detail, every brush stroke, every use of color and light as if etching the painting into his mind to revisit again and again . . .

You care for a monster.

She crossed her arms over her chest. "What do you want?"

He tilted his head, the moonlight casting deep shadows beneath the sharp cliff of his cheeks visible just below the mask. "Why did you run away back there?"

"You seemed to be having a grand time without me."

"Did I?"

Her mind flashed to all those half-naked females writhing behind him, desperate for his attention, for—

Nope. She didn't care.

His nostrils flared delicately and then he took another step toward her. "You've been crying."

She couldn't talk about this right now, not with him—especially not with him. Already she felt ready to crack open. Bell's hurtful words and her cruel reply repeating over and over in her mind.

Shaking her head, she turned her back on him—something she would never normally do—and faced the ocean. "It's nothing. Do you have the translation finished?"

Bell had said she clung to him because she was too afraid to learn who she was or her purpose in life. And in some way, perhaps he'd been right. All these years, she'd convinced herself that, if not for Bell, she would have left to find her family.

It had been a convincing lie.

So much easier to let herself believe she had a family waiting for her somewhere than take the chance she might search for them, only to realize they were dead.

The scroll the monk handed her . . . deep down she knew whatever words were written on that ancient paper, they would help unlock her past.

Something slid over her bare shoulders. Stolas's jacket. The silk was cool and heavy against her flesh, the dark inner lining imbued with Stolas's exotic scent of irises, blood mandarin, and musk.

She felt Stolas come up right behind her, felt her imprisoned dark magick lurch at his nearness. His breath was cool against her neck as he said, "The translation will be finished tomorrow morning. I will hand it off at the trial."

She whirled to face him. "What if you are otherwise engaged tonight?"

A wicked smile lit up his features. "All night?"

"I mean, I'm sure there are hundreds of females here who would love to share your bed." Her voice came out brittle and sharp. She was taking her anger out on him. "Sleeping with the Lord of the Netherworld must be such a novelty. Unless your wife isn't okay loaning you out."

He didn't so much as flinch, even though she knew how much he hated that word.

Why was she being so hurtful? But the bitterness was pouring out of her, a dam let loose.

"Sharing would imply she's *had* me." The steel in his voice should have warned her away, but it did the opposite.

"Hasn't she, Shade Lord?"

"Never. That is the one thing she could never have."

A low growl rumbled in his chest as he pinned his arms on either side of her, long fingers flexed over the marble banister. "If you need to hurt someone, to slake that rage I feel blazing inside you, go ahead. Say anything you desire to me, anything at all, except that."

"Why?" she demanded. She was being so very awful and she knew it. *Knew* it. But she couldn't stop. She needed to prove to herself she didn't love him. To prove that Bell had been wrong about that.

Stolas inched closer. "Because when I am with you, I do not want to think about *her.*"

"Then what do you want to think about?" Haven asked, dangerously needling him.

His eyes darkened. "Would you prefer the truth or an acceptable lie?"

She was teetering on something precarious, a ledge that led to a place she wasn't quite ready to visit. "The truth, if you are capable."

"I have never lied to you, Haven. Never."

Her name on his lips—not Beastie, but her *name*—sounded decadent, a song. No, a prayer.

"Haven't you? It doesn't matter. The truth. What do you want to think about with me, right now?"

Those predatory eyes fell on Haven's lips. "I am wondering what you taste like."

The air between them shivered with anticipation. Haven knew then that she wanted to kiss him, wanted to prove the desire coursing through her was just that—desire, and nothing more.

He was a novelty, a forbidden novelty, that was all.

You care for a monster. And if you don't love him yet, you will.

She brushed her lips over his, violently, as if her mouth was a weapon she could use to destroy everything Bell had accused her of.

The moment her mouth collided with his, the moment she caught the scent of moonberry liquor on his breath, felt the softness of his lips, felt his hands instinctively brace on either side of her hips, the coolness of his flesh bleeding through her too-thin dress—

Something inside her roused. A primal yearning that terrified her.

She gasped, and he jerked away, his hands leaving her hips and flexing over her wrists, pinning them to the banister.

His breath was ragged, his eyes dangerously black as he growled, "Not like this."

"Like what?" she snarled, shame and rage and disappointment crashing through her. She wanted to rake her fingers down his face; she wanted to kiss him again, harder, until he took her in his arms and flew them somewhere private.

Oh, Goddess help her, she was losing it.

"I will not have you kiss me out of anger or to satisfy some morbid curiosity."

She blinked. "That's not what I'm doing."

"Isn't it?"

Her silence condemned her. How she hated him at that moment. Hated him for being right. For making her feel things out of her control. Wild, impulsive, powerful emotions.

She trembled as he brushed the pad of his thumb over her bottom lip. "Just for that, when the time comes, I will make you beg for my touch."

Furious, she tried to bite his thumb, but he moved his fingers just out of reach.

"Never," she hissed.

"Am I interrupting something?"

Haven flinched at the male voice behind Stolas, her heart racing. Archeron.

No. No. NO.

She met his furious stare. He wore a crisp white tunic over a gold brocade vest, his shoulder-length honey-gold hair hanging loose. His mask was crafted from azerite and shaped like the face of a bear, his gilded skin contrasted against the pale, silver-veined material.

Even now, his face hidden and emerald eyes blazing with rage, he was beautiful.

Ducking beneath Stolas's arms, Haven went to Archeron. To explain, somehow, this wasn't what it looked like. If that was even possible.

Stupidly, she said, "Did you get my letters?"

The part of his face she could see was emotionless. "The ones that claimed this was all a misunderstanding? Yes."

Soft. His voice was too soft.

Runes. She tugged on the bottom edge of her mask. Her skin felt feverish, her body ached. Jolts of fire nipped at her spine . . . but she needed to make this right somehow.

"It wasn't a lie. I did come that night to meet you, but I was late."

"I know." He smiled, a hollow grin that ratcheted her heart into her throat. "I saw you."

Saw her—which meant he saw Stolas carrying her.

His focus went to Stolas's black dinner jacket hanging from her shoulders. "How long, Haven?"

She swallowed. Her tongue felt like dried leather. "How long what?"

"How long have you been fucking the Lord of the Netherworld?"

The sound of Stolas's wings flaring came from behind Haven, and then she felt the Shade Lord's presence, electric blue tendrils of his dark magick churning the air.

"Careful what you say next, Archeron," Stolas said, the softness of his voice unable to mask the menacing undertone.

"Or what, Shade Lord?" The full extent of Archeron's wrath fell on Stolas. "Will you curse me like your mother did mine?"

"What are you talking about?" Haven asked, looking from Archeron to Stolas.

"Oh, Stolas didn't tell you?" Archeron asked, the vein in his temple bulging. "His mother cursed mine to die at the hands of a male heir. Because of her, my life has been a living hell."

"My mother didn't create that curse," Stolas amended, and again Haven picked out the warning tone beneath the quiet calm. "She was a powerful seer, and she told your mother the truth. A male heir would be her downfall."

"Out of spite," Archeron snarled. "She must have known the bloodshed that would follow, the innocent babies that would die."

"Perhaps your mother shouldn't have tried to seduce my father, then." Stolas's wings twitched. "The Seraphian race does not whore themselves out like the Solis. When we mate, we mate for life, and we do not share our mates with *anyone*."

Stolas looked pointedly at Haven as he said the last part, and she knew then he was taking a dig at Archeron wanting both Avaline and herself.

"Stolas, I can deal with this," she said as a sudden calm came over her. "Despite what you believe, Archeron, I have never disrespected you. Never. I know how this looks. I know you must be hurt and angry. But I understand now that I could have never been with you, Archeron."

The second the words left her lips, she felt the heaviness on her shoulders lift. And she knew then. Knew with absolute certainty it was true.

Archeron stepped closer, and the bright blue snakes of magick around Haven swirled protectively. Archeron's gaze went to Stolas's magick, to Stolas, and then settled on Haven, his jaw clenched so hard the muscles trembled. "I gave up everything for you, Haven. Everything."

His eyes were dark, almost black, and pitted with horrible shadows. His cheekbones hollow and temples sunken. His hair was unwashed, a week's worth of stubble clinging to the too-sharp edge of his jaw.

This was not the Archeron she knew.

"I know," she said, trying to make her voice calming. "And I will never stop being grateful for this second chance at life you gave me or the friendship we share."

"Friendship?" Archeron spit the word from his mouth like poison.

Haven pulled at her mask.

Hot—she was so hot. And cold. Shivers wracked her body.

Surai. She needed to find Surai and recarve the runes. But first she had to make this right.

Somehow, she *had* to.

"Why?" Archeron demanded, and the anguish in his voice yanked her from the descending fog. "Is it because I'm a slave? Is the one thing I gave up for you the thing that makes you unable to love me?"

"No." Her throat was raspy, her pulse crashing in her ears. She needed to hold on to something. She was going to fall . . .

"Admit it. You despise seeing me forced to grovel at your mortal king's feet. Forced to do every depraved wish he commands. It disgusts you. *I* disgust you."

"No." Her head was pounding, the darkness swelling inside her, splitting her open. She wrapped her arms around her chest, her skin burning to the touch.

"Say it. Say you despise me."

"I don't." Gasping, she ripped the mask from her face. The sound of the porcelain shattering as it hit the floor came from so far away.

"Liar." His voice warbled from the end of a tunnel. "Coward."

"No, I just—I can't, Archeron," she panted as the truth suddenly surfaced with perfect clarity. How had she not seen it sooner? "I cannot be with someone promised to another. We both deserve more than that."

Anguish flashed inside Archeron's eyes. "What has Stolas been saying to you?"

Archeron reached to grab her arm—

An unseen force sent Archeron crashing into the table across the balcony like he weighed nothing. *Nothing.*

Stolas.

The Shade Lord's roar sent fresh adrenaline spiking through her veins.

No.

She tried to conjure her magick. Tried to stop the oncoming bloodshed.

Raging fire burst across her flesh. Fire that was hot and cold and all-consuming.

Couldn't breathe—she couldn't breathe.

A scream tore from her throat. It felt as if the dark magick were ripping her in half. Her knees buckled. The marble floor rose to meet her.

Before the floor could connect with her face, Stolas had her in his arms.

SIXTY-SIX

The barley wine Bell had forced down his throat in copious quantities soured his stomach and threatened to come back up. Groaning, he leaned back against the trellis of wisteria, closed his eyes, and listened to the bees buzzing around the fragrant flowers.

"Shadeling's shadow, you're pathetic."

Renk's voice cut through Bell's solitude, and he opened his eyes to his half-brother staggering a few feet away. Two males flanked him, and unlike Renk, who could barely stand up, they were entirely sober.

Bell's blood chilled as he first took in the drunken cruelty in Renk's shiny, deep-set eyes, then his companions.

Both males were dressed simply in black, no wings or horns, their hair magicked into the fairer colors of the Solis native to Effendier. But, even with the barley wine making his senses sluggish, Bell felt the darkness swirling around them.

They were Noctis.

Why would Noctis be with Renk?

Bell straightened, trying to exude strength. "What do you want, droob?"

Renk laughed, a sloppy, cruel sound that usually preceded him hurting something. "Why do I have to want anything? We're brothers. Perhaps I want to wish you luck tomorrow."

While Renk talked, Bell slowly positioned his hand over the Hadrassian dagger at his waist. He had practiced drawing it quickly for days on end, and he felt comfortable he could at least retrieve the weapon before the first Noctis struck.

"Okay." Bell glared at Renk, refusing to show an ounce of his usual discomfort in the bully's presence. "You've said it. Now leave and go make a fool of yourself or find someone smaller and weaker than you to beat on—you know, what you usually do at parties."

"Oh, brother." Renk stumbled forward, clapping a huge hand on Bell's shoulder, the four inches Renk had on Bell never more apparent. "I'm going to enjoy tomorrow so much."

Something hung in his words, and Bell frowned as the two Noctis shared a look and then physically dragged Renk away.

What the hell was that?

Releasing a tense breath, Bell straightened his dinner jacket, prepared to leave the ball early. Tonight had to go down in history as the worst party ever.

Bell made it two steps before he changed his mind. Xandrian sat along the balcony rail, smirking casually despite the deadly drop behind him. He was resplendent in a topaz and silver outfit the exact color of the sea below, a mask of colorful orange and blue fish scales covered his face.

As Bell realized Xandrian was watching him—and probably had been for a while—a faint flutter started just beneath Bell's ribs.

Grabbing a lungful of courage, Bell plucked two deep purple drinks from an attendant's tray and strolled over.

You can do this, Bell.

Xandrian studied the drinks in Bell's sweaty hands and then met Bell's nervous stare. "Don't you have a trial tomorrow to win?"

"Right." Bell quickly got rid of the glasses, his mind suddenly on Haven. Without her, he didn't stand a chance in the Netherworld of winning. "And what if I lost. What if I end up staying here, indebted to your aunt?"

Xandrian rubbed the back of his neck. "Do you not want to win? Become a king among kings? Even your father would have to obey you."

Bell laughed. "Of course that would be amazing, it's just . . ." Bell scraped a hand through his hair, his fingers snagging in the curls. "What if my magick wasn't as strong as it seems?"

Would you still like me, Sun Lord? Bell thought but didn't dare say.

"Hmm." Xandrian leaned back slightly, the normal amusement in his deep blue eyes bleeding away to something serious. "Tell me, Cursebreaker, why do you want to become ruler of the Nine?"

Bell shifted on his feet. He'd had a lot of time to think about that. At first, his only motivation was winning so he could escape being bound to the Sun Sovereign. He hadn't thought much past that. But lately . . . lately he'd spent nights dreaming of what he might do if he were in charge of all the mortal lands.

"If I win the tournament," Bell said, "I hope I could make my world a better place. Not just for the kings and noblemen, but for everyone."

"A naive answer," Xandrian commented, but his tone didn't

match the disdain of his words.

If anything, he almost sounded impressed.

"Anyway." Bell glanced back at the dance floor inside. Maybe it was the wine in his belly, or the oncoming trial tomorrow, but he suddenly wanted very much to dance.

With Xandrian.

Clearing his throat, Bell offered his hand, proud that it didn't even tremble. "I don't want to dwell on that tonight. Would you . . . would you like to dance?"

Bell was prepared for Xandrian to say no, was prepared for him to use some cutting remark, but it was worse than that.

Pity flashed inside the Sun Lord's eyes. Pity and surprise. And Bell knew then that every smile he thought was for him, the accidental touches and lingering stares, the gifts—none of that had meant anything.

"But the book you helped me find," Bell said. "And the dagger you gifted me. You sought me out, you showed up wherever I was. I thought . . ." Bell took a step back, breathless, face on fire as he tried to process how he had gotten this so wrong.

"There are reasons for that, Prince. Reasons I cannot get into here."

In Bell's periphery, he caught Xandrian's friends watching them with barely contained amusement. Bell took in the laughter seconds from erupting from their smirking lips. Their faces red from holding it all in.

Reasons. Of course.

This had been some twisted joke. His throat ached. They were toying with him.

The gifted dagger hung heavy at his waist. He ripped the weapon from its leather binding and thrust it at the Sun Lord. "You can have this back."

Xandrian shook his head. "It was a gift."

"I insist." After Xandrian took the dagger, Bell forced the hurt from his face, forced his lips to smile. "Goodnight."

Runes, he was such an idiot for thinking Xandrian could ever feel something for a mortal—or for anyone other than himself. Shame heated Bell's face, but he lifted his head high, forcing a confidence he didn't feel as he stormed off.

If Xandrian thought Bell was beneath him, then Haven was right, and the Sun Lord didn't deserve Bell.

Haven.

What a fool he had been. What a huge, embarrassing idiot. Now all he could hope was that she'd forgive him.

SIXTY-SEVEN

Agony rippled over Haven's body, wave after wave of pain. Her consciousness blurred in and out; shadows strangled her vision.

She saw things in snippets.

The warbling darkness of a portal.

Then a hallway.

Someone's room. *Her* room.

Stolas smashing the door in and then clearing everything off the dining table—plates, a decanter of wine, a tureen of soup.

All of it crashed to the floor.

Demelza rushed into the room wearing a linen nightgown, her hair tufted out wildly in every direction, a war cry on her lips. When she saw Haven, when her eyes took in whatever panic and pain twisted her face, Demelza froze.

"Grab a pot of hot water and some clean towels," Stolas barked, sending Demelza scuttling off. He set Haven on the smooth table face down and tugged off the jacket he'd given her. Another scream burbled from her throat as he shredded the back of her dress, the air like liquid fire over her bare back.

The silence told her how bad her back was.

"What the hell is that?" Acheron asked.

Archeron. Archeron was *here*. He must have followed them through the portal.

Stolas snarled. "She bound her dark magick, weren't you aware? I assume you are half the reason."

She tried to lift her head to look at them, tried to speak. Nothing. She could do nothing but suffer the unending agony crashing through her body.

"I didn't know she was in pain. I thought—"

"What?" Stolas growled as his hands rested lightly on her ruined back. "You thought dark magick as powerful as hers would happily lie dormant? Magick like hers cannot be caged like a hunting dog. It will find a way out any way it can. If the runes fail and it releases now, as powerful as it is—she could die."

"Don't you see?" Archeron snapped. "The darkness is a malignancy growing inside her and this just proves that. If I could carve it from her soul, even if it meant risking her life, I would do it without hesitation."

Despite not being able to see Stolas's face, she felt his rage as he said, softly, so very softly, "A malignancy? It's a part of her. You cannot cut it out. Cannot send it away just because it makes you uncomfortable. But the idea that you made her think it was necessary, that you ever made her feel an ounce of shame for who she is—if she didn't care about you so deeply, I would shred you from existence."

Haven wanted to say he wasn't to blame—not entirely. Except the words shriveled on her tongue and became a groan.

She could feel her flesh mending together, feel the blood evaporating, the snapped tendons pulling taut as they reconnected. Who knew the Lord of the Netherworld could heal as well as he hurt?

Demelza rushed into the room carrying a pot of steaming water. Haven cried out at the first touch of the wet towel over her sensitive flesh.

Prayers rushed from Demelza's throat, and for some reason, her worry made Haven want to cry.

Archeron raked a hand through his hair. "I didn't know this could happen," Archeron said, his voice softening as she felt his gaze on her. "I didn't know," he repeated. "What can we do?"

"First I need to heal the torn flesh the magick has destroyed. Then I must reopen the scars to halt the influx of dark magick, but the pain will be excruciating. I'll try to mask the effects with a soothing spell—I'll do what I can."

"Why not let the scars fully heal?"

"I warded off the dark magick's reemergence, but not for long. Without those runes, it would do the same thing again, only this time worse."

"So it's punishing her?" Archeron growled, making his distaste for dark magick incredibly clear.

Stolas was quiet for a few breaths. "Something like that."

Dread fell over her like a shadow. If that were true, she may have to reopen the runes for the rest of her life.

Archeron suddenly clutched his chest before huffing a dark laugh. "Speaking of mortals, the king calls. As much as I hate leaving her with you, Shade Lord, she made her choice, and when you turn on her like the rabid dog you are, there will be no pity in my heart left for her."

Haven shivered at the brittleness of his voice, as if he were on the verge of shattering completely.

She would have said something . . . would have found the words to at least say she was sorry, but before she could muster the strength, the door clicked shut behind him.

She felt the loss of their friendship nearly as much as she felt the wounds on her back.

But flesh could be healed, given the right magick. Hearts could not.

Stolas's footfalls were soft against the wooden floor as he crossed to the window and opened it, letting in the sea breeze. Then he turned to Demelza and ordered her out. She protested, but Stolas explained that, if something went wrong and Haven's dark magick found a way out, it could kill her.

After Haven promised to get Demelza when it was safe again, her lady's maid left for Bell's room downstairs.

"Tell me," Haven rasped, watching Stolas lock the door behind Demelza and then cross toward her. "How bad is it?"

"If I hadn't halted its progression, the dark magick would have probably killed you. You don't lock a beast up, starve it until it's lust for blood is all-consuming, then forget to lock the door one day. Not unless you are its master."

"I didn't want to bloody the dress Bell bought me." Saying it aloud, she realized how stupid she had been. For all of it. Binding her magick without understanding the consequences. Thinking she could control it.

"I promise you, as gorgeous as you were inside it, that dress is not worth your life." She felt his hands move to her lower back. The pain had become a dull ache, like a giant bruise pooled just beneath her skin.

She felt his hands slide up again, his fingertips pressing between her shoulder blades. The last shreds of pain fell away as her flesh finished mending. A sudden blanket of coolness fell over her.

Tears of relief blurred her vision.

"Thank you," she whispered, her breath scraping over a raw, blistered throat.

Stolas exhaled. "Never again, Beastie. Do you understand? If you choose to hate yourself, to risk death rather than accepting your gifts—then perhaps you do not deserve them."

"Sorry to disappoint you," she whispered, "but it seems failing those I care about is what I do best."

"Self-pity doesn't suit you."

"And smugness doesn't suit you."

"Oh, but it does."

"Shadeling curse you," she seethed.

A dark chuckle. "Too late; he already did." Then his voice lowered as he murmured, "Get ready."

He was about to reopen the scars. What would he do it with? His talons? A blade? Magick?

"I can handle—"

A blinding agony ripped through her entire being. She gritted her teeth against the pain, tears wetting the corners of her eyes. After the first onslaught, the torment lessened into a throbbing that emanated from her core.

Then came the cold.

An aching, unrelenting cold. Her jaw snapped shut, teeth clinking, body thrashing with shivers.

Arms slipped below her neck and waist and then Stolas was carrying her across the room. She leaned her head against his crisp white shirt, unbuttoned at the top.

When he got to her bed, he stripped back the covers, gently laid her down on the mattress, and then, after the briefest of hesitations, settled in behind her.

SIXTY-EIGHT

She felt the mattress depress. Felt his dark magick licking over her shivering flesh. His wings flared to cover them, greens and blues catching in his feathers. He breathed a runespell and heat flooded the air. Seeping into her muscles. Chasing away the gnawing cold until only the pulsing ache deep within remained.

His arms were locked around her stomach, his breath tickling the nape of her neck. They lay like that for countless heartbeats.

"You stopped shivering," he remarked, and then, "How's your back?"

"Better. The pain is . . . different now. Like it's buried deep inside me."

He began pulling away, slowly, readying to leave. "You need to sleep."

A jolt of panic hit her. Despite the constant throb of pain, her body reacted to his nearness, pressing into him.

She wondered if he felt it too. That building tension between them. Wondered if he fought it like she did. If that's why he was so quick to put distance between them.

Turning in his arms, she found his gaze; his wings curved around them blocked the light, and in the near-pitch dark, the yellow ring around his eyes danced like fire.

"Don't leave," she whispered.

"Haven—"

"Don't. Leave."

His expression turned feral—a wild beast who'd stumbled upon wounded prey. His pupils elongated and became feline, his eyes flashed red, and the tips of incisors peeked below his upper lip. "Still want me to stay?"

"Yes."

He was trying to scare her, but it wasn't working. Or maybe it was. Maybe she relished how everything else faded away except this moment and the adrenaline searing her body.

Masking her pain. Her worries. The upcoming trial and Archeron and . . . everything.

Stolas was a drug, a balm to forget.

"What if I told you that, right now, without your dark magick masking your light powers, I can feel them coursing through your veins, begging for me to drain them from your fragile body?"

"I would say I'm safe with you."

"I thought you were smarter than that." His lupine gaze shifted from her eyes to her lips. "What, exactly, do you want from me, Haven?"

"Distract me," she whispered, her inhibitions untethered by the night's events and the pain—and by the gentle way his fingers had run over her flesh only moments ago. But more than a distraction, she wanted to prove this thing between them was desire, nothing more.

"How would you like me to do that?" he breathed, his elegant voice low and husky.

"Make me feel something other than the pain. Make me . . . forget."

"*How?*" he insisted, lifting a devilish eyebrow as he forced her to say it.

Another wave of throbbing pulsed through her body, but she couldn't tell if it was from the pain or her need. It was all mixing together.

"Kiss me," she murmured. "Kiss me until I forget the pain."

She could see in his eyes he knew the pain she mentioned wasn't really physical. He'd smelled her tears earlier, sensed the anger and hurt coursing through her. And his soothing spell had dulled the effects of the newly carved runes on her back to a quiet ache.

"I told you I would make you beg the next time I touched you," he reminded her, a roughness fraying his normally elegant voice.

"Bastard."

His sensual lips parted in a wolfish grin. "I tried to warn you."

Never in her life would she beg for anything, but—

"*Please.*"

That single word destroyed any last reservations Stolas had.

With a low growl, he dragged his lips against hers. Their softness in contrast to his power. Teasing her. Pulling away before she could taste him.

It wasn't enough. Not nearly.

Frustrated, she tried to slip her hands behind his neck but he caught both her wrists in one large hand.

For a wild heartbeat, he stared at her. His control never more evident than now.

Then, holding her gaze, he gently flipped her on her back.

Watching her face, he slowly guided her arms over her head and pinned them above her pillow. Moonlight danced across the jewels of her dress.

A wicked smile played across his face as he began to languidly map her body with his eyes. Taking every inch of her in. His expression was unreadable, his only reaction a slight intake of breath.

The realization hit like a lightning bolt. She was completely at his mercy.

Her pulse jumped, and his head canted sideways as he detected the change, the watery light refracting off his onyx horns.

Then he positioned himself above her, still staring into her eyes with that savage, primal look, not bothering to hide his true nature.

Daring her to react. To cower from what he was.

"Are you sure you want this, Haven?"

Her mind was a chaos of alarm. *Predator*, it shouted. *Run.*

But her body—her traitorous body felt alive. Every nerve ending on fire. The flesh hidden beneath her too-thin dress yearning to be touched.

Holding his stare, she wrapped her legs around his lithe waist in answer.

He went inhumanly still.

Something in his raw gaze hinted this wasn't a game. Not to him.

He started with the hollow between her breasts. His lips tracing that bare swath of skin that mortified her only hours earlier. Yet now—now she relished the way his lips and tongue traced the naked flesh up her neck, her jaw, trailing along the shell of her ear . . .

When his mouth found hers again, it was still soft and teasing, but there was an intensity that wasn't there before. He didn't pull away.

And this time, when she parted her mouth for him, his tongue eagerly slipped inside.

Caressing. Claiming. Plunging deeper.

His teeth tugged at her lower lip. Gently. Reminding her of what he was. She returned the favor, nipping, relishing the way he snarled low as she bit hard enough to draw blood.

A rough laugh trickled from his mouth. "Wicked Beastie."

"That's for teasing me," she breathed.

His one hand still held her wrists, but the other began to roam her body. Slowly. Reverently. The slight pressure of his fingertips charging through the thin silk of her dress. Again teasing her.

She ground against him, trying to twist her arms free so she could touch his body, trying to pull him into her with her legs—

His breath hitched as he hardened against her.

She groaned, an intoxicating mixture of pleasure and pain overwhelming her senses.

He pulled away to stare down at her. He took in her flushed cheeks, her parted lips, her ragged breathing.

One corner of his lip lifted in amusement. "Should I stop, Haven?"

Her name on his lips sent a shiver rippling down her middle. And it all became so real. The line they were crossing.

Bell's words whispered in her skull. *You care for a monster.*

Only, Stolas didn't look like a monster. Not with his ivory hair tousled to the side, his full lips parted, silver eyes heavy-lidded with desire. His white shirt was unbuttoned at the top, the muscles peeking through hinting at raw, unchecked power.

"More," she whispered—no, *pleaded.*

One arm broke free, and she plunged her hand into his hair.

Her fingertips brushed the base of his horn. Stroked higher, all the way to the metal tip.

He shuddered at the contact, and then his mouth came down on hers. Deeper. Possessive now.

This had gone way beyond a simple distraction or proving her feelings for him was lust instead of love—and yet, she couldn't stop.

She arched her back, hips hooking into him, grinding against that considerable hardness. His wings flared to fill the darkness.

Tearing her hand from his head, she began working on the buttons of his shirt. Runes, it was impossible with only one hand! Growling against his mouth, she slipped her fingers beneath his shirt hem, dragging them across his ridged abdomen, over his side, and up the swell of his back.

His breathing became ragged. He ripped his head away and again stared down at her. His nostrils flared, a predatory gleam in his eyes. Without breaking her gaze, he found her free hand, laced his fingers with hers, and tugged her hand out to the side.

She tried to reach up and touch him again, but he shook his head.

And then silky strips of his power gently wrapped around her wrists, trapping her arms on either side of her head. She twisted, but he disentangled from her legs and then his powers fell over her like a soft blanket, holding her entire body below her head immobile.

She was completely at his disposal.

"Shadeling Below, I'm going to devour you," he growled.

Beneath the barely-there fabric of her dress, her chest rose and fell. And that's when she saw the luminescent tinge to her skin and realized—

Goddess save her, she was *glowing*.

"My light magick," she said, apologetic as she realized how that would affect him. "I'm sorry, it—"

"No," he admonished, clicking his tongue. "Never apologize for what you are. Not to me or anyone else."

"It doesn't . . . bother you?"

His eyes flashed. "Haven, there is not a single part of you that isn't glorious."

As if to prove that point, he brushed his lips over the glowing portion of her neck, then moved on to the exposed hollow between her breasts where beads of sweat shimmered.

Her breath caught in her throat as she watched him prowl lower. Watched his eyes darken as he took in the slit of her gown, so high up on her thigh.

"I've wanted to do this since the moment I saw you in this dress," he murmured.

She could do nothing as he dragged his mouth, his teeth, his *tongue* over that bare strip of flesh. One hand slipped beneath her gown, his fingers bunching over the silk as he languidly began gliding the fabric up her thigh.

His other hand began stroking the inner portion of her leg.

Circling.

Higher.

Higher.

His eyes held hers. Glazed as they took in her reaction.

When the hem of her dress reached her butt, he loosened his power's hold on her so she could lift her hips. She was bare from the navel down. Only a slip of underwear covering her lower half.

Hooking his fingers beneath the sides, he gently removed those too.

Pressing his hand flat on her belly, he ran his tongue over her stomach, his fingers teasing now as they caressed between her thighs.

"Focus on every sensation," he ordered, sliding his fingers closer. Closer. Still watching her. His pupils slits; his nostrils delicately flared as they breathed her in and—

The pad of his thumb grazed that spot at the apex of her thighs. *Oh, holy Goddess Above.*

Her head fell back, her hips bucking, pressing into him. "Don't stop."

"So demanding."

"Bastard!"

She cried out as he found the spot again, her entire focus narrowing to that one sensation. Her fingers clawed the sheets.

She was going to rip right through them. Going to shred—

"What was that?" he purred . . . just as he slid one finger part way inside her.

She moaned, lifting her hips, head arching back. Her light magick leapt off her skin and illuminated the room, sparks dancing across the ceiling.

"More. Please, Stolas."

"Better," he whispered, still toying with her. His thumb circling, grazing. His finger moving so slowly. Never going deep enough. Never quite satisfying her.

And the entire time he appraised her, drinking in her reaction. His mouth parted and eyes black with hunger.

"You have no idea how long I've wanted to watch your face while I touched you," he whispered. "Although I have to admit, I never imagined I'd be the first male to make you *glow*."

She growled in frustration. "Who says you're the first?"

"Liar." He slid his finger in all the way, and a hiss of pleasure fled her lips. But it wasn't enough.

"Stolas—"

He slid in a second finger, and her head sank into the pillow. The pain was gone. Her mind wholly focused on the gathering ache between her thighs. On his fingers, warm and long and hard. Soft, gentle strokes in and out. In and out.

"Is this what you wanted, Haven?" he murmured.

"Yes."

She lost herself in the feel of him. In the boldness of his stare; the gentleness of his touch. The shock of desire she felt every time she dared look up and meet his eyes.

And then, the sensation of his lips dragging down her belly . . .

I'm going to devour you.

Her heart boomed in her chest. Her skin was on fire. Her mind whirling. That throbbing pressure growing between her legs. Begging for release.

And when he brought his mouth down where his fingers worked—

I'm going to devour you.

Nothing mattered. Nothing but the inferno of warmth and pleasure and sensation billowing over her, surging through her limbs, her entire world honing in on his fingers as they plunged deeper with every thrust, and his tongue . . . it swept over her in long, claiming strokes.

I'm wondering how you taste.

His words from only hours earlier were enough to nearly undo her.

And then she glanced down and met his eyes, still watching her with that merciless intensity, greedily taking in her face, her moans, feeding off her enjoyment—

A wave of blinding pleasure hit as release shot down her middle. She cried out. Her light magick flared to fill the room. Every muscle in her body clenched, her thighs trembling, her heart pounding in her skull.

She gulped for air as if she hadn't taken a breath since this whole thing began. The world came crashing back. She became all too aware of the sweat pooling between her breasts and behind her knees. Her dress bunched around her waist.

A light breeze from the open window cooled her sweat-damp bare calves and thighs.

The powers that held her fell away, but her body didn't dare move, her limbs limp and shaking. Her skin no longer glowed, but it was flushed and sensitive to the lightest touch.

When he removed his fingers, she barely swallowed her whimper.

Without a word, Stolas gently began peeling off her dress, his knuckles brushing her ribs as he worked.

"Lift your arms," he ordered softly.

She obeyed, and he tugged the dress over her head.

Then he lifted her into his arms and carried her to the bathroom. Water filled the tub already, and he ran a hand over that clear surface until it steamed.

It wasn't until he lowered her into the tub and the hot water seeped into her flesh that she realized the worst of the pain was gone.

She looked at Stolas, his shirt unwrinkled, wavy white hair still neat, as if none of the last thirty minutes had transpired—

Before she could say anything, he cleared his throat. "Did I . . . satisfy your needs?"

"Yes," she murmured, suddenly awkward, her thoughts impossible to translate into words. "Thank you."

A flicker of emotion rippled over his face, too fast for her to read it. And then he said, a little too smugly, "Glad I could be of service, Haven." He padded to the door. "I'll have the translation finished by the trial."

"Wait." Her tongue felt like dried leather as he turned to face her, his face unreadable. "Did you . . . satisfy your curiosity?"

I'm wondering how you taste.

As understanding dawned, something dark and dangerous flickered inside his silver eyes, and he brought the same fingers that had, moments ago, been inside Haven, and sucked on them.

"For now," he murmured.

Netherworld take her. If not for the upcoming trial, she would have dragged him into the water with her for a repeat.

Instead, she watched him leave, feeling as if she were caught in a dream. One where, impossibly, Bell's outlandish prediction came true.

You're in love with a monster.

A monster that, in a few short hours, would try to take everything from her.

SIXTY-NINE

An hour later, Haven sat propped on the windowsill, wrapped in a silk robe. The wind blowing off the river helped distract her from her tumbling thoughts.

Now that she was bathed and no longer in pain, her mind balked at her actions with Stolas. What in the Netherworld had she been thinking?

And yet . . . every time she allowed herself to relive the experience, a new surge of warmth spread over her. She could feel his hands on her flesh. His lips parting hers.

And her bed still reeked of his scent . . .

She sighed. She'd barely broken it off with Archeron, and now she had done the very thing he accused her of.

Shame washed over her, but it was nothing compared to the ache in her heart as her thoughts turned to Bell. He was all she had. His words about her using him to hide from her past may have had a ring of truth, but that didn't erase their bond of love and friendship.

Just get through today and you can find a way to fix this.

Releasing a breath, she stared down into the waking city. Runelights twinkled from the townhouses and lamps lined the streets, mirroring the stars above.

The sun would rise in a few hours, bringing with it the final trial.

A few hours. She blinked sleepily at the tendrils of smoke rising from chimneys. Shopkeepers were already washing the sidewalks, and vendors were setting up tents to sell their wares. Even from her high perch, the scent of baked bread and other exotic spices perfumed the air.

The city was preparing for the celebration tonight to crown the Ruler of the Nine—whoever that ended up being.

Bell. It has to be him.

Even after their argument, after he severed her oath to him, she would still fight to the death to keep him safe and put him on the throne.

The Ruler of the Nine would possess immense sway over the original Nine royal Houses, plus they would serve as the conduit between Solissia and the mortal lands.

It has to be him.

The room filled with the bitter tang of Demelza's twisted version of coffee. Demelza shuffled over, a steel tumbler sifting steam into the air. "You need sleep."

Haven reached out for the cup. There was no point in even trying to refuse the vile drink. "I can't. Not now."

"After what you went through, you must."

Haven noticed the way Demelza's eyes kept going to the bloody pile of towels on the table and Haven's heart sank. "I'm sorry. You must think I'm . . . an abomination."

Demelza tsked. "I have seen true abominations, girl. You are not one. Now drink."

Pulling a soft bristled brush from the pocket of her robe, Demelza began combing Haven's hair. It was still wet, and drops of water splattered over Haven's bare thighs as Demelza worked.

"I used to do this for you when you first came to the palace," Demelza said. "Do you remember?"

Haven shook her head. She had been such a mess then, haunted by nightmares and the fear of Damius finding her, and much of those first years were blocked out.

"You were this wild, broken thing trying to bite and claw anyone who came near you. I used to sing you the lullabies I sang for my daughter. My words would calm you enough that we could bathe and clothe you properly, at least."

Haven shut her eyes as bits of the songs came to her. Only it wasn't Demelza's sharp northern accent forming the words . . .

"I think my mother sang to me," Haven said suddenly. "And when you did the same, I recognized some of the songs."

"There was one lullaby that could quell even your most savage tempers." Demelza set the brush down on the side table, took Haven's untouched coffee from her hand, and motioned to the bed. "Lie down and I will sing you to sleep. You must rest."

Haven obeyed without a word, her body suddenly so tired. When she was in bed, the light silk sheets childishly tucked around her, Demelza began to sing.

"The stag in wood, the bear in the field, they all bow down to her. The ravens up high, the Shadowlings of nigh, they all swear oaths to her. The mortal kings, they fall, one and all, to worship at her feet. But those that don't heed the shadow of wings, the bite of fiery eyes. Her wrath will come and swallow them whole, the girl of fire and ice."

As the words filled the night, Haven was surprised to feel tears wet her eyelashes, and she stopped fighting sleep.

An hour later, something woke Haven. Watery half-light streamed across the floor. Nearly sunrise, then. A knock sounded at the door, and Haven jumped from her bed before the sound could wake Demelza who was slumped in the bedroom chair, snoring.

Surai waited on the other side of the door, and something about her eyes . . .

Alarm shot through Haven. "Is it Bell? Is he okay?"

"No, Haven—" Surai's voice broke, but then she cleared the emotion from her throat, lifted her chin, and said, "They found him."

"Who?"

"The betrayer, Bjorn."

SEVENTY

The palace prison wasn't like the dungeons inside Fenwick Castle. Instead of deep underground, the cells were high above the city, set into the same mountain range where the museum resided.

Instead of rats and stench, there was silence.

Haven discovered why when she passed a prisoner and noticed his missing tongue.

The metal cages were similar, at least. Made from spelled iron, the cages inside the prison gave off a dark, ancient magick that prickled Haven's bones. Surai explained the dark magick imbued in the iron constantly drained the prisoner's light magick so they couldn't escape.

Only they could escape, if they wanted. Windows lined each cell, open to the outside, which explained the fresh air.

It wasn't a kindness. The drop from the window was nearly a thousand feet.

The jailer led Haven and Surai to a heavy door with fiery runes carved deep into the iron. As soon as they entered, wind blasted over Haven, tugging back her cloak and whipping her hair around.

The room was open on three sides to the air. In the center of the room, Bjorn was strung up to the rafters by chains that glowed molten hot. Haven could feel the corrupted magick flowing from the chains. As she took in Bjorn, stripped down to his pants, his back flayed open and limbs jerked spread eagle, she flung a hand to her mouth.

Her gaze shifted to Archeron where he leaned against the only wall available. He met her eyes, and if he were glad she was okay, the harsh lines of his face said the opposite.

Surai was quiet as she circled Bjorn. When she came into his periphery, Bjorn lifted his head. "Surai."

"No!" Surai snarled. "You do not get to say my name. Not after what you did."

Worried for her friend, Haven crossed to Surai, and Bjorn's gaze whipped to Haven.

"Ah," he groaned, pain making his voice breathy. "Mortal girl. Tell me, how do you like the Sun Court? Is it much better than Spirefall? Sunnier, maybe."

His ability to see through her illusion spell rendered her momentarily speechless.

He blinked at the rising sun, hovering just below the edge of the Solaris cathedral. In a few minutes he would be bathed in light. "I still marvel at the sunrise, the way the sky changes colors before your eyes. I missed that the most when my sight was gone."

His arrogance, his flippant tone—she wanted to rip his eyes out all over again. "I hope every day of freedom you felt was tainted by your shame, and every sunrise you saw with your new eyes made you think of Rook. And I very much hope they leave you to rot inside this cell."

A haunted smile played across his face. "You might want to get used to this view."

What in the Netherworld did that mean?

"Enough." Archeron pushed off the wall and prowled toward Bjorn. "He won't be here long. When the sun rises and its rays fall over his flesh, he'll burn alive from the inside out."

Burn alive? Haven noticed the way Bjorn flinched at Archeron's approach, an instinctual reaction. Archeron must have been with him for a while. Must have been the one to inflict the deep gashes in his back, the bruises mottling his dark flesh.

Gritting her teeth, she pushed any pity she might feel away. Why wouldn't Archeron beat and torture him after what he did? And burning alive wasn't near enough punishment for what he did to Rook.

What he did to *her*.

A terrifying fury seethed inside Archeron's face as he slammed a fist into Bjorn's side, right in the middle of a dark purple bruise.

Dark purple—the color of an older bruise.

Bjorn groaned, pain rippling across his face. His eyes—now deep, rich brown—looked to her. "I am sorry."

Surai had never looked so fierce, so cold as she peered at him without a single shred of sympathy. "You do not get to absolve your soul so you can die easy. I do not forgive you, betrayer."

"I do not apologize for Rook's death. To do so would take away the honor and bravery of her sacrifice."

The noise that fled Surai's chest was a mix between a cry and a growl, and Haven thought the girl would fling herself at him and tear him to shreds.

But she kept her dignity as she snapped, "What game do you play now, Seer?"

Bjorn gave a weary sigh. He looked so ragged, as if he'd been chained for much longer than a few hours. "No game." His eyes once again flicked to Haven's. "I apologize because I made a mistake. A costly one. That is why I came here. Why I let myself be taken, knowing the price."

Let himself be taken? One look at Archeron's face and Haven knew Bjorn spoke the truth.

"Enough lies," Archeron growled, and Haven had to look away as Archeron hit Bjorn so hard in the mouth that blood splattered the walls.

"I want to hear what he has to say." The high mountain winds nearly swallowed Surai's soft words.

Frowning, Archeron stepped back. He was still wearing his clothes from the ball, and blood dotted his gold brocade vest. More blood than could be explained by that one hit.

"Everything I did was for a future not far from now. Every act carefully thought out to ensure the evil that threatens to consume our world is stopped. But, Haven, I did not steal you from your family. You were given to me by the same order I work for. Given for a purpose."

"You work for Morgryth," Surai spit.

Archeron's eyes blazed, and Haven thought he would hit Bjorn again. "Shut up, heretic."

Heretic . . . the same word the Gold Shadows used for the monk, and for Xandrian.

"When I pushed you and Archeron together and made him think he cared for you, I thought that was the only way to make him sacrifice his wish and break the Curse."

"Liar," Archeron snarled. "You seek to hurt us even now—"

"Ask Surai. I pointed her in the same direction, planted the seed so that when it came time, she would nudge you toward the mortal girl. I knew it would hold more weight coming from her."

Surai's eyes went wide, and again Haven knew he told the truth.

Bjorn's gaze was still on Haven's as he continued. "I knew Archeron in his brokenness would cling to you, knew he would believe you could heal him. And when he made his wish and brought you back, I thought I had read the fates correctly."

"You're saying what I felt for Archeron—what he felt for me, the sacrifices he made, it was never real?" Haven felt cold all over. Had none of it been real? "It doesn't matter, because whatever you did worked. If not for that, the Curse would still be unbroken."

"I thought the same." A dark shadow passed over Bjorn's face even as the sun's rays crept across the ceiling toward him. "But something kept nagging me. And then I searched for the original writing of the Curseprice, before it was translated into many languages. The final item on the price was not the sacrifice of two lovers. It was the sacrifice of two *mates*."

The sunlight burst onto the rafter above, slowly creeping down down down. He only had a few minutes left.

"What does it matter?" Archeron seethed. "My wish broke the Curse. We all saw it."

Bjorn just shook his head. "Was another bargain not made? A sacrifice?"

Haven blinked, unable to process everything he was saying. None of it made any sense.

"Like Archeron said, what does it matter how it happened?" Surai demanded.

Bjorn tore his gaze from Haven to stare at Archeron. "Because, my mistake created a monstrous king who will upset the balance of power. He will serve the dark one. By trying to follow my oath to the Goddess, I may have set into motion the one strand of fate that will destroy everything, and I cannot see how to stop it."

Could he be talking about Stolas winning the tournament? Surely not.

She looked to Bjorn again. His entire body trembled. Haven's focus went to the bruises darkening his torso, and her eye caught on the tattoo just above his heart. A black serpent wrapped around flames of gold.

"I don't understand," Haven said, but they were running out of time.

He smiled at her, his rich brown eyes full of light, hope, even. "You will, *King Maker*. And remember. To master the beast is to master thyself." Those beautiful eyes shifted to Surai. "I am glad it is you here at the end."

Then he stared out into the rising dawn. "I swear an oath to the child of ice and fire, to guide her toward her destiny. I will gladly give up my life—"

That molten curtain of sunlight fell over him, and his body began to bubble and crack, molten fissures splitting his flesh from within. He screamed as fire leapt from the cracks and licked out, screamed as hungry flames of death consumed every inch of him.

Magickal heat flared against Haven's skin. She blocked out the screams. Blocked out the stink of burning flesh and clothes. Blocked out the memories of the man who cooked her stew or laughed with his friends—all but one of which were present to watch him die.

It was only after she had fled, after she had bathed the smoke and ash from her hair and scrubbed it from her flesh, that she realized where she had seen that tattoo before.

Xandrian. She had thought then that the snake and that bright inferno warred with each other, but she realized now it was the opposite: they were entwined in perfect harmony.

SEVENTY-ONE

Despite the sun having already risen, Archeron's mother and sisters had yet to leave the ballroom where the party still raged. Heavy red curtains had been drawn to block out any hint of day, and her current favorite courtesans whirled and leapt across the dance floor, no doubt ordered to dance until she grew bored of the spectacle.

Archeron stepped around the runelight candles scattered over the floor, their soft red lights illuminating the dancers and throwing shadows across the ceiling.

Such a waste. Of power and magick. His anger surged as he stalked through the mess of bodies, most in various states of undress, some copulating right in the open like beasts.

Lilith was sprawled on a bed of cushions wearing only a flimsy red scrap of gossamer that wrapped over her breasts and between her legs. As a child he remembered being forced to attend the balls all night, the way his mother used her magick to force revelers to stay for as long as she wanted.

The way she sometimes forced husbands to service her in front of their wives.

And now his sisters, spread out among the cushions, suffered from the same corrupted sense of power. Shiny-eyed males drugged with magick and drink littered at their feet.

Powerless. Disposable. Humiliated.

That was what his mother loved the most. The shame of others. Watching the light slowly die in their eyes as they understood they had absolutely no dignity. That she could do whatever she wanted to them.

It was a lesson he learned a long time ago.

He strode through the path toward his mother, ignoring the surprised looks from those in her court who knew who he was— and his mother's outspoken loathing of him.

Archeron paused when he spotted King Horace slumped in a chair, and the familiar spike of humiliation and rage the king's presence caused surged through Archeron's veins. The king was drunk beyond recognition, probably magicked too, which explained why Archeron had not been called by the king all night.

Only his mother would dare toy with a mortal king just for entertainment.

His sisters saw him first. Once, there were a few he might have called friends, but he'd been away too long, and his mother's perverted influence was too powerful.

Now they sneered at him from where they lay, not even bothering to cover themselves.

It took all his power to tamp down his rage at what this once glorious court had become as he bowed before his mother.

His mother's favorite concubine, Lysander, said, "Kneel before your sovereign."

Archeron kneeled, choking on the stench of incense and wine. His mother waited until his back ached and bruises burned his knees before she lifted her gaze to acknowledge him.

"What is it that brings you here, my son?"

Son. The word was wrong. His nostrils flared. He had to keep his emotions hidden. If she caught even a whiff of his desperation, she would destroy him.

"I have come to ask you to end my punishment and sever my enslavement to King Boteler." He kept his eyes on the marble tiles at his feet.

She lifted onto her elbows. "And why would I do that when the king seems so very fond of you. We are friends now. Did you know? Oh, he is rather boring at times, but his mistress makes up for his dullness. Just tonight, I made him watch while she willingly made love to another male."

The court laughed.

"Of course he won't remember any of that tomorrow. But he would remember if I took away his favorite dog, and then where would we be when I needed a favor?"

Archeron felt sick. He was here to discuss his freedom and she played silly games. "I could serve you better here. I could—"

"You could what?" The icy tone in her voice scraped down his spine, and her concubines, all too aware of her changes in mood, retreated quietly. "You could serve me in court? Help me make decisions? Help me rule?"

"No." Gritting his teeth, he focused on the gold lining between the mosaic tiles, on anything but her.

She clapped her hands together. "Let us play a game. Lysander, bring the truth vipers."

Archeron's head whipped up in time to see Lysander carrying over a wicker basket. Hisses came from inside.

Dread coiled in his gut. This was a mistake. He had been desperate, but he should have come when she wasn't drunk.

It was too late.

The sound of the two snakes hitting the ground filled Archeron with quiet terror. The serpents were massive, larger than normal pit vipers, their hooded heads the size of melons. Their black scales scraped softly against the marble as they approached.

He was still kneeling, and when they reached within striking distance, they raised on their bellies until they were inches from his face.

Two pairs of serpentine eyes stared into his, filled with the ethereal glow of magick.

"A gift from the Morgani Queen. Aren't they spectacular? They only strike when a lie is told. You would be surprised at how many in my court have tasted their venom. A painful death, truly."

The entire court had gone still, even his sisters. How many of their friends had they watched tormented and killed by these creatures?

"Don't believe me? You, kneel next to my son." She jerked her head at a young male concubine. Trembling, the concubine rushed to take his place next to Archeron.

How fast they obeyed.

They were terrified. Every single one.

"What is your name?" his mother asked.

"Jereth," the boy answered.

"Jereth, tell a lie. Say you love me."

The poor boy's chest wobbled as he tried to breathe; Archeron could hear the boy's pulse bouncing erratically in his veins, his frightened thoughts whirling as he realized he was about to die.

"Go on," Archeron's mother pressed, gently, as if he was the most beloved person in her life.

Jereth's hands shook at his sides as he looked at the sovereign, a horrible finality in his expression. "I . . . I love you."

The vipers struck instantly, over and over. Jereth screamed as he curled into a ball. The sound of hissing, of the serpents' fangs puncturing the poor boy's skin . . . over and over and over.

It was all Archeron could do not to cover his ears, but he forced himself to watch until finally the boy went still.

"Now," his mother purred as the vipers lifted, settling their deadly gaze on Archeron once more. "Tell me again, do you think you would make a better ruler than me? It's okay, son. You can be honest. We are family after all."

Archeron looked her straight in the eyes as he said, "Yes."

"And what would you have done differently?"

"I would have never let the Noctis into our city. They are plotting something. Our people are in danger."

"Is that so?" Her lips pressed together. "Our court is the strongest it has ever been. With the Curse broken, the Donatus Atrea thrives, its power coursing through every citizen. The Noctis wouldn't dare strike in Solethenia. They would be crushed, annihilated from existence. What do you say to that, son? And be *honest*."

Fear spiked through his blood, fear and loathing. The serpents' tongues tasted the air, waiting to test the veracity of his words.

"I say, Mother, that your ego will be the destruction of Solethenia."

"And would you stop me if you could? Would you take my place?"

His gaze shifted to the vipers and then back to his mother. He had never been more certain of anything in his life as he answered, "Yes."

She smiled, a cold, dead thing.

The gesture sent waves of panic crashing over him.

A low whistle called the vipers back to her. When they were safely inside the basket, she settled back on the cushions and took a slow sip of her wine. A dangerous silence suffocated the room.

"If that is all," she said with a dismissive wave of her hand. "You may leave."

Disbelief made Archeron hesitate. The tension in his muscles softened. Sensing her wrath had been sated, the concubines settled back onto the cushions beside her, and his sisters once more busied themselves with their guests. A low, tentative chatter eroded the silence as the party resumed.

He made it only a few steps before Lilith called out, "Wait."

A pit of true terror opened in his core, and he was a child again, skulking in the shadows, trying to hide from her unending wrath.

Archeron turned, his heart booming thunderously in his chest. Instinct had him counting the Gold Shadows lurking in the dark corners along the wall. He could fight—he would die proud, at least.

The sovereign snapped her fingers. "King Horace, come here, please."

The king stumbled over. And through the sheen of magick and drink in his eyes, Archeron caught the flicker of true fear.

"Force my son not to move an inch."

Before Archeron could react, the mortal king said the words and Archeron felt every traitorous muscle in his body obey. Just like that, he was a statue, unable to fight what was coming.

Helpless. He was helpless.

"My son wanted to leave your service," his mother continued. "What punishment do you suggest?"

A nervous laugh. "A whipping?"

"No."

The king swallowed. He was trying so hard to focus through the fog of magick and fear. "A day in the cells—"

"No." Her voice was steel.

"I do not—what would the appropriate punishment be?" the king stammered.

"Perhaps your mistress can help you?" Archeron's mother offered, nodding toward Cressida as she strolled up behind the king.

Cressida's lipstick was smeared, her dress askew, and her eyes were dull with wine, but her voice was still composed as she said, "Why not a choice?" She slid her hungry gaze over him, lips parted, enjoying the power that came with such an act. "He wanted to take something precious from you, King, now he can lose something precious to him. A choice, say his eye, his hand . . . or that beautiful face of his?"

Something inside Archeron went cold and dark.

"Very good," his mother praised, impressed by the king's mistress. If Cressida were a Solis, she would be one of his mother's favorite courtesans.

His mother rested her focus on him. She still wore that warm smile, the kind he would have given anything as a child to see from her just once. "Rulers often have to make hard, sometimes impossible choices. Which will it be? Your eye, your sword hand, or that lovely face of yours?"

Archeron felt a part of himself die. That cold pit growing bigger, splitting him open, consuming anything left inside him that still cared.

He would not let them see how much this cost him. His voice was steady as he gave his choice. His mother smiled again. His sisters smiled. The entire court laughed as if this was some big joke.

Even unable to move, with his sisters and mother and the

entire demented court watching, Archeron showed no emotion. Even when Lysander approached with the flaming blade, the fire licking at Archeron's skin, he didn't give them the satisfaction of his fear.

He didn't scream as his punishment was meted out. He didn't make a sound. The pain was there, but he watched it happen to someone else. A stranger.

And no one saw as the Sun Lord finally, truly broke.

A few hours later, when Magewick found Archeron in his rooms and saw the state of him, the Shade Lord tsked. "Mothers can be so . . . cruel sometimes. It's how they show their love, I suppose."

Archeron said nothing. He felt nothing. No more unending rage. No more shame. He was hollow, empty. Even the voices had left him.

It was a relief. To finally not feel anything at all.

"Are you ready to discuss breaking your bond to the mortal king?" Magewick asked, his voice conversational, as if they were friends. "Or do you prefer to wait until he has taken everything from you?"

Archeron looked past Magewick to the mirror on the wall, his new reflection like a monster smiling back at him. One of his teeth had chipped. Probably he'd bitten down too hard from the pain earlier. He hadn't even noticed.

"What do I need to do?"

"Only procure one tiny dagger beneath the vaults. That is the only thing that is powerful enough to break the king's hold on you."

"The Godkiller?" Archeron watched the reflection's lips move. It was like someone else speaking. "It's highly guarded."

"Most of the guards will be at the final trial."

Archeron dragged his gaze from the mirror to Magewick, trying to root out his true intentions. And yet . . . this could be his only chance to be free of the king.

Refuse and centuries could pass before the opportunity arose again.

He would no longer be a slave. No longer be that helpless child quaking beneath his mother's shadow. He imagined the king's expression when he tried to command Archeron, the fear that would overtake the king when he realized Archeron was no longer his plaything.

For the last countless nights, he'd dreamt of putting his hands around the king's throat and squeezing, dreamt of terror flickering inside the king's eyes.

Archeron ran his tongue over his broken tooth. "Breaking my enslavement bond has consequences."

Dark consequences.

Magewick's eyes settled on Archeron's face. "Worse than what you have already been forced to do?"

"How can I be sure you won't use the weapon against me or Solethenia afterward?"

Magewick grinned. "You know the weapon is cursed. Only someone with both light and dark magick can wield it. And unless someone that rare and special exists, you and your court are safe."

Archeron thought he could no longer hurt, but as Haven came to mind, the scab inside him broke open.

His chest ached. Haven.

She betrayed you for the enemy. She's an abomination. She chose her side.

And now she could become a weapon against his city. She hurt him once and she would do it again.

You can find another way.

But it didn't matter how guarded the dagger was, if they knew there was someone to wield the weapon, they would stop at nothing to get it. Perhaps they already knew. Perhaps that's why they were here.

Perhaps Haven had already made some type of deal with Stolas, or he'd used his dark magick to influence her, to seduce her.

He ground his teeth, the chipped canine slicing the inside of his lip and filling his mouth with blood.

He had helped create her, which meant he was responsible for the risk she posed to his city, the kingdom he'd sworn to protect at all costs.

There was only one way to ensure the Godkiller could never be used—but it would cost him the last remaining piece of his humanity.

Good, a dark voice whispered. *Let your heart match your face.*

"I will get you the dagger," Archeron said, "but if this is a trick . . . I'm coming for you first, Noctis."

Magewick gave a dark chuckle. "So untrusting, Sun Lord. I think enslavement has made you unnecessarily suspicious. What will you do with your newfound freedom?"

"Protect my city from her many enemies, including you."

Archeron waited until Magewick left his room and then the Sun Lord calmly walked over to the mirror, appraised himself, and smashed his fist into his ruined reflection.

SEVENTY-TWO

For the final trial, the disc-like arena had been moved to the city below the castle, beneath the enormous shadow of the Tree of Life. The streets on all sides swelled with citizens from every nation waving flags for their favorite contestant. Their voices charged the air, so loud Haven could feel the rumble in her chest.

Her hair hung in a thick braid decorated with jasmine and primroses, and she wore supple pine-green leather pants and a golden tunic with metallic thread that made her blouse glitter beneath the sun. A polished breastplate of silver clung to her torso like it was made for her.

Each finalist had been prepped this morning by the Sun Sovereign's own attendants, their clothes and hair carefully chosen to represent their nation. Avaline and Stolas wore ink-black armor, the tips of their wings dipped in silver and gold. Bell looked dashing in a black and gold ensemble, his curly hair tied back in a gold ribbon. And Ember, Rook's sister, wore red and black, the green stripe across her eyes outlined in gold.

The five finalists waited in the middle of the arena. Haven stood on the far-left side, followed by Avaline, Ember, Bell, and . . . Stolas.

She had yet to gather enough courage to look in his direction. To acknowledge him—or what happened a mere few hours ago.

She could feel his gaze on her, feel the prickling bite of his magick. Just thinking about him made her feel dizzy and warm, and she needed all her wits in the coming hours.

Directly behind and above them, the highest-ranking members of their courts sat in a mezzanine draped with wisteria and honeysuckle.

The too-sweet fragrance made the pounding inside Haven's head worse, and she shaded her eyes from the sun as she glanced up at the Tree of Life. The trunk alone was twice as thick as the taverns on the other side of the street, and it rose nearly as high as the palace. Roots and branches snaked throughout the city like arteries, intertwining with nearly every structure.

Even from here, she could feel its magick pulsing through the air. And if her nerves weren't frayed to bits, its essence might have calmed her.

Haven's fingers brushed the pommel of the sword she wore. A present from Archeron. The simple yet beautifully made weapon had been delivered to her room early this morning with a note:

I hope this sword helps you accomplish everything you desire.
Archeron.

Knowing that Archeron didn't hate her was a huge relief. Whatever mess lay between them, she could fix it. They could be friends again.

Haven looked to the stands hoping to catch a glimpse of Archeron. Instead, her eyes met Surai's gaze, and the girls shared a long, emotional look. After Bjorn's violent death and Haven's bath, she had found Surai in her bed, bawling.

They curled up together, the stench of that horrible incident still clinging to Surai's hair, her skin, and sobbed. Afterward, Demelza helped Haven put Surai in the bath. They washed her hair while Haven told stories about Rook, how fierce and lovely and bright she had been. Surai mentioned the extravagant dresses Rook had planned to buy for their wedding—three, one for the night before, one for the event, and one just for Surai's eyes afterward. And eventually Surai's tears had dried and she'd fallen asleep with a smile.

Yet, even now, Haven could see the rawness in Surai's face along with the doubt Bjorn's words created.

Damn seer, sowing chaos until the very end.

Focus, Ashwood.

A horn blew, drawing Haven's attention to where Lysander entered the arena, the Sun Sovereign following behind. She'd traded her usual gown for ceremonial armor, the kind Haven imagined she would wear into battle. The walnut sized rubies embedded into the neckline sent sparks of red flickering over everything in her path.

The din of the crowd became a roar as they cheered, parents holding up children to catch sight of their queen. The sovereign basked in the glow of adoration, a snake sunning itself on a rock.

She held up a hand and silence reigned. "Citizens of Solissia, we welcome you to the final trial of the Praetori Fiernum. This tournament has been an interesting one, and for the first time in history, two mortals have advanced to the final round." The mortal section of the stands went wild. "For the last trial, I have chosen a very special place. Five finalists will enter the Forest of Broken Souls, but only one will come out first to claim their title as Ruler of the Nine."

Forest of Broken Souls? Haven's mouth went dry. She had no clue where that was or what to expect, but its name alone conjured tendrils of panic.

Beside Haven, Avaline laughed. "You are so out of your league, mortal. I cannot wait to watch this haunted forest eat you alive."

Well, then. Haven snarled at the Skeleton Queen. "You first."

Smiling, Avaline flared her gray wings as she prepared to jump through her portal. Haven did the same, readying her mind and body for the trial ahead.

You ready for this, Beastie? Stolas's voice purred inside her mind.

Are you? she shot back, refusing to look at him. If she allowed herself to meet his eyes, she might remember last night. How he carried her. How he healed her with such gentleness.

The things they did afterward.

She could feel his laughter as it whispered through her skull, and then, *Is this really the time to think about last night?*

Screw you.

Happily, he purred. *But later, when there's not a crowd.*

If they didn't have an audience she would have thrown her sword at his arrogant, infuriating head.

Remember, he added, all traces of humor scrubbed from his voice. *It's not real. Cling to the unbreakable bonds between you and your family.*

Haven frowned, not expecting the cruelty of his words. He knew she didn't have a family. *Go away. I have a trial to win.*

Another sultry laugh. *That's the spirit.*

As the portals flared to life, those ominous rings of fire heralding the start of the final trial, the streets erupted in yells. Each person in the crowd chanting the name of their favorite finalist until the shop windows rattled and the floor of the arena shook.

Haven locked eyes with Bell. There had been no time to apologize this morning. As soon as they'd arrived each finalist was ushered off to be dressed and made ready for the spectacle.

Now, she barely had time to nod before they all leapt through the flames to the other side where destiny awaited.

SEVENTY-THREE

The smell of the forest hit Haven first: wet, rotting leaves and overgrown moss, woven with the fainter stench of stagnant water and a hint of putrefaction. As if something had died here recently.

Moist air drew sweat to her skin, soaking the nape of her neck where her braid hung. Above, the branches from the massive oak trees were woven tight enough to strangle all but a few shafts of light.

Something ancient and vulgar stirred just beyond the trees. And far off, so faint she could almost imagine it was in her mind, came a terrible weeping.

Her body recoiled from the wrongness. The heavy pall of death and corruption blighting the forest. Each breath felt like drawing in poison. Each lungful of that wet, rotted air making her limbs heavier, her soul dirtier.

A flutter of wings drew her focus upward. Ravens cawed from

the highest branches.

They watched her try to determine which way to go. Watched as she spun in circles searching for landmarks, a path, anything.

One impossibly large bird dropped to a branch near her head. This close, she made out the white film of death inside the raven's eyes, the bits of missing feathers and flesh where decay had already set in.

Revulsion slammed through her.

It's just part of the illusion.

So she tipped her head at him, the flowers from her hair spilling onto the carpet of dead leaves and moss, when she really wanted to vomit.

She needed to move. There was no path. Brambles, thickets, and the roots of the trees tangled together to form a dense wall. Sweat stung her eyes as she began hacking at the mess of thorns and roots, some as thick as her legs.

She could swear the forest shuddered with each bite of her sword. Its branches tightening above, its underbrush tangling in her legs. The first true whisper of panic twined around her heart as the forest closed and the space around her shrunk.

It was going to swallow her alive.

Avaline's laughter echoed from somewhere nearby. A single raven cawed, the piercing sound ricocheting off the trees. Stolas's barely-audible voice rustled through the branches, the sound like dead leaves stirring.

Can you love a monster?

A strand of light broke the darkness and she lunged forward, hacking and sawing her way toward it.

She stumbled forward—and broke into a clearing.

A group of people stood around a fire. Her heart leapt as she recognized them. Surai and Rook stood arm and arm next to

Archeron. Bjorn smiled at her from above the steaming pot of stew he tended.

Even Bell was there. He sat on a large, mossy rock reading from a book. When he saw her, his face lit up.

"Come," he offered, patting the rock. "Join me. I think you'll like this book."

Something was wrong. How could this be? She had just been . . . where?

Where where where—

Her mind blanked. Somewhere important. She had been somewhere important.

And yet . . . what was more important than this?

Surai laughed. "Haven, my sister. Look who's come back to us. My mate. We are getting married. Isn't that wonderful?"

"Yes," Haven said automatically, even as she frowned.

Something is wrong. I need to . . . need to . . .

Her mind kept wandering.

What was she doing? These were her friends.

Archeron smiled at her and beckoned. "Little Mortal, I've missed you. Come here."

He'd been angry with her—but why? Maybe that was a dream.

His grin was a balm to a wound she couldn't remember. She wanted this, so why was she fighting it?

She took a step. Another. Dead leaves crunched beneath her boots.

That's it, a voice whispered. *This is what you want. Stop fighting.*

Another step. She could smell the rich, meaty promise of soup, the smoke from the fire comforting.

Surai grinned at her.

And yet, her eyes—

They were completely black inside her face. Hadn't they been another color once?

Haven gasped as Rook turned to face her. Maggots squirmed and wiggled inside empty sockets.

"I gave up everything for you," Rook said. "Now give me my bride."

Grinning, Surai handed a knife to Haven. "Do it. I'm ready."

Bell stood, grinning as well, his eyes twin pools of night sky. "Me too. I'm ready to die for you, Haven. That's what you want, right?"

No, this was a nightmare, it wasn't real. She had to get out of—

"Rose. My rose. Come here."

Terror filled her veins as she slowly pivoted to face him.

Damius.

This was his camp. How did she miss the stench of blood magick in the air?

"No," she snarled. "I got away."

"Did you, though?"

He stood between her and the rift, his crimson cloak sputtering the air like spurts of blood.

He reached out a hand. "Come here, my rose."

Someone kneeled at his feet. Recognition shot through Haven.

Cyra.

Her friend's eyes were huge, pleading. "Please don't let him kill me. Do what he says. Please. I don't want to die."

Haven rushed to Damius, hands held out and ready, but nothing happened.

Her magick was gone.

"That's a pity."

"Wait, please," Haven begged.

Cyra pierced Haven with an accusatory gaze. "You kill everyone you love."

Cyra stood and began backing toward the cliff.

"No," Haven whispered. "Don't do it."

"You did this," Cyra said. "My blood is on your hands."

Haven fell to her knees.

Unbearable—the guilt was unbearable.

You're a failure, the voice whispered. *You're an abomination that poisons everything you touch. Your family gave you away. Your best friend doesn't want you. You let Rook die.*

You love a monster because you are a monster.

No.

Then prove it, the voice whispered. *Kill him.*

And there was Stolas. Not the Lord of the Netherworld, not the menacing Shade Lord married to Ravenna, but the prince. He wore simple clothes—a peasant's tunic and tan pants—his white hair pulled back, horns unadorned.

He was scribbling on a piece of parchment, his bottom lip caught between his teeth, the poem nearly finished.

Kill him.

Tears blurred her vision.

He glanced over at her, smiled, and said, "Do it just the way I taught you. End my suffering. You owe me."

SEVENTY-FOUR

Bell had known from the beginning what to expect from the cursed forest. He'd read about it years ago, how travelers that entered the woods became overwhelmed with sorrow, the dark magick of the forest replaying their greatest fears until they went mad.

He used that knowledge to fight off the hallucinations, tethering himself to a single, constant source of love in his life.

Haven.

Her undying loyalty to Bell pushed him on, and he stabbed at the branches that reached for him until the forest freed him.

He rushed to the top of a knoll—

Something made him turn back.

And there, through a hole in the wall of underbrush, blazed Haven's shirt, bright green against the darker hues surrounding her. Filaments of her rose-gold hair twined with the earthen colors of the forest.

His heart lurched as he made out the scene.

Her eyes were closed. Her body caught inside a writhing nest of roots and branches that tangled around her body like serpents.

As he watched, the branches tightened, more joining the others. They turned her over and over as they wrapped around her, an invisible spider entombing its prey.

The forest was consuming her.

"Wake up!" Bell yelled.

He tried to shove through the trees to reach her, slashing at the branches, the thickets, but the woods refused to give up its prize.

New undergrowth took the place of the cut ones, faster than he could hack—

"Haven!"

Only her face was left. She looked to be sleeping. Her face peaceful.

He willed her eyes to open. Willed her to wake up.

"Haven, fight!"

At his words, her expression twisted in some unseen agony. But still she didn't open her eyes.

Branches encircled her throat and began sliding up to cover her mouth. Slender, green-leafed vines slipped inside her parted mouth—

No. "Fight back, Haven," he screamed.

She couldn't die. She would never know how sorry he was for what he said last night. She would perish thinking he hated her.

Falling to his knees, he screamed her name.

Over and over and over.

Haven's nightmares played on repeat. She stumbled from one

sickening scenario to the next, trying to anchor herself to reality. To grasp a tether of hope in a sea of terror.

This isn't real.

This can't be real.

Stop fighting, a voice ordered. *As soon as you stop resisting the pain will go away.*

She struck out at the voice, but her magick was gone.

Without it, she was powerless.

You are nothing.

That voice—

You are a failure.

Where did she know it?

Even your family didn't want you.

And then it hit her—

Could it be?

The voice was her own. The words her own.

Which meant—

She was creating her own nightmares.

She alone was responsible for all the terrible hurt that was slowly drowning her.

What does it matter who's responsible when it's still the truth? Her voice echoed all around her. *You are an abomination.*

No.

Admit it. Admit you are powerless against the evil inside you.

No.

Admit you are too weak to control your beast.

No—

Admit your friends would be better off without you—

NO!

Remember, it isn't real. Stolas's words boomed inside her mind, warring with her own voice. *Cling to your family.*

Her *family.*

She quickly spoke their names, "Bell, Surai, Archeron, Stolas," and with every name, a piece of the darkness shattered. "Demelza," she added. "Nasira."

You will be their undoing—

"You're wrong," she yelled, her voice banishing the last of the shadows as her anger surged out. "I am the weapon that will save them."

All at once, she was back in the forest. Vines wrapped around her body. Her lungs burned. Blackness shrouded her vision.

The pressure at her throat was cutting off her air—

Refusing to panic, she conjured a burst of light magick.

This time, her magick obeyed, and she'd never witnessed anything quite as beautiful.

The woods around her exploded with light. As the fire swept over her cage of branches and vines, the forest groaned, and she sprang free.

"Haven!"

She jolted into a sprint toward Bell's voice. Her boots smacked on bones—so many bones. The forest was littered with them. Limbs reached for her, vines and thickets clinging to her legs, but she didn't stop running until she was free from the forest's deadly embrace.

Bell slammed into her, his hug tearing the breath once more from her lungs. "Don't ever do that to me again."

"Goddess Above," she panted. "Remind me to never come here."

Bell laughed, but it was part sob. "I couldn't get to you. I tried—"

"No, Bell. You did, believe me." She pulled away and glanced up the hill where the light from the portals glowed against the heavy fog. "We can talk about this later. C'mon, we have a king to crown."

They made it to the top of the hill before Haven saw Stolas. He stood by the far portal, one hand behind his back, looking every bit the conquering hero. A wily grin carved into his jaw.

Her heart sank.

No.

"Bravo," he called, strolling over. Behind her, Bell stiffened. "Resisting the forest's ghastly magick isn't easy."

Ignoring the way her body purred in his presence, she jerked her head at his portal. "Why haven't you entered yet?"

He shrugged. "Perhaps I don't want to be the Ruler of the Nine."

She exhaled, trying to work out his angle. "Then why enter the tournament? No, I don't believe you would give up access to your homeland when you are this close to winning."

"Still don't trust me, Beastie?" There was something in his voice, an emotion she couldn't decipher.

"What do you want in return?" she asked carefully.

"Nothing."

"You will be the sovereign's slave."

"As will you."

Haven blinked. They were wasting time. Any moment Avaline or Ember would race through the portal and win.

And yet . . .

"Go," she ordered Bell. "It's okay. I trust him."

"Are you sure?" Bell glared at Stolas.

"Yes, because he knows if there's a trick in this, I will murder him with my bare hands."

Stolas's eyes glittered above a crooked smile. "As enjoyable as that would be, rest assured, there is no trick in letting the prince win." He bowed low, showing off the tips of his horns. "Congratulations, little rabbit. You've transformed into a lion."

Bell's nostrils flared as he appraised the Shade Lord, uncertainty written all over his expression.

Haven nodded, mouthing, *Go.*

Bell hugged her a final time, and then she watched him disappear through the portal. She smiled as she imagined the cheers and surprise on the other side.

They had done it. Finally.

"Thank you," she said as she prepared to enter her own portal.

His fingers brushed her arm. She met his gaze, letting her guard drop just for a moment, the memory of last night burning between them.

Then he slid something into her pocket. "The translation."

She swallowed. "Then I guess I should thank you twice."

"No. I should be thanking you."

She shifted on her feet. "For what?"

"When the time comes, you will understand."

Mentally exhausted, she didn't even want to ponder his cryptic words. "See you on the other side?"

He nodded. "See you on the other side."

Thunderous applause still shook the arena as she entered, and any final lingering doubt fled as she saw Bell being showered with bouquets of flowers from the crowd.

Dahlias, his house flower, littered the ground at his feet. Someone had draped him in a velvet cloak of gold with the Ruler of Nine crest, a roaring lion surrounded by every house flower from the Nine Houses.

She'd never seen him smile so hard or so bright.

Her chest swelled with pride. *We did it.*

He would be crowned the ruler tonight, and then they could

start making plans on moving to Shadoria. Her smile stretched from cheek-to-cheek as she approached Bell, ready with some quip about never doubting this moment, when he glanced over at her and froze.

Terror rippled across his face.

That's when she noticed the thunderous applause had died to a few random claps.

Someone near her gasped.

Bell's horrified gaze traced down her exposed skin.

"Your fleshmarks," he whispered, even as he was tearing off the golden cloak from his back, ready to thrust it at her.

Time slowed to a crawl. Her heart ratcheted into a hammering din that drowned out the gasps as the crowd stared at her. Their wide-eyed gazes tracing the fleshmarks dancing over her flesh. No longer hidden but *glowing* for all to see.

It was too late to hide the truth.

The Sovereign's eyes cut through Haven, and on some unseen order, the Gold Shadows rushed forward.

She hadn't been expecting to fight, so her reaction was slow. By the time she tried to conjure her magick, it was too late.

The Sovereign's magick billowed over Haven, entombing her in a crystal cage. She was frozen in place.

Pain jerked through her body as the Gold Shadows wrenched her arms back and forced some type of spelled shackle over her wrists.

The darkness inside the iron bindings felt wrong, their power like the ancient kind in Bjorn's chains.

You might want to get used to this view. Bjorn's words clanged through her skull, along with what he'd called her. *King Maker.*

He'd seen this coming. All of it. She made a king . . . and lost her freedom.

The arena was completely silent as the sovereign stalked toward

Haven. Outrage burned in her faded green eyes. When she neared, she flicked a finger and Haven fell to her knees. Pain sliced through her body. Another flick of the sovereign's fingers and Haven's tunic shredded into scraps that fell away.

She tried to twist, to hide her fleshmarks, but the stunning metallic runes she'd once admired condemned her. In full sunlight, they glittered like rivers of magick tattooed over her flesh.

Clenching her fingers beneath Haven's jaw, the sovereign twisted Haven's head to look at the crowd. They were furious, a few booing. But most simply stared in stunned silence, unable to comprehend what was happening.

"When Freya gave mortals the gift of magick," the sovereign said, her voice carrying over the arena, "the Solis nations supported her decision. A decision we went to war to uphold. We bled, suffered, and died to ensure the mortal kings and queens could possess this rare and beautiful gift of magick."

The audience was completely still, as frozen by her words as Haven was by her magick.

"Fleshmarks, however, have always been off limits," the sovereign continued, her voice rising. "A birthright not shared by mortals. Were our laws not clear?"

Her wrath fell upon the section of the mezzanine where the mortal courts—only moments before celebrating—had fallen deathly silent. Their faces pale, mouths pinched.

Not a single one met Haven's eyes.

The sovereign shifted her focus to King Horace, and the blood literally drained down his face and below the high purple collar pressed tight against his fat neck. "This girl is your son's friend. Did you or anyone in your court know she was fleshmarked?"

King Horace couldn't answer quickly enough. "Of course not. I've never seen that girl in my life."

"Then no one from your courts will mind when she is put to death? Say, after the coronation tonight?"

Haven caught Bell's incredulous gaze and shook her head. *Don't.*

His hands curled into fists at his sides, but he knew what she did. Speaking up for her would only incriminate himself and the mortals of Penryth.

"Good." The sovereign smiled, the gesture so warm, so inviting that Haven blinked. "Renfyre of House Volantis, for crimes against the Goddess's law, I sentence you to death. Your execution will transpire during the soulless hour, your soul condemned to the Shadeling for all eternity." She gestured to the Gold Shadows holding Haven. "Take her away."

As they dragged Haven across the arena through the crowd, their hateful curses and shouts filling her ears, she found Surai's face in the stands above.

Get Demelza and flee, Haven mouthed. She could only hope her friend, her *soror,* would honor her and do this one thing.

Haven wanted to look into Surai's face forever. Wanted to take comfort in the eyes of someone who didn't hate her. But she dragged her gaze away before the sovereign noticed and punished Surai too.

Haven whirled on her guards. The shackles binding her arms behind her back limited her mobility, but she could still fight.

She slammed her forehead into the closest guard's nose, enjoying the squelching sound as the bones snapped and blood exploded everywhere. Rearing her knee, she caught the second guard between his legs—

Bright white pain burst behind her eyes as something hard slammed into the left side of her head.

Her body went numb; the sky tumbled across her vision.

And everything went dark.

SEVENTY-FIVE

Haven was going to kill Stolas. Murder him with her bare hands.

Her cell—the same one where Bjorn was held only hours earlier—was freezing. Whatever horrible magick was imbued inside the stone amplified somehow so that the air was near freezing.

A white cloud spilled from her lips as she tilted her head to appraise her binds. Two thick, heavy chains strung her arms out wide. Two more splayed her legs spread eagle.

She'd been in the same uncomfortable position for hours, shivering, half clothed, yet a thick fog of rage numbed her to the discomfort.

Stolas—

This was all *his* fault.

Why had he betrayed her?

Even now, the memory of last night seared into her. His mouth dragging over her skin, his fingers—

Snarling, she jerked her chains, more out of frustration than actually thinking they would break. They jingled, and a shock of horrible, cold magick poured through her.

The pain fueled her rage.

There would be nothing left of Stolas when she was through except feathers. No, she would burn those too. Burn every last piece of the bastard.

He must have somehow broken the spell that hid her fleshmarks when he dropped the translation in her pocket.

If she escaped this blasted cell—no, *when* she escaped, she would thank him properly for his betrayal.

A growl spilled from her lips, and she tried to work out in her mind why he might have done it. She had been so sure she could trust him. Where did she go wrong? But the chaos of emotions whirling inside her made thinking rationally impossible.

She needed to calm down. There would be time to figure out Stolas's plan.

Sighing, she focused on the canvas of stars in front of her. Night had fallen an hour ago, and, ironically, the evening sky from Haven's vantage in her cell was the most beautiful she'd ever seen.

She imagined this was meant as a cruelty—freedom so close yet just out of reach.

You better get used to this view. Bjorn's cryptic warning bounced around Haven's skull, aggravating her pounding headache. Being knocked unconscious had its drawbacks.

Her thoughts drifted to Surai, Nasira, Demelza. Had they made it out of the city yet? Were they safe? If the Sun Sovereign chose to punish them for Haven's transgressions . . .

She lunged at her binds and a shock of dark, vile power

reverberated through her.

That was the worst part of this all. Beyond the stink of Bjorn's death still clinging to the wall and the black burn marks no one bothered to scrub away. Beyond even her own dark magick scraping against her healing wounds.

A primordial magick seeped from the chains into her flesh, burrowing deep. The poison wormed into every part of her—her bones, her blood, her muscle—devouring the light magick from her body. Stealing her warmth.

Making her weak and sick.

She had the vomit around her feet to prove it.

She glared at the stars. At least the *view* could be worse.

Footsteps echoed from the other side of the cell. The door creaked open. She glanced back as far as she could turn. The mountain wind blew strips of her rose-gold hair across her vision. Her milky breath filled the dim air.

By now, her identity illusion had been broken. Anyone who entered her cell would see her true features.

Her eyes narrowed as she tried to make out her visitor through the shadows. With her arms held spread eagle above her and her legs pulled taut mirroring her arms, she was completely exposed.

Something about the footsteps, the presence was familiar. Achingly so.

Archeron?

Her rapid pulse slowed, and a tiny flicker of hope warmed her chest.

Archeron was a friend. He would find a way to help her.

"Archeron?" she called, hating the way her voice frayed, the hopeful lilt.

Dark shadows cast by the moon laced his features in inky darkness. She twisted despite the chains, the fresh wave of agony, desperate for a friendly face. The light from her newly revealed fleshmarks cast a soft, silvery glow over her bare, stippled flesh.

They hadn't even seen fit to give her an extra shirt, and only her bra covered her upper torso. Not that Archeron hadn't seen it all before but . . .

Why wasn't he saying anything?

His silence stretched out, the only sound the wind swirling inside the cell and the faint rush of his breathing.

Haven waited, a part of her aching to hear his voice.

"Why are you so quiet?" she finally asked.

Her voice cracked; she needed water.

"They are extraordinary, aren't they?" he whispered, his voice distant, almost sorrowful. "There was a time I imagined kissing your fleshmarks, imagined seeing them—and you—in my bed every morning. I thought you were a marvel, *my* marvel."

Her muscles ached from forcing her head back, and she turned her head to face the stars, panting.

The magick inside the chains was draining her energy.

Footsteps echoed off the stone as he neared. His breath was wonderfully warm on her neck. She shivered as he traced a finger over a fleshmark curving her shoulder, pressing into the heat, into him.

His fingertip glided down her back until it reached the runes cresting her spine.

She nearly cried out as he jerked his hand away and then retreated.

"Archeron, *please*."

Only for Archeron would she use that word. Only for him would she lower herself to plead, her heart longing to breach the distance she felt between them.

A sigh. "I warned you, Haven. I told you not to come here. I told you not to trust *him*. Why didn't you listen to me? Why did you have to be like everyone else in my life? Could you not have respected me just this once?"

At the mention of Stolas, another sharp spike of anger warmed her veins. His betrayal stabbing her over and over. Reopening the same wound.

She had trusted him beyond reason, beyond comprehension . . . and why? Because he took her to some museum and shared her dreams?

No—it had been more than that.

"Don't worry," she answered, licking her dry lips. "When I get out I'm going to rip him limb from limb."

"Optimistic even till the end. I think that's what made me fall for you. It was real, you know. I don't care what the seer said, what I felt for you was as real as those chains around your wrists. As real as the stars above."

Felt—not feel. And comparing their relationship to chains seemed a bit ominous.

Haven shivered, her chest tight. "Why won't you face me, Archeron?"

The sound of paper rustling filled the night air. "They said they found a note in your pocket. I thought it was from him, but it looks like some ancient, fake prophecy."

"What?" Haven wrenched her head back, trying to get a good look at him. But he was once more veiled in shadows. "What does it say?"

"You haven't read it then?" She heard him move closer. "It's an old prophecy from the time when blood augurs were still allowed in our realm. My mother thought she had all the apocryphal scrolls burned, but apparently, this one survived."

She jerked at her chains. "What does it say?"

His laugh was devoid of warmth. "I'll indulge you, Little Mortal. Why not?" Paper crinkled as she imagined his long fingers smoothing out the scrolls. "The prophecy is one of the oldest in existence. It says a child born of two gods, ice and fire, dark and light, would decide the fate of the world. This child would either be a weapon or salvation, and they would be more powerful than all the kings and queens combined."

"That's it?" Haven released a disappointed breath.

"I tried to tell you, it's an old, vague prophecy. It's driven rulers mad over the years. They've had children murdered, cities burned. Eventually the world realized it was just like most blood augur prophecies—a lie, smoke and mirrors meant to divide us."

"I don't understand, why would he give this to me?"

"Who?"

"I don't know, a monk." She didn't want to get the monk in trouble, so she added, "He found me in the streets. I think someone called him a heretic."

"The order of Soltari?" Archeron's laugh cut through the mountain wind. "I'm afraid you've been taken for a fool. The order is filled with madmen. My mother wiped most out centuries ago, but a few remain, hidden in the city. They're like crawlers, infesting the city, impossible to kill."

She shook her head. "What makes them mad?"

"They believe in apocryphal texts. They claim after Odin poisoned Freya in battle and she escaped, Odin sent his most trusted general, his brother, Varyssian, to hunt her down. But when Varyssian found her, instead of taking her prisoner, he fell in love and helped Freya hide while she recovered."

"That explains the statue," she remarked, recalling the feathered wings. "But how is that so apocryphal?"

"There's more. According to the order, Freya was with child.

It wasn't the first time. As a god, she could conceive, but she couldn't bear children like mortals and each baby died in her womb."

Haven leaned into his voice, his words. "Go on."

He scoffed. "Are you sure this is how you want to spend your last hours?"

"Yes."

"Freya knew there was only one way to have the baby."

Haven closed her eyes, imagining what a mother might do for their child. "She became . . . mortal?"

"Yes, at least, according to the order. They want us to believe Freya, the divine Goddess, would give up immortality for a child, knowing that once she became mortal, she would die."

"The poison."

"Exactly. To believe their claims, one must believe Freya was willing to sacrifice everything for her child."

Haven found herself smiling. A male would never understand a mother's love. "What about the rumor she became a statue?"

"They even have an answer for that. They claim she had a spell drawn to preserve her and her unborn child until the stars indicated the time of the prophecy was approaching. Only then was she to be awoken to give birth."

"And then die," Haven whispered.

"According to them. They claim their order was born from an oath. The Solis villagers along with Varyssian's soldiers swearing to protect Freya's body. And when the time was right and they woke the Goddess, their oath then fell to protecting her child. A child both mortal and god, ice and fire."

"The child of the prophecy."

"So they claim."

Haven drew in a breath. "What happened to the baby?"

"Nothing." His voice was hard, almost cruel. "It was never born, Haven. Freya died after the battle, there was no baby, no secret lover, no oath. The order uses those stories and the prophecy to trick people into giving them money and power. There's a thousand offshoots just like it, all claiming Freya didn't die or came back to our realm. For every heretical order that the Gold Shadows destroy, ten more pop up."

Bjorn's tattoo came to mind. "Was Bjorn one of them?"

She heard Archeron go still behind her.

"Did you torture him before we came because of it?"

"I never knew he was a heretic." Archeron's voice changed, became bitter. "Then again, I never knew he was Morgryth's puppet, either. It seems I have a knack for trusting those who do not deserve my trust."

A gust of cool wind blasted the cell, blowing Haven's hair back and drawing another round of gooseflesh over her bare stomach.

"Archeron," she began, willing him to hear her, "if you release me, I will hunt down Stolas and then I'll leave. Your mother will never find me."

She despised the pleading tone of her voice. But he was her friend, he'd forgiven her. Why else give her the sword before the final trial?

A sigh. "I'm afraid I cannot allow that to happen. You are a weapon, Haven, a weapon that can be used against Solethenia, against all of Effendier and everything I care about."

"What are you talking about?" She craned her neck trying to see him. If only she could read his expression . . .

He took a step away from the shadows. "In all fairness, you should know it wasn't Stolas who broke the spell hiding your runemarks."

She was shivering. Cold all over. Her breath frosting the air.

If it wasn't Stolas . . .

"Then who?"

Another step.

Only a few others even knew about the fleshmarks.

Including Archeron.

SEVENTY-SIX

A piercing pain shot down Haven's middle as the full extent of the betrayal became clear. "The sword. It was spelled."

"Yes," Archeron admitted.

"Why?" she panted. She couldn't catch her breath. Not Archeron. Not after all they'd endured, all they'd overcome together.

She had nearly given him everything. Her heart. Her dignity. Their stolen moments in the Ruinlands flashed in her mind. She told him things she'd never told anyone else.

Netherworld take her, she was going to be sick again.

Another step. "I lied when I said I would have no more pity in my heart for you. I still care for you. I think I even might still love you, despite your betrayal. Your death will most likely haunt me forever."

"Then why?" Haven growled, twisting against the chains as she tried to face him.

"I told you I could never love anything as much as I do Effendier." Another step. The shadows stopped just below his chin. "And anything that puts my kingdom at risk—even if it is something I love—I will destroy it."

"I am not your enemy," she said, breathless, her mind trying to wrap itself around what was happening. "Archeron, it's *me*."

Even cloaked in shadow, she could see he had to look away from her. "You are a weapon, Haven. It's why Morgryth wanted you, why Stolas has taken such an interest in you. It's why Magewick is undoubtedly at this very moment trying to find a way to get to you."

"What are you talking about?" She shook her head. None of this made any sense.

"There is a dagger, a killer of gods, with enough power to destroy cities. And you are the key."

The Godkiller. "It's locked away."

"Not anymore. But it doesn't matter if it's buried thousands of feet beneath the ground. As long as you are living, as long as someone can use you to wield it, no one is safe."

"Who would use me?" Her head was spinning. If only she could rip off these chains. If only she could face him properly.

"Everyone. My mother, Stolas, the Noctis . . . even I'm tempted. Whoever holds both you and the dagger possesses immense, unstoppable magick."

"Then destroy it."

His voice was soft, hollow as he said, "Not possible. And even if I could, the dark forces will never stop finding ways to use you against everything I love. If my mother discovered what you are . . . I can't even imagine the weapon you'd become. You are worse than the Godkiller because you possess unchecked magick to both sides. The only difference is your mortality means I *can* destroy you."

She sagged against her shackles. "You gave me my fleshmarks. You knew what I was, and yet you did it anyway."

"I was blinded by love, Haven, and I take full responsibility for that mistake, which is why I have to be the one to end you. You don't see it now, but killing you is an act of mercy. I am saving you from what you would become."

He took that final step into the moonlight, and as his face was revealed, a shock of horror trilled through her. If she could have moved her arms, she would have thrown a hand over her mouth.

The right half of his face was the same stunning visage she remembered, a face crafted by the gods themselves.

But the left side . . . once perfect flesh was burned beyond recognition. It couldn't have happened long ago, but the flesh had been healed—if that's what one could call the melted, shiny skin sagging down his cheek like candle wax. What once was an eyebrow of beautiful gold was now a lump of drooping skin hooding his eye.

And his lips—

Lips she'd once kissed. Lips that once pressed behind her knee and spoke words of love and humor and kindness—

His lips on the ruined side of his face were nothing now except a wrinkled hole.

"Who did this to you?" she hissed, but she already knew. Only one person possessed the cruelty to disfigure him.

His mother.

Perhaps that was why he didn't believe the story of Freya giving up her life for her child. All he'd ever known from his mother was pain and torment.

Something horrible shined in his eyes as he laughed. *Laughed.* And that's when she noticed just how dark his eyes were.

"It's only fitting they stripped my vanity away along with

everything else, I suppose. Now I am nothing, and I have nothing except this one singular purpose."

"What's wrong with your eyes, Archeron?" The burns on his face didn't explain the coldness there, pools of shadow and emptiness where once was humor and life.

Another thought occurred, and she said, "Why aren't you with the king?"

With such a public event, King Horace would want to show off his favorite toy.

Archeron's smile made the wounded side of his face appear to be snarling. "I no longer answer to him."

"He gave you your freedom?"

A dark chuckle. "No. I took it back."

Her heart clenched. "Don't you see? This isn't you. Breaking the bond inside the ring changed you."

"Yes. Now I see things so clearly."

Large *pops* drew her attention to the stars where the first of the celebratory fireworks etched against the sky. She should be down there with Bell. Bell would be worried, thinking about Haven during the most important moment in his life.

Archeron's madness was to blame. For the first time since he'd admitted his part in her imprisonment, she felt the first seeds of rage sprout inside her.

"I have to go," Archeron murmured.

Her nostrils flared as he suddenly approached, his ruined face inches from hers. He mistook her expression for sorrow, not fury, and his too-dark eyes softened. "I'm sorry. I never wanted it to end this way."

"Coward," she growled, leaping forward, the chains biting into her arms and legs. When she couldn't reach him, she spat in his face. "You're no better than Bjorn."

He flinched at that. "I don't expect you to understand. You're an orphan. You'll never know what it is to sacrifice everything for your homeland."

She gasped as he leaned forward and kissed her. A snarl ripped from her mouth as she tried to bite him, but he pulled away, grinning as if this was all some game.

Then he uttered a runespell—a *healing* runespell.

It took a moment for the ramifications of his actions to sink in. As the wounds at her back began to mend, the skin tightening and pulling taut, she felt the dark magick inside her stir.

"It will kill me," she said, stupidly, as if he didn't already know the consequences of his actions.

"I know. Consider it a kindness compared to what my mother was going to do. Goodbye, Little Mortal."

SEVENTY-SEVEN

The prison stairwell was dusty and cold, barely large enough for Surai, much less Nasira and Demelza. The small space was tactical. In case of a breach it was much easier to cut intruders down one by one as they ascended.

So far, that hadn't been a problem, thanks to Nasira.

They came to the final level, and Surai carefully peeled open the door. She cursed beneath her breath as she recognized the shimmer of a devouring spell, a shieldgate that prevented the use of light magick inside the prison.

That hadn't been here when she'd come to see Bjorn meet his end.

The sovereign was being careful.

"Our magick is useless," she whispered, pulling out two short, fat daggers. Her katanas were too long for close combat.

Behind her, Nasira laughed. "Speak for yourself. My magick works just fine." To prove her point, she sent a spark of ice-blue flame zipping around Surai's head.

Surai snarled at the girl. Goddess help her, why had she accepted Nasira's offer of help? The girl was a mistake. A horrible, bloodthirsty mistake. Already the five guards she'd eviscerated proved that point. She hadn't just killed them, she'd strung their entrails around their bodies, playing with the corpses.

And the things Nasira did afterward. The slurping noises as she drank their blood and more—

Surai shuddered. But if unleashing Nasira meant saving Haven then the carnage was on the sovereign.

Surai stopped near an empty cell and listened, careful not to touch the iron bars.

Haven was close. Surai knew from Bjorn's prediction that Haven would be in the same uppermost cell. She didn't relish going back to that place of horror and reliving Bjorn's death.

Desperation twisted her gut as she imagined Haven strung up similar to Bjorn. Whatever depraved execution the sovereign had planned for Haven . . .

Surai picked up her pace. That would never happen. She would die before she let anyone hurt her friend.

Nasira was silent, and in Surai's periphery she caught the girl crawling along the walls like a spider.

She wasn't just killing guards, but prisoners—

No. Surai had known using Nasira would inflict casualties. She would ask the Goddess for forgiveness later, once Haven was safe and they were far away from the sovereign.

Hard footsteps sounded behind Surai, along with wheezing as the plump older mortal woman tried to catch her breath. Surai cringed. Demelza had insisted on coming—Haven would be pissed—and her mortal clumsiness was sure to alert every guard on this floor.

Surai was about to instruct her to go back and wait inside the stairwell when a scream pierced the air.

Haven's dark magick did nothing at first. The runes carved into her spine were gone, the scars probably already faded into faint white lines that would disappear in a few minutes. But her magick waited, hesitant this time.

It sensed the strange *other* magick inside the chains.

She felt it unfurl from the place inside her where it burrowed, felt it stretch, testing the other magick. Testing her.

What is this? it whispered. *I do not like it.*

"Go back," she ordered.

No!

And then the pain hit blindingly fast as the dark magick ripped through her, the force rattling the chains and ripping her head back.

Her mouth wrenched open, but nothing came out. The pain was indescribable.

It stole her breath. Her consciousness. Her will to do anything but beg it to stop.

Please, oh, Goddess, *please*.

She was slipping in and out of darkness. Black shadows pooled on the floor of her cell.

Stolas's words whispered across the wind.

You don't lock a beast up, starve it until it's lust for blood is all-consuming, then forget to lock the door one day. Not unless you are its master.

Another shock of pain ripped through her and she groaned.

Bjorn's words came next, so clear she thought his ghost was in the cell with her. *Remember, to master the beast you must master thyself.*

Master. But to be its master, she would have to accept that darkness was a part of her.

A surge of icy power scraped across her back, but she fought the scream of pain on her lips. She would not cower from herself.

Herself.

More groans rushed from her lips. Fire consumed her.

Not unless you are its master.

Her magick was part of her.

They were one and the same.

Why would it hurt itself?

As understanding dawned, an ache opened inside her heart.

The darkness wasn't hurting her; she was hurting herself. Lashing out at her body because she despised her darkness. Because she had let Archeron make her feel less than.

But that was a lie. Whatever she was, she was made this way for a reason. And it was her choice what she did with it.

She was the master of all her magick.

Enough.

Just like that, the pain stopped. The fiery inferno ripping through her back ended, and the raw power inside her began to purr.

Another realization hit, and tears stung her throat.

She could have stopped the pain after the ball with one single word. Could have ended that unrelenting agony.

Except a part of her had thought she *deserved* the pain. That torment was just punishment for possessing vile magick.

All along, she had been punishing herself.

All along, her dark magick had only been following orders.

Not unless you are its master.

She had feared her dark magick. Hated it. Wished it gone.

Her self-loathing had nearly killed her.

Not anymore.

Her dark magick whispered through the air, seeping over the chains that bound her. The *other* magick inside the iron didn't stand a chance.

Her chains were silent as they crumbled to ash that blew away on that relentless wind. The jangle of keys in a lock drew her attention to the door behind her.

Her dark powers purred in anticipation.

A beast lived inside her, she accepted that now. And sometimes it was okay to let it out.

The dark silhouette of two guards framed the doorway. They were so sure she was still chained they didn't even glance her way as they paused. "He said to kill her if she wasn't dead in an hour," the first one was saying. "But it's only been half that."

"Once she's gone, we can join the celebration in the city. Why wait?"

"He prefers it to look like an accident."

Cursing, the first guard shut the door, locking it from the inside. "Let's get this over with."

They both turned to find Haven a few feet away, unbound.

Dark tendrils of magick danced around her as she grinned.

When Surai got to the cell door where she knew Haven was being held and heard the muffled cries, she flung herself at the iron. Locked.

Whatever they were doing to Haven—

She would kill them. Magick or no magick she was going to rip their heads off.

Surai jerked her chin at Nasira where the girl leaned against an open cell door, dabbing at the blood on her lips. "Open the door!"

Nasira cocked her head, listening to something Surai couldn't hear, and then shrugged. A quick wrench of the girl's hand and something inside the lock clicked.

Surai ripped the door open so hard it slammed against the opposite wall, her dagger ready in her left hand.

The wind barreled through the open doorway, whipping back her cloak and carrying the startling scent of dark magick: cinnamon, bergamot, and blood.

But the blood scent was by far the strongest. The metallic tang choked the air, rising above the other scents. Surai's gaze went to the red puddles streaking the stone floor. Stars and a near full moon reflected in their depths.

Which meant it was fresh blood.

No.

She followed the bloody stars to the bodies. Her eyes taking in the two male guards. Both very, very dead.

"Haven?" Surai called, her voice swallowed by her pounding heart.

And then she caught the flash of rose-gold hair.

"Haven!"

Her rose-gold hair blew wildly around her face. She wasn't wearing anything above her pants but a tan bra, and the muscles of her stomach trembled, as if she had just run a long distance.

Surai was unused to seeing Haven with her fleshmarks, their beauty and intricacy beyond anything Surai had ever witnessed.

For a heartbeat, Haven's eyes glittered with raw, overwhelming magick. The air around her consumed with her power.

A flicker of fear sparked inside Surai.

But then Haven called out Surai's name, her golden eyes changing back to normal, and Surai rushed to her friend.

"Soror," Surai murmured, releasing a heavy sigh as she stripped off her cloak and rested it on Haven's shoulders. "I heard the screams and I thought . . ."

"They weren't my screams," Haven finished, and Surai saw the way Nasira regarded Haven, the Noctis girl cocking her head as she hung back.

Nasira's eyes never left Haven. Something had changed and Nasira sensed it.

For the first time since Surai had met Nasira, she looked almost afraid.

Haven glanced past Surai to Demelza standing near the far wall. "What is she doing here? I told you to get them to safety."

"You did," Surai admitted. "And I ignored you."

"Looks like she didn't need our help after all," Nasira murmured.

Muttering a string of mortal curses, Demelza ran to Haven and began a search for injuries.

"I'm fine, Demelza," Haven growled, but the woman ignored her protests. "Really," Haven continued, looking at Surai. "Archeron healed all my wounds."

Archeron? "He was here? When? Why did he not free you?"

Surai had assumed when she couldn't find Archeron that he was with the mortal king. But if he'd been here . . . she couldn't imagine him leaving Haven to die.

The smile bled from Haven's face. "He found a way to break his enslavement to the king."

"Found a way? But that would mean he—no, only the darkest of magick could do that, and he would need to destroy part of his soul . . ." She shook her head. "He would never."

Surai could feel the anger radiating off Haven from here. "He's the one who revealed my fleshmarks. He came here and healed my wounds, *all* of them, because he hoped my dark magick would kill me. He wasn't even honorable enough to do it himself."

No. Surai massaged her forehead. She'd known he was struggling, that he hadn't been himself lately. But this?

"I should have done something sooner," Surai said. "Should have found a way to stop the king's abuses. Being here, with the trauma from his youth and then his unending humiliation . . . no. I cannot believe he would do this."

"Maybe before he broke his enslavement, but after—"

"No." Surai shook her head even as the truth slowly crept inside her. Her friend. Her loyal companion. "I should have done more."

"He made his choice, Surai." Surai could hear the barely leashed anger in Haven's voice, the fury at what he'd done. "He chose to give in to the darkness. And now, the Archeron we know, the Archeron we love"—her voice broke at that—"he's gone."

Shouts came from somewhere in the tower below.

"I think it is time we left," Demelza pointed out. "The change of guard will come any minute, and I would rather not watch that demon child over there"—Demelza slid her disapproving gaze to Nasira—"play with their insides."

Haven just shook her head. "No. When my dark magick returned, a memory came back. A plan. I need to find Stolas. There's going to be an attack. Ravenna—"

"It's already happening," Nasira interrupted, and Surai followed her curious gaze through the open cell door to the night sky. Shadows streaked toward the city, dark gashes slashing the star-studded tapestry of night.

"Shadeling's shadow," Surai hissed.

A screech shredded the air not far from the prison, the sound awakening a primal terror in Surai. Her people told stories of the Dark Night when Odin's otherworldly army blotted out the stars over entire cities.

But that was thousands of years ago.

"Demons," Haven growled. "And they're going for the Tree of Life."

She frowned at Nasira who was watching the demons a little jealously, like she yearned to join them.

"Nasira, are you on our side or theirs?" Surai demanded, tensing as she waited for the girl's answer.

Nasira rolled her eyes. "Really? How often do I get the chance to feed off demons?"

Haven nodded. "You get all the demon blood your little heart desires, but first . . . how are you at portals?"

Nasira flashed her sharp teeth in a grin. "It's my specialty."

Haven turned to Surai. "And that illusion spell you helped me with, the one that disguised my face. How hard would it be to do on a Noctis?"

Surai frowned, confusion drawing her dark brows together. "It could be done, I suppose."

"Good. Because I have a plan."

"What about the prince?"

For a heartbeat, Haven looked torn, and Surai waited for her to rush to his side, his faithful protector. But then she pressed her lips together and shook her head. "The prince is stronger than I've given him credit for. I have to trust that he'll pull through the attack."

SEVENTY-EIGHT

"**D**rink your wine, Bell, or is it too strong for your sensitive stomach?" Renk whispered, out of earshot of their father, who was seated nearby.

Bell's hands flexed over the gilded arm of the most uncomfortable throne in existence. Normally he would have snapped at the idiot by now, but he was preoccupied.

All he could think about was Haven and how to use this newfound power to save her.

"Where is my Sun Lord?" his father said, absentmindedly rubbing the dark red jewel inside his ring. "Bell, have you seen him? I've been calling him for hours."

Bell shook his head, ignoring the way his father slurred his words. That was the third time his father had asked the same question, and each time, his tongue had gotten sloppier.

The Solis wine was getting to the king. If only Cressida didn't keep filling his cup with more. It was like she wanted him to make a fool of himself.

Or, perhaps she didn't want him to notice her wandering eye as she flirted with every male in the room.

Fighting back his revulsion for his father's mistress, Bell turned his attention back to the coronation party. Around him, the grandest celebration he'd ever seen raged. Kings and queens from nations ranging from the Ashari steppes to the tip of Freya's Spear came to pay their respects to the new Ruler of the Nine.

Him. How was that even possible?

It was a whirlwind of languages and dialects, names and faces, some kind, some curious, some flagrantly disdainful that a mortal had taken the coveted position.

And all he could think of while they bowed to him, whispering in his ear of alliances and trade, was Haven.

Was she hurt? Scared?

You're the only one who's scared, he corrected. And it was true. He was terrified his best friend would die for his mistake. And that she would do so not knowing how much he loved her.

His hands shot up to the dark crown weighing down his head. He would give it back in an instant if that meant she could live. He would give it all back. His father's fickle love; the adoration; the way everyone suddenly looked him in the eye and listened to him speak.

He shot an impatient glance at the nearest clock.

When Surai told him her plan, he'd wanted to go with them to help. But his absence would have only alerted the sovereign that something was wrong.

So he was forced to sit here and smile and do what he could, in case they failed.

All night he'd been searching out who could help him. What could he promise from his new position to free her? He would give away everything in his power to secure one person who could help him.

But his careful digging came up with one answer: no one would defy the Sun Sovereign.

Bell glared through the haze of incense permeating the room and found Xandrian. The Sun Lord had been avoiding him all night.

That beautiful, arrogant man may be your only hope left, he told himself, trying to override his ego. Xandrian was the sovereign's nephew, a favorite of her court.

Perhaps if Bell offered him something, he would talk to Lilith. Persuade her to spare Haven's life.

Bell had just conjured up enough nerve to go speak to Xandrian when Eleeza performed an elaborate bow in front of him. For a moment, he blinked, unused to such decorum.

Get used to it, he reminded himself. Even his father was expected to bow before him now.

"Congratulations," she said, her dark hair spilling over her forehead. "Maybe we can go somewhere private later? To celebrate?"

He felt his lips tugging into a frown and forced the corners upward. "Uh, yeah, sure."

He would tell her tonight that he couldn't marry her. She deserved the truth.

As soon as Eleeza was gone, Renk sniggered. "When are you going to tell her she doesn't have the proper equipment?"

Nostrils flaring, Bell looked Renk straight in the eye. "Renk, one of these days you and I will come to an understanding, and it won't involve words."

Renk laughed, spittle dotting his lips. "Was that . . . a threat?" But behind his smile his eyes were dark and cruel.

Bell glared out through the open balcony doors into the night. As he took in the too-dark sky, which moments before had boasted countless stars and a swollen moon, his annoyance gave way to unease.

"What's wrong with the sky?" his father asked, his voice thick and breathy.

Renk chuckled, and something about his laughter chilled Bell's blood.

The wail of sirens cut through the air. The music stopped. The dancing halted. Someone screamed. And then the first creature hit the balcony with a tremendous thud, and Bell knew what it was.

"Demon," he whispered. The thing was massive, larger than five Solis males. Crafted from the deepest black, the demon had a reptilian face with six yellow glowing eyes. Its body was twisted and hunched and uneven, mangled wings protruding from its misshapen back, as if its creator had derived pleasure in its imperfections.

Its *wrongness.*

More demons followed. The balcony filled with wings and claws and primordial eyes. Every creature crafted from the same nightmarish parts, yet somehow different.

Bell leapt to his feet just as the room erupted in chaos. Guests fled in every direction. Bell watched a Solis female get trampled a few feet away. Some of the more powerful lightcasters conjured their magick—but instead of using their powers to fight the invading demons, they used it to save themselves. Knocking others out of their way as they fled.

Tables were knocked over. Decanters of wine shattered. Guests were shoved into the pools of water and drowned beneath the crush of bodies.

The Gold Shadows rushed to the sovereign, retreating into

the throne room with the flowing river. They formed a circle, working to create a shield around her. The shield shimmered in the air, but something was wrong with it.

Holes appeared in the layer of solid magick. Holes that grew larger with Bell's every breath.

An iron gate fell with a loud crash, cutting off the sovereign and her guards from the rest of the hall.

Anger shot through Bell. That room could protect hundreds of innocent guests, but anyone who tried to approach was incinerated by the Gold Shadows.

Weapon—he needed a weapon. He patted his waistband before remembering he'd armed himself with only the throwing knives Xandrian had given him and a vial of the enhanced poison he'd been working on.

He had hoped that if Surai failed to break Haven out, he could use the poison to trade for Haven.

He'd also had the forethought to tip the throwing daggers with the poison, but that meant nothing if he couldn't hit his target, and his newfound skills from practicing daily wouldn't help him when it came to unearthly fast demons.

A hand grabbed Bell's arm, and he pivoted to see his father pulling him toward the door. "Lady Thendryft knows of a hidden room," his father panted.

Capillaries broke over his nose and cheeks, his speech slurred. He stumbled, and it took all Bell's strength to keep him upright.

The crush of bodies pushed Bell and his father toward the back doors. Behind them, unholy screeching pierced the night, and shadows danced over the marble walls of the throne room as more demons landed outside.

When the hallway split, Eleeza led them to the right, away from the crowd. Cressida and Renk followed close behind. Bell tried to recall where the other direction led . . . another balcony? There were so many places the demons could breach here.

All those people were running toward danger.

Bell turned to go back. If there truly were a hidden room where they could be safe, he had to help some of the guests find it.

"Bell!" Eleeza called. She was limping, her face twisted in pain. "Bell, my ankle."

"You're hurt?" Sliding an arm beneath her armpit, he helped her down the corridor. "How close is the room?"

"Almost there," she breathed. A long stretch of hallway opened up, and she nodded at the marble wall. "Push into the wall. There's a door there."

She was right; as soon as his fingers brushed the cool marble, a door-sized panel slid open. On the other side was a dim chamber that looked like it hadn't been used in ages. Dusty chaise lounges were situated around the room in groups of three and four, and a pool tinkled from somewhere in the corner.

Moonlight spilled from arched windows onto the marble floor, and Bell tried not to look at the monstrous shadows as he helped his father onto the nearest couch.

Muffled screams trickled from the other side of the thick wall. Renk huffed a high-pitched laugh. "Poor idiots. They don't stand a chance."

Bell rounded on him. "Open the door. We can offer sanctuary."

"And risk letting a demon in here?" Cressida shrieked. "Don't be foolish, Prince."

"It's king, now," Bell reminded her. "And I order you to open the door for those people."

His father pushed up onto his elbows, and shock hit Bell as he took in his purple face, swollen lips, and blood red eyes.

"Do not talk to my son that way," he shouted, but his words

jumbled together. "He is better than . . . better than . . ."

The king slumped onto his back, his chest shuddering with each ragged breath.

Cressida strolled over to the king, towering over him. "Or what, my liege? What will you do?"

His lips moved but only gurgles came out. When finally his lips formed proper words, he mumbled, "Where is Archeron?"

"What did you do to him?" Bell snarled.

Cressida smiled, still watching his father as he began to convulse. "It's called wraithwort. Terrible stuff. It's rare and expensive, and it doesn't kill the Solis, only steals their power for a short while, so it's hardly used. Which is why the sovereign didn't test the wine for that particular poison."

Bell's heart lurched into his throat.

"It does, however, kill mortals."

Bell positioned himself in front of Eleeza. Thank the Goddess her limp had gone away and she was able to flee. "Eleeza, make a break for the door. I'll fend them off—"

Cold laughter drowned out his words. Eleeza's laughter.

"In my host's mind, you were such a weakling, Bell. A poor, pathetic, cowering prince. But now, look at you. Playing at being brave. It's adorable."

Slowly, Bell pivoted to face Eleeza. Except this wasn't Eleeza. "Who are you?"

She blinked and when her eyes reopened they were all pupil, and huge, twice their normal size. "You saw my mark, remember, Prince?"

Her voice was no longer high and lilting but gravelly and loud, like a thousand voices crashing together. She ticked her head, the animalistic movement twisting Bell's guts, and he caught the dark markings curving the nape of her neck.

A nest of snakes wriggled and hissed against her skin, just above her collar. He didn't need to see the full tattoo for the realization to hit.

Eleeza was the blood mage.

SEVENTY-NINE

Archeron was in the gardens when he saw the demons attack. He rushed to the palace, erecting portal after portal as he threaded inside. Hundreds of guests sprinted past him, screaming, some bloody and others severely wounded.

The scent of blood choked the air.

The grand hall was empty. Beyond, the giant gate used for attacks such as this had been deployed, and he spotted his mother and sisters on the other side. When his mother saw him, she flung her arm through the gate.

"Archeron! Son, let us out. Hurry."

As always, even in crisis, his mother's voice was calm and demanding. Not a shred of doubt he would do exactly what she commanded.

He strolled to the gate, taking in the way his sisters and the concubines shoved and pushed at the bars. The terror barely hidden in their eyes.

Where were the Gold Shadows? And why weren't they using magick?

When he was close enough he could touch his mother's long, outstretched fingers, he halted. Without magick, her beauty spell had fallen away to reveal sunken cheekbones, her normally youthful appearance aged and hard. Her once lustrous hair was thin and brittle.

Lysander stood behind her, his eyes pleading. As far as Archeron knew, her favorite concubine had never held a sword, but he held one now.

Ready to give his life for the sovereign.

"Unlock the gate," she ordered. Her voice sounded different now, breathy and wild.

He stared at her, unsure why he was hesitating. "Where is your magick?"

A flicker of something—fear?—darted across her face. "Our powers were stripped by poison."

He peered past her to the throne room where black lumbering shapes scurried over the walls. Demons. More clawed up from the river inside the throne room, the water black with the creatures.

It had always been assumed demons avoided water, and yet, they had discovered a way in through the water system.

Clever.

Gold Shadows scattered the ground, some torn in half, others missing limbs. Blood was everywhere.

A few Gold Shadows still lived, and they fought the demons valiantly. But without their magick, they were powerless against the onslaught of creatures.

A hunched demon with a reptilian body and enormous, twisted horns killed the last two guards. His tail dragged through the carnage, smearing blood across the floor as it sniffed through the bodies, picking out pieces it deemed edible.

The sound of bones snapped between teeth echoed off the walls.

One of his sisters, the youngest, reached out and grabbed his shirt. "Please, brother. We're trapped, without magick, and the lock requires a lightcaster to open it."

Archeron flicked his gaze to the lock and then back to his mother.

Her anger sizzled the air between them. Even now, at his mercy, and she still thought she was in control. "I am your sovereign, now open the lock."

His sisters, sensing the approaching demons, grabbed their swords and turned to face the horde. One began praying.

The vile beasts were everywhere now, the air thick with their putrid stench. Their snarls and whines and howls creating a grim song of death.

"Tell me, Mother," Archeron said. "Do you love me? You can tell me the truth. We are family, after all."

For the first time in his life, true fear glinted in her eyes. He hated how much he liked it. Hated how much pleasure the pungent scent of her terror gave him. He wanted to breathe it in, wanted to etch her terrified face into his memory for eternity.

"What game are you playing?" she hissed, the panic in her voice matching her eyes.

"No game."

A demon darted toward the gate, grabbed one of the concubines, and dragged him by his foot into the churning mass of creatures. A frenzy erupted over his body. He never even had the chance to scream.

More crunching of bones. More blood. The scent of fear was now everywhere.

His mother calmly watched the attack, and when she turned

back to face him, her eyes had changed. Become loving. Affectionate. "Yes, I do love you. You are my only son. Now, enough of this game. The *gate*, Archeron."

A thousand nights he'd wished for that look. Those words.

He loosed a breath as if coming out of a trance.

His heart jolted. What was he doing?

He reached up, ready to send his magick to release the lock, when he caught the look in his mother's face. The absolute contempt in her eyes.

Contempt for him, when she was to blame for all of this.

She let the Noctis inside the city.

Her insidious pride was responsible for the carnage, the dead and dying in the streets. And so much more. Hundreds had died because of her. Unborn children ripped from the womb. His brothers.

If he let her out, he was dooming his kingdom to centuries of her unchecked depravity. Centuries of fear while she sated her lust for power.

She was a threat; they all were. Each one molded into a version of her. Each one capable of filling in her shoes.

He retreated a step. "What should your punishment be for lying, Mother?"

She watched him, a sudden finality coming over her face. "The Empress's prediction was right. I bore a monster. I should have murdered you in my womb."

Archeron gave a bitter smile. "Whatever I am, you made me into it."

She gripped the bars, a mad glint in her eye. "You will regret this, Halfbane. It will haunt you all your immortal life."

"I killed the woman I loved earlier tonight to protect this city. That will haunt me. Not this."

The screams started almost as soon as he turned to walk away. He heard the scrape of steel as his mother drew her sword. She would go out like a lioness.

Cowardice had never been one of her failings.

He was giving her a good death. A heroic death. It was better than she deserved.

And she was wrong. Whatever he should have felt as their horrified wails of pain echoed off the marble walls, stretching out into countless minutes, the demons *playing* with them—

He felt nothing.

Only a wonderful sort of emptiness, and the sense that his work to purge Effendier of its rot had only just begun.

EIGHTY

Bell couldn't stop staring at Eleeza—

No. Not Eleeza. A monstrous imitation.

Renk chuckled as he pointed at Bell. "Look at his face. Shadeling's shadow, this is more entertaining than the attack out there. Hurry up and kill him. I want to see how loud he screams."

Bell's disbelief gave way to reality. Eleeza was the blood mage. The books on blood magick said a powerful mage could take someone's identity with enough of their blood.

The blood mage killed Eleeza. Kind, strong Eleeza.

A chill passed over him.

He stole a breath, his fingers hovering over the breast pocket of his velvet vest where the closest knife was hidden. He might only get one chance.

Distract her.

"What did you do to Eleeza?" he asked, steeling himself for her answer.

"Now she was a fighter, that one." The blood mage flicked up her eyebrows, *Eleeza's* eyebrows. "I took her the night you nearly killed that one over there." The blood mage nodded toward Renk. "Or should I say, your protector nearly killed him."

"Why?"

"I needed to get close to you, and who better than the girl rumored to be your intended? I had no idea at the time you didn't love her."

The boat. The ball. Tonight.

Every chance encounter now played through his head.

His father groaned. "What is happening? Where is Archeron? He should be here by now." His eyes were rolling back into his head, but he managed to focus on Bell. "Son, what are you waiting for? Use your . . . magick."

Cressida's sneer was all teeth as she brushed a finger down his father's swollen cheek. "Oh, didn't you know? He's a coward. And all the magick in the world cannot change that. He's abandoned you just like your beautiful Sun Lord."

His father gaped at Cressida as her betrayal slowly sank in. "Why?"

"I gave you every opportunity to make Renk the heir apparent. But you insisted on giving that sniveling brat chance after chance. Never underestimate what a mother will do for her child."

His father's eyes fell on him, pleading. "Please, Son. Help me."

Bell's chest ached. He wanted to tell his father he was barren, that if he could, he would use all the magick he possessed to save him.

Convulsions wracked the king's body. A second before his eyes rolled back into his head and a final breath shuddered from his body, an emotion flashed over his bloated face.

Disappointment.

"I thought he'd never die," Cressida remarked casually, and Bell wanted to rip her throat out.

Renk laughed, the bastard.

He would kill them both.

Rage steeled his nerves, and Bell chose the moment to act. The slim dagger was cold between his fingers. *Pretend this is practice with Nasira in your room.*

He stilled his mind, his breathing, even his heart as he loosed the weapon at the blood mage.

And missed.

One side of the blood mage's lips twitched up. "See. It's like he's trying to be a hero all of a sudden. What happened to the sniveling, lying prince? I liked him better."

"Kill him," Renk whined. "That was the deal. Kill him and give me his magick, and when I take the mortal throne, we send your master mortal slaves every year."

Snake. Murderous snake.

When the blood mage didn't respond, Renk tugged at his collar. "What does he do with the mortals anyway?"

The blood mage pinned Renk with a cold look.

Renk lifted his hands, his tone less sure than it had been moments ago. "Just curious. We don't need to know. Just give me his magick like you promised and we'll conclude our deal."

It was Bell's turn to laugh. "She's a blood mage, idiot. I'm just guessing here, but I don't think they uphold their bargains to mortals."

The blood mage's eyes glittered as she clapped slowly. "A hero and smart. Well done. You might have actually made a decent ruler, much better than that slab of flesh."

Renk blinked, a whisper of fear rippling over his fat face. "Now, wait a minute."

The blood mage snapped her fingers. A crack followed as Cressida's head jerked ninety degrees, her neck breaking. Her eyes were open as she slumped next to the king, dead, a thick ribbon of blood unspooling from the corner of her still smiling lips.

Renk backed toward the door, shot a panicky glance at his mother, and fled.

"Shadeling Below, he talked too much. But she—she got on my nerves." The blood mage took a step toward him. "Now, come here, boy."

"Screw you."

This time his dagger was aimed true, but she froze it inches from her throat. The dagger clattered uselessly at her feet, and she kicked it without breaking her gaze from his face.

Crap. He took out the last throwing dagger, gripped like an ice pick, and lunged for her throat.

She flung him back with dark magick, and he slammed into a couch, the dagger crumbling in his hand. His head throbbed, his shoulder ached.

Get up.

"Jokes on you," Bell snarled, jumping to his feet as he scoured the room for a weapon. "I don't have any magick. I'm barren."

She lifted her hand, and a force latched onto his neck, dragging him toward her. His boots scuffed the stone as he tried to free himself, bucking and jerking.

But she was too strong.

"You should have consumed the wine," she remarked. "Then you wouldn't feel a thing. I'm afraid this is going to hurt."

A stabbing pain pierced his chest. He clutched the area above his heart.

"Whoever your mother was, she must have loved you dearly because she gave her life for you."

He fell to one knee as fire ripped through his chest. "What are you talking about?"

She was standing over him now, her face twisted in pleasure as she watched him suffer. Her black eyes churned like storm clouds caught in a globe. "You do have magick, Prince. Powerful, dormant magick. I thought I had been misled at first when I realized it was your personal guard feeding you your powers, but when I realized who she was and saw your birthmark, it all made sense."

Bell ripped his collar down and stared at the flesh just above his heart. Blinding light poured from the lines of his birthmark, the feeling like a brand being shoved into his skin.

"You're one of Freya's chosen. The bitch gave your mother that spell while you were still in her belly. Your mother bound your magick in the womb so that you would be protected from the Curse. The price, of course, was her death."

The world seemed to tilt beneath him. "You said chosen. Chosen for what?"

The blood mage sneered at him. "You mortals know nothing. You are *her* chosen protector."

A wave of relief washed over him as the torment stopped. "Who? Who am I supposed to protect?"

"The bitch's daughter," the blood mage said, kneeling beside him. "But never mind that now. I've just freed your magick, and now I'm going to take it and then kill you. Actually, the process of ripping out your magick will probably kill you first, but if it doesn't, I'll finish the job. A deal is a deal, right?"

"Why?" he demanded. "You broke your deal with Renk, so why do you need my magick before you kill me?"

Everything he'd just learned clanged inside his mind. His mother had died for him, and for the magick inside him—magick that was about to be taken away.

If he let that happen then his mother died for nothing.

The blood mage shrugged, her hands positioned palms forward toward his chest. Obsidian talons capped her fingers, the only hint at the monster beneath. "Because now that you are the Ruler of the Nine, my master's plans have changed. I'm not just going to kill you, Prince. I'm going to *become* you."

Bell shuddered as her face changed. Her eyes turned round and blue, rimmed by thick black lashes, her nose elongated and thickened, her ridged dark eyebrows filled in and settled.

It was like looking into a mirror.

"Now," the blood mage said as inky tendrils of magick sprouted from her clawed fingertips and spiraled toward his chest. "Try not to scream too loud."

Bell threw his hand up—as if that could stop her from taking his magick—and the back of his hand hit something hard inside his breast pocket.

The vial of poison.

One second the blood mage was smiling. The next, the vial was hurtling toward his nose. It seemed to break apart in slow motion, the glass shattering into tiny shards, and Bell held his breath as he watched the red-tinged poison splatter over his stolen face. Watched as that face began to melt into something else.

Black eyes, gray corpse-like skin, and a bald head took the place of his image. The creature shrieked, clawing at its face, and then its skin cracked open as flames rushed out.

Bell stumbled back away from the smoldering flesh as it crumbled into ash. When he was sure the blood mage was dead, he ran to his father. His eyes were half open, his skin already mottled and cold.

Grieve later.

He closed his father's eyes and then rushed into the hall.

He'd barely made it twenty feet before he found Xandrian on the floor, a demon tangled around him. Black ichor oozed from several stab wounds in the creature's thick, scaly hide.

Xandrian's eyes fluttered open. "I followed you. I was trying to—"

"Don't worry about that."

"It's dead, right?"

"Yes." Bell dropped beside him. "Can you walk?"

Xandrian nodded. "If you can get this stinking corpse off me, I can. I'm still weak, but whatever poison was used has almost left my system."

Bell grunted as he heaved the demon corpse off Xandrian. A wave of revulsion hit as his fingers pressed into the demon's slick, meaty flesh. "Runes, this thing is disgusting."

Xandrian grinned. "Try lying under it for half an hour."

Xandrian got to his feet. Blood seeped from a gash in his silver and black shirt, and he clutched the wound, grunting low.

"You're hurt."

"A mere scratch." Xandrian's face brightened as he forced a smile, and Bell felt his heart flutter.

Even now, with the world overrun by demons, Bell was still susceptible to the Sun Lord's charms.

Xandrian thrust something at Bell—the Hadrassian dagger. "Take this."

"No, I—"

"You don't have a weapon, and it was happier with you, I promise."

Bell accepted it. "Thank you."

"Look, I need to explain," Xandrian began as they worked their way silently through the palace.

"You don't have to—"

"Yes, I do." Xandrian paused beside a tapestry splattered with blood. "At first, I took an interest in you because of the purity of your magick. I thought—I thought you were the runecaster I've been searching for. But then, when you impressed my aunt with that water display, I knew it wasn't your magick but *hers*."

Bell swallowed, that familiar shame that came from lying weighing him down.

"But still, whenever I was around you, I felt something. So I gave you two tests. The book and the Hadrassian blade. Both required magick to use."

Bell blinked down at the weapon in his hand.

"That's when I asked to see your birthmark, and I realized who you were."

"And who is that?"

"One of Freya's chosen."

"Chosen for what?" Bell asked, searching Xandrian's face for the truth. Even now, the hurt from the ball lingered.

"To protect the most important thing in the world to Freya— her daughter."

Not expecting that, Bell loosed a nervous laugh, but Xandrian wasn't finished. "I want you to know, *need* you to know that the only reason I rebuffed your offer to dance is because I could never be in a . . . relationship." Xandrian pressed his hand into his injured chest. "I have lived a lie for too long, pretending to be the sovereign's puppet while I informed against her to the Order of Soltari."

The stolen memory of Xandrian killing the Gold Shadows made so much sense now.

"Once you pretend to be something for long enough, that is what you become. And you deserve more."

Any words Bell could muster died on his tongue.

A nearby shriek shook the hall, and they rushed down the corridors, Xandrian's revelation tucked away for later.

They rounded a corner—

Bell recoiled from what awaited them, the scene straight from one of his nightmares. Mangled bodies were everywhere, the rotten stench of demons and blood poisoning the air. Long swaths of black charred the walls where the guests had tried to fight back. But their magick, weakened as it was, did little to save them.

They halted at the threshold to one of the grand halls. On the other side, demons lurked, feasting on the dead. They fought each other over the bodies. Their otherworldly hisses and whines scuttling down his spine.

Xandrian held up a finger to his lips.

All at once, the demons lifted their heads in unison, listening to some silent signal only they could hear. With a blood-curdling roar, the creatures shot into the air.

Bell waited for the last creature to disappear out the balcony before sagging against the door frame.

"Maybe the attack is over?" Bell offered, praying it was true. "Now that the wraithwort is wearing off, perhaps they know it's a losing battle."

Xandrian shook his head. "No, whomever is controlling the demons would be prepared for that. They're amassing for something . . ." His jaw ticked, and then his eyes widened in horror. "No."

"What?"

"The Donatus Atrea. If they could destroy it—" Xandrian suddenly took Bell's hand, and Bell ignored the urge to lace his finger through the Sun Lord's. "I can portal us close. Have you ever threaded with anyone before?"

Even though they were probably minutes from certain death,

Bell found himself grinning. "Never."

Xandrian winked. "I'm honored to be your first."

A dark hole yawned open, as if a sharp blade sliced open the air, and then they were sucked through.

EIGHTY-ONE

Fire brightened the night sky as it consumed the city, a symphony of screams playing in Haven's ears. Demons were everywhere; dropping from the stars, crawling from the canals and rivers, exiting windows of homes where she could only guess at the carnage left inside.

Buildings were torn apart, flames licking from the gaping holes. Bridges fell into the water with booming crashes. People sprinted past her. Their eyes glazed with shock. Others huddled in the open, frozen in place by panic.

Wave after wave of dark magick slammed into the city. Stripping the light magick from its bricks, its flowers, its people.

Blinding rage crashed over her as she sprinted through the streets toward the Tree of Life. The demons ignored her—probably because of her dark magick—but they weren't so lucky. She took them down, slaking her rage with every spark of her power.

She boiled them from the inside out.

Turned their bones to ash.

Their blood to dust.

She felled swarms of them in the sky, watched as they splattered to the cobblestones.

It wasn't just demons; Noctis infested the city. Golemites with their bat-like wings and gnarled horns emerged from alleyways, their battle armor coated in blood. They were destroying anything they could: buildings, monuments, people.

And Freya's beautiful cathedrals—the bastards amassed in the hundreds around the ancient churches, picking them apart like maggots on a corpse.

A snarl loosed from her throat at the sight. She was going to murder them all. Rip them to pieces.

Around the corner she spotted a male Golemite enter a bakery where citizens huddled behind the counter.

She shattered the shopfront window and filled his body with every single shard of glass. Another Noctis flung a Solis woman over his shoulder and started to take to the sky—until Haven ripped his wings from his back.

He writhed on the ground. Blood spurted from his wounds. When he spotted Haven, he growled, gnashing his teeth. Grinning, Haven choked him on his own blood, funneling it into his mouth until his lungs burst.

Haven ignored the woman's shrieks as she crawled away from the dead Golemite . . . and Haven, just as terrified of her as she was of the Noctis.

When Haven neared the palace and the Tree of Life came into view, panic whispered through her. A thousand demons swarmed the tree like termites. Even from here she could see its large buds shriveling, its branches convulsing all around the city as it fought to withstand the onslaught.

Deep inside her chest, her light magick guttered, and she clutched her heart.

The tree planted by Freya, the gift that gave mortals magick, that gave the Solis their power and balanced out dark and light.

If it were destroyed . . .

The entire city would fall.

No, the entire realm.

But the tree was strong, and it fought back. The demons who got too close to its branches caught fire, and they plummeted around the base like falling stars, their screeches splitting the night.

She was sprinting now.

The arena flew by on her left.

Up ahead rose the tree, and all around it writhed the Noctis army: Golemites with their membranous wings: Seraphian, their horns capped silver and radiating blue light; demons of every type; and Shadowlings. Fights broke out between the different species as the promise of victory—and the bloody carnage that followed—grew stronger.

This close, she made out the glint of a shield erected around the tree. It was all that kept the dark army from destroying it. A tremor rippled through her core as she heard the tree groan.

She felt the tree's anguish, its pain as the dark magick surrounding it pierced the shield, seeping through weak spots.

The tree couldn't stand this attack much longer.

It was up to her now to stop them.

Her dark magick acted like a veil as she approached the front, pushing through the mass of creatures.

She was a monster just like them. There was no denying that now.

A strange sort of calm washed over her as she broke from the crowd and Ravenna appeared. The breastplate and shoulder pads of her armor were crafted to look like hundreds of metal feathers, each one sharp enough to cut through bone. Her cloak of creatures—scorpions, beetles, spiders, centipedes—hissed and clicked as it churned behind her.

And standing next to her, looking every bit a dark, vengeful god, stood Stolas.

Clad in metallic armor seemingly crafted from the night, his wings fanned out behind him. Power rolled off him in waves. It charged the air and permeated Haven's bones, making her dizzy.

Like a wolf awoken from its den by the scent of another apex predator, her dark magick stirred.

Stolas's primordial gaze fell on her; it felt like being raked by claws of ice. She was drawn toward him on some invisible thread, and when her powers collided with his, a shock went through them both.

Someone let their beast out, he whispered inside her head, so softly it could have been her imagination.

She didn't dare respond, but her dark magick purred in answer.

Firelight danced inside Ravenna's black eyes as she approached Haven. "Kneel."

Haven dropped to a knee and bowed her head, hoping her thundering heart didn't betray her.

Ravenna's wings twitched as she stared down at Haven. "Stolas said he turned you, but I didn't truly believe it. I still don't."

Stolas prowled over, his sneer revealing sharp fangs. "She'd already let me inside her mind. After that, it wasn't hard to break down her will in the cave."

Ravenna laughed. "I wish I could have been there for that, my love." It took everything Haven had to bury her revulsion as Ravenna reached over and kissed Stolas, a deep, violent, claiming kiss.

"Still," Ravenna said as she halted her assault and focused back on Haven. "The Shadeling needs proof that she's turned."

The Shadeling. Haven had suspected the dark god was involved.

"Magewick, bring the prisoner."

Magewick loped toward them, the prisoner in his arms bucking and flailing. Haven's mouth went bone-dry as she took in Demelza's terrified stare. Demelza's mouth gaped open as she tried to talk.

"You are sure this is her lady's maid?" Ravenna asked, glancing at Magewick.

He nodded, his fear of the new Shade Queen palpable. "Yes. This is her. The one who brushes her hair at night."

He dies first. Haven's fingers clawed into fists, and her arms trembled as she forcibly made her hands relax.

Not yet.

Ravenna turned to Haven. "Kill her."

Even the slightest hesitation would condemn Haven. So she held Demelza's stare as she used her dark magick to reach inside her chest. When Haven felt the prisoner's heart beating furiously, squirming and twitching like a frightened rabbit, she crushed it.

Demelza's face slackened, the light drained from her eyes, and she collapsed to the ground.

Don't look. Don't look.

Clearing every emotion from her expression, Haven raised her stare to meet Ravenna's predatory gaze.

With a pleased grin, Ravenna reached into a small iron box and pulled out something. A knife.

The Godkiller.

Moonlight swam along the curve of silver horns that made up the hilt, and Haven shivered as the red eye blinked, roving around until it fixed on her. The slashed pupil dilated, and a pulse of depraved magick slithered over her skin.

You.

For a horrible moment, she was trapped in her repeating nightmare. Unable to resist the dark forces inside her. The bloodlust and malice that came with her dark magick.

Ravenna offered the weapon to Haven. The second her fingers wrapped around the cold hilt, her body contracted as the weapon's corrupted magick began probing, trying to find a way inside her.

Let me inside, the Shadeling whispered. *Give yourself to me.*

Blood pricked her taste buds as she bit into her cheek, fighting the evil presence even as a part of her longed for it.

The dagger spoke of cancer and rot, power and destruction. It sang of a world drowned in blood, of skies choked with hideous creatures, and a dark, bent, perverted god.

You are mine, the Shadeling said. *Mine. Serve me and I will make you queen of shadows and lies. You will be my most magnificent weapon, and they will all bow to you, Daughter.*

Daughter.

No.

Nausea twisted her belly. She had suspected after Archeron read her the prophecy, but she hadn't had time to soak in the truth.

Daughter of both the Shadeling and Freya.

She blew out a wild breath. With everything happening, she couldn't begin to deal with that yet.

Focus on what you need to do.

Her muscles froze as the eye's pupil constricted, its gaze burning into her flesh. She could feel the vile god watching her from his Netherworld prison. Taking her in.

When she'd imagined a reunion with her family, this had not been it.

Her chest ached as vile fingers of magick reached inside her, probing, clawing, claiming.

Filling her with an overwhelming need for power.

For chaos.

For control.

I could kill them all, she thought. *I would no longer be powerless. They have no idea what I can do.*

As if in a dream, she walked toward the last line of defense against the invading demon horde. The shield shrunk from her presence, from the ancient weapon inside her hands.

Do it, the insidious voice urged as sweat soaked her skin, her body fighting against the onslaught of darkness. *Do it, Daughter.*

The handle was like ice against her palm, a terrible cold penetrating her body. Her hand shook as she lifted the weapon. The sliver of her reflection she caught inside the double-edged blade terrified her: wild eyes blotted out with darkness, mouth twisted in a grimace of either pain—or pleasure.

The eye watched her, pleased, so sure she would do its bidding.

I made you, it whispered.

Everything hung in the balance.

"Do it, girl," Ravenna hissed. "What are you waiting for?"

Stolas came up behind her and grabbed her arm. "Do it." Only instead of his fingers digging painfully into her skin, they were gentle. As was his eyes as he pleaded with her.

"Do it," he breathed again. "My one favor."

Then, so softly, she couldn't be sure she heard him, he whispered, "I added the Godsbane, just in case."

His words from the other day trilled through her, drowning out the Shadeling's whisper, Ravenna's voice, even her own doubts.

It would take the most powerful weapon in the realm to truly kill me, and then—only then—would the curse binding me to the

Netherworld be broken.

A vehement snarl ripped from Ravenna's lips as she realized what Haven was going to do, but it was too late.

Haven rounded on Stolas, their eyes locked, and she plunged the Godkiller straight into his heart.

EIGHTY-TWO

The impact of steel against armor, muscle, and bone slammed through her palm. She jerked her hand back as if stung.

Stolas's eyes went wide, but his lips were curved in a faint smile. Even now, dying, he was trying to make this easy for her.

Gasping, he clutched at the weapon, and a part of her yearned for him to pull it out.

But she knew he was only trying to ensure Ravenna couldn't remove the blade before its poisonous magick stopped his immortal heart.

Haven caught Stolas, lowering him gently to the ground as she spoke to him.

Stupid stuff, like how big of an idiot he was for talking her into this, and how much he would pay later.

Because there had to be a later—there had to be.

She ignored the corpse beside them. Before she arrived, Nasira had captured a Golemite soldier and Surai spelled her face and body to look like Demelza's.

The spell had appeared so real that, even now, Haven's hands shook from the act.

A few feet away, a portal appeared beside Ravenna and Nasira leapt out, followed by Ember, Surai, and Demelza. To Haven's shock, Bell and Xandrian followed.

A look of recognition and then horror overtook Ravenna's expression as she stared at Nasira. The rightful heir to the Noctis throne.

Her shock gave Nasira time to rip the necklace from Ravenna's neck.

Nasira slammed a burst of dark magick into Ravenna, sending her hurtling into the stunned army. The second the Shade Queen was out of the circle, Surai erected a shield.

Nasira held up the necklace like she would the bloody head of her enemy and, with a war cry, set fire to the dark jewel binding the Seraphians to Ravenna. As the necklace burst into shards and Ravenna's hold on the Seraphians broke, chaos erupted.

Seraphians turned on Golemites, Shadowlings attacked demons.

Just as Stolas promised they would.

Haven kneeled beside the fallen Shade Lord, careful not to crush the delicate feathers of his wings which were spread behind him like his cloak, the one made from his mother's own wings.

Her heart clenched. He looked . . . peaceful. A fallen Seraphian prince.

His full lips were parted slightly, giving the false illusion that he still breathed. His eyes were closed, his dark gray lashes fanned out over the sharp rise of his cheekbones. If not for the fish-belly white of his skin, she might have thought he was sleeping, not dead.

"Why did you have to bear this plan all alone?" she whispered as she pried the silver caps from the tips of his horns. The strange jewelry no longer thrummed with the dark magick Ravenna used to keep Stolas obedient.

The memory from the bridge attack had resurfaced in her cell right after her dark magick returned. How Stolas had saved her. How he'd flown her through a giant waterfall and then told her everything.

Ravenna's plan to steal the Godkiller and use Haven to wield the powerful weapon.

The attack on the Tree of Life.

When the Curse was broken, he explained, the injured Shade Queen was desperate. She went to the darkest pits of the Netherworld and awoke the Shadeling, hoping to bargain with the dark god.

Instead, he was loosed from his cell and into the Netherworld along with his demon army.

After months of torture, Ravenna finally found a way to break Stolas by threatening the lives of the remaining Seraphian slaves. As long as the dark jewel at her throat remained intact, she could destroy the last of his people with a word.

That's when he warned Haven in the dream not to trust him again.

And yet, as soon as he gave himself to Ravenna and she explained what the Shadeling had planned, a dangerous idea surfaced. One that required the utmost secrecy until the very end.

Which was why Stolas hid Haven's memory of the cave and their scheme until the right time.

And now . . . now Haven had to finish the final part of the plan and bring Stolas back to life so he could fight beside her.

Except she suddenly felt so small and inexperienced, his body terrifyingly cold.

What had she done?

Haven's chest ached, unshed tears burning her throat. Gritting her teeth, she yanked the dagger from Stolas's chest, ignoring the rage that emanated from the weapon, and slipped the horrible knife in her waistband.

"Help me," she hissed, her mind spiraling with the possibility they wouldn't be strong enough to bring him back. Everyone but Surai—who was responsible for upholding the shield—and Xandrian gathered beside the fallen Shade Lord, all careful to step around his wings.

Tears blurred her vision as doubt crept in. Stolas spent the entire two hours inside the caves teaching her the spell to bring him back. Still . . . he'd admitted it was a long shot.

"It's time I took a stand. I would rather die than be a weapon for her," he'd said before flashing a grin and adding, "Plus, they will sing songs about me, the heroic, sexy Shade Lord who saved the entire Solis nation."

She swallowed down the sob in her throat and blew out a breath. *Focus.* Her fingers shook as her friends joined their hands with hers. Combining their powers to bring him back. Even Demelza kneeled, her hand clenching Nasira's. Ravius had appeared from somewhere and was perched on Demelza's shoulder.

For once, the talkative bird was quiet as he stared mournfully at his master.

Nasira let out a sob. Never had the girl looked so vulnerable, so mortal before. "Haven, please," she begged. "Bring him back."

Around them, Ravenna and Magewick led the charge, hurling lightning bolts of power at Surai's shield.

Surai grunted, her eyes squeezing tight. "Hurry, Soror. I'm a badass shield layer, but even I have my limits."

They needed more power.

"Help us," Haven growled to Xandrian. "Prove you deserve my friend's adoration."

Bell winced, and Xandrian snuck a sideways glance at Bell before saying, "Happily. Once someone tells me *why* we're resurrecting the Lord of the Netherworld."

"Because once he crosses the threshold into death," Haven quickly explained, "the Netherworld curse will be broken, meaning Ravenna no longer has control over him. If we bring him back, all his glorious power will be unleashed upon our enemies."

"And we're sure he won't use that power against us?" Xandrian added, pale blue eyes narrowed.

Another blast of dark magick billowed over the shield, inky tendrils spearing all around them, searching for an entrance.

Haven met his eyes. "Trust me."

The tension left her shoulders as Xandrian knelt beside Bell and, after the briefest of hesitations, took his hand.

Time to come back to me, Stolas.

Closing her eyes, Haven blocked out the cacophony of battle that raged around them. The snarls, clash of steel on steel, and explosions of magick faded into silence. The rush of her heartbeat grew louder, the thrum of magick pulsing through her veins filling her with power.

She crafted the runes in her mind and then spoke the words to increase the strength of the spell. Dark and light magick coalesced over Stolas's form, swirling together faster and faster until the flame transformed into a deep shade of amethyst—like the third flame that night during the festival of light.

"I can't hold it much longer!" Surai growled.

Come back, Stolas, she whispered, searching the darkness for his presence as desperation crept in.

587

She said the words louder, the others chanting the spell. The flame of magick leapt higher, amethyst light rippling across the feathers of his flared wings. Opening her eyes, she focused on his slightly parted full lips. On his storm gray eyelashes. Willing him to take a breath, to open his eyes.

To look at her the way no one else dared.

The others were watching her now. Urging her to admit the truth. He was gone. Surai cried out, and a portion of the shield bowed inward as demons surged toward them.

She stared at the fallen prince, her desperation awakening a ferocity inside her. *I won't lose you*, she thought. *I refuse.*

She pictured him that night in her bedroom. Remembered the way he carried her in his arms. His surprising gentleness.

The words between them she'd left unsaid. And now she might never have the chance to say them.

Bell touched Haven's hand. "Please, Haven. He's gone."

"No!" She wouldn't stop. She refused to give up on him.

Even Nasira had stopped chanting. "Haven . . ." Tears shone in her eyes. "Haven, please. Enough."

A roar split the air as a demon broke through the shield. Snarling, Haven sent a fiery spear into its throat.

The demon shrieked as flames licked its black flesh.

Surai finished it with a flash of light magick, but the demons knew there was a weak spot now, and more piled through. They fought each other, snarling and gnashing their teeth as they pushed against the hole.

Hundreds all trying to thrash their way inside.

Surai fell to her hands and knees. "Haven! I can't hold it!"

And then a *whoosh* announced the shield's destruction just as the demons surged toward them.

EIGHTY-THREE

Haven leapt to her feet, cutting down five demons where they stood. Bell joined her, Xandrian flanking him. Surai, Ember, and Demelza faced the dark army on the other side. Nasira took to the air, protecting them from attacks above.

The twin Seraphians Haven met at the ball, Bane and Delphine, shot through the air and joined their true Empress, Nasira.

Together, Solis, mortal, and Noctis repelled wave after wave of demon.

A bellow split the night. Haven whirled to face Ravenna. A large, twisted black horn was pressed to the Shade Queen's lips as she called the demons from every part of the city.

Haven watched in horror as the sky around them turned black with the entire demon horde. Surai gathered enough power to form another shield. But with Stolas no longer alive, the Shadowlings had stopped fighting the demons. And the Golemites had beaten back the Seraphians by sheer force of numbers.

Ravenna, free now to use her powers without distraction, began picking apart the tenuous second shield. Talons of dark power scraped down the side, taunting them. She stood just outside the translucent wall of magick, black hair swirling around her, eyes bright with the promise of destruction, as a thousand beasts converged.

Ready to slaughter them all the moment Ravenna broke the shield.

Ravenna's smile was horrifying as she peered at Haven a few inches away. The only thing separating them a thin, dying layer of power. "The Shadeling wants you alive, so I can't kill you. But I can hurt everyone else inside this shield. Can make them scream in torment. You know I can."

A snarl ripped from Haven's chest. That would never happen.

Understanding the hopelessness of their situation, Xandrian grabbed Bell's hand. "I can thread us out of the shield one by one."

His magick flared around him as he created the portal—

Nothing. Xandrian tried again.

Again, nothing.

"There's too many demons," Ember growled, her blonde braids flipping over her shoulder as she looked around, her sword held firmly between her hands. "The dark magick is devouring our light magick."

It was true. The beautiful amber flame licking down her blade was guttering and hissing.

Ravenna pressed a talon into the shield, her curved claw indenting the surface. "Drop the shield, and I might let one live."

Haven bared her teeth as inky shadows rippled from her body. Her dark magick worked just fine. But there were too many demons. She couldn't protect everyone. They would be picked off individually.

Ravenna's powers surged to surround the shield, clawing, stabbing, poking at the weakening bubble of magick.

Surai gasped, her eyes squeezed tight as she fought the attack. Pain wrenched her mouth into a groan.

"I'm sorry," Surai cried out. "Haven, I'm so sorry."

The shield disappeared. Haven braced herself for the demons, her dark magick ready. She would fight to the death protecting every person inside their circle.

But the demons didn't come.

The creatures hovered a few feet away. Hissing. Clawing at the ground. Great bellows piercing the air.

But they didn't attack.

What was Ravenna playing at?

Haven looked to the Shade Queen and was confused by what she saw. Ravenna's expression had changed.

Gone from that of a conquering god's to . . . raw, unmitigated fear.

"Hello, wife."

Stolas's voice charged through Haven, alighting a glorious spark of hope, and the sound was its own sort of magick.

Alive—he was alive.

"You're dead," Ravenna hissed, her hands held up defensively.

"Apparently not." His gaze met Haven's. Just for a moment. A nameless emotion passing between them. Ravius had alighted on Stolas's armored shoulder, his chest puffed out, dark eyes glittering.

Casually, as if waving someone off, Stolas gestured with his fingers and the demons raining down on them burst into hungry blue flames that lit the night.

They writhed as the fire consumed their putrid flesh to ash.

Horrible, terrible noises erupting from their dying throats.

More caught fire. More. Heat kissed Haven's flesh. The demons shot to the air in a swarm of wings and claws, but that didn't save them.

Nothing could.

They burned, every single one, until it seemed the very stars were aflame.

Everyone inside the circle stumbled back from the risen Shade Lord, even Haven.

He was a sight to behold. The Netherworld chains must have stifled his powers along with his control because surge after surge of unfathomable magick shot from his being. His eyes were pure black, his wings wrapped in shadows and blue lightning, his bone-white hair falling around his face.

And his expression—like a vengeful god raining down judgement on all who'd wronged him.

Realizing her leash on him had snapped, Ravenna stumbled backward, her leathery wings beating at the air as she prepared to flee. Compared to him, she was hideous, a thing that slithered in darkness and hid beneath rocks.

Stolas's grin was a thing of nightmares. He let her go about ten feet in the air, watching, one hand stroking the tip of his horn. His wings stretching to their full, massive spread, as if remembering how she tried to destroy them.

He let her make it just high enough to think she might escape. Let that hope build inside her—

With the crook of his finger, Stolas rendered the Shade Queen's daughter, one of the most powerful Noctis in the realm, powerless.

The sound of the hollow, delicate bones of her wings snapping all at once pierced the night, followed by Ravenna's scream.

Useless wings streaming behind her, she wrenched through the air and fell at Stolas's feet.

In the presence of such power, the creatures of her cloak fled, their dark bodies scuttling over the ground.

Ravenna held up a hand, her eyes pleading. "Please, I never wanted to do those things to you. It was my mother. She's to blame. I never hurt you. Please, *husband*."

If Ravenna thought using that title would somehow soften him, she was wrong.

Stolas's all-black eyes burned with fury. Haven thought of how the word 'wife' pierced him. How he flinched beneath its weight.

No more.

He didn't say a word, didn't show a flicker of emotion as a blade appeared in his hand. Fear rippled over Ravenna when she recognized the dagger, the same one that shaved the sliver of horn from her mother. She began panting. Panting and writhing as she tried to get away.

He stalked toward the vile creature who had tormented, tortured, and controlled him for thousands of years. The female who helped murder his parents, forced him into marriage, and turned him into an irredeemable monster.

Invisible shreds of his power lashed around her; he held her immobile the same way he had Haven the night before.

Except this time, instead of pleasure, he planned to inflict pain.

Only Ravenna's head could move now, and it thrashed side to side as he leaned down, almost intimately, and brushed his lips over her ear.

Then he whispered something only Ravenna could hear.

Ravenna's head whipped up, her eyes full of fury as they found Haven—

Stolas used that moment of distraction to drive the blade deep beneath Ravenna's ribs.

This time Haven heard what Stolas whispered as he said, "That's for what you did to my sister."

He yanked the dagger out, black blood spraying his face, and plunged it down again. "That's for my wings."

Ravenna was cursing and begging between screams. Calling for Magewick, who'd long abandoned her.

Nasira strolled over, and Ravenna took turns looking from brother to sister. There were no more words left inside her.

She was gasping for air.

But the dying Noctis still saw everything, including Nasira as she bent down, took the hilt of the blade between her small fingers, and twisted, the bones in Ravenna's chest cracking.

"That's for my parents," Nasira breathed, her words so soft Haven had to strain to hear them.

Ravenna's mouth parted, bloody foam wetting her lips, as if there was something she could say to make right thousands of years of cruelty, torment, and death.

Haven prowled toward Ravenna. When Ravenna saw what glimmered in Haven's hands, she shook her head. "No, not that. No, please, anything but that."

The demonic eye inside the handle rolled to stare at Ravenna, its cat-like pupil dilating. Haven could feel its excitement as it reacted to the blood in the air.

"This is for Bell," Haven whispered as she slammed the Godkiller into Ravenna's heart.

Unlike Stolas, Ravenna shrieked with pain as the blade's crooked magick entered her body.

And then her face went slack, and Ravenna Malythean died.

EIGHTY-FOUR

As soon as Ravenna took her last breath, the demons scattered. The night filled with the flapping of their bony wings, their otherworldly grunts and shrieks. The sky opened up. Delicate shafts of moonlight piercing the shadows.

The dark magick that poisoned the air lifted.

Stolas came up beside Haven. The edges of his immense powers reached out, stroking, affectionate.

Her own magick purred in greeting.

The yellow ring around his silver eyes blazed as he said, "Thank you, Haven."

Overwhelmed by the intensity in his voice, she switched her focus to the Godkiller, wiping the wetted blade on her pants and then slipping it back into her waistband.

A scuffle of footsteps drew Haven's attention to Nasira as she darted into Stolas's arms. He embraced his sister, the girl he'd given up everything to help escape imprisonment, and she buried her head in his shoulder.

Then she pulled from his arms and approached Haven.

Expecting Nasira's usual rancor, Haven stiffened. But Nasira surprised her with a violent hug. "You gave me my brother back and for that . . . you will always have my loyalty."

Nasira jerked away, her magnificent onyx wings beating the air as she took to the sky, a tiny, vengeful god more terrifying than any demon.

Haven looked to Stolas, still at a loss for words. "I never thought that would happen."

"Every beast has a pecking order. My sister accepts her place below you. They all do." His smile was positively villainous as he added, "Now, ready to do what only beasts can?"

Haven looked to the others, waiting for her to lead them into battle. Her gaze darkened with fury as it shifted to the army of fleeing demons and disoriented Noctis. The Golemite forces seemed confused as they observed their fallen queen.

Their hesitation cost them greatly.

Haven and her friends moved as one, a spear of unchecked power. No one questioned their roles as Haven led. Stolas flanking her right side. Surai on her left. Followed by Xandrian, Ember, Bell, and Demelza.

Above, Nasira charged through the sky, shadowed by the twin Seraphians, their movement marked by dying screams. Bits of demon gore littering their path.

By the time the Golemite soldiers realized what was happening, it was too late.

They didn't stand a chance. Not with Surai's defensive orbs and shields dismantling their offensive strikes and Ember's light magick pounding them from all sides.

Xandrian drowned them with spears of water. But he used

blood just as often—it was, after all, mostly water. Nasira and the twins' dark magick streaked across the canvas of night like bolts of lightning. Their wrath like something from a myth.

Stolas was the only one who held his powers in check. Somehow, he knew Haven needed to be the one to obliterate their enemies, needed to slake her primal thirst for violence and revenge.

She took the Golemite soldiers' wings first. A wave of light magick wrapped in darkness shredded the flesh from their beloved appendages.

They dropped from the sky in the hundreds. The impact shaking the earth.

Twisting her fingers, she broke their legs. Their pelvises. The bones in their clawed, bloodstained hands. The rhythmic sound of snapping echoing through the streets.

Finally, as they dragged their twisted, broken bodies across the cobblestone streets, crawling through the blood of their victims, the citizens hiding in the shops and homes realized what was happening and descended.

The Golemites were powerless against their once victims turned attackers.

Still not satisfied—not even close—she took the horn, the one Ravenna had used to call the demons, and blew.

As soon as the bellow from that ancient horn left her lips, a tether between her mind and the demons snapped taut.

Rage—a terrible, unending rage filled her mind as she shared the demons' thoughts. Their thirst for blood and carnage and chaos revolted her. Hot bile slammed against the back of her throat. Feelings of nothingness, a horrible, unending nothingness, drowned her soul.

The beasts' minds were of one thought: *Kill kill kill.*

But she held on, forcing the bond between them to solidify.

I am like you, she purred. *A beast of darkness and rage. I am your master. Obey me.*

Revulsion coiled in her gut, but she continued. Cooing to the demons, urging them to trust her. They were desperate for a master. Their bloodlust crying out for someone to command them into battle.

She cringed as their twisted minds merged with hers.

Darkness. So much hatred and darkness and anguish and malice—

She gasped; her legs buckled.

Stolas took her hand.

Drawing from his steadying presence, she grasped that tenuous bond between herself and the demons, nurturing it. Feeding it.

I am a beast like you. I am eternal darkness. I am the night.

As she drew the demons in, she searched the sky.

There. A black cloud rising high above the city.

And below it, feeding the heavens with oily smoke, was Freya's temple, the Solaris Cathedral.

Ruined—completely, utterly destroyed. The most beautiful monument in the realm reduced to charred remains.

A pulse of fury slammed into her as she took in the inferno that raged from the landmark's once beautiful spires and licked out its broken stained-glass windows.

An inferno large enough to kill thousands of demons.

Large enough to obliterate the Shadeling's army.

There, she whispered across the tether, steeling her mind. *Go there. Into the smoke. Into the fires of hell.*

The demons hesitated. She could feel their confusion. Their fear of the light.

And on the other side of that tether, a distant growl sounded as the Shadeling realized what she was doing.

Go, she soothed. Urging them into those hungry flames before the Shadeling could stop them. *Go.*

I command you.

And just like that, the demons surged toward the cathedral. The sound of their wings battering the sky in tandem filled the night. Citizens stumbled from the shattered buildings to watch the screeching horde.

They held hands. Some of them making the sign of the Goddess. But most simply watched silently, shaking. Not quite believing that the nightmare was finally at an end.

When the first creature hit the flames, its torment ricocheted inside her skull. The others followed. Unable to stop themselves.

Their panic echoed inside her mind, the excruciating pain as the fire consumed their flesh filling her.

The agony—oh, Goddess save me.

But she held strong, focusing focusing focusing—

Until the tether between her and the demons snapped.

And, at last, the sky was clear.

A faint roar rumbled through her mind. The Shadeling's demonic voice a fading promise of revenge as he whispered, *We will be reunited soon, Daughter.*

The tide of despair caught up with her; she staggered, her eyes closing.

And then Stolas was wrapping his arms around her, bracing her body with his unimaginable strength.

"Well done, Beastie," he murmured against her ear.

She forced her eyes open. Startled to find the citizens of Solethenia had gathered around them.

They were . . . cheering. Bloodied, injured, some barely able to stand, others still clutching their makeshift weapons, and yet they conjured the strength to praise the band of warriors from every nation.

As if the dawn had been heralded by their victory, the first light of the sun poured over the battered city. Haven's heart broke at what she saw.

Not a single building untouched by the horror and destruction of the Shadeling's attack. Fingers of smoke clogged the skyline; buildings ripped apart, some taken down to their foundation; the rivers and canals tinged red with blood.

Bodies littered the streets, their race indistinguishable. The faint knell of keening drifted in the breeze, as if the city itself cried.

The crowd of onlookers parted suddenly, and Haven whirled to face whatever new threat this was.

Gold Shadows marched down the sweeping marble stairs of the palace. They held spears and golden shields, the orange glow of their magick glittering around them.

Haven's gaze went to the figure leading them.

She was expecting to see the sovereign flanked by her daughters, and she braced herself for the confrontation.

Still, however ready she'd been to meet the queen, when she took in who led the royal soldiers, a shock of fresh pain crashed over her.

Clad in golden imperial armor, a purple cloak fastened to his shoulders, Archeron towered over the army.

His army.

A few steps behind him strolled Avaline, her halfling entourage poised on the stairs beside the Gold Shadows, ready to take to the air and fight.

As Archeron appraised Haven the same way she did him, surprise whispered across his otherwise emotionless face. A smile twitched his ruined lips, but the coldness in his eyes chilled her blood.

Her focus went to the azerite crown atop his head.

The crowd recognized it too. Even injured and battle-weary, the citizens of Solethenia dropped into a reverent bow.

For their new King and Sun Sovereign.

King Maker, Bjorn had called her. She'd assumed he meant Bell.

A monstrous king will come to power, cloaked in light to hide the beast within, and he will serve the great darkness.

She shivered as Bjorn's prediction became clear.

Surai joined Haven. Her face smudged with smoke and blood, her eyes worn from battle.

And when she looked to this newly crowned king—Haven saw the flicker of understanding dawn, followed by the ripple of grief.

"You're right," Surai said, her voice raw. "He's gone."

The Gold Shadows stopped marching, but Archeron continued down the steps until he was close enough Haven could make out the shadowy darkness inside his once vibrant eyes.

Eyes that held hers. There was nothing inside them that hinted at their shared past, the warmth, respect, and affection they once shared.

Only a strange emptiness.

Xandrian refused to bow as he regarded his cousin. "Where is my aunt?"

"Dead."

"And your sisters?"

"Also dead."

Haven shivered at the calm way Archeron spoke of their deaths. His flat eyes never leaving hers.

"How convenient," Xandrian remarked. He didn't bother hiding his revulsion as he added, "And what happened to your face?"

"It doesn't matter. Those responsible have been punished." Archeron's eyes narrowed. "Do you refuse to bow to your new king, cousin?"

"I only bow to one sovereign ruler, and that person isn't you."

Archeron shifted his focus to her, and Haven was once again disturbed by the nothingness behind his eyes. "I'm glad you lived. Especially now that I see how powerful you are. All the ways you could service the Sun Court."

"Screw you!" Haven seethed.

The good side of his lips curled. "Haven Ashwood, by the laws of the Praetori Fiernum, you are mine for the entirety of your mortal life." He held out his hand, the gesture almost affectionate, and she stared at those fingers that once stroked her flesh. "Come willingly, and no one else has to die today."

Before Haven could respond, she felt the collective powers of the others ready themselves behind her. Dark and light converging as one into a fierce weapon. The twin Seraphians began to circle Archeron, black shreds of their magick dancing around them.

Xandrian, Surai, Bell, and Ember formed a protective circle around Haven.

Nasira's ominous shadow streaked across the marble steps toward the Gold Shadows, multiplying as the freed Seraphians joined her. The Gold Shadows nervously scanned the sky.

And Stolas—the Shade Lord did nothing but flash a lazy smile at Archeron, but she felt the threat in his gesture most of all.

"Her promise of servitude died with your poor mother," Stolas drawled. "Goddess rest her immortal soul."

"Haven is mine," Archeron growled, the confidence in his tone suggesting he'd been king for years, not hours. "Even without the bargain, she has broken the Goddess's law and I have every right to claim her."

"I'd like to see you try," Stolas replied, his rage masked beneath a dangerous calm. "She just took out a horde of demons to save this godforsaken city. What do you think she would do to your cowering army over there?" His wings flared proudly as he slid his attention to the army and then back to the new Sun Sovereign. "Then there are the rest of us. Each one willing to die protecting her."

An ache opened inside Haven's chest, and she proudly surveyed the warriors—her friends, her *family*—ready to give their lives for her.

No matter how this ended, she would never forget this moment or their sacrifice.

"Surai?" Archeron said, and Haven could have sworn his face softened. "We've fought side-by-side through countless wars. I've nursed your wounds. Slept next to you, grieved with you. Don't do this."

Surai didn't respond. She simply lifted her chin and looked beyond him, her disdain painfully clear.

A muscle popped in Archeron's jaw, and he shifted his anger to Xandrian, his eyes hardening. "Xandrian. Are you really willing to fight against your kingdom for an abomination?"

Xandrian shook his head. He was injured, blood staining his tunic, his shoulders sagging. But there was a ferocity in his ice-blue eyes that surprised her. "An abomination?" He laughed, clutching the wounded side of his chest. "You really have no idea who she is, do you?"

Something about Xandrian's words registered with Bell, and he turned to stare at Haven, surprise and something else—Awe? Reverence?—gleaming inside his blue eyes.

"You call her an abomination," Xandrian continued, "but others call her something else."

Archeron's gaze snapped behind her just as a murmur rose from the crowd.

Haven followed their focus to the street behind them. Hundreds of people kneeled, their heads bowed—to her.

The monk who'd given her the scroll stood at the front of the group. He gave a wry grin as he, too, bowed.

Haven glanced at Archeron. She refused to believe the Sun Lord she knew wasn't still inside him, somewhere.

"Archeron," she said, willing him to listen. Willing her voice to break through to whatever remained of his humanity. "There's a great evil coming. I felt the Shadeling's thoughts, his desires. He will find a way out of the Netherworld, and when he does—we need to be ready. Fight with the mortal kingdoms against this new threat. Together we stand a chance."

Three breaths passed as they regarded one another.

For a wild, hopeful beat of her heart, Haven thought she glimpsed the Archeron she loved in the wry curve of his lips, the sarcastic humor brightening his face.

Then he laughed, and the cruelness in his tone snuffed out the last spark of hope she'd allowed herself.

Gone—he was gone.

The ruined side of this new Archeron's face twisted as he shifted his focus to Bell. "Didn't they tell you, Prince? For the crime of murdering your father, the kingdom of Penryth has turned against you. Your half-brother, Renk, is now king."

Bell flinched at the news.

Archeron continued, "By the law of the Praetori Fiernum, you might technically be the Ruler of the Nine, but without a kingdom to fall back on, you are a king of *nothing*, Kinslayer."

Haven's heart clenched at this new information, but she knew one thing for sure: Archeron was lying.

Bell would never have murdered his father.

Anguish pooled inside Bell's eyes, but he forced his head high. "Then I will spend my every waking moment as Ruler of the Nine proving my innocence and reclaiming my kingdom."

Stolas's wings flared, casting shadows over Archeron. "We'll be taking our leave now. You're welcome to try and stop us. In fact, Sun Lord, there's nothing I'd like better."

Not Sun Sovereign. Not king.

Sun Lord.

Archeron's eyes narrowed. Behind him, the Gold Shadows readied themselves for battle. "And the Godkiller?"

"I'm rather fond of the weapon," Stolas drawled, hiding the fact that the dagger was with Haven. "Think I'll hold onto it for a while. Keep it safe from those who would abuse its powers."

Stolas's eyes pointedly drifted to Archeron.

Wrath twisted Archeron's face into something unrecognizable, and she saw it then. The glint of madness burning in his eyes.

The years of pain, of being unwanted, hated, unloved—and then being abused and humiliated over and over by the man who murdered his friend until . . . until he was forced to shatter his soul just to end his misery.

It had made him deranged.

A monster—no, worse than a monster. A murderous ruler cloaked in the guise of righteousness.

"You may go," he answered. "Just know, whoever leaves with her will be branded a traitor against all of Solissia." His focus drifted from Surai to the citizens still bowed behind Haven. "You will be systematically hunted down, tortured, and executed. And your nightmare will not end until I have her back, along with the cursed Godkiller."

Until I have her back. Haven shivered at the words.

A threatening snarl rumbled low in Stolas's chest, but Haven shook her head, and he refrained from ripping this new king to pieces—which is exactly what she knew he longed to do.

Too much blood had already been spilled, the collective horror of the night rotting the air. She would not be responsible for Archeron's death.

Not today, at least.

The people of Solethenia deserved the bloodshed to end, and killing the last true heir to the throne would only sow chaos and more despair.

So she would let him hunt her, this new, depraved king. The brother-in-arms she once fought beside, the friend she would have died for, the almost-lover she nearly let herself love—

She would let him declare war on her.

And when the time came, she would end him—and it would be a mercy.

EPILOGUE

The setting sun painted the sea in wide strokes of pink and gold. Haven leaned over the stern of the boat they sailed on, watching the great obsidian cliffs of Effendier's northernmost tip grow smaller on the horizon.

In two days' time, they would be in Shadoria. Stolas would discover what was left of his fallen kingdom, and Bell would learn who, if anyone, would dare ally with the new, kingdomless *kinslaying* King of the Nine.

They did have an army . . . of sorts.

Haven, her friends, and about four hundred Seraphians and citizens, including the monk, all packed into five container ships.

Threading would have been faster, but it was impossible to take that many people through portals.

Haven still couldn't believe anyone would have willingly chosen to follow her after Archeron's dire threat.

Sighing, she turned her attention to the sea. Three shadows

streaked over the rich topaz waters—Nasira, Bane, and Delphine. They patrolled the skies while Xandrian watched from the crow's nest above, ready to use the ocean around them as a weapon—if necessary.

But Haven knew Archeron wouldn't come after them. Even now, with all the wrongs he'd done, he would consider breaking his word dishonorable.

He would allow them to leave. And then, today, tomorrow, perhaps a week from now, he would begin hunting those who left with her.

She flicked her gaze to the ships flanking theirs. Innocent people strolled the decks, normal citizens who believed the apocryphal texts. Who thought she was part of some prophecy to save them.

Yet, she worried the opposite. Just by joining her, every single soul on board those ships had doomed themselves.

All because of a myth, a fable she couldn't quite fathom.

Not yet—maybe never.

Daughter of both Freya and the Shadeling.

Beside her, Stolas watched her quietly, as he had since the moment they boarded. Ravius was hunkered down on Stolas's shoulder, for once not saying a word. She had needed time to gather her thoughts, time to scrub the traumatic images of death and destruction from her mind.

But now, now she was ready to face the truth.

"How long have you known?" she asked, the wind blowing off the ocean threatening to swallow her words.

He didn't even ask what she meant. "I think, deep down, I suspected you were Freya's daughter the moment I saw you."

She nodded; she had thought as much. "In the forest?"

He shifted his unreadable gaze to the sea. Sensing a shift in mood, Ravius took to the windy air. The orange light of dusk danced inside Stolas's onyx horns and coaxed out the indigo in his black feathers.

"No. The first time we met was years before that."

"Where?"

When he looked at her, she was surprised by the anguish in his eyes. "In the Ruinlands."

She blinked, confused. "I'm not following."

"Do you remember after you fled the Devourer's camp? You found the white snakeroot and made a poison for yourself."

"Yes," she answered carefully, wondering how he could know that. Did he listen when she told Archeron the story? "But I didn't drink it. I saw a falling star and was reminded of Freya's— my mother's love."

He held her gaze, a deep sorrow welling behind his eyes. "You did drink it, Haven, and then you died. It was a quick, merciful death." He paused, perhaps to let the shock sink in, and then continued, "When I came to collect your soul, however, Freya appeared to me. She bargained fiercely for your life."

The sun had finally submerged into the horizon, and a silvery light had fallen, painting Stolas in shades of gray.

Haven shook her head. "What could she have offered you, the Lord of the Netherworld, in return?"

A dark laugh. "Countless things, every one of which I denied. There was nothing material she could offer me, and my powers were already greater than nearly every Noctis in the realm."

"Then what?"

"Finally, after I had assured her there was nothing that could tempt me, she presented one final offer. The chance to do a single good act. The chance at . . . redemption, I suppose." His black gaze caught on something in the distance, and he tugged his long fingers through his moon-white hair. "She said if I let you die, I would be extinguishing the spark that would someday chase the darkness from our world."

The stars above seemed to tilt, her world spinning. "How did you answer?"

"I laughed at her, spit in her face. I had turned down all the riches and power in the world, and she thought that would tempt me? Filled with rage, I promised her I would drag your soul to the deepest belly of the Netherworld and then, well, I won't elaborate on the horrible things I threatened to do after that."

Her mouth was bone-dry as she imagined that side of Stolas. "But you didn't."

His gaze dropped to his fingers where they clenched the side of the hull. "When it came time to take your bright soul to that pit of hell I called a home—"

He met her gaze. And something delicate shimmered inside his eyes.

"I couldn't. The thought of watching your essence wither and fade inside that awful place—I couldn't," he repeated. "I told myself letting you live was a curiosity, nothing more. At Freya's insistence, I guided you to Penryth, made sure you found the young prince she claimed was the beginning of your destiny, and then told myself I was done with you."

She could hardly breathe; her chest ached from thinking that she had killed herself. "But?"

"But I found myself checking on you. Shadeling's shadow, you were this beastly thing, ill-mannered and uncouth, wild beyond reason, and I thought the Goddess had played a trick on me. You were no savior. But a hidden, desperate part of me dared to believe anyway. I was furious with you for making me hope. And every time I visited you, I promised it was the last."

He paused, studying her expression, but she nodded for him

to go on.

"You became an . . . obsession. I spent years interrogating new souls in the Netherworld, priests and educated men, until finally, an Ashari priest familiar with the Order of Soltari told me their belief that Freya bore a child. He swore it was just a myth—but I couldn't get the idea out of my mind. That's when I first suspected you were her daughter. But I didn't connect you to the prophecy until much later."

"After you tricked me into tasting your blood?" she asked.

He nodded, his eyes never leaving her face as he gauged her reaction to the revelations. "I knew my dark magick would awaken any dormant powers inside you, if any. But it wasn't until you brought me back to life that I knew, without a doubt, you were the savior promised."

"Why not tell me?" she asked. A flurry of emotions clashed inside her, but above everything was hurt. Knowing he hid something so important from her. All those years yearning for her family . . . wondering who her parents were.

"Because I couldn't."

"Why?" she pressed, taking a step closer. "We shared our dreams, I visited your hidden home, we fought together. I trusted you. Why couldn't you be open with me?"

"Because, Haven," he began, his voice soft, his eyes pleading with her to understand, "to someone as wicked and broken as I was, there's nothing more terrifying in this world than . . . hope."

He was still—so very still. His only movement coming from the wind as it blew his pale hair across his forehead and ruffled his glossy feathers. He didn't blink as he waited for her to react.

But, inside his eyes, a whirlwind of emotions raged. Guilt. Sorrow. And . . . vulnerability, the kind only someone who has just bared their soul feels.

She stared at him, this Prince of Night, Lord of Nightmares, Son of the Fallen Empress. She held his gaze as she reached toward him.

A flicker of shock widened his yellow-rimmed eyes as she took his hands in hers.

"You said 'was'," she pointed out. "Someone as wicked and broken as I *was*. And now, Shade Lord?"

An emotion rippled across his beautiful countenance, perhaps hope, perhaps something even more powerful.

And then he dropped to his knees, tipped his horns toward her as he bowed his head, and said, "I'm still irredeemably wicked, a beast, but you shattered my chains and set me free. So now I am *your* beast, Haven, wholly and completely. Your wrath, your weapon, your protector, your soldier, your friend, and . . . when the wounds from the Sun Lord heal and you're ready, I'll be your everything else too."

Warmth cascaded through her at the implication of what *everything else* meant.

"What did you say to Ravenna right before you killed her?" she breathed. "She looked at me with such hatred."

"I will tell you *that* when you're ready." He rose, a wicked smile brightening his face.

Between the warring emotions of desire and anger, she couldn't quite find the words to respond. But it wouldn't matter if she possessed a thousand words because behind him, she suddenly noticed, waited a line of people.

Her friends—her family.

With a triumphant grin, he gestured at them. "Every single person you see is ready to swear an oath to you, daughter of ice and fire, moon and sun, dark and light."

It was hard to feel worthy of such a gift, especially from some of the most powerful runecasters in the realm.

I will fight every second of every day to earn their loyalty, she promised herself.

Haven was speechless as they came one by one to pledge themselves to her.

Demelza, her eyes misty and lips full of curses. The Seraphian twins, Bane and Delphine, finally freed from thousands of years of oppression. Xandrian, his eyes bright with a fervor she wasn't expecting.

Even Nasira kneeled, surprising everyone, including Stolas. The girl hadn't stopped watching Haven since she'd unleashed her dark magick.

When Haven asked her why she, the rightful Empress to the Noctis throne, made such a promise, Nasira simply shrugged and said, "Because until a few hours ago, I was absolutely sure our world was doomed."

"And now?"

"Now, I see what my brother did all those years ago. A chance, however small, that you could save us."

Ember's turn came next. The Morgani princess had left everything she loved behind—her homeland, her title, her family—to follow Haven. She was so regal and so much like Rook that Haven could barely hold back the wave of emotions that flooded her.

But when Surai came before Haven, there was no holding anything back. Both girls let the tears stream down their faces—tears of sorrow, grief, and love.

"Soror," Surai said, taking her hand, "friend of my heart and soul, I pledge my life to you now and forever. Your destiny is my destiny, your fate my fate."

Haven couldn't find the words to respond to such a gift. And when Bell appeared last—her brother and best friend—she thought her heart would burst with gratitude.

"Haven Ashwood," Bell said, kneeling before her. "You swore an oath of protection to me once, and now it's my turn to give my life for you. I, King of the Nine and rightful King of Penryth, friend and brother to the most fearsome girl in the realm, swear by the Goddess—your mother—I will guide you to your destiny, protect you from harm, and serve you until the day I die. Which is, hopefully, a long time away."

As soon as he stood, she embraced him. He had just lost his father, his kingdom, and yet he was pledging himself to *her*.

She would fight every breath to be worthy of such blind love.

A throb of light magick surged from his flesh, and she pulled away. "What is *that*?"

He grinned. "I'm not sure you can handle any more surprises today."

Haven flicked up her eyebrows. "Try me."

"I'll tell you the story during dinner," he added. "Or whatever they're calling the slop they're trying to feed us." Then he held out his arm. "Coming?"

"In a minute," she promised.

She watched them disappear below deck, her heart full, then stared out into the dark waters. She was buoyed by the love of her friends, but a part of her still felt the loss of Archeron deeply.

"Goodbye, friend," she whispered.

She understood now that they all had monsters inside them. Desperate, clawing, ravenous beasts that craved power and control. They fed off shadows and hatred, fear and jealousy, and rage—that most of all.

And only the steady light of love could keep them in check. As long as she had that, her monster was hers to control.

The waves broke over the bow in a steady, rhythmic rush. The wind tugged at her cloak, her hair.

Loosening the constraints on her magick, she let her powers seep out. Let them fill the sky. The ribbons of bluish-black and luminous gold streaked through the night, a lightning storm of contrasting magick.

Shadows and light. Ice and fire.

I am the daughter of Freya and Odin, the Goddess and the Shadeling, and I am not ashamed anymore of what I am.

Part beast; part flame; part mortal.

And when the time comes, I will unleash my beast on you, Father.

Somewhere far in the distance, or perhaps in the deep recesses of her mind, a growl sounded, reverberating through her very bones.

The Shadeling was coming.

He would break free from his cage.

He would wreak havoc on the realm and devour all the light in this world.

He would kill and kill and kill without remorse.

And she would be ready for him.

After all, who better to put down a depraved god than his bastard daughter?

THE END

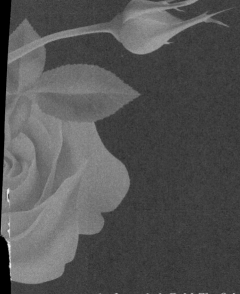

Book four, L I G H T S I N G E R , will release November 2020. You can pre-order it on Amazon.

In the meantime, you can keep up with Haven and Archeron's world and all things Kingdom of Runes by signing up for my monthly author newsletter!

GLOSSARY

- **The Bane** – The central region of Eritrayia and a barren wasteland, it acts as the buffer between the Ruinlands destroyed by the Curse and the untouched southern kingdoms protected by the runewall

- **Curseprice** – The items that must be collected and presented to the Shade Queen to break the Curse

- **Dark magick** – Derived from the Netherworld, it cannot be created, only channeled from its source, and is only available to Noctis. Dark magick feeds off light magick.

- **Darkcaster** – One who wields dark magick

- **Devourers** – Mortals with Noctis blood who practice demented dark magick and worship the Shade Queen; live in the bane and guard the rift/crossing into the Ruinlands

- **The Devouring** – The dark magick-laden mist that descends when the Curse hits and causes curse-sickness and death in mortals

- **Donatus Atrea** – All-Giver, or runetree of life where all light magick springs from

- **Eritrayia** – Mortal realm

- **Fleshrunes** – Runes Solis are born with; the markings tattoo a

Solis's flesh and channel their many magickal gifts

- **The Goddess** – Freya, mother of both Solis and Noctis, she is a powerful and divine being who gifted mortals with magick and fought on their side during the Shadow War.

- **Heart Oath** – Oath given before an engagement to marry. Can only be broken if two parties agree to sever the oath and at great cost

- **House of Nine** – Descendants of the nine mortals given runeflowers from the Tree of Life

- **Houserune** – Rune given to each of the Nine Houses and passed down from generation to generation

- **Light Magick** – Derived from the Nihl, it cannot be created, only channeled from its source, and is only available to Solis and royal mortals from the House Nine.

- **Lightcaster** – One who wields light magick

- **Mortalrune** – Runes mortals from the House Nine are allowed to possess/use

- **Netherworld** – Hell, where immoral souls go, ruled over by the Lord of the Netherworld

- **Nihl** – Heaven, ruled over by the Goddess Freya

- **Noctis** – Race of immortals native to Shadoria and the Netherworld who possess dark magic, they have pale skin, dark wings, and frequently horns

- **Powerrune** – Powerful type of rune forbidden to mortals

- **The Rift** – Chasm in the continent of Eritrayia caused by the Curse that leads to the Netherworld and allowed the Shade Queen and her people to escape

- **Ruinlands** – Northern half of Eritreyia, these lands are enchanted with dark magick and ruled by the Shade Queen

- **Runeday** – The eighteenth birthday of a royal child of the Nine Houses, where he or she receives their house runestone and potentially come into magick.

- **Runemagick** – Magick channeled precisely through ancient runes

- **Runestone** – Stones carved with a single rune—usually—and imbued with magick

- **Runetotem** – Tall poles carved with runes, they are used to nullify certain types of magick while enhancing others

- **Runewall** – A magickal wall that protects the last remaining southern kingdoms from the Curse

- **Sacred Heart Flower** – Given to the Solis at birth, this sacred bud is kept inside a glass vial and worn around the neck of one's intended mate

- **Shade Lord** – A powerful Noctis male, second only to the Shade Queen

- **The Shadeling** – Odin, father of both Solis and Noctis, he once loved Freya but became dark and twisted after fighting against his lover in the Shadow War. He now resides in the deepest pits of the Netherworld, a terrifying monster even the Noctis refuse to unchain.

- **The Shadow War** – War between the three races (mortals, Noctis, Solis,) sparked by the Goddess Freya giving mortals magick

- **Shadowlings** – Monsters from the Netherworld, under the control of the Lord of the Netherworld and the Shade Queen

- **Solis** – Race of immortals native to Solissia who possess light magick, they are more mortal-like in their appearance, with fair eyes and hair

- **Solissia** – Realm of the immortals

- **Soulread** – To read someone's mind

- **Soulwalk** – To send one's soul outside their body

- **Soulbind** – To bind another's will to yours/take over their body

- **Sun Lord** – A powerful Solis male who enjoys special position in the Effendier Royal Sun Court under the Effendier Sun Sovereign

- **Sun Queen** – A powerful Solis female who enjoys special position in the Effendier Royal Sun Court under the Effendier Sun Sovereign

SOLISSIAN WORDS AND PHRASES

- **Ascilum Oscular** – Kiss my ass (maybe)
- **Carvendi** – Good job (more or less)
- **Droob** – Knob/idiot
- **Paramatti** – Close the door to the Nihl, used during a light magick spell
- **Rump Falia** – Butt-face
- **Umath** – You're welcome
- **Victari** – Close the door to the Netherworld, used during a dark magick spell

THE NINE MORTAL HOUSES

- **Barrington** (Shadow Kingdom, formerly Kingdom of Maldovia)
- **Bolevick** (Kingdom of Verdure)
- **Boteler** (Kingdom of Penryth)
- **Courtenay** (Drothian)
- **Coventry** (Veserack)
- **Halvorshyrd** (unknown location)
- **Renfyre** (Lorwynfell)
- **Thendryft** (Dune)
- **Volantis** (Skyfall Island)

KINGDOM OF RUNES PLAYERS

Mortal Players

- **Haven Ashwood** – orphan
- **Damius Black** – Leader of the Devourers
- **Prince Bellamy (Bell) Boteler** – House Boteler, crown prince, second and only surviving heir to the king of Penryth
- **King Horace Boteler** – House Boteler, ruler of Penryth
- **Cressida Craven** – King Horace Boteler's mistress
- **Renk Craven** – half-brother to Bell, bastard son of Cressida and the King of Penryth
- **Eleeza Thendryft** – Princess of House Thendryft of the Kingdom of Dune, House Thendryft
- **Lord Thendryft** – House Thendryft of Dune Kingdom
- **Demelza Thurgood** – Haven Ashwood's Lady's Maid

Noctis Players

- **Stolas Darkshade** – Lord of the Underworld, husband to Ravenna, son of the last true Noctis Queen
- **Avaline Kallor** – Skeleton Queen, Ruler of Lorwynfell, half Noctis half mortal, promised to Archeron Halfbane
- **Remurian Kallor** – Half Noctis half mortal, brother of Amandine, died in the last war
- **Malachi K'rul** – Shade Lord, Shade Queen's underling

- **Morgryth Malythean** – Shade Queen, Cursemaker, queen of darkness, ruler of the Noctis
- **Ravenna Malythean** – Daughter of the Shade Queen, undead

Solis Players

- **Bjorn** – Sun Lord of mysterious origins
- **Archeron Halfbane** – Sun Lord and bastard son of the Effendier Sun Sovereign
- **Surai Nakamura** – Ashari warrior
- **Brienne "Rook" Wenfyre** – Sun Queen, outcast princess, daughter of the Morgani Warrior Queen

GODS

- Freya – the Goddess, ruler of the Nihl, mother of both Noctis and Solis
- Odin – the Shadeling, imprisoned in the Netherworld pits, father of both Noctis and Solis

ANIMALS

- Aramaya – Rook's temperamental horse
- Lady Pearl – Haven's loyal horse
- Ravius – Stolas's raven
- Shadow – Damius's wyvern

WEAPONS

- Haven's Sword – Oathbearer
- Stolas's Dagger – Vengeance

ABOUT THE AUTHOR

AUDREY GREY lives in the charming state of Oklahoma surrounded by animals, books, and little people. You can usually find Audrey hiding out in her office, downing copious amounts of caffeine while dreaming of tacos and holding entire conversations with her friends using gifs. Audrey considers her ability to travel to fantastical worlds a superpower and loves nothing more than bringing her readers with her.

Find her online at:

WWW.AUDREYGREY.COM